# THE LOVE I CRAVE

## HENSON DREAMIER

@Copyrights 2021

IBSN 978-1-7368122-0-4

Other books by Henson Dreamier

The Missing Years

The Found Years

The Secret Years

Book Design by Aqib Awais

Editing by Sue Soares

# CONTENTS

# PROLOGUE

There they were every time I closed my eyes. His intoxicating eyes, his gorgeous face, and that sexy smile. The one when his lips curled up into a half smile, and I could just see a little of his white teeth. It made me melt every time. He was always there behind my eyelids, haunting me. I hadn't seen those eyes in eight years, but I remembered the day he stole my heart. The eyes that haunted me belonged to a boy. He was now a twenty-six-year-old man. I needed to stop thinking of him, stop dreaming of him, but I couldn't—it was too hard. I met him when I was sixteen years old at LABA, Los Angeles Business Academy. He was there for the summer, and I was there with my three best friends: Sasha, Sophia, and Damon. They were the best things that came out of my fucked-up life.

When my eyes met Hunter's for the first time, he made my heart stop beating. When Hunter grabbed me from behind, catching me from falling on my face, his touch sent a shock of pleasure up my spine, causing me to lose my breath. It was intoxicating the way his lips moved when he asked me if I was all right. I had never felt anything like that before. The way our hearts screamed out for one another, I knew it was love at first sight. We were inseparable that summer. That summer, our lives changed forever. We fell in love, and we were going our separate ways. We both knew we wanted to spend the rest of our lives together. He had promised that no matter what, he would find me. No matter where I was in the world, he would find me. It was funny how life seemed to get in the way of things.

I felt like an idiot waiting for him, believing he would come for me. I believed deep down in my heart that he was telling the truth… and I still did. I was a young girl back then, and now I was a woman scorned. A woman who had been through hell and back. A woman who had been hurt so many times. Shit, I hadn't had sex since the day I ran for my life, and my kitty screamed for some attention, to the point where I would have an orgasm at the gym on an exercise bike or riding in my car over a damn speed bump. I had to carry spare panties around just in case. Probably the reason I didn't even bother to wear them half the time. I'd waited a long time for Hunter, and I had no idea why I was still waiting. I guess I was chasing that feeling again when I was with him. I also had no idea how I would react if I saw him. I might run for the hills or smack him for taking so damn long.

My entire teenage life was a blur. Most of it I blocked out to protect myself from the heartache and pain. I traveled all over the world and had seen so many beautiful places and experienced so many wonderful things. Sad to say, I didn't remember most of the good times, just the bad times. I had done things in my life I knew would come back to bite me in the ass. The only good thing that came out of my blurred years was Hunter Javier Grayson. Yes, that was his name, and I never forgot it, and I never would.

Starting a new life on the run and looking over my shoulder wasn't a life at all. The only thing that kept me sane was knowing I wanted to be successful and start my own publishing company. The dedication and the fight I had in me kept me going. I felt like giving up, and that was when I got the call that changed my life. I got a call from a man named Jason, who had a special letter for me. I went to his office and from that day, all my dreams came true. I had been living a good life, just waiting for Hunter to come along and swoop me up. A girl could dream, right?

*To: Baby Girl*

*I've dreamt of this moment for a very long time now. Time will heal all wounds. I thought this day would never come. Words could never explain how I feel about you. I meant it when I said that one day, I would find you and make you my wife. I promised that I would always take care of you, and this is my first step of fulfilling that promise. Our world will be much brighter now since we have found each other. I wanted to be there with you right now, but business called. I know what it is you want to become, and now you have that chance. I love you with all my heart, and I always will. See you later.*

*PS. Don't spend all the money in one place.*

*LOVE H.*

# FACE FIRST

Hope, wake up." I heard my name called. It brought me back from the eyes I dreamt about every night. They were so close, I thought he was here with me, snuggled up with me under the covers. Calling me baby girl and brushing my hair back from my face. I stared in his eyes like a school crush.

"Leave me alone." I yawned, turning over and putting the covers over my head. The lights came on, but I didn't want to wake up. I was sleeping wonderfully, thinking of that day I got that three million dollars. I had thought long and hard over the last three years of that day and that letter signed H. It still gave me chills. God, I missed him.

"Hope, your alarm has been going off for the last half hour. You can't hear that loud ass thing?" Sasha yelled. I heard a smack, then a clunk sound. I didn't look to see, but I was sure Sasha smacked my alarm clock off my dresser. It hit the floor with a clunk. "Hope, get your ass up. You're going to be late for your nine-thirty meeting." Sasha was my best friend. I had met her in foster care when we were teenagers. The word meeting was all I needed to hear for my eyes to open. I shot up from the bed, snatching the covers off.

"Well, why didn't you just lead with that?" I smiled. I had gotten on her nerves over the years, but she was my best friend and like a sister to me. I gave a quick glance at the alarm clock that was now silent and turned upside down on the floor.

If I was correct, the time read 8:32. I ran into my bathroom and closed the door behind me. I took a deep breath looking at myself in the mirror. My hair was a mess of brown bed hair curls. My eyes were light brown, but my friend Damon said they were the color of butterscotch. My eyes went to my face and neck, to my scars. I looked away immediately. One day, I would be able to look at them and not think of HIM, but I doubted it. HE was a major part of my life and why I was stronger than I had ever been. The dark circles and the bags under my eyes had cleared up from last night. I had cried myself to sleep again. It wasn't just because I missed Hunter, but I missed everyone I had lost. My mom especially. I snapped out of my slumber.

I didn't have time for a shower, so I took what I had time for, what I used to do back in my modeling days. I took a hooker's bath, where I washed up in the sink, just the necessities. Face, underarms, under my breasts, and between my legs, coochie and ass. Ten minutes, and I was done.

When I exited the bathroom, Sasha already had my clothes set out on the bed. A true best friend. Sasha had always been there for me, and she always would no matter how annoying I could be. She knew me in my worst of years. Sasha was smart and beautiful. She had that light, bright skin, with dark eyes. Her hair always flowing down to her shoulders. Her hair a natural highlighted brown and blonde. She set out red high-waisted pants with a black shear shirt that went together perfectly. I threw on my Jimmy Choo shoes. I sat at my vanity to put on my accessories while Sasha brushed my hair and put it in a bun. Once she was done, I looked myself over in the mirror. I was ready to go. I gazed at the time: 8:52 a.m.

I grabbed my things and headed for the front door of our house. Sasha and I bought this house when we moved back to California. I spent my last dollar on this house, and it was something that I owned. I had wanted a house on the beach, but there was no one selling their home at the time. This three-bedroom, two-level house was ten minutes from the beach. My parents had a beach house growing up, which was one of the reasons I wanted one. When I saw this house, it made me feel like home. It was almost like the one I had grown up in, with a big living room and the open-space kitchen leading into the dining room. I cried when I saw it, and Sasha said we had to buy it. Sasha stopped me before I squeezed through the garage door.

"Call me and let me know how the meeting goes. I feel the need to celebrate," Sasha said, which didn't surprise me. Now that we were older and more mature, she always felt the need to go out and party. We did when we were teenagers, but she was always the responsible one.

"I sure will. I have a good feeling about today," I said, leaving through the garage door. Even though I was crying last night, I still felt good. I wasn't sure if it was the nice weather or the client I had been trying to land for the past year.

I hit the unlock button on Silvia, my silver 2011 Range Rover. I opened the door and hopped in. I put my seatbelt on, then checked my mirrors and put on my sunshades. It was nine o'clock by the time I hit the freeway, and I dodged and dashed in and out of traffic. I couldn't be late for this meeting. I connected my phone to the Bluetooth and dialed my office.

"Melissa," I called out when I no longer heard the ringing.

"Yes, boss lady," Melissa, my assistant, answered. I smiled because she had called me that since she started.

"I should be there at nine thirty on the nose. Have what I need ready when I arrive."

# THE LOVE I CRAVE

"Of course," she said. I hung up. It was 9:25 when I pulled up to the building. The building offered valet parking and private parking. I used valet because it was cheaper per month. I stopped the truck and tossed it in park as a black limited-edition Range Rover was pulling away. I grabbed my things and got out.

"I see you're running late as usual this morning," Rodney, the valet parking attendant, said. He gave me a smirk as I walked around my truck.

"Well, you know me, always running late. LA traffic is terrible," I said, and Rodney laughed.

"There could be no cars, and you would still be late," he said. Rodney was about my age, give or take a year.

"Catch you later." I ran toward the glass doors into EQ Skyscraper, an office building I had tried to get into for a long time. I swung the door open and ran to my right, toward the elevators. EQ Skyscraper was one of the tallest buildings in LA. The doors to the elevator were open, and people had already exited, and other people were already gathering inside.

"Hold the elevator please," I yelled out as the doors were closing. Someone put his arm in the doors for them to open back up, and I leapt through. It felt like I did this every morning, but I would never admit that to anyone. "Thank you," I said, catching my breath.

"Anytime, Hope." I turned around to see who had said my name. It was Trevor from the twentieth floor, who I always seemed to run into.

"Trevor, how are you?"

"Wonderful. I have no complaints, and you?" he asked with a smile, and I smiled back.

"No complaints here either." I turned to survey the elevator just to see who I was riding up with. To my right in the far back were devouring eyes. I quickly looked away. I waited until one person left before looking again. It was a dark-chocolate-brown man whose eyes seemed remarkably familiar. I turned my head back toward the front. My heart raced as an explosion erupted in my chest. Could it be? The glimpse of those eyes gave me chills. I went to focus on the light-up number and noticed I didn't push the button for my floor.

"Shit," I said, pushing the button for the fortieth floor. I heard someone snicker and assumed it was Trevor. I turned to him and gave him a soft smile. To be honest, I just wanted to look to my right again in the far-back corner. Our eyes connected, and I gasped quickly and turned my head away. God, were the eyes there? The eyes that had haunted me for years.

The elevator stopped on the seventeenth floor, and two people got out. I looked around, and there were only five people left inside. The doors closed, and the elevator went up.

# THE LOVE I CRAVE

I waited for my floor, but I felt like someone was staring at me. I moved a little to the left and slightly turned my head to the right. I saw those eyes again, and they were undressing me. I quickly turned my head back to the elevator doors. It opened again on the nineteenth floor. One person got off. Then it stopped again on the twentieth floor, and Trevor and another guy got off.

"See you later, I hope." Trevor smiled, and I smiled back as he got off.

Trevor had asked me out once before. I told him I wasn't ready to date anyone, which wasn't a lie. I didn't trust men at all, and it had a hell of a lot to do with HIM. I was a fool who was still waiting for Mr. Right. The elevator doors closed, and we went up again. My heart raced as I realized it was just me and those eyes left. I wanted to turn all the way around but was afraid. I was afraid that it was really those eyes, and I didn't think I was ready.

"Come on, come on," I mumbled to myself impatiently.

I heard a snicker behind me. Someone found my impatience amusing, and that irritated me. I wanted to turn around and ask him what the hell was so damn funny. I was relieved when the ding came, and the doors opened to my floor. I didn't even let the doors open all the way before I slid between them. I couldn't wait to get out of that elevator. He was sucking up all my oxygen.

7

# Henson Dreamier

I turned around to finally see who was standing behind me. I slowly looked at him, starting from his feet. The first thing I noticed was his black Prada dress shoes. They were probably a size twelve, maybe. One leg was up against the wall of the elevator. His long legs were covered with black slacks. His white collared shirt had three buttons undone at the top, and I could see a little bit of chest hair peeking out. One hand held his Armani jacket while the other held his cell phone. His hair was all over the place as if he hadn't had a haircut in months.

The doors were closing, and I took the opportunity to look into his eyes. He was already watching me with that smirk on his face. My heart leapt out of my chest. My mouth hit the floor, and my eyes popped open. I gasped. My eyes had to be playing tricks on me. Was it really him? He was sexy as hell. My heart beat rapidly in my chest. That face, it couldn't be. When I realized what was going on, the doors were closing. I leaned forward to get one last look as the doors closed. I had no idea I was still leaning over until I fell face first to the floor.

"Holy shit," I mumbled to myself, trying to pick my face up from the floor. I shook my head a few times. I stared at the closed elevator when I felt hands on my arms.

"Hope, are you okay? You look as if you saw a ghost," Aimee said. Aimee was my receptionist. A ghost, you could say that. Aimee helped me up to my feet.

# THE LOVE I CRAVE

"I think I just did." I turned back to the elevator for one more look, but nothing was there. I straightened my clothes and turned to say thank you to Aimee. I rushed past her to my office. Melissa was already there with my necessary paperwork. I needed to focus on this meeting.

"Are you okay? You look a little flustered." Melissa handed me a cup of hot tea and a folder.

"Yes, I'm fine."

Melissa gave me a contemplating look. "Okay, the meeting is being held in conference room three. I just escorted them in, so they haven't been waiting long."

"Thank you." I left my office to head down the hall to conference room three. Melissa followed me.

"You look sick. Are you sure you're okay?" she asked.

"I'll be fine," I said, entering the conference room. I greeted everyone with a handshake and got straight to business.

The meeting lasted longer than I expected. Maybe it was because my mind was still in that elevator. I sat at the head of the table trying to land this important client. The only thing I could think about was those eyes, but there was something different about them. There was no love, no passion behind them anymore, not as I remembered. I wondered what had happened to him since the last time I saw him. It was a night in New York, I was there for work. I was a senior in high

9

school. I guess life since then had gotten to both of us. My name brought me back to the present conversation.

I looked up to see both accountants staring at me. They had been talking, and I wasn't hearing a thing. How rude and unprofessional could I be right now? Just the quick glimpse of Hunter had me squirming in my seat, thinking about what happened the last time I saw him. My kitty kat purred for him. Why did he still after all these years have that effect on me. My body tingled from his last touch, igniting my body like flames. Helen called my name again.

"I apologize. What were you saying?"

"I think this will be a wonderful opportunity for the both of you." Helen gave me a concerned look from across the table. She handed me the contracts, and I looked over them. The contract stated what I wanted for my magazine Javier. The interviews and the photographs and what I could and couldn't say or ask.

"Mr. Miles, how does that sound to you?" I asked once I was done scanning over the contract. Mr. Miles was the lawyer for Carmen, a successful businesswoman who owned a night club in Las Vegas called Club Candy. I wanted to land this contract. Carmen had Club Candy remodeled, and I wanted to be the first to write about it and interview Carmen.

"I think it's a wonderful decision, Miss Hope." Mr. Miles was a fifty-year-old man with salt and pepper hair. He stood from his seat, offering me his hand. "I'll keep in touch concerning the dates and times of the interviews. I'll call you in a couple of days to let you know what weekend Carmen decides." I accepted his hand.

"Thank Carmen for the wonderful opportunity," I said.

"Of course. Have you ever been to Vegas before?" Mr. Miles asked. A horrible memory came back to me. One I wish I could have blocked out long ago. I shook the thought away.

"Yes, a long time ago. I don't remember that much of it. You know what they say, what happens in Vegas stays in Vegas." I gave him a smile as laughter filled the room.

"Yes, indeed," Mr. Miles said. I led the way out of the office and down the hall. We entered the reception area, heading toward the elevator. "Well, it'll be a pleasure to have you back again. I'll keep in touch." We shook hands again as the elevator doors opened, and he stepped in.

"Wonderful, have a great flight back," I said. I waited for the doors to close to get excited. I turned to see Aimee behind her desk. I gave her a quick smile, and I ran back to my office.

I closed the door and thought about the client I just landed. I started Javier right after I got the money from Hunter. I sank into my seat as I thought of the name Javier. It belonged to the man I loved. I just saw him, why wasn't I excited about it? Quite frankly, I was terrified. I'd been in love with that man for as long as I could remember, and now here I was, feeling like a shy school kid. I thought repeatedly of the possibility of traveling the building to find him. Then I remembered seeing the button that he pushed on the elevator. The eightieth floor. I remembered being told that the top floors were held by the owners of the building, whom I'd never met before. I needed to get through the rest of the day with my head out of the clouds. Hunter made me lose focus already. I picked up the phone and called Sasha and informed her of the good news.

Sasha was excited for me as always. She said she would make reservations for us at Obsessions tonight, one of our favorite spots here in Los Angeles. After I hung up with Sasha, I headed upstairs to my magazine and newsletter. I informed them of the good news. I would have my manager Abby call the printing company to let them know. My newsletter was called LA Days, which consisted of news that had happened yesterday, today, and what may possibly happen tomorrow. I also ran a few charities and owned two floors in EQ Skyscraper. The fortieth and the forty-first floor.

As I made my rounds on the forty-first floor, informing everyone of the new client we just landed, I also used that time to catch up with my employees' lives. I tried to do that every two weeks. Being a major publishing company with many employees, I picked a handful of people to travel with me. I tried to give everyone who worked with me a chance. I told them that I'd be in touch regarding who would be traveling with me to Vegas. I conversed for a while longer before I headed back downstairs to my office to finish up some work.

# THE LOVE I CRAVE

"Hope, you had a visitor while you were gone," Aimee said as soon as I stepped off the elevator.

Aimee had an uncontrollable smile upon her face. I stopped at her desk, and she handed me a small white envelope. I gasped when I saw the familiar label. The moment my hands touched it, I got chills. This was the second envelope I had received, and I knew who it was from. Hunter, the love of my life. I slowly opened the envelope with nerves traveling to my fingers. I was nervous and excited to see what it said. My heart stopped as I read the first words. The name, he was the only one who ever called me that.

*To Baby girl: Our time has finally arrived. I know I'm late, but better late than never, right. I'm still in love with you, and I hope you're with me. There's no stopping us now. Congratulations, Zollah, you deserve all the great things that has and will happen to you. See you sooner than later.*

*Love H...*

No one had called me Zollah in a long time. I smiled and put the note back into the envelope and looked around the lobby.

"He didn't stay. He said he had to get ready for tonight," Aimee said.

"What?" I paused "What's going on tonight?" I stood there in shock.

# Henson Dreamier

Why wouldn't he stay? Why would he come when I had left? I fought the urge to get back on the elevator and march around the eightieth floor. I looked around the receptionist area again. I looked down at the letter as I went back to my office. I closed the door behind me and paced the floor like a mad woman. I was determined to go upstairs and find him. Just when I got the nerves to go upstairs, the intercom came on, and Melissa told me that my next meeting was in five minutes. Lucky him, or maybe it was lucky me. I knew I wasn't the same person I was when I left California at the age of fifteen. I was damaged goods now. HIM, my ex-boyfriend, fucked my whole world up. I had no idea there could be life after HIM. Hunter's eyes kept me sane, believing that my life could get better, and it had.

Was I ready to meet the new Hunter, and was Hunter ready to meet the new me? I looked around my office. I wouldn't have any of this. I loved my floor-to-ceiling windows. I had them all around the reception area, my office, my meeting rooms. Even Melissa's office had them too. Not many floors offered fireplaces, but I was thrilled with mine. Damon, my best friend, was a painter, and I had all his paintings around the office and along the hall. I loved the plants decorating my office. I loved the pale-blue paint on the walls. I loved my huge black desk with my massive chair. I owed Hunter everything.

My next meeting didn't last long at all. I scored another client, so my day was a successful one. I had a couple of conference calls to make and several emails to complete. My day was finished by four. I told Aimee and Melissa I was heading home, and to switch all my calls until after noon tomorrow. I had a feeling I wouldn't make it in on time. I called Rodney and told him I was on my way down and to have Silvia ready for me. By the time I hit the glass doors, Rodney was ready. I was disappointed I was leaving without seeing Hunter, but I was ready to go out and celebrate. He said he had to get ready for tonight, so did I. What was more important than seeing me?

"Have a great evening, Hope," Rodney said.

"You too. See you tomorrow." He smiled and held my door open for me. I hopped inside and headed home.

I made it home before Sasha, so it was my turn to cook. We made that rule years ago. Whoever made it home first would be the one to cook dinner. So, I guess that would be me tonight. I made a simple stir fry. Once I was done with that, I hopped in the shower and picked out something sexy to wear tonight. I decided on a black skintight strapless dress. As my girl Bey called it, a freak-em dress. Sasha got home at six thirty, and we ate and had a glass of wine. I got dressed while she showered. I put on some red, red bottoms shoes with my red lipstick and my mother's diamond earrings, necklace, and bracelet. I was ready to hit the dance floor and take some shots of tequila.

It was nine p.m. as we pulled up to Obsessions. Sasha and I took my truck. She loved my truck because it rode as if it floated on water. The line was around the corner; you would have thought it was a Friday night, not a Monday. We parked in our usual spot and walked right on in. Henry, of course, was there at the door.

"Miss Hope, Miss Jordan." Henry had been the bouncer of Obsessions since we started coming here. Henry was a big guy, and he loved him some Sasha.

"How is it going, Henry?" I asked, taking his attention away from Sasha.

"I have no complaints. Would you ladies be having your regular table in VIP?" he asked.

"Of course, and also tell Jesse to send us a bottle of Dom Perignon and a bottle of Patron," I said as Henry opened the door for us, and we headed toward the VIP section. We took the long hallway down and the steps up on our left. As we walked, men stared the entire time. Sasha and I had been approached by all types of men: broke ones, crazy ones, toothless ones, cheap ones. All the ones that were no good, they came our way. By the time we reached our table, Jesse had finished setting up.

Jesse was the owner of Obsessions and was like a father to me. In his early fifties, he had always looked out for me since I started coming here. I loved Jesse, and I loved the way he knew his way around the dance floor.

"How are my two favorite ladies doing tonight?" Jesse asked as he pulled out our seats. Jesse was dressed in one of his colored suits. He reminded me of Steve Harvey. He was always sharp and always had a suit on.

"Great," I said.

"What are we celebrating?" he asked, placing one bottle of tequila on the table while he opened the bottle of Dom and placed it in the bucket of ice.

"Well, I landed a new client today. A wonderful opportunity for Hope's Publishing Company," I said.

"That's wonderful, Hope. Congratulations. I'm so happy for you," he said, pouring us two glasses. Then he placed the bottle back inside the ice.

"Let's make a toast," Jesse said as we held up our glasses. "This is for the two daughters I'll never have. May your lives be blessed and stress free. May you two be as successful as me. To Sasha and Jordan's Technology being a success, and to Hope having one of the top publishing companies in LA. Hope, I pray that you find a man that will sweep you off your feet and treat you like the queen you are." We all tapped our glasses.

"Amen to that, Uncle Jesse," Sasha said before taking a sip. Jesse was a little familiar with my past. He knew how far I had come from being with HIM. What he said made me think of Hunter and how much I forgot to update Sasha.

"Are you guys starting without me?" I turned to see Melissa walking in, looking amazing as usual. Melissa had on black high-waisted pants and a baby-blue shirt with some baby-blue and black pumps.

"Honey, the party waits for no one," I said as Jesse pulled her seat out for her. Ten minutes later, Aimee strolled in with skintight jeans and a half shirt and high heels. We all sat and finished up the bottle of Dom Perignon.

The DJ was setting up, and it was time to get our party on. I wasn't the type to hold up the wall; I held up the dance floor. I loved to dance and so did my mother. We used to dance around the house, singing to some Patti Labelle and Chaka Khan—mostly anything from the 70s or 80s. The night was going well until Aimee opened her mouth.

# GIRL, TONIGHT

S o, did Hope tell you she has a secret admirer?" Aimee said, sipping from her glass. All their eyes turned to look at me. I nervously sipped from my glass. It wasn't that I didn't want to tell; I just totally forgot.

"No, miss thang didn't tell me," Sasha said, giving me that holding out on me look. The one she had been giving me all my life.

"I forgot to mention it over dinner," I said, not trying to look at her. I knew she was burning a hole in my head trying to get inside. "You remember that summer at LABA?" Once I said that, her eyes lit up.

"Yes."

"Well, he showed up at the office today and left me another note. Saying congratulations, see you sooner than later." I took another sip.

"Did you find him?" Sasha asked.

"Well, he always seems to find me, which I find highly interesting," I said. Sasha turned to Aimee.

"How did he look? What was he wearing? Where does he work?" Sasha asked Aimee. I didn't have the time to say anything before Aimee spoke.

"Drop-dead gorgeous. I mean finger-licking good." My eyes turned Aimee's way, listening to how she described my Hunter as "...tall, dark, and mysterious. He has the most beautiful russet-color eyes I've ever seen before... short haircut, long fingers, and big feet," Aimee said, and I saw a glint of admiration in her eyes. We all stared at her and the way she described Hunter.

"And you got all of this from just three minutes of him in your presence," I said.

"Two minutes and hey, I know something good when I see it. Plus, this guy was all smiles when he said your legal name Zollah, as if he was mind fucking the shit out of you," Aimee said.

"Aimee." I gasped with shock. Sasha had her phone in her hand, pressing them buttons like a maniac.

THE LOVE I CRAVE

"I'm just saying, and he was dressed from head to toe in Armani. He had on a Winston Rolex worth two hundred thousand dollars and a Harvard graduate ring on his finger. Should I go on?" Aimee said, taking a breather so she could take a sip from her glass.

As they talked, I thought about my elevator ride. That was him this morning. It was Hunter, my Hunter. Well, I didn't know about mine. He was the reason why I fell on my face. I looked over at Sasha, and she was in deep thought. Her eyes lit up, and I knew she had something. She downed her glass and poured herself another one.

"How could I have been so stupid? I've been so tied up with myself that I didn't put two and two together. Holy shit, how could I have missed something this big?" Sasha said, and we all looked at her. Waiting for her to say what she had come up with, she looked up from her phone. Sasha was good at finding out information.

"I remember the night you met Hunter. I'd never seen two people look at each other the way you two did. I can't even explain because I never had that before. At first, I thought you were crazy for believing in him. I thought you were a fool for waiting. Remember when you tried to get two floors in EQ Skyscraper?" Sasha asked.

"Yes, they were full."

"Yeah, full. Then not even a week had passed, and you received a call saying there was a vacancy." All I had ever known about the place was that it was owned by two millionaires. I never bothered to look up the names. I was happy to have a space. Sasha was right; just like that, I was moving into the building which was ironic. I had received a call from Asher Ross' assistant. As soon as I said the name, a lightbulb flickered. Asher Ross, why didn't I think of that at first?

"Have you ever met the owners of the building?" Sasha asked.

"No," I admitted. Everyone was quiet for a moment as we took in what Sasha said. I was nervous as hell. For what reason, I didn't know. I just sat there, my mind wandering as I sipped on my glass.

"You got that call from Asher Ross' assistant. Asher Ross was one of the owners of the building with his partner. Asher is Hunter's best friend from LABA." As she spoke, I remembered Asher. Tall, light-brown skin, funny, and smart. It all made sense to me now. So much I had blocked out of my mind, and some things were knocked out, but it was all coming back to me.

"Oh my God." I knew Hunter gave me the money, which I used to start my business. I never knew he was the one behind me getting into the building.

"Hope, I really thought he just wanted to get in your panties. I knew you were in love with each other, but..." she

22

said as she grabbed the bottle of Patron. "Do you know what this means, Hope?" Sasha asked, opening the bottle.

"That we're taking shots."

"No."

"That I should be running for the hills," I said.

"Hell no, it means that all these years, you've been in love with the multi-millionaire Hunter Grayson, one of the wealthiest black men in America. You go, girl," Sasha said.

"You go, girl," Aimee and Melissa said in unison.

"And you got all of that from your cellphone?" I thought about what was to come. Was my time here? Would I finally be with Hunter Grayson? It scared me because I wasn't sure if I was ready for a relationship. A relationship with Hunter meant being publicized. If people saw me and knew my name, then HIM would find me. Now that was the scariest shit ever.

"Let us make a toast," Sasha said as she poured us shots of Patron. It was time to get twisted. I didn't want to get drunk, but tipsy sure. Maybe a little stumble but not a fumble, if you know what I mean.

"I want to go first," Aimee said as she passed out the shots. We all held up our shot glasses. "I want to toast to Hope for giving me the chance no one else would give me; for that I'm grateful. I'm happy that this Hunter is back, and you could finally be happier." We all tapped our glasses, then downed our shots. I loved Patron Silver; it was smooth and went down easy. Sasha poured us another shot as Melissa went next.

"I want to toast to finally having real ladies in my life. I know what the meaning of true friends means. Friends I know who would have my back no matter what, and I'm thankful for having such a wonderful job that I love so much. Thank you, Hope." We all tapped our glasses together and downed another shot. I was beginning to feel nice as the Patron made its way through my body. Sasha poured us another shot, and she went next.

"I want to thank my best friend for always being there for me. We've been through hell and back with one another. Each moment I wouldn't change for the world. It made us the women we are today. This is to you finally having Hunter in your life. To him finally fucking you and knocking them cobwebs out of your pussy. To him sexing you senseless and to having you screaming until you're unable to stand up," Sasha said. Now I knew that would be the type of toast she would make. I ignored her and took my shot.

"Amen to that, sister," Melissa said before taking her shot.

We ordered our second bottle of Patron before the music called me to the dance floor. DJ Mani always played the mix to get all the women on the dance floor. Men were sure to follow. Aimee, Melissa, Sasha, and I danced around each other, feeling the music. As I danced, I felt someone watching me, but I figured it was some guy. I was always being watched by some guy or somebody else's guy.

We danced through a few songs before we headed back to the table. Before I even stepped foot off the dance floor, I was snatched up by somebody. I turned to look, and it was Jesse, of course. Jesse and I always shared a dance when I came. He was the one who actually taught me how to hand dance. I was a little girl when my father tried to teach me. That was a long time ago, so I needed a refresher course. It was hard at first to learn, especially when he said I should let the man lead. That was hard for me to do. I couldn't let a man lead. The last time I did that, I ended up running for my life.

DJ Mani played some oldies but goodies, and we twisted and turned all over the dance floor. I could work up a sweat dancing with Jesse, but I loved it. I still felt like I was being watched. It felt like eyes was burning through the back of my head. Our time was over, and Jesse made his way back to his office. I made my way over to the bar to grab a glass of water, but I never made it. I made one step, and my head started to spin. I felt like I was burning up. I stood in place for a moment to get myself together. I closed my eyes just for a second and counted to ten when I felt someone come in front of me. The hairs on the back of my neck stood at attention. A hand touched my arm, and I felt butterflies fill my stomach. The way the hands felt on me brought back good times. I was afraid to open my eyes. In my mind, the music disappeared, and all I could hear were two hearts beating in sync. When I heard my name, I could have lost it.

25

"Zollah, baby girl," an intoxicating voice said. I slowly opened my eyes to see a tall, dark, handsome, hunk of a man standing before me. The butterflies flew around in my stomach. His hand left my shoulder as he fed me water from a straw. I saw those eyes that took my breath away. I couldn't speak. I just leaned in, drinking the water before me. I finished the glass of water, and he placed it on the table next to us.

"Zollah, you're scaring me. Can you please say something?" he said, but I couldn't say anything. His eyes hypnotized me, just as they had always done, especially the first night we met. I knew I had bright brown eyes, but I'd never saw anything like his before. I felt like that sixteen-year-old teenager all over again.

I stepped back from him just to take all of him in. He was dressed in all black and looked Tony the Tiger great. He was dressed in Armani from head to toe. He had a fresh haircut with waves as deep as the ocean. He had two buttons undone on his shirt. His arms looked strong; I could tell through his shirt that he worked out.

"Sorry, do I know you?" I said, trying to play coy. I was smiling, unable to control myself, but I was fighting him already. He gave me that smirk, and my heart melted.

"I told you years ago that I didn't like my future wife getting drunk in public. I think you've had enough for tonight," he said, grabbing for my hand and pulling me with him. I planted my feet on the floor.

# THE LOVE I CRAVE

"Excuse me, I'm not sure if you've noticed or not, but I'm not that same person anymore. I grew up," I said, pulling my hand away. I was trying to sound serious, but it was hard. I watched him as he moved closer to me. Oh my, I could smell his essence. He smelled amazing. He was so close to me that his chest grazed against my breasts. A sigh escaped my lips.

"Oh yes, I noticed that you're no longer that young girl from LABA. You've grown to be such a beautiful, amazing, sexy, and successful woman." He smiled at me, and I melted. He moved closer as if that were even possible. He was up close and personal. "I watched the way you moved on the dance floor," he whispered in my ear. "My God, that dress you're wearing is hugging every inch of your body. Every inch that I want to lick." He closed his eyes, and I could tell he was imagining some freaky things. His eyes shot open. "You're making me hard." My eyes widened at his choice of words.

Not even knowing, my eyes glanced down at the tent building in his pants. Oh my. My legs just turned on its own, and I began to walk away. I made three steps before I felt his hand on my arm. He turned me back around to face him.

"Zollah, don't run. We've waited too long for this moment. We can finally hold each other in our arms. We can finally be together," he said as he pulled me closer to him. Every time he said my name, it was like my vagina moved two inches toward him. He grabbed my face with his hands, and our eyes met. "Zollah, I'm not going to hurt you. I would never. I can see that you've been hurt and wounded tremendously. All I want to do is protect you and help you heal from the pain. Then hopefully, you can make me the happiest man alive," he said, and I knew he meant every single word of it. I believed him just like I did all those years ago. His hand grazed the scar on my cheek, down to the scar on my neck. I didn't have the scars the last time I saw him, and they didn't seem to bother him. Well, not until I was naked, and he saw the rest of my body.

I was afraid, and I turned my head away so I couldn't look him in the eyes. How could I say what I wanted without being rude? I did want this, but I was terrified.

"I'm… I'm not the same. I've changed. I've been through hell and…" I was saying, but he cut me off by putting his finger up to my lips.

"We've both been through some things that changed us," he said, but all I could think about was that I wanted another drink. Hunter had my body screaming. I felt alive. My brain was working overtime on what I wanted. I got the strength to look up in his eyes.

"I'm going to get another drink. Would you like one?" I asked, and a scared look appeared on his face.

"No. I don't drink, and I think that you've had enough tonight," he said.

"You keep saying that. Why?"

"Zollah, I'm scared for you. You were and still are the girl who stole my heart that summer. I will never love another as I love you," he said. I lifted my hands up to his face as if I were showing him his heart. Then I lowered my hands to his chest and put his heart back where it belonged.

"Now you can have it back. I must get back to my friends. It was nice seeing you again." I turned and walked away. I couldn't believe what I just did. Each step I took away from him was like stepping on needles. I picked up the pace until I got closer to my table. When I got there, Aimee, Melissa, and Sasha were having a conversation about God knows what.

The moment I wasn't in his presence anymore, I felt sick. Like a part of me was missing. I felt whole again for about ten minutes, and now I felt empty. Tonight made a hell of a turn. I was breathing heavy by the time I sat in my seat. How could I just leave him standing there like that? What was wrong with me? I shook my head. I grabbed the bottle of Patron and poured a shot. Sasha turned toward me. I down the first shot, then poured another one.

"What the hell is wrong with you?" Sasha asked.

"You won't believe what I'm about to say," I said, finishing the second shot.

When I looked back up to continue talking, I saw a tall figure floating my way. It was like he was gliding across the room. My eyes locked with him, and he took my breath away. Damn, the brother was drop-dead gorgeous. My heart fluttered watching him walk toward me. His eyes were glued to mine. He looked like a Greek god. I picked up my napkin to wipe the drool from my mouth.

"Oh my God," I said, turning my eyes away.

"That's him," Aimee said as she turned to look at me. Sasha turned to look at me.

"I can't," I said.

"What? Hope, stop acting like a big baby," Sasha said, turning to face Hunter who was now at the table.

"Hello, ladies. Melissa, Aimee, it's a pleasure." He held out his hand as they shook it. Then he turned to Sasha. "Sasha, it's a pleasure to see you again," he said as he shook her hand.

"The pleasure is all mine. Please have a seat," she said. I glared at her. There were only four chairs at the table and out of nowhere, here came another chair, thanks to Melissa. Sasha rolled her eyes at me. What were we, like twelve years old? Melissa grabbed an extra champagne glass and poured him one.

"He doesn't drink," I said, snapping at them. Melissa's eyes widened as if she'd never heard such a thing before. I was irritated for no reason, maybe more like scared.

"Oh, I'm sorry to hear that," Melissa said. We all looked at each other, then burst into laughter. Even Hunter laughed, which made me think he still had his sense of humor. I tried not to watch him, but the man was FINE.

"So, Hunter, what brings you here to Obsessions?" Sasha asked, and his eyes landed on me.

"I came to finally claim what's mine. I've been out of the country for a while," he said. then his facial expression got serious. "You promised me," he said to me in a stern voice.

"I was sixteen years old."

"The first time, but don't forget the second time in New York," he said, and my whole body jerked at the thought of that day. The last time I saw him. "So, what you're saying is you didn't mean it?" he asked.

"No, I mean you said…" I paused for a moment. I inhaled a deep breath. "I mean it took longer than I expected, and now I'm…"

"Whatever, Zollah." He snatched my right hand from across the table and looked at the black and gold band on my ring finger. I gasped. His eyes widened with shock, but his heart sure sang at the sight of the ring. Then that smirk appeared on his face. I tried to snatch my finger back, but he held it tight.

"You're ready, and you've been ready. You're still wearing the promise ring I bought you that summer." Yes, I was, and it was one of the things I left with when I ran.

"I said I will never take it off, and I never did." I was finally able to snatch my hand back.

"You're just fighting me because you're scared."

"Stop talking like you know me," I said.

"So, you're not scared?" he asked, and I looked around the table. Everyone's eyes were on me.

"And you're not?" I asked, ignoring them.

"Yes, but I know what I want, and I'm staring right at it." I felt tingling all over my body when his hand touched mine. I looked at everyone at the table, and they were staring at us, like we were some damn soap opera.

"Zollah," he called my name.

"Stop calling my name like that," I said. My pussy moved two inches every time, and now I was damn near straddling him.

"How am I saying it? That's your name, right? Zollah Piper Hope. Born April 7th, 1985," he said. What was he going to do, tell the whole damn world who I was?

"Okay, okay, Hunter, what do you want?"

"Dance with me." He stood and held out his hand for mine. "I'll tell you." I looked at his hand. "Please, Zollah," he begged after I left him hanging for a moment. Two more inches, and I was out of my seat.

"Okay, Hunter, but I hope you still know your way around the dance floor. I don't like a man with no rhythm," I said, taking his hand, and he led me toward the dance floor.

## THE LOVE I CRAVE

"I got all the rhythm you'll ever need, believe that," he said as he pulled me closer to him, and then the music immediately slowed down.

Tony Toni Tone came through the speakers. That song took me back to that night when we first met. When his arms formed around my waist. I felt safe again, like he would protect me from the world itself. I always felt that way when I was with him.

"Whatever you want, girl. You know I can provide," he sang into my ear. We moved to the beat as the DJ mixed a bunch of slow songs together. Hunter Grayson still had some moves on him. The way Hunter danced was getting me hot and bothered.

"Zollah, I want you to be able to trust me," he said, holding me close. Roger came over the speaker. I knew the song well. My father used to sing it to my mother. He asked me to trust him as if he knew I had trust issues. Maybe I had mentioned it before. I put my head down because I knew it was true.

"Zollah, look at me," he said, lifting my head up with his finger. "I want to be the man in your life. I can't be that if you ignore me or run from me. I want you to open yourself up to me. I'll never hurt you."

"That's a lot to ask from a fucked-up individual with major trust issues," I said.

"We all have issues," he said, holding me tighter in his arms. A sigh escaped my lips as we moved to the music. He sang the song in my ear.

"I want to be your man." Those words sent chills down my spine. "I missed you so much," he moaned in my ear as our bodies became one to the music. I could feel his chest against my breasts. "Come home with me tonight please," he asked. I tensed under his touch.

"No, I can't," I said in a hushed tone.

"No?" he said, pushing me away from him. He turned me around, so my back was against his chest. I could feel his manhood growing against my ass.

"I just want to be your man," he said as his voice sent a shockwave through me.

His hands ran all over my breasts, making my nipples erect. His hands ran from my breasts to my thighs, making me feel so good. My kitty was screaming at me. She wanted some attention, and she wanted it now. She had waited too long for some male stimulation.

Hunter lowered his head, and I felt his lips against my neck, then my shoulder. Oh my, he made me feel so good. I moaned out to him. He used his hand to spin me around again, and now I was facing him. His face was full of determination.

"Zollah, you look so sexy in that dress. I just want to rip it off you." He was turning me on. We were grinding manhood to vagina. Then the song changed again to a one by Twista. My arms were around his neck, while his arms were around my waist. I felt his warm breath against my neck. Every time he sang to me was like a lullaby. He rubbed his hands all over my back. He'd always had a seductive voice.

Hunter had me moist between my thighs. We were in a bubble, floating away to another world. Hunter had me open like a layaway plan at Christmas time. He turned me back around, his chest against my back. His hands massaged my breasts through my dress. A moan escaped my lips as my nipples hardened. I felt his hands move down past my stomach to my cave. Oh no, what was he doing? His hands eased under my dress, and I didn't even try to stop him. His hand slid under my dress and massaged my pebble. I leaned my head against his shoulder as Hunter's soft lips kissed my neck. I shivered when his lips kissed my scar. I hadn't felt this good in a long time. I felt wanted and needed at the same time.

"Zollah, you're so wet for me," he moaned into my ear. Yes, I was; I couldn't deny that.

"You have that effect on me." I felt his hands slip away from me. My eyes were closed as I found myself facing him again. I gazed into his eyes and noticed that they had gotten brighter. He pulled me closer to him, then smiled at me.

"Sounds good to me," he said.

Every song the DJ played was like he was setting me up. Our eyes were connected, never wanting to let go. We were so close, he slid his right arm between our bodies. He stopped once he found my pebble again. Another moan escaped my lips. My eyes melted in his. His lips nibbled on my ear.

"Come home with me, baby girl." I felt his fingers pull my sex lips apart. I shivered, and my body fell against him. I wrapped my arms around him.

"No, I can't," I moaned out. I wasn't saying *I can't* come in the middle of a dance floor.

"No," he repeated what I said. I was enjoying every moment of this. Why not go home with him. You'd been waiting to fuck his brains out for a long time now. My train of thought was broken when I felt his thumb rub circles on my pebble. I wrapped my arms tighter around his neck. His long fingers massaged my cave.

"Shit," I moaned into his ear as his finger found its way inside my cave. I tilted my head back as my eyes rolled in the back of my head. My kitty purred from the attention. She let him know it to. "Hunter," I screamed his name. It wasn't a loud scream; it was a soft, sexual scream.

"Yes, baby girl, let it out all over my hand." I held on tight to him. My knees were giving out. After I came all over his hand, he never stopped. In and out of my cave with his finger as his thumb ran circles on my clit. My nipples were so hard they hurt. My hips moved with the pace of his hand, helping him go deeper and deeper inside me. I wanted every part of him, but something was fighting it. I knew it wasn't my kitty. She was ready and down for whatever.

"Oh, Hunter, please," I moaned out to him. The next thing I knew, I was coming again. My juices rolled down my thigh. I held on to him as if my life depended on it.

"Come home with me, Zollah. My house is lonely without you there," he whispered in my ear. "You promised me forever, and I'm here to collect." I couldn't speak. Maybe if he removed his fingers from inside me, I could function properly, but his fingers were still inside me.

"Please stop."

"Not until you agree to come home with me," he said as his thumb moved faster on my pebble.

"No, you can't make me." I never liked someone making me do something I didn't want to do. That was my life with HIM, and I hated every moment.

"Say yes," he said. His pace picked up. His fingers moved faster inside me as I felt my pebble swelling up.

"Don't give in. Don't give in," I kept telling myself. My whole body tensed up. I tossed my head back as my eyes rolled in the back of my head. I was on the verge of screaming. My climax was on the edge, waiting to rip through me. When he leaned down, he bit my neck. My body couldn't take it anymore. That orgasm ripped through me like nothing

I felt before. I lost my breath for a quick moment and if he weren't holding me, I would have fallen to the floor.

"Hunter, I'll go home with you," I said. How could I say no to such an orgasm? My body was alive, and it was seeking for more.

"Good girl," he said, removing his hand from inside of me. "Oh my God." He lifted his hand to his mouth, slowly sucking my juices from his fingers. Oh, he was nasty, and I found that such a turn on. Then he saved his last finger for me. He held it out to me to see if I would do it. I smiled before I slowly opened my mouth, closing it around his finger. I pulled my mouth back slowly with my tongue.

"My nasty girl, I knew you'd do it. You taste delightful, don't you?" He removed his finger from my mouth and smiled as he wrapped his arm around mine. "Now let's go home."

"Home?" He made home sound like I was never leaving. I had my own house I shared with Sasha. I was just going to his home for a night. Maybe a couple of times out of the week.

"Yes, home," he said. I had no idea where he was going with that, but I didn't care at the moment.

"Alright," I said. I probably would have agreed to anything now. "Let me tell Sasha that I'm leaving," I said as we walked hand in hand back to the table.

# THE LOVE I CRAVE

"Of course. I wouldn't let you leave without telling your friends," he said. Every time he spoke, he sent chills through me. When we got back to the table, they were in conversation. Sasha was the first to look, as her eyes gazed over me.

"Umm hmm," she said as if she knew what had taken place on the dance floor.

"It was nice meeting you, ladies," Hunter said.

"A pleasure," Melissa and Aimee said.

"I'm leaving," I said, cutting them off as they gawked over my man. I grabbed my red handbag from the table. I opened my bag, pulled out my keys, and handed them to Sasha. I turned to look at Aimee and Melissa who made little faces at each other.

"You put a scratch on my baby, and I will put a scratch on you," I said.

"Your truck should be the least of your worries. You should worry about yourself." Sasha gave me a wink. Then she snatched the keys from my hand.

# SWIMMING

The night air felt good when it hit my skin. I was burning hot inside from all the body-on-body contact. The breeze sort of woke me up. I felt nervous as each foot made its way to the curb. I noticed an all-black 2012 limited-edition Range Rover at the curb. It had tinted windows with all black rims. Damn, that thing was sexy. I'd seen this model before, right outside of EQ Skyscraper. It was sexier and prettier than mine. I was officially jealous. There was a tall, handsome man with light-brown skin waiting at the truck for us. He came around to open the back door for us. He had a smile on his face. What was it with everyone smiling tonight? I guess tonight was a good night for many. The smile I rocked made my cheeks hurt. I hadn't been able to smile in a long time. I'd laughed, but never smiled.

# THE LOVE I CRAVE

"Julius, this is Zollah. Zollah, this is Julius. Julius is my personal driver. He takes me wherever I want to go, and he'll soon do the same for you, if you need him to," Hunter said, and I turned to Julius.

"Hello, Julius."

"Hello, Miss Hope," Julius said. We finally climbed in the backseat, and Julius closed the door. I watched him walk all the way around and climb in the driver's seat. I wondered why Hunter didn't drive himself around. I didn't mind driving my truck, and I sure didn't need someone else driving me around.

"Where to, Grayson?" Julius asked.

"Home," Hunter said as we sat side by side. Our arms rubbed against each other. We held hands, never wanting to let go. He pulled me closer to him, and our eyes met. I gazed into his eyes and said the first thing that came to mind.

"I thought I would never see you again. I want to say how I appreciate everything you've done for me."

"I'll do anything for you, baby girl. I got your back just like I know you'll have mine," he said, rubbing his other hand through my hair.

"Always," I said.

"Always." At that moment, everything moved in slow motion.

Our heads slowly moved toward each other. This would be the first time tonight our lips met for the first time in years. My heart raced. My kitty purred. My God, I still loved this man. My eyes closed as our lips finally connected. It felt like something exploded inside me. His lips devoured mine. I sucked on his bottom lip.

Damn, his lips were as soft as a cotton ball. I opened my eyes and saw fireworks. We held the kiss for a moment as I slowly opened my mouth to accept his tongue that forced its way through. I almost forgot how it felt to kiss someone, especially someone you were in love with. I forgot how sweet a kiss could be. Hunter brought back everything I'd been missing in romance. In intimacy.

"Oh Zollah, I've missed you so much," he moaned between the kiss.

"I've missed you more." He smiled. I couldn't lie to myself anymore. I was happy, and I did miss him like crazy. I finally felt somewhat whole again after feeling so empty for so long. I loved Hunter, and I didn't think I would ever stop.

The ride to Hunter's house didn't take long at all. We pulled up to this beautiful house after a twenty-minute drive from Obsession. His house sat alone while the others were connected. I guess the man needed his privacy. His house was also bigger than the others. It looked bigger, better, and newer. It wasn't a house I thought a multi-millionaire would live in. I was thinking a house on the hill, with a pool in the back with a gym or something. I thought his house would be more secluded from the rest. Well, it was a gated community. I rolled the window down to get some fresh air. I inhaled and could smell moisture in the air. The beach had to be close by.

Hunter didn't wait for Julius to open the door for us. He grabbed my hand and led me out. He pulled me all the way to the door. He was very anxious to get me inside. I smiled as I turned to see that Julius was trailing behind us. I hadn't noticed how built he was. I guess they must also be workout buddies. Julius looked to be in his thirties, and he looked good. We all waited for Hunter to get his keys out to unlock the door. My mind wondered what would happen once I got on the other side of that door. Hunter finally got out his keys, and he turned to me.

"Julius, you're done here. I'll see you in the morning," he said.

"Yes, Grayson," Julius said, turning around and walking back to the truck. He got inside and pulled off. I turned back to Hunter and imagined him touching me all over and kissing every spot on my body. I imagined him behind me, stroking me with everything in him. Pulling my hair and spanking me at the same time. Sucking on my nipples while I played with myself. Just the thought made me come.

"Shit," I mumbled, realizing I had my eyes closed. He finally got the door opened. I looked at Hunter, then down at myself, and noticed little drops of liquid rolling down my thigh.

"Did you just?" he asked, staring at me. I couldn't say anything. I shook my head yes. He quickly pulled me through the door, slamming it shut and dropping his keys on the small table.

His mouth was on mine before I knew it. This kiss was filled with so much aggression and determination. Everything I ever felt for him came back to me in full force. I wrapped my arms around his neck as I pushed him up against the door. The last time I saw him was in New York. I thought about that day in the piano room. I pulled back the kiss. There was no going back now; I was with the one I'd waited for.

"I want you, Hunter Grayson," I said in his ear. He pulled me in for another kiss. Our hands were all over one another. His hands found their way to the back of my dress.

"Did I tell you how much I wanted to rip this dress off you earlier?" he said. I looked up into his eyes. I was so wrapped up in his essence that when I heard a rip, my eyes widened with surprise. He... he ripped my dress straight down the middle. He was now pilling it off my shoulders. I watched as it fell to the floor.

Hunter's moans were like music in my ears, and I knew from this moment, I would be lost in him. Lost in his world. Lost in the life I always wanted with him. I hadn't been naked around Hunter since that night in New York. My body wasn't the same anymore. I feared how he would react to all the scars. My kitty purred like a tiger. I stood there in front of him, wearing nothing but my pumps.

# THE LOVE I CRAVE

I watched Hunter admire my body. His eyes trailed from my face down to my feet. Everywhere his eyes met, I ignited in flames. This wasn't the first time he had admired me. I used my arms to wrap them around me. I didn't want to fall shy or embarrassed, but my body didn't look the same. Of course, my body filled out as I got older, but there were scars on me that weren't there before. I wanted to hide the evidence of HIM. Hunter hadn't once asked about the scars or what happened to me. He didn't care, and that almost made me tear up.

"Don't be ashamed. You don't have to be with me. I don't see them; I just see you," he said, placing his hands on my face to pull me in for a passionate kiss. Even though his words meant everything to me, I saw the vengeance burning behind his eyes. I knew one day he would ask me who, and I wasn't sure if I could tell him.

He lifted me up in his arms, laying me slowly on the couch. I gasped, feeling his body against my naked body. He pulled back the kiss and trailed them down to my neck. Fire erupted through me. His soft lips against my skin made me crave for more. Hunter latched onto one of my breasts, while one hand squeezed the other. He took his precious time on my breasts, making sure they got the attention they deserved. When his lips moved further down south, I ached with anticipation. His lips on my stomach made me trimmer. My legs spread like butter as his lips moved down past my belly button.

45

"Oh my." A moan escaped the moment his tongue found my cave.

I opened my legs even further, one leg hung over the top of the couch and the other dangled on the floor. I tossed my head back as his tongue lathered me up. God, it had been a long time since I let anyone pleasure me in such a way. The day I ran away from my ex was the last day I had sex. It was the day Sasha finally got me out of there. Thank God she did. If she didn't, I wouldn't be alive to experience something so powerful. I felt powerful with Hunter. I felt I was worth something to someone.

"Hunter," I moaned his name as his tongue fought with my swollen pebble. My hand gripped the couch, holding on as something exploded from me. I closed my eyes, hoping he would stop but no. Hunter kept going, sending my head thrashing back and forth on the pillow. I remembered everything there was about Hunter Grayson, and I knew he sure had gotten better than the last time. He finally pulled himself away.

"I'm going to have so much fun with you. I can make you come just by a single touch." He touched my face with his hand. "Just by a kiss." He lowered his head again and kissed my kitty. Then he looked back at me and smiled.

"I'm happy that I amuse you." Hunter got up from the couch, pulling me with him. He was so big and so strong. He sat me on my feet and snatched my hand up in his.

# THE LOVE I CRAVE

"Come take a walk with me, Mrs. Grayson," he said. I turned to look at him when he called me Mrs. Grayson. He pulled me tight in his arms.

"Mrs. Grayson already. So soon." I smiled.

"So late," he replied. I was finally able to get a good look at his place now that I wasn't on my back. His living area was spacious and had floor-to-ceiling windows just like the building. All the furniture was in dark colors like black and coffee. When I first come through the doors, I realized it was an office, and to the right was the kitchen with all stainless-steel appliances and a long island with four barstools. A chandelier hung in the living area. I couldn't see the dining room since he took me straight for the steps.

"Where are we walking to this time of night?"

"You'll see; it's a surprise."

"A surprise for me. But I have nothing to wear. You tore my dress, remember?"

"A lovely dress it was; you should buy another one," he said, sounding too thrilled about it. I could tell he was thinking about ripping it off again. If he had a thing for that, we were sure to have some problems. Clothes cost money, and that dress was a hundred dollars.

Hunter led me up the stairs of his house. As I walked, I turned to see pictures on the way up.

"Zollah, you never have to worry about anything again. You'll never be without, ever." He spoke. I just smiled as I looked at the portraits on his wall. The two women looked just like him. They had to be his sisters, but I knew he only had one from the stories we shared long ago.

"Who are they?" I asked, pointing to the pictures. He turned to see what I was referring to.

"This right here is my sister Leena, and that beautiful creature right there is my mother Carrie Grayson," he said.

"That's your mother? She looks amazing." The woman didn't look a day over forty. She must have a good skin regimen. Beautiful skin and beautiful brown eyes. I could see now where he got those dreamy eyes from.

"She takes good care of herself," he said as he pulled me along. Taking care of herself was an understatement. The lady was a vampire, and I was convinced. I smiled to myself as we stopped at the first door on the right. He opened the door, and I looked around. *Why would he bring me to an empty room?* He led me across the room to the closet and opened the door. He leaned forward and turned on the light. I was confused at first because I had no idea what I was looking at. A closet full of women's clothes. I stepped back to look at him.

"Hunter, what is this?" I asked.

"Well, while I was away, I had my designer do a little shopping over the years. I knew one day I would have you. I got you everything I could think of. So, pick something out and meet me downstairs in five minutes," he said, turning away. I looked in, and the closet was filled with all kinds of clothes and shoes in different fabrics. Silk, satin, lace, and denim.

"This is all mine?" I asked, confused.

"Yes, and you have your own bathroom to freshen up. Don't take long. I've waited…"

I cut him off and said, "Long enough." He smiled and left the room, leaving me to my thoughts which were running wild right now. This was all happening so fast. Was it really when I had waited for this day? I finally had Hunter, and I was excited and scared at the same time.

I paced the room. Was this real? Was this a dream? Was all this really mine? For a moment, I got sad. I didn't know why thoughts of my mother came to mind. I missed her so much. My father too, but my mom was everything. I wished my mother were here. I wanted to talk to her, but if she were here, I would have never met Hunter in the first place. Just thinking about it, I would have never met Sasha, Sophia, Damon, or even HIM. I missed my mother so much, it pained me to think of her. I had to think about the moment at hand.

I slowly examined the closet. I didn't have time to look at everything, but the one thing that caught my eye was a long, silk, pink robe. I pulled it out from between the long silk nightgowns. I held the robe up by the hanger. I could tell it was specially made. The upper left-hand side held the initials

ZHG. When did Hunter have time to get this made? I guess since the day he found me and gave me that money.

Zollah Hope Grayson. At least he knew I was keeping my last name. I took the robe off the hanger, then scooped up a pair of slippers. I cut off the light of the closet, then closed the door. I hung the robe behind the door of the bathroom and set the slippers next to it. I gazed around the bathroom which I noticed was very spacious. The bathroom was painted black with gold trimmings. The shower was separated from the tub and had a glass door with three different showerheads. I would love to have that in my house. I could do wonders with that. I smiled, thinking of Sophia. She was my best friend. She taught me that masturbation was best in the shower, especially with removable showerheads. She was such a freak. I held back the tears. I missed her too.

I checked the cabinets and nearly fainted when I found all my favorite soaps, creams, perfumes, and lotions in the cabinets. This freaked me out. How did he know all the things I used? Someone must have been keeping uncomfortable tabs on me. I pulled back the door of the shower and turned on the water. I laughed at how the water came out as if I had never seen one before. I didn't have one in my house. I would have to change that. I washed up, trying not to think of everything I had been through to get to this moment. I didn't want to think about all the people in my life I had lost. I wanted to think about this moment, the moment of finally having the one thing I always wanted—Hunter Grayson. I quickly finished up and cut the water off. I grabbed a towel from the shelves by the door. I lotion up in my favorite Shea butter cream. I put on my robe and my God, it felt good against my skin. I brushed my hair down and gave myself one last look. I slipped on my slippers, then turned to open the door and saw a tall figure standing there.

"Hunter, you scared me." I jumped back with my hand over my chest.

"You're late, I said five minutes."

"Well, you can't give a girl such fancy clothes and expect her to be on time." He grabbed my hand and pulled me from the room and back down the stairs. I noticed he was wearing grey sweatpants, a white tank top, and he was barefoot. Sexy. I could see the print of his manhood, telling me he didn't have any boxers on. Damn. Commando.

"You'll need to learn to be punctual with your time. Not to run late for everything," he said, leading me to the back of the house through the kitchen to the patio door.

"Excuse me, I'm always on time," I said, defensive.

"I saw you this morning running for the elevator. I want my wife to be noticeable of time. I don't like tardiness," he said, and he was absolutely serious from the looks of it.

"Oh, we're setting rules already. I like." I smiled.

"Do you like punishments, Mrs. Grayson? Those are the consequences of tardiness," he said, winking his eye at me. I had to pay close attention to what he was saying.

# Henson Dreamier

"Punishment? I'm not a child, Hunter," I watched his every move. We stood at the patio doors just staring at one another. He finally turned his head because I wasn't backing down. He pulled the string to the curtains, bringing them back.

"Then don't act like one," he said. I made a face at him behind his back. He turned to look at me, and I smiled like I wasn't doing anything. "For being one minute late, I will show you what punishment is," he said.

I was about to tell him how I wasn't acting like a child and that I wasn't afraid of him. There was only one man I was afraid of, and I hoped I never saw him again. Hunter unlocked the patio door and slid it open. We both stepped out, and my focus left him and turned to gaze outside. I couldn't believe it.

"Hunter." I was so wrapped up in the amazing view. The sound of the ocean beating against the shore. There were many things I loved, and a beach house was one of them. "You have a beach house. I'm jealous. I tried to get one on the beach, but no one was selling." I moved past him. I kicked off my slippers and exhaled when my feet touched the sand. It had been awhile since I could make it to the beach. The sand felt good between my toes. I looked around, and it was an amazing night. There was a soft breeze blowing. The moon and the stars shine bright. It was a night for love. Hunter came up beside me and grabbed my hand as we walked up the beach.

# THE LOVE I CRAVE

"I always wanted to live on the beach," I said as he turned to look at me.

"I know," he said with a glare behind his eyes. We walked and enjoyed the peace and quiet, just the sound of the ocean. I watched every house as I walked by, and all the lights were out. I guess everyone was asleep; it was kind of late. I had no idea what time it was. I focused all my attention back on Hunter.

"Can I ask you something?"

"Anything," he said.

"What did you mean when you said my room?"

"It means that anytime you're here with me, and don't want to sleep in the same room as me, you have your own. Just tell me what you want inside it, and it's yours," he said, squeezing my hand tight in his.

"Hunter, I don't need anything. Just you, that's it. That's all I ever wanted," I said, squeezing his hand back.

"And you'll have me forever, but I want to take care of you in every way possible," he said, stopping at this cliff of rocks. Water ran through it, and it was a beautiful sight to see. He climbed up, then he helped me up to the top.

"Sit," he ordered. I hesitated for a moment before I sat.

"I can take care of myself. I know I'm not that girl you met long ago, sorry to say." I looked away, turning my attention to the water. Hunter came and sat next to me.

"No need to apologize for changing. Everyone does." He wrapped his arm around my waist to bring me closer. We sat in silence for a moment, just admiring the view.

He must have a million questions for me. I was waiting for him to ask me why I didn't show up to Harvard. I got accepted, and I was ready to go. Hmmm... my ex wouldn't let me leave. He didn't want me so far away from him. I was waiting for Hunter to ask me about the scars. I waited, and none of that came. Hunter knew I was with my ex at the time we met, but there was still much he didn't know. And I knew I couldn't tell him.

After a while, I turned to look up at him. God, there was nothing different about him. His brown skin still was smooth. His russet eyes were as intoxicating as they had always been. If this was real, and we were going to be together, I had to get a few things off my chest. I had to say this, and I wanted him to understand where I was coming from. I wouldn't get into full detail. I wasn't ready for that, not just yet. I must take this one day at a time. That's what my therapist Dr. Stevens would say. So that's what I planned to do. I had to tell him what was going on in my head.

When I first met Hunter, a light turned on in my heart. I was cold and meeting him had lit a fire in me. From the moment our eyes connected, I knew he was the one for me. I knew when he touched me, he had a home for my heart. I couldn't and wouldn't live a day without him. I'd lived a life of hell just to live a life of heaven. That craving feeling I'd had for so long just to see him again. Just to talk to him. If only I could tell Hunter what I had been through with HIM.

"Hunter, I need to know this is real and not some game," I said, looking down at my hands. All of this was moving fast. Yesterday, it was just me, working hard, going out, then coming home and being lonely with my vibrator, waiting for this moment here. Now I have this wonderful man who wants me. All of me.

"I don't play games. Zollah, I want you like I have never wanted anything in my life. And I have almost everything a man could ever dream off." His hand reached up to move a lock of hair.

"Almost everything?"

"You were always the final piece to my dynasty. Now that I have you, I have everything." His words whispered in my ear, they ignited the flame. "I know you'll have my back. I know you never cared about how much money I had, or my family had. I want you to be my wife, Zollah. I have always wanted that, and I always get what I want." His voice sounded so serious and demanding. He kissed me, and it was like lemonade on a hot summer's day.

"The final piece," I said.

"Yes, all I ever wanted was you. Any other women I've had relations with it had never been serious. Only once." My heart leapt, and the questions formed. I wanted to know about the one. The one that almost took him away. I shook my head. The thought of him loving another woman made me sick to my stomach. I couldn't imagine another woman being kissed by those lips. "I've never wanted someone as much as I want you. I want you all to myself. I'm selfish," he said with a smile. He kissed me passionately, and I closed my eyes and took him in. I couldn't fight this or him anymore. This was what I wanted, and I knew that. He pulled back the kiss, and my eyes were still closed. I was thinking too much. "What are you thinking about?" How could I say this?

"I just have to say something before this... our relationship goes beyond this rock," I said, opening my eyes. I had to get myself together before tears rolled down my face. I didn't want to cry in front of him, looking as broken as I felt. "Hunter, I'm going to say this once. I have a hard time trusting anyone, especially men. It's not your fault. You're the first guy I've ever opened myself up to, and I hope you're going to be the last. I really want this, I think we both do, but I don't want to be used up and sent on my way when you're done with me." He opened his mouth to say something, but I put my finger on his lips. "I'm not a jealous girl. I don't care who your male friends are. I don't care who your female friends are. I know you probably have a lot of female friends; all I want for you is to be honest with me. I want you to be able to talk to me about anything, and I will try to talk to you about everything. I also have male friends and don't need you to be jealous either. If I'm with you, I'm with you," I said, and he made a face.

"I'm going to have to work on that, the jealous part. I don't like to share my toys," he said, rubbing my inner thigh. I laughed. I could see him being a selfish little boy. "So, from this night forth, you're mine forever. No one gets to have you." Hunter slid from the rock, so he was in front of me. He pushed my legs apart and squeezed between them. He grabbed the back of my neck and pulled my head in for a kiss. It was so aggressive. A moment later, he whispered in my ear, "Are you soaking wet for me right now?" he asked, trying to slide his hand through the slit of my robe.

"No, I'm not," I lied. I was soaking wet, and my kitty purred for some male penetration. He eased his hand down to touch my cave. I caught his hand in mine.

"Oh no, don't be shy now." He gave me that smirk. The top of my robe fell off my shoulders. Every time the man kissed me or touched me, the heaven gates opened. My right breast slipped out from the top of my robe, and Hunter was like a dog in heat or a breast-fed baby.

"I love the fact that you're always ready for me. I hope you'll be that way for the rest of my life," he whispered in my ear. My mind was on Mars right now, and I wasn't thinking straight.

"Anything you want," I moaned in his ear.

"You shouldn't tell me such things like that. I have an adventurous imagination," he said. I smiled, thinking back when we were at LABA together. He always found or made up a game for us to play.

"I'm not scared of you, Mr. Grayson." He pulled back and looked at me. Maybe I shouldn't have said that.

"Oh really," he said.

"I did have somewhat of a life before you," I said with a smile, but it wasn't anything to smile about. It was a dangerous sex life.

"Don't make me sick. That's nothing compared to the sexcoaster you'll experience with me." He grabbed my hand and helped me down the rock.

"Sexcoaster?" I asked; I was intrigued.

"Remember we went to Disneyland and rode all the rollercoasters there?" I looked up at with a smile.

"I would never forget it. I got sick, and you took care of me. You always take care of me," I said, trying not to make it seem sad. I never thought I would need to feel that with the man I loved. Losing my father at a young age, I guess I was looking for that. I couldn't say if it was a good or a bad thing.

"Yes, you had too much funnel cake." He laughed. I smiled, thinking about that day. I had so much fun. "So, imagine yourself on a rollercoaster, and you're at the moment when your adrenaline is at the highest. Then imagine you're having sex, and you're about to reach that mind-blowing orgasm. Can you imagine sex on a rollercoaster? You're riding at the top, ready to take our first leap. That orgasm will rip through you, causing you to black out. That's what sex is like with me," he said as we reached his house. I stood there trying to figure out if I understood what the hell he was saying, but you know what? I was intrigued. Damn, that was sure a rollercoaster I wanted to try out. I would ride him every chance I got. I laughed.

"What's so funny?"

"You say this as if we haven't had sex before. Twice if I'm correct."

"Well, more like four times, but we've only seen each other twice, but anyway, I was an amateur."

"Our first time was the best time, but that second time was sure mind blowing."

"I visited that piano room a lot afterwards, hoping I would run into you again." We never saw each other again after that, not until now. A sting hit my heart.

"And now you're a professional,"

"Well, I don't want to brag, but yes. I talk to the body with my mind," he said, and I laughed again.

"Well, I'm ready for my first sexcoaster ride," I said, trying to use my sexy, seductive voice. I looked up at Hunter, and he was undressing himself. Muscles ripped and popped out from everywhere like microwave popcorn. My mouth watered for a taste of him. He had a physique that I knew he was part of a gym. Shit, I used to work out three days out of the week and still didn't have abs of steel like him.

I watched carefully as he pulled his sweats down halfway, letting them fall on their own the rest of the way. My eyes popped out of my sockets when I decided to get a sneak peek. A lot of things had changed. His manhood was at attention, and it looked as if it could do some damage. My kitty tingled at the thought of it inside her. I feared what he could and would do with that weapon. I noticed he was staring at me, giggling. The expression on my face must have told him what I was thinking. He walked up to me.

"Oh, you scared now," he said.

"Never," I lied. He pulled me close with one hand and used the other hand to untie my robe. He moved fast, and my robe fell to the sand, but he still held the belt in his hands. He grabbed my hand and pulled me toward the water.

"Excuse me, where do you think you're going?" I asked as if it wasn't obvious.

"For a swim." I planted my feet into the sand to stop.

"No, I can't swim." I pulled away from him. He looked up at me, and I knew what he was about to say.

"You never learned, and I was supposed to teach you." He was right. He was supposed to teach me that summer at LABA, but we never got around to it. "I'm sorry."

"And what exactly are you sorry for?"

"For never getting around to teaching you and not being here for you to do so." He reached out and pulled me close again. His hand ran up and down my back. "Let me teach you now."

"What? Hunter, it's pitch black out here."

"Best time to learn."

That made no sense to me, but it meant a lot that he was still willing to teach me. No one had ever considered teaching me how to swim. Shit, I never thought about teaching myself. I guess I was too worried about staying alive. I pulled him closer with aggression, and he liked it. Our naked bodies were one for a moment. I leaned in and kissed him. I wanted to let him know that he meant the world to me. I was nervous as hell thinking about learning to swim at this time of night.

"Okay, teach me." His smile showed me those pearly white teeth. He pulled me with him into the water.

"You're not worried about your hair, are you?"

"First of all, don't come for me like that, and second, no, I'm not worried about my hair."

"All right, you're a little feisty I see."

"No, just a little nervous."

I didn't care about my hair. All I wanted was to be next to him. It didn't take him long to teach me, especially when I was addicted to learning new things. He taught me how to doggy paddle first, then to swim under water. Then after a hundred times, I had it down. I was swimming. I couldn't believe I was swimming in the middle of the ocean. He said that I had to pass a test first to make sure I was an excellent swimmer. I had to save him from drowning. I didn't think that it was a good idea.

"How can I do that without panicking? I'm going to freak out."

He moved closer to me in the water. He held my face in his hands. "If you love me and can't go another day without me, you'll save me," he said as he laid a hell of a kiss on me. Hell yeah, I'd go to hell and back for him. I couldn't live another day without his lips on mine. I'd die. I closed my eyes for a quick moment and when I opened them, he was gone.

# DARKNESS

I did the first thing he told me not to do, I panicked. Why would he do this to me? It was dark out, and the only light was from the single buoy in the ocean. One was next to me that lit up the ocean around me, so I could see a little, but I didn't think it was enough to save the love of my life. *How long had he been under there?* I moved my arms around me to see if I could feel him, but nothing.

I sucked in my fears, held my breath, and sank underwater. I slowly opened my eyes. Remembering what he taught me, I made a circle around, and I saw nothing. I didn't want to panic so I sank down some more and circled around again. I saw him. He was right by the buoy. When I reached him, I grabbed his arm, pulling him up. He helped because there was no way I could have done it alone. He was faking as if he were unconscious, and I thought it was cute. It felt like forever for us to get to the top. We finally made it through, and I caught my breath to curse him out for pulling such an idiotic stunt. I turned and saw the smile on his face that just made me smile.

"I knew you could do it." He pulled me close for a passionate kiss.

"I would never let you go again."

He stopped at the buoy. I should be scared that a shark was coming to eat us, but I felt fearless with Hunter. The buoy was long with three poles on it. It was hard for me to describe, but it floated in the middle of nowhere. I didn't even notice that Hunter still had the belt to my robe with him. He climbed up first, then helped me up next. I had no idea that the both of us could fit on this thing. In fact, we couldn't without holding on for dear life.

"Put your back up against this pole." He ushered me, showing me which one. I gave him a strange look.

"Do it and spread your legs apart," he ordered. "Wider." I did as I was told.

"What are you going to do to me?" I asked.

"Taking you on your first ride."

I watched as he tied both of my wrists together, then tied them to the pole. What was he going to do to me in the middle of the California ocean? I was tied to a buoy. What kind of freaky fuckery shit was this? Whatever was going on, I liked it.

"Tonight, you're going to learn discipline. To do only what I say when I say. Only moan when you've been told to. Only scream my name when you've been asked to. To only come when you've been told to," he said as he finished tying my wrist to the pole. That was impossible. He stood there admiring his handiwork. It was impossible, especially for someone who hadn't had sex in years. I was like a virgin all over again.

"You look beautiful tied up," he said. My attention snapped his way. All the fear that tried to creep up died the moment I saw who was tying me up. This was Hunter, not my crazy and deranged ex. I got that out of my head and remembered what he just said.

"Whatever, I already learned discipline, and you already taught me a lesson tonight. A swimming lesson."

"Oh no, that was a life lesson. This is a sex lesson 101." His hands held onto the pole by my waist. My legs were spread, and his legs were in the middle of mine. He leaned in and kissed me, and I knew my lips had to be swollen by now. The hard and aggressive kiss didn't last long before he pulled away and made his way to my neck. He slithered his tongue out, tracing the scar on my neck, and I erupted with fire. I gasped.

# Henson Dreamier

God, why did he make me feel so damn good? He moved his kisses to my shoulder, and his tongue ran along my scar there. A tear formed in my eye, but it didn't fall. His tongue ran traces all over my breasts, making my nipples protrude. He kissed every inch of my body, making sure he missed the one place I wanted him to kiss. He teased me, knowing how much I wanted him inside me. My vagina was sealed shut these days from lack of attention. Only from me and my vibrating friend. Hunter licked and squeezed my nipples, letting the juices flow. I moaned out. I couldn't help it; he made me feel so good.

"Strike one," he said, nibbling on my ear.

"What?"

"Only moan when told to."

"That isn't fair. I'm going to be bad at this," I said.

"You'll learn to get better," he said as he went back to sucking, licking, and pinching my nipples. I wanted to moan, but I held it in. I had no idea how many strikes I had. I guess three.

He lowered himself down as he laid kisses on my stomach, making it tremble. He stuck his tongue in my navel. I braced myself because I knew what was coming next. As much as I wanted him to lick me down there, I was afraid he would. One lick, and I would come, and that would be strike two.

# THE LOVE I CRAVE

"Let me apologize now," he said.

"For what?"

"What I'm about to do to you. I'm going to show you how much I missed you, how happy I am to have you. I'll try to control myself, I promise." I looked down at him with surprise in my eyes. Nervousness shot through me. I looked up at my wrist tied up, then back down at him. His eyes were brighter and begging.

"What are you going to do to me?" I was scared to ask, but I wanted to be prepared. I braced myself.

"I'm going to eat you alive first. Then I'm going to fuck you until you can't take no more. Until you're screaming my name and shedding only happy tears, baby girl." My heart fluttered, and my insides turned to mush. He was face to face with my cave, and I could feel his breath on me. I closed my eyes the moment I saw his tongue slither out like a snake. I held on to that moan. I didn't want a strike two. He wrestled with my pebble, begging for me to scream. I closed my mouth tight, holding back the scream I wanted to let out.

I fought back that moan, and I was doing great until he slipped his finger inside me. My nipples were so hard, they were like missiles. I closed my eyes again, but that intensified the feeling. So, I opened my eyes. I looked down, and he was eating me as if he had entered a pie eating contest, and he was fighting to be number one. I felt the muscles in my body tighten. The orgasm was building up in me, ready to erupt. I couldn't moan, say his name, or even come. I thought he was about to stop when he pulled back, but nope. He lifted my legs up and brought them around his neck.

He went to work on my kitty as if it were a million-dollar client he was trying to land on his team. My eyes rolled back in my head. I couldn't take this amount of satisfaction. The more I was quiet and couldn't scream out, the more I wanted to explode. Oh my God, he knew what he was doing. He knew what a pussy and a tongue were made for.

"Please, Hunter," I moaned out, but it was more of a scream. It felt good to release what I had been holding in.

"Strike two," he said as he still went to work on my cave. I felt it; it was coming.

"Hunter, please, I'm about to…" I couldn't even finish what I was going to say when I screamed. The orgasm ripped through me like a tidal wave. It felt amazing.

"Oh, naughty, naughty girl, strike three," he said with a smile that I wanted to smack off his face.

"This isn't fair. You've made me come at least ten times since the club, and you haven't even fucked me yet," I said, trying to catch my breath.

"Good things come to those who wait," he said, licking his lips and fingers as if he were licking the icing on a cake. Hunter totally turned me out.

# THE LOVE I CRAVE

"Best pussy I've ever tasted in my life." He stood in front of me. He leaned in and kissed me on the lips, letting me taste my own juices. He whispered in my ear, "Do you still want me?"

"More than I've ever wanted anything in my whole life," I said as he continued to kiss me all over. Then something dawned on me. I hadn't been on birth control since the day I left Florida.

"When was the last time you've had sex?" he asked as if he were reading my mind. It was hard to hold a conversation tied up in the middle of the ocean.

"Three years ago. I'm not on any birth control," I said.

"Three years ago. Almost like virgin kitty."

"You know what virgin kitty feels like?" I asked, knowing damn well he knew what virgin kitty was like.

"Yes, Lord, I do. I remember our first time as if it were yesterday. Oh, and you don't have to worry about getting pregnant. I can't have any children." Lightning struck the night, and I could have sworn he said he couldn't have kids.

"But..." I felt him crown me. "Shit," I moaned as he filled me up nice and slow.

"Strike one," he said as he slid back out and inside again. I lifted my legs and wrapped them around his waist to accept all of him.

"Baby girl, you're a perfect fit," he moaned into my ear.

"Yes, you are." I wanted to touch him, caress him, but I couldn't.

"Strike two."

"What?"

"You came, and I didn't tell you to."

"I didn't mean to," I pleaded as he moved in circles in and out of me.

He found one breast with his mouth. I was building again. I'd be damned if I came again. I was going to hold onto this orgasm. I had a feeling if I came, I would explode, and my organs would be splattered all over the ocean. How would he explain that to Sasha or even the police? The deeper he went inside me, it was like he was tapping on that orgasm, and I was holding on tight. Why not just ask if I could come?

"Hunter, can I come, please?" I begged him.

"Good girl, you asked for permission," he said but didn't answer me. He just worked the tip of him inside me, which sent us both over the cliff. He held on tight to his orgasm that wanted to be released. He picked up his pace and held onto the poles as he worked my inside as he sucked hard on my nipples. I screamed out his name, and I was sure some shark heard me and was now coming for us.

"Strike three." It should be illegal for someone to make you feel this damn good. When I looked at him, he smiled. "Are you ready?"

"For what?"

"For that powerful orgasm you're never going to forget," he said, removing one of his hands from the pole, using it to rub against my pebble as he worked me fast and hard. I moaned uncontrollably. He leaned in and whispered in my ear, "Remember what I made you do on the piano?" I gasped. He rubbed me until he saw my kitty erupt like it did in the piano room. I screamed loud, and I sprayed Hunter like a hose.

My eyes rolled in the back of my head. He wouldn't stop; it was like sensations coming from all over my body, turning my brain into suds. The way he worked every inch of my body sent my body convulsing.

"Hunter," I screamed out, waking up the whole California.

My whole body went numb. I couldn't feel anything anymore. I was drained of everything in me. My memories, my organs, and my fluids. That wasn't what took me by surprise. My heart was racing fast, my brain was sudsy, my eyes closed, and I fell into darkness.

# Henson Dreamier

\*\*\*

I blinked my eyes open, trying to get them to adjust. I realized I was in a bed with comfortable sheets. I reached out my hand to caress them. They were silk. Who lays in a bed of silk sheets? I sat up from the bed, looking around. The bedside clock read four in the morning. I stretched my arms out over my head. I was in Hunter's bedroom. The room had white walls and cream-colored furniture. The nightstand and dresser were cream with his king-size bed. The bed sat in the middle of the room, and my heart melted. His room was set up like the hotel room where we first had sex. *God, why do I feel like I don't deserve him?* Maybe I didn't, but I had him, and I was going to do everything in my power to keep him. I finally exhaled. I was in bed all alone. Then last night came back to me. How in the hell did I end up here? I eased out of the bed, taking my time since my legs were weak. I gazed around the room, looking for the bathroom. He wasn't there. I pulled open the cracked bedroom door.

"Hunter," I called out, and there was no answer. I eased out of the door and made my way down the hall and down the stairs.

I stepped off the last stair and made my way to the living room. I came around and saw him lying on the couch. He was asleep. He was lying with one hand behind his head and the other one across his chest. His laptop was on the table in front of him with two cell phones beside it. He must have been doing some work. Damn, I thought I worked hard. I moved closer so I could admire him. He was wearing boxers and some white socks. He looked so damn sexy lying there asleep. I wanted to lick every inch of him.

"Hunter," I called out to him. His eyes slowly opened, then widened when he saw it was me.

"Zollah, are you okay?" he asked, sitting up from the couch.

"I'm fine, but the bed is lonely without you." I stood at the end of the couch.

"I apologize, baby girl. I was doing some work, but I'm done now," he said. He sat up from the couch and turned to close his laptop. "I must have fallen asleep." He turned back to me, blinking his eyes. "You're naked." Was it a question or a statement? "Come on, let's go to bed. We have to work in a couple of hours." He got up and came for me.

"I'm not due in until noon," I said as he wrapped his arms around me.

"Then so am I." He smiled as he lifted me up in his arms. He tossed me over his shoulder. I loved being in his arms; they were like home.

It was funny how long I had lived without him, and now I couldn't live another day without him. How sick did that sound, but I loved him. I always had. Hunter pushed the door open to his bedroom, and he placed me gently on his bed. He climbed in next to me as he pulled the covers over us. I lay on my side as he wrapped his arms around me. We held each other tight like we never wanted to let one another go. I wanted to savor the moment because as visions of the night came back to me, everything he did to me, it felt like I owed him something. Maybe I owed him the last ten years, but he owed me that too.

"Hunter," I said, rubbing my hand up and down his arm.

"Yes." I adjusted myself so I could look him in his eyes.

"What did you mean when you said you can't have children?" I asked, and he tensed under my touch. I stopped rubbing my hand up his arm. I could see in his eyes that it was hurtful to talk about.

"I can't have any children," he repeated what he had said earlier. I waited for him to say more, but he never said anything else.

"Is it because something you needed to do or something you wanted to do?" I asked. I knew it wasn't something he wanted to do. Not a smart, sexy, successful businessman like Hunter Grayson. He should be allowed an heir to his throne. My mind rewound to four years ago. My hand touched my stomach. I took a deep breath before I lost it. I couldn't go back there, to that dark place.

"It was something I chose to do." I tried not to gasp, I caught it just as it hit my lips. A tightness squeezed at my heart. Why would he choose to do something like that after everything we had talked about? I know life gets in the way, but he had no idea if we would ever see each other again.

"Why?" He put his head down. I touched his chin with my finger, pulling his eyes back to mine. I didn't want him to hide from me.

"It's a long story, but to sum it up, I've met a lot of women who just wanted me for my money. Some wanted to get pregnant to guarantee them stability, and I didn't want to be used. The one I got serious with, she did something that I still can't understand till this day. But…"

I reached out and pulled him in my arms. I could tell there was more to the story, but I let it go. I didn't want to hurt him. It was a painful subject, and I of all people knew about painful subjects. I wouldn't rush him to talk about it when I knew there were things I wasn't ready to talk about. I didn't think I would ever be ready to talk about HIM. My mind traveled all around the world, trying to figure out how he could make such a major decision like that. So young and rich and could afford to have lots of children.

"Baby girl, what are you thinking?"

"Nothing," I lied. I was afraid of how this may work. I wanted children, a lot of them. Maybe five or six of them running around the house, and the man I want to marry doesn't want any. Cannot have any. A sad look came upon my face.

# Henson Dreamier

"We had plans to have children," I said, touching my stomach again. He pulled back the embrace and looked at me.

"I know. We planned to have lots of kids, and we still can. If you want children, then we shall have them. I only want children with you," he said as our foreheads rested against one another. I looked in his eyes, and he was scared. "I will do anything for you, Zollah."

"But you can't."

"I can." He held my face in his hands. "Whatever you want, I will do. If you want children, then we shall have them. Just let me know when you're ready, and we'll do it."

"I don't want you regretting the decision you've made. I want you to want this. If not, I guess we can adopt," I said with a straight face but didn't mean it. I wanted Hunter Javier Grayson babies. All of them.

"Zollah, I've never been sure about anything in my life. If you want my spoiled-rotten babies, then so be it." He kissed me, taking my breath away. That was the end of that conversation. We lay quiet in each other's arms for a while. My mind went back to last night.

"Hunter, how did you get me inside after I passed out?" That had been gnawing at me since I woke up. He smiled.

"I swam with you on my chest. Then once we made it to shore, I carried you inside," he said as I smiled for a moment. I felt so embarrassed. How could I pass out like that?

# THE LOVE I CRAVE

"Have you ever had sex like this with other women?" I asked, but I didn't want to know the answer.

"I've had plenty of sex, but never of this magnitude. You're so sensitive to my touch." He touched my breasts. "No one has ever passed out from an orgasm. It's a first, and I plan on having a lot more first moments with you." His hands ran through my hair.

I looked over at the bedside clock. It was almost six in the morning. I could get at least a couple of hours to be at work at noon. I ran my hand up and down his chest. It was now my turn to show him a few things. I tossed my leg over him and climbed on top. I leaned in and kissed his lips as I slid down on his chest to be face to face with his manhood. I admired it as if it were a million-dollar dick. Then I realized it was a million-dollar dick, and I held it in my hand. My mouth watered instantly. I needed him inside me. Before I rode his ass to sleep, I wanted to know what a million-dollar dick tasted like.

# BREAKFAST

I woke up to the sun shining through the curtains of the floor-to-ceiling windows. When I eased my eyes open again, I smiled when they landed on the most beautiful man on the planet. Then all the feelings from last night and this morning came back to me. I realized that he was still inside me. We fell asleep in this awkward position, and it was lovely. I could wake up every day like this with his arms around me. I lay there for a moment just staring at him sleep.

How would I slip out from under him without waking him? I had to be careful, I didn't want him waking up and wanting more. I didn't think my kitty could handle that. I slipped from under him, climbed out of bed, and made my way to my room. I needed to take a shower after the night I'd had. Well, I needed a bath to soak this kitty, but a shower would have to do. I soon realized this was the best shower I'd had in a long time. All those showerheads felt like a miracle. When the hot water hit me between my legs, it was heaven.

Once I was done with my shower. I headed to my closet to find something to wear. I couldn't believe everything in here was mine. I had the time to look around, and there was some of everything in here. It was hard to choose. A tan V-neck Vera Wang dress that caught my attention. I pulled it off the rack to look at the size, and I'll be damned, it was a size eight. How could Hunter know the right size?

I chose a pair of black peek-toe shoes in a size seven. Hunter knowing my size was freaky. As I finished oiling myself, I put on some panties and a bra set I found. As I dressed, something kept telling me to look at the price tag. I loved the dress, and it was my taste. I found the price tag hanging from the left side of the short sleeve. When I lifted the tag, I could have choked.

"Three thousand dollars for a dress," I mumbled to myself. That didn't keep me from snatching the tag off and putting the dress on with a smile.

I checked the time, and it was ten o'clock. Neither of us had eaten since dinner, and I was starving. I wanted to make him breakfast to show him that I could cook as well. I didn't want to go downstairs in heels, so I chose a pair of sandals. As I made my way down the hall, I went to check up on him first, and Hunter was still asleep. I closed the door and headed downstairs. As I got to the bottom of the steps, I heard noise in the kitchen.

# Henson Dreamier

Who could be in his house this early in the morning? When I hit the corner, I saw an older lady in the kitchen. She was pulling things from the cabinet and saw me standing there. I was more surprised seeing her than she was seeing me.

"I'm sorry," I said as I turned to head back the way I came. I had no idea who this lady was in his kitchen.

"No, Zollah, stay." I stopped, my body tensing up. I turned around to face her slowly. The lady had a huge smile on her face.

"You know who I am?"

"Yes, of course. Come, have a seat," she ordered me to sit at the breakfast bar. I walked in past the living room into the kitchen. "What would you like for breakfast dear?" she asked. I was still speechless that she knew who I was. I knew she wasn't his mother. I sat there staring, not knowing what to say.

"I'm sorry, you took me by surprise. I wasn't expecting anyone to be here. I was coming to make Hunter something to eat." The older lady looked to be in her early or late fifties. She had long, salt and pepper hair with dark-brown, bubbly eyes. She had her glasses on a string around her neck.

"Oh, no, honey. That's what I'm here for. I'll take care of you just like I have Hunter all these years," she said, whipping up something in a bowl. I was totally confused right now. I wanted to know how long she had known about me. How long had she been here? Did she have a key, or did she live here? There were a thousand questions running around in my head.

"How about some scrambled eggs with cheese, turkey sausage, fried potatoes, and onions, and some waffles?" she asked.

"I'm more of a pancake, French toast gal." I smiled.

"Oh wonderful, pancakes it will be then," she said as she went to work in the kitchen. I just sat on my stool and watched. But the question in my head forced its way out of my mouth.

"How long have you known about me?" I asked. As long as he had been looking for me? As long as he had been studying me to know so much about me? I guess since Jason found me. She turned to face me.

"Let me see, about ten years, I think." I held onto my seat. I was stunned. I never thought he would tell his family about me. I put my head down and thought about my life after I left LABA that summer. What if I would have left with him then like he wanted me to? Like he wanted me to in New York. My life would have been so different. What if Hunter had found me in Florida? My chest tightened thinking what HIM would have done to Hunter. I was so pressed to be with Hunter, I had no idea how I would leave HIM.

"Zollah," she called me, snapping me back. "I know he talked about missing the one girl who got away. The one girl he wanted so bad, but he couldn't have. He said her name was

Zollah." She paused for a moment while she cracked eggs and put them in the pan. "Hunter's a good, good man. He will give you the world and everything in it if you allow him. Piece of advice. It has always been about you. Everything he has ever done had been for you." She gave me a wink. I knew she was telling me this for a reason. "I'm happy to finally meet you. You're even more beautiful than he described." I blushed.

"Thank you." I paused for a moment. "Do you mind if I ask your name?"

"My name is Phoebe." I gasped. The name hit me like a hammer. The name that came from her lips sent a cloud of sadness over me. I held the tears back that wanted to fall. I thought of my mother and how much I missed her. I needed and wanted my mother here with me.

"That's a very special name you have," I said, fumbling with my fingers.

"I thought it was a weird name growing up, but my friends wanted to change their names to mine," she said, smiling as I watched her flip the pancakes in the pan. If I wanted to be with Hunter, I needed to know everything about him. His favorite color, his favorite food, what made him happy and sad. I was already so attached to this man, it was a shame. Nothing, not even a chainsaw or an axe, could separate us at this point, I think. Mrs. Phoebe stacked up the pancakes, then moved over to put eggs inside the pan.

"Are you making an omelet for Hunter? Is that his favorite thing to eat in the morning?"

"Yes, it is." I watched her stuff the omelet with sausage, bacon, diced tomatoes, green peppers, and onions. "I'm happy the two of you finally found each other. I'm sure Hunter is so ecstatic." We were quiet for a moment. "He has never brought anyone here before. I mean women wise. He said if he did bring someone here, it will be the one. So, I guess that's you." She giggled to herself. "You wanting to know how he likes his food tells me you have agreed to let him woo you." I was lost for words. How much did Phoebe know?

"He's pretty convincing at the wooing." I smiled just thinking about the last several hours.

"Oh, honey, the sex is half the battle. You haven't seen anything yet. Get ready for a hell of a rollercoaster." That made me think of what he said last night. About sex with him was like a sexcoaster. How did she know how good his sex was? This wasn't no innocent old lady. I just burst out into laughter. I could see now that this would be a wonderful friendship.

"What's so funny?"

"Just thinking that we may just be good friends." I smiled, and we both burst into laughter. She set my plate in front of me and my God, it smelled good. My stomach was growling at the delicious smell. I said my grace. I was starving for something other than sex.

"Phoebe, this is delicious." The home fries were so good, I finished those first. As I was complimenting Mrs. Phoebe on her cooking, I felt arms around my waist.

"Doesn't taste as delicious as you do, Mrs. Grayson." The whisper in my ear sent chills all over me.

"Good morning," I said as I continued to eat my food. I slanted my eyes to the side and watched him as he sat. He was wearing sweatpants, but no shirt this time. Damn, he was hot.

"Morning, Phoebe," he said as she put his plate in front of him. "Thank you," he said, never taking his eyes off me. He leaned in and kissed me all over my face. I couldn't even eat my food.

"Let the girl eat. I'm sure she's famished after a night with you," Phoebe said as she laughed to herself.

"Yes, ma'am," he said as he turned around in his seat and started to eat his food. He obeyed as if she was his mother. He was very respectful of his elders.

"So, what were you ladies laughing at?" he asked, biting into his omelet which was cheesy as hell.

"You," Phoebe said.

"Me?" His eyes widened, looking between me and Phoebe.

"Yes, she wanted to know how you liked your omelet," she said, leaving us alone in the kitchen. He turned to me and lifted his hand up to my cheek. A warm feeling came over me.

"How often does Mrs. Phoebe cook for you?"

"Five days a week," he said, staring at me. How could he even eat when he wasn't even looking at his plate? The man sure knew how to multi-task.

"Five days, I think that's a lot."

"No, it's not. It's regular working hours, and she gets paid a lot," he said, smiling.

"I bet you do pay good and yes, five days is a lot for a woman of her age. Does she have a family?" I asked.

"Yes, a husband and two children who are grown," he said, turning back to face me. "You are the most beautiful woman I've ever laid eyes on." He rested his hand on my thigh.

"Oh no, you don't." I pushed his hand away. It was Tuesday morning, and I knew that Mrs. Phoebe had better things to do. Maybe home relaxing or running some errands or doing some things with her husband.

"She fixes you breakfast and dinner?" I asked, finishing my food.

"Yes, and she's gone by three," he said. When Mrs. Phoebe came back in the room, she had chicken and some asparagus that she set on the counter. I asked her if she had any plans for today and of course, she did. I felt as though Hunter had been holding her hostage in here. I was done with my plate, so I went to clean it, but Mrs. Phoebe took it from me.

I wasn't surprised that she did, but I took things into my own hands. I told her that I was to handle things for the rest of the evening. I would cook Hunter's dinner while she ran her errands and spent some time with her husband. She was taken aback and looked at Hunter for permission. He just shrugged his shoulders. I asked her what she was cooking him for dinner. She told me as she headed for the door. I told her that I would see her in the morning. She winked at me and said, "Thank you, Mrs. Grayson," she said, laughing on her way out the door.

I could totally get used to that name. In my mind, I'd always been Mrs. Grayson. It was all I ever wanted. I turned toward the sink and finished the dishes. After that, I put the chicken in the refrigerator for later.

"That was nice of you. You haven't been here twenty-four hours, and you're taking control of things. That's such a turn on," he said as he came up behind me. "You're making me horny." He grabbed my ass.

"You're always horny."

# THE LOVE I CRAVE

"Yes, I am. You have that effect on me," he said, picking me up in his arms. He carried me upstairs to his room and threw me on the bed. He stripped out of his sweatpants.

"No, Hunter. I'm going to be late for work," I said, trying to get up from the bed.

"It's only eleven o'clock. We have time, baby girl," he said, pulling me by my legs and spreading them apart as he moved between them.

"I have to make it home to pick up my truck, then go to work." He licked my lips to stop me from talking. I wouldn't give in to him. It wasn't like we were going to have a quickie when he was long winded.

"No," I said. The way his face tightened was like telling a child no, they couldn't have any candy.

"Okay, just let me get a little taste then," he begged, looking so innocent. He had a sad puppy face. How old was he, three? His eyes were bright and full of determination. How could I say no to him?

"Okay."

He pulled me all the way to the edge of the bed. His manhood was hard and ready for a taste. I gazed at his manhood, and it was like the tip winked at me. Yes, I was a sucker, and this man had me whipped. I just sent his cook home for the day and agreed to cook for him, which meant I agreed to stay another night.

"You look so good in this dress."

"Come get it then."

He wrapped my legs around his waist. He lifted me, holding me tight. I kissed those soft lips as his hands traveled my body. He gripped the back of my dress. The next thing I knew, rip, there went another dress.

"Hunter, I liked this one," I said as he ripped the rest of the dress off me. I knew now not to wear nice things around him.

"Sorry." He smiled.

# ELEVATOR

Julius was in the truck waiting for us when we came out. He still had the same smile as he drove us to my house to pick up my truck. Hunter and I made out the whole time like teenagers. I could never get tired of kissing him. It took us almost thirty minutes to get to my house from his. I opened the garage door, jumped in my truck, and headed for the parkway. Julius followed me the whole way. It was almost one o'clock when we pulled up to EQ Skyscraper. I could see Julius when he pulled up behind me. I grabbed my things from the passenger seat, and Rodney came over to open the door for me.

"Thank you, Rodney," I said as he helped me on the curb in my five-inch heels.

"Long night?" he asked.

# Henson Dreamier

"You can say that," I said as he made his way back around to the driver's side. I made one step back from the curb, and arms were around me. I turned and saw Hunter next to me. He leaned in and kissed me on my forehead. Rodney stared his wide eyes at us. I didn't even see Hunter get out of the truck.

"Good afternoon, Rodney," Hunter said as he noticed the look on Rodney's face.

"Mr. Grayson." Rodney nodded as he hopped inside my truck and drove off, heading to the garage.

Hunter held me tight as we made our way through the glass doors. It felt so surreal walking in. I was usually running for the elevator. I'd never noticed so many people in the lobby before. Now it seemed so crowded. I noticed all eyes were on us. All the attention made me stop in my tracks. I was nervous, but Hunter didn't care who was watching us. He squeezed my hand and pulled me toward the elevator.

"Okay, the show's over," Hunter said to everyone who was watching. Just like that, they all went back to doing whatever they were doing. Hunter and I made it to the elevator just as the door slid open. We stepped inside, and two guys came up behind us. Hunter put his arm out.

"Next elevator," Hunter told them. They stopped and took a few steps back.

"No problem, Grayson," one guy said as the doors closed. Was this how it would be with him? He was the boss, and people knew it.

"Does everyone always do what you tell them to do?" I asked, leaning back against the railing of the elevator, holding my purse and bag in my hand.

"Of course, don't you?"

"No," I said, and I could feel the mood shift in the elevator.

"No," he repeated, moving closer to me. I stared into his eyes. They burned with determination to prove something.

"No, I do what I want to do," I said, knowing I shouldn't have, but I did anyway.

"No," he repeated. He backed away from me and moved closer to the wall of buttons. I watched him pull something from his pocket.

My eyes widened with shock. He wasn't about to do what I think he was. I watched the elevator go from the eighteenth to the nineteenth floor. Then it stopped on the twentieth. I waited for the doors to open, but they never did. I turned to him, and I noticed the little key he pulled from his pocket had stopped the elevator. He walked slowly back over to me. I was still up against the railing of the elevator. I saw the look in his eyes. They were glowing, and I knew what that meant.

*Oh God, please let me make out of here with my dress in one piece.*

"Please don't rip my dress off me," I begged.

"If I tell you to spread your legs, will you do it?" I looked at him to see if he was joking or not. From the looks of it, he was dead serious.

"Hunter, I can't. Stop playing and move this elevator," I said, trying to get away from him, but there was nowhere to go.

I tried to sound serious, but I smiled at the same time. I had no idea what to expect from him. He leaned in and looked deep into my eyes. I didn't have a change of clothes with me. I changed into a Versace champagne color V-neck dress. It was similar to the one I had on at first. I had no idea what to do.

"Spread those legs wide and hold on tight to the rail," he ordered.

"Hunter, no, please."

"What did I say? Spread those legs... now," he demanded. I felt as if I was being hypnotized by his eyes. His demanding words made me shiver, and instantly I spread my legs.

Hunter wore a navy-blue suit with a grey shirt and a blue, black, and grey tie. He looked scrumptious. He came up to me as his chest brushed against mine. He slowly lifted his hands to touch my breasts. A sigh escaped my lips. Then his hands slowly moved down to my legs and under my dress. He pulled my panties down, and he went down with them. He slid my thong from my feet and put them inside the pocket of his slacks. I smiled.

"Still a panty napper, huh?" I said as I remembered him doing exactly what he just did.

"And I still have them." My eyes widened.

"No."

"Oh, yes." He got down on one knee and lifted my dress up to my waist. This wasn't what I expected when he got down on one knee.

When his tongue licked me one time, then blew on my cave, I was sent on a rocketship to the moon. This whole scene was intense. My eyes closed as my bags hit the floor, and I gripped the railing of the elevator. And why the hell was there a railing in the elevator? I gasped when his tongue ran circles around my pebble. Here I was, the president of Hope's Publishing, in an elevator getting her kitty eaten out by the president of Grayson's Industries. Hunter took one leg and lifted it over his shoulder. It didn't take long for the orgasm to build and erupt, making me moan.

"Hunter." His name was like ruffles escaping my lips. I opened my eyes when my foot was back on the floor and my dress was pulled down back in its place. Hunter's eyes locked with mine as he stood up to his feet. He pulled my panties from his pocket to wipe my juices from his face. He… he was so nasty.

"See? Everyone does what I tell them to do," he said, pulling his key out and the elevator continued up. He came back over to me, and I was still catching my breath, clinging to the railing for dear life. He kissed me, making my knees even weaker than they were. I heard the ding letting us know that the doors were about to open. I pulled the kiss away, grabbed my things, and headed out as the door opened. I felt him grab my hand and spin me around to face him. I gasped.

"I'll see you later, Mrs. Grayson." He smiled as he kissed my forehead. He held the elevator door with his hand.

"Of course, Mr. Grayson." I stepped out and before the doors closed, I felt a smack on my ass. I turned around, but the doors had closed. I stood there for a moment to take everything in. How in the hell would I keep up with this man? I had no idea what to expect from him.

"You're a nasty girl." I turned and saw Aimee watching me from her desk. "You had fun last night and this morning I see, and you're late." I didn't say anything. I just smiled and walked past her desk. I went straight to my office where Melissa was setting up my tea. I felt like a new person. I wasn't in my office two minutes, and Aimee and Melissa stood, staring at me at my desk.

I knew they were here for the juicy details of my evening, but I couldn't tell them without my bestie on the line, so I called her. I kept things simple when I told them about my night. I didn't want to get into everything, but I told them what I wanted them to know.

"He fucked you senseless," Sasha said.

"He sure did that." I smiled.

"Oh, he did all right. The elevator was held on the twentieth floor for about ten minutes," Aimee said, laughing as she sipped on her coffee.

"Shut up," I said, feeling embarrassed for a moment.

"Don't be embarrassed. I'm all down with elevator sex," Aimee said.

"Hey, me too. Tell me more," Sasha said.

I gave them a preview of my night, leaving out the conversations we had about children and the fact that he had a vasectomy done. I told them that he taught me how to swim. I told them about my room in his house and my closet full of clothes. Everything in there had to be over a million dollars.

"Bitch, I'm going to need to raid that closet," Sasha said from the speaker. "So, Zollah Piper Hope, you're no longer single."

"Nope. I'm off the market," I said with a smile.

"To be honest, you've never been on the market, but I'm not going there," Sasha said with a laugh, and she was right. I never put myself out there as if I were available. I never dated anyone since running, and I sure wasn't planning to. I guess I was always waiting. All Sasha could keep talking about was the fact that I blacked out.

"I want to find me someone who could make me black out like that." We all laughed at Sasha. "I'm serious. I'm adding that to my bucket list."

"You have a bucket list at twenty-seven years old?" Aimee asked.

"Yup, I do, and finding darkness is one of them. That is Hunter's new name for me—Darkness." After another five minutes on the phone, I ended the call with Sasha, telling her that I wasn't coming home tonight. Then I sent Aimee and Melissa back to work.

I sat back in my desk, wanting to stay focused. This sadness just came over me. I knew if someone deserved to be happy, it was me. Being with my ex was a nightmare itself. I had done bad things in my life, but I was still a good person. I sighed thinking about Hunter finding out all the stuff I had done with HIM. The drugs, the abuse, drinking, the sex. A lot of things were forced upon me and believe me, when I said I tried to leave, I did. I placed my hand around my neck, thinking how I almost lost my life. I would have loved to die though; it was a way out, and I could have seen my parents again. If I did die, then I wouldn't be here now to be with Hunter or to finally be a position to find my sister and brother.

# THE LOVE I CRAVE

I was twelve years old when my parents died in a car accident. An earthquake had erupted, and they were at the wrong place at the wrong time. Their car was destroyed, and they died. My sister Brooke was eight, and Ryan, my brother, was six years old. That day was the first time I had ever lost people I loved. The hurt and pain of losing a parent still hurt me, and it had been years since they passed. That was where my life of foster care started. That was where I met Sasha and Sophia. I missed my sister and my brother, and I knew that one day I would see them again. I was fourteen when they were adopted, and I was seventeen when I stopped hearing from them again. I had to find them; it was about time.

My workday went by fast. No meetings, just sending and responding to emails. Making phone calls and setting up appointments. I had a conference call with Melvin who owned a place in New York called Martin's, a nice, elegant restaurant and jazz club. I'd heard so much about his place. It was one of the hottest places in town. A lot of people couldn't afford tickets to get in. Melvin called his place a jazz club experience. I wanted Martin's in my magazine. The conference call didn't take long. He was highly intelligent and forthcoming with his story. I couldn't wait to interview him. He suggested that I come to New York and see his place first. I thought it was a wonderful idea. He told me that this weekend was good and asked if I could make it. I informed him that this weekend was acceptable. I would see him on Saturday at seven thirty. After hanging up with him, I called Melissa and had her call for available flights for Friday and to email me a list. I was getting hungry, and I was thinking about what to eat when my phone rang. It was a number I didn't recognize, but I had to answer it. It could be important.

"Hope's Publishing," I answered.

"Your panties smell so good. I'm visualizing you at your desk, working with no panties on. It's making me hard." Hunter's sexy voice came through the phone.

"You're so nasty," I said, smiling.

"I'm nasty? Baby girl, you're the one with no panties on." He chuckled.

"What do you want, Mr. Grayson? I'm a busy woman."

"I want you up here now in my office," he demanded.

"Well, that will have to wait until tonight."

"Why are you torturing me?" he said, whining as Melissa walked in with a small envelope. It was the same one I had seen twice so far. Melissa handed me the envelope and turned to leave. The envelope was a little heavy. I pulled out two keys on a gold Z keychain. Was it real gold? What the hell?

"Hunter, what is this?" I asked, pulling a piece of paper out with the numbers 4, 7, 8, 5 on it.

"You got my note?"

"Yes, I just got it."

# THE LOVE I CRAVE

"I'm going to be a little late getting home. I have a late meeting. I want you home when I get there," he said. As he was talking, I thought of something I wanted to do for him.

"A last-minute meeting, huh? It must be important."

"Yes, it is," he said.

"Well, Mr. Grayson, I know the meeting will go well. So, I will see you at what time?" I asked.

"Seven."

"Okay, see you at seven then." We said our goodbyes and hung up. I finished a few things before I looked at the time, and it was four o'clock. I called Melissa and informed her that I was leaving for the day, and to move all my calls to the morning. Melissa said that she would have all the flight information on my desk in the morning. I grabbed my things, turned off my computer and lights, and headed for the elevator. I called Rodney for him to bring Silvia around.

Rodney was there waiting with Silvia. We said goodbye, and I headed for the mall. There were a few things I needed to pick up. I made good timing since I still had to cook. I arrived at Hunter's house a little after five. It felt good pulling up in front of his house. I told Hunter those years ago that I'd always wanted a house on the beach. I grabbed my bags from the backseat and headed to the door. I pulled out that heavy-ass Z keychain and unlocked the door. The alarm came on as soon as the door opened. I set the bags on the small table next to the door and pulled the paper out with the code: 4,7,8,5.

# Henson Dreamier

The alarm settled, and I smiled when I noticed the four numbers again. I realized that the code was my birthday. Hunter Grayson always surprises me.

Once inside, I kicked off my shoes, washed my hands, and took out all the food. I wanted to listen to some music, and it took me ten minutes to figure out that his stereo was hooked up to his TV. Once I was finished cooking dinner, I put me a bottle of wine on ice after fixing myself a glass first. I checked the time, and it was six thirty. I turned the oven down low, grabbed my bag, and headed upstairs to take a shower. I lotioned up with my Shea butter cream that smelled amazing. I pulled out the bag I got from Frederick's of Hollywood. I bought a sheer red body suit with three strategically placed holes in it. Could you imagine where those three holes were? It was sexy and exotic and sure to knock his socks off.

I put on some red lipstick and some come fuck me black pumps. To go with the sexy tail in the back, I had the nerve to buy some devil horns. I put my hair up in a ponytail and looked at myself in the mirror. My God, I looked HOT. I wanted to fuck myself. How would I make it out of here alive?

I went back downstairs to check on dinner, which was now ready. Al Green came through the speakers as I fixed myself another glass of wine. I lit some candles around the living room and dining room to soften the mood. I watched as the minutes went by, waiting to hear keys jingling at the door.

"I want to know what turns you on," I sang with Joe. I knew what I had on would turn him on. I was singing my life away when I heard keys at the door. I stood up from my seat. I turned to look at the time. It was seven o'clock on the nose. How punctual he was. I couldn't even punish him for being late. I heard the door open and close, and I heard another door open and close. He came around that corner looking as good as chocolate. When he looked up and saw me standing there, he stopped in his tracks, and I swear his heart stopped. His eyes were a hazel brown that turned to that russet glowing color. He was excited.

"Welcome home, Mr. Grayson," I said, walking over to him. I handed him a glass of ginger ale that I put inside a wine glass. He grabbed me into his arms.

"I can come home every day like this," he said and kissed me.

"You can if you're a good boy," I said, kissing him back.

"You're a sexy little devil," he said, pinching one of my nipples. I had to get him off me before he ended up taking me right here, and I wanted him to eat dinner first.

"No, dinner first, Mr. Grayson." I pulled him to the dinner table. I set my glass down as I removed his suit jacket. I wanted him to be relaxed. I fixed our plates as he washed his hands. I set our food down on the table. "How was your meeting? Are congratulations in order?" I asked as we sat.

"Yes," he said, holding up his glass to mine.

"Wonderful," I said as I tapped his glass.

"Baby girl, this looks and smells amazing."

"Thank you." We said grace and enjoyed our food. Once again, he kept his eyes on me. How could one eat like that?

"Hunter, can you stop staring at me and eat your food?"

"I'm eating, and it's quite delicious I might add," he said. I could tell he was making love to me in his head, ripping my clothes off. I totally forgot about that. I may never see this outfit again. "I'd rather be eating my dinner off you." He paused for a moment, taking a bite of his food. The way he ate made me shiver. "You remember red is my favorite color?"

"No," I lied.

"Lie. If I may say, red has never looked better." He smiled, and I poured myself another glass of wine. I was going to need it. Once we were finished, I cleaned the kitchen. I didn't want Phoebe coming in the morning to a dirty kitchen. I turned around, and Hunter was standing in a t-shirt and his slacks.

"Why don't you drink?" I asked. His facial expression changed. I could tell he was a little irritated by the question, or maybe the reason behind it irritated him. "Sorry. I don't want to pry. It's okay if you're not ready to tell me. I was just curious," I said as I saw him put his head down. He was now up on me. My chest against his chest. He lifted his head back up.

"No, it's okay. I had a bad experience drinking as a teenager, so I just chose never to drink again," he said. He wrapped his arms around me. It had to be after I left LABA because we drank a lot that summer. We didn't get a chance to do anything in New York.

Shit, I'd had plenty bad experiences drinking. I'd been all kinds of drunk, and I still drank. How wicked was that? I refused to do anything else. Drugs... I could never go back down that road again.

"Did something bad happen?" I pried. I felt his posture tense. I wanted to know everything about him. But I didn't want to hurt him. "It's okay, Hunter. I've been through all of that." His eyes stared me down. "I've been through more than you can imagine. So, don't think I wouldn't understand." I pulled him in closer to me and kissed him passionately. Behind his eyes, I saw hurt and pain. And I wanted to erase it all. I grabbed his face with my hands, and he put his hands on top of mine. We stared in each other's eyes, and I could tell he saw the same pain in mine. We were two hurt individuals who needed and loved each other. We kissed for a long moment, just letting each other know that we would be there for one another.

"Let's go to bed," I said.

"As long as you're coming too."

"I wouldn't want to be anywhere else." He smiled and lifted me up in his arms. He blew out the candles as we walked past them. I laid my head on his shoulder. I wanted him so bad that I could taste it. We entered the bedroom, and he set me down on my feet.

"Take off your clothes," I ordered.

"Yes, ma'am." My eyes widened as he stripped.

"Lie down on your stomach." He did what he was told without a fight. I pulled out the oil from my bag. I climbed up and poured oil on his back.

"My man deserves a massage after a long day at work." I ran my hands all over his body, getting all his kinks out. I could tell he was loosening up. I wanted him to know that he could trust me with anything. I wanted to make him as happy as he had made me in the last forty-eight hours. I must have been making him feel good as he moaned with pleasure. I climbed off his back and told him to turn around.

He stood on the side of the bed facing me. He leaned in to kiss my neck while his hands traveled all over my body. His hands rubbed and pinched at my nipples.

"Damn," he moaned as I heard my body suit go down in shreds. After we made love, we lay in each other's arms. We were quiet for a moment until I broke the silence.

# THE LOVE I CRAVE

"Hunter, have you ever been to a place called Martin's in New York?" I asked as I lay on his chest, and he rubbed his hand through my hair. I'd been thinking about this trip all day. I'd been to New York City before, but in my past. Hunter was from New York; we ran into each other once there.

"Yes, of course. Martin's is a lovely place. Would you like to go?"

"I have a business meeting there this weekend and would like for you to come with me. If you're not busy."

"I'm never too busy for you. I'll go anywhere in the world with you," he said as he held me tighter. I felt safe in his arms, something I hadn't felt in a long time.

"You're so sweet. I'll have my secretary Melissa to call you about the flight arrangements."

"Don't worry, I'll handle all of that. Just let me know when you want to leave and what time," he said. Just when I thought I had my hand on things, he was taking over like always.

"Friday, any time after noon. My meeting is at seven on Saturday."

We made love again. Hunter never lied when he said that sex with him was like a rollercoaster. My adrenaline was up when I exploded from that orgasm. My body reacted toward him in ways I'd never thought possible. I tried not to think of losing him. I got afraid that my past would bite me on the ass.

# Henson Dreamier

How could I have so much baggage so young? It was time to pay my therapist a visit about this change in my life. Dr. Stevens would be surprised. She said that one day, I would meet someone who would help me build my trust back in men. When should I tell him that I see a therapist? Being as though he knew so much about me, he probably already knew. I didn't want to lose him. I'd lost so much in my life, and to lose Hunter probably would send me off my rocker. I held him tighter in my arms.

"What's wrong?" he asked. How could I lie when I told him to be completely honest with me?

"I'm scared I might lose you. I've lost too much already. My parents, my sister, my brother, Sophia." I felt myself tearing up. I didn't want him to see me crying. He lifted my head up to his.

"Zollah, I don't care about your past. And I'm sorry about Sophia. I… I liked her. She was always there for you. I'm sorry about your siblings. I know something happened to you, and I know you may not be ready to talk about it," he said with much sadness. His hand reached up to touch the scar on my face, neck, then the one on my shoulder. I shivered under his touch. "Whatever it was, I know it was what stopped you from coming to Harvard. I know you got accepted." I sat up from his chest.

"Hunter, I promise you I was going to come, I was. I just…" I turned away. "I just couldn't leave," I said so defeated. HE stopped me. Hunter pulled me into a hug. We lay back and just held each other. God, we were fucked up.

"Thank you…" I paused for a second. "for everything," I said. He didn't know half the shit I had been through. He sensed something in New York and begged me to run away with him. There was no way in hell I could have left at that time. Sasha and Sophia were still there, and I couldn't leave them to be upon HIS wrath. New York was before I was supposed to leave for college. I was about to graduate high school. I had told Hunter that I would see him in Harvard. That was where we were supposed to start our life together. But I never showed up.

"No, thank you for believing me in LABA when I made you all of those promises. I meant them. Everything I've done wasn't just for myself, but for you and the family I know we'll have together. I never had to struggle in my life, but I know you have, and I never want that for you again."

"You know how to make a girl swoon. You spoil me."

"We spoil each other, especially if you dress up like that every night."

"You've destroyed two dresses and a lingerie; you cannot have more nights like this." He chuckled. I moved over to turn off the bedside lamp. We were now in complete darkness, but I found my way back into his arms. "Good night."

"Good night, Baby Girl." I fell asleep to the sound of his beating heart, which was music to my ears.

# CRAZY, DERANGED, MOFO.

Today was Thursday, and my week had gone by pretty fast. I'd spent every night with Hunter since Monday. Quite frankly, I was exhausted. Staying up late and having sex all night, I wasn't getting a lot of sleep. Even though I hadn't been sleeping well for a long time. I had just left work and was now on my way to see Dr. Stevens. I needed to see her before my weekend with Hunter. I had to; my emotions were all over the place. One minute, I wanted to be with him. The next minute, I wanted to run away, just to protect Hunter from HIM. I felt as though this was too good to be true. I just kept thinking how someone like him would want to be with a girl like me. I wasn't perfect, but I considered him perfect. He was in my eyes.

# THE LOVE I CRAVE

I hadn't seen Sasha since Monday, and I missed her. Tonight would be my first night without Hunter, and I was already having withdrawal symptoms.

"Miss Zollah, aren't you glowing," Mrs. Clark said as I walked in to Dr. Stevens' office. Mrs. Clark was her receptionist.

"Am I really glowing?" I asked, smiling from ear to ear. I knew I was glowing. I had heard it all day today.

"Yes, you are. She's ready to see you," Mrs. Clark said, opening the door for me.

"Thank you," I said as she closed the door behind me.

"Zollah, what a pleasure." Dr. Stevens got up from her seat as we embraced in a hug. "How have you been?" she asked as I went to sit on my favorite couch. "You look… brighter."

"I feel brighter but also confused and scared." I didn't waste any time opening up. I didn't have time to bullshit; she was paid whether I talk or not. I started seeing Dr. Stevens a couple of months after moving back to California. Sasha found her for me once she couldn't handle the nightmares anymore.

"Scared and confused, why is that?" she asked. It was time for me to get down to it.

"A few things have changed since my last visit." I couldn't help but smile thinking about my last few days with Hunter.

"Really? I'm guessing they're good things from that smile."

"Well, I'm no longer single. I have a boyfriend," I said. Her eyes widened at the news and nearly jumped from her seat. She never thought I would get to the point to trust a man, let alone have a boyfriend.

"Boyfriend, a serious one?" she asked as if she didn't understand.

"Yes, remember I told you about the boy I met that summer at LABA."

"The one you've been waiting for most of your life." I could tell by the look on her face that she believed that I'd been wasting my time all these years. No one ever believed me when I said he would find me. She thought it was a coincidence that I received the money three years ago from someone called H.

"Well, we ran into each other and have been together since Monday. When I saw him, all my feelings came back in full force. I knew I was still in love with him, and he was with me." I paused for a moment. "It was difficult at first, but I couldn't fight it anymore. We've spent every day together, and I can't go a day without him anymore," I said as I finally stopped talking.

# THE LOVE I CRAVE

"So, what I got from what you said is that after waiting this long for the man, now that the wait is over, you're scared shitless because of your past. You're afraid that if you put everything you have into this relationship, you'll end up losing. You have a fear of loss and losing the people you love. You're confused because you don't feel as though you deserve to be happy. Is that it?"

"Yes." She hit all of that on the nose. She was the only one I could open up to about my ex. Damon and Sasha were the only other people who knew what I had been through with HIM.

"So again, this is all about HIM?" Everyone called HIM that because his name wasn't allowed to be said in my presence. That name sent me into a dark place.

"Yes, it's always because of HIM. HE has ruined my life. I was scared to commit when everyone in my life had left me, been taken away, or had died. I know Hunter is different. He is sweet, charming, passionate, handsome, smart, and sexy. I'm scared that if HE finds me, he'll hurt Hunter, and that will be unacceptable. I'll die if anything happens to Hunter because of me."

"I can see that your thing here is fear and commitment. You cannot dwell on the past, which I've been telling you for the past three years. You have to find it in your heart to forgive HIM for everything HE has done to you, and I mean everything." I felt a tear roll down my face. How could I forgive HIM for what HE had done to me? It was

111

unforgiveable. "If you really want this to work, Zollah, you have to and not just for Hunter, but for yourself." I knew she was right.

"It's going to be hard to forgive someone who has hurt me emotionally, verbally, mentally, and physically. It hurts to even think of HIM. I haven't had any nightmares for a while now, and I hope and pray they're over with," I said.

"Okay, Zollah. I want you to listen and listen carefully. First, you need to take one day at a time. This won't be easy, you know. I've heard of Hunter Grayson. He's one of the wealthiest bachelors in the world. I want you to be prepared for HIM finding out about you and Hunter. Hunter is in the spotlight. HE will find you and know where you are." Just her words made me afraid. I never wanted to see HIM again.

"Your relationship is going to be public. Don't do things to make Hunter run because you're afraid. All I want you to do is open yourself up to him one day at a time. Tell him little by little of your past. You have to so it won't be such a big surprise if HE returned in your life." Her words ran around in my head. She was right, but to tell him meant I would have to relive what I'd been through, and I couldn't do that. It made me feel... dark.

"Maybe I can try this weekend. I have a business meeting in New York City, and he's coming with me."

"I can see that you seem happier than I've seen you in years, so don't ruin it because of your past. Not because of your parents or because of your siblings or even HIM. This is going to be a rough change in your life, but I think it's going to be for the best. You're confused because things are moving fast. Open your eyes, ears, and heart. Let Hunter decide what he wants, and from what you say, he isn't going anywhere. Things will get worse before they get better, and I want you prepared."

I took everything she said with me when I left. I thought about it on the way home. She said that she was quite sure that Hunter had his own issues that he needed to settle. She didn't think they were as severe as mine, but she wasn't sure. Well, I could agree with her on that. My mind ran as I drove home. I was in dire need of a glass of wine. I knew my past would come forth. I just hoped that I would be ready, but who was ever ready for their psycho ex-boyfriend to come back and try to kill them? That's what he probably had to do because I wasn't giving up without a fight. I wouldn't let anyone, or anything, come between what I'd waited a lifetime for.

I listened to one of my favorite songs, 'Stronger' on the ride. Even though the pain I'd been through, I was still alive, and that's all that mattered. I was jamming to some music when my phone rang. I turned my music down to answer the phone.

"Hello."

"Hey, where are you?" Sasha asked.

"On my way home."

"Well, get here soon. I have a surprise for you."

"What is it?"

"If I tell you, then it wouldn't be a surprise." Sasha hung up. Then my phone rang again.

"Yes, love," I answered, smiling when I noticed who was calling.

"I miss you so much," Hunter said.

"I miss you more. I'm on my way home," I said.

"Our home or your home?"

"My house."

"How sad. Can I come and see you and get a little taste? I'm going crazy. I haven't seen you in almost nine hours," he begged. He was crazy.

"No, absence makes the heart grow fonder."

"No, there goes that word again. We'll see." He hung up. Now I was nervous not knowing what he may do to me, but it excited me. Whatever it was may cause me to lose consciousness and blackout.

I turned my truck around so I could back into my garage. I spotted a 2012 Charger with the Hemi parked in front of our house. I gave the car one last look, spotting the paper tags. I opened the door that led from the garage into the house and heard music playing but no conversation. I saw a man standing in the kitchen, holding a glass of wine. Sasha was leaning over the island, staring at the man with a big smile on her face. I examined the guy from head to toe. Tall, light-brown skin with short, curly hair. Then the man spoke, and I heard his voice. My heart leapt.

"Damon," I yelled out. He turned around and I'll be damned, it was Damon.

"Hey, Z," Damon said, setting his glass on the island.

"Damon." I dropped my purse and bag. I ran over and jumped into his arms, and he spun me around. I held him tight in my arms. Damon was my best friend. I met him when I was fourteen years old on the bus to modeling camp. There were no more seats, so I had to sit next to him. We had been friends ever since. I missed him so much. I finally pulled back the hug, and he let me down to my feet. "Oh, my goodness. Where have you been in the last two years?" I asked.

"Just seeing the world and all."

"Yeah, forgetting about the little people," I said. I was upset that Damon left even though I knew it was a good decision for him, for the both of us maybe. Damon knew everything I had been through, all my secrets. He was there with me through most of it. He begged me to leave, even he tried. Everyone tried.

"I'll never forget about you guys, my two best friends. The world is a big place. We shouldn't be limited to just

America," he said as he sat at the bar and poured me a glass of wine. "So, how has your life been since we last saw each other."

"I've been enjoying my life, my career, my friends. I…" I paused for a moment. "I'm doing great." Damon gave me a weird look. There was silence, then he spoke.

"So, you and Hunter finally," he said, and my eyes widen.

"Umm, yes, finally."

"That's good, and it's about damn time." He smiled, holding his glass out for mine. We tapped, and my body relaxed. I stared in Damon's eyes to read him, to sense how he was feeling. The only way to know was to ask, but I wouldn't right now.

Damon had always cared for me since the day we first met on that bus years ago. He had seen me at my worst and my best. He was a great friend to me even when I wasn't to him sometimes. Sasha, Damon, and Sophia lived that life with me. Damon and I shared a kiss twice. It meant something to us, but we could never act on it. I was scared that HE would find out. It wouldn't have been a good outcome. HIM being in my life made me miss out on being just a normal teenager. Maybe if I were a normal teenager, I wouldn't have lost contact with Hunter. I probably wouldn't have met any of them. Damon wanted to be with me once, but I was a lost soul. The person I was before HIM was no more and was never coming back.

# THE LOVE I CRAVE

We sat and talked while we waited for Sasha to finish dinner. Damon and Hunter had gotten close that summer. We all were together like white on rice. Hunter, Damon, Sasha, Sophia, Asher and me. The six of us went everywhere unless Hunter and I wanted to sneak off. I couldn't say they became best of friends, but they tolerated one another. When Sasha finished with dinner, we sat around and ate and had more wine. It felt good to sit and chill with my friends. It was like old times but without the fireworks, which was Sophia. She was the feisty Latino who was always ready for whatever.

Damon's career took off right after graduating UCLA. He graduated the same year Sasha did. I followed the next year. He graduated with honors like the rest of us. He made a nice living as an artist, painting everyday people. They loved his work. He started off with a birthday gift from a wife to her husband. That was when a major celebrity came to him for a painting. She wanted it for her husband as a birthday present. She wanted him to paint her nude. Damon knew he could do it but thought he shouldn't. He turned her down. She offered him ten grand, and he couldn't say no. I told him he'd be a fool to not take the money. It was one of the best decisions he had ever made in his life.

She brought him a lot of work, and he ended up making hundreds of thousands of dollars on his paintings. Then one day, the first lady that brought him all the work came back to ask him for a favor. She was a famous actress who was producing her first low-budget movie overseas. She asked him if he could take the leading role because the original actor broke his leg in a major accident. Damon said that he had no acting skills, but that didn't stop him from saying yes. She was the one who changed his life with his paintings. He said he owed her this. That was the second-best decision he made in his life.

"I have two tickets for a red-carpet premiere in a couple of weeks. Would the two of you like to go?" he asked.

"Hell yeah. You don't have to ask me twice," Sasha said from the recliner. She was rocking, sipping on her wine. Damon and I sat on the couch. He had his shoes off and was very relaxed. I turned to look at the clock, and it was ten o'clock. Damn, how time flew when you were having fun.

Sasha excused herself to the bathroom. While I realized I hadn't called Hunter, I know he was freaking out right now. I got up from my seat to reach for my purse. I had to get my phone out to call him immediately. I had ten missed calls. They all were from Hunter. Right when I was about to call him, the doorbell rang throughout the house, and my heart stopped. I looked over at Damon, who stared at me.

"Do you want me to get it?" he asked.

"No, I'll get it," I said, walking slowly to the door. The bell rang again. There was no need to look out the peephole I knew who it was. I unlocked the door slowly, then opened it. When I looked up, I saw Hunter standing there. My mouth watered. He was wearing what seemed like his workout gear.

Oh my God, he looked good with sweat dripping all over his body. I wanted to lick every inch of him. I snapped out of it.

"Hunter, what are you doing here?" I asked, stepping out onto the porch and closing the door behind us. He kept looking inside to see who was in there. I knew where this was about to go.

"I was worried about you. When I called, you didn't answer your phone," he said. I had no idea why my heart was racing. "Do you know how fast I drove over here? Like a mad man." He turned to peek inside the glass of the front door.

"I'm sorry. I lost track of time."

"Time passes fast when you're having fun," he said, trying to look through a closed door. "Who is in there?" he asked, and I was taken aback.

"You came all the way over here to make a damn fool of yourself." I was happy I took this conversation outside, but Damon was sitting by the window, and I was sure he could hear us.

"Are you alone in there?"

"No, I'm not. Sasha is in there, and so is someone I haven't seen in two years." I looked into his eyes and saw something I didn't want to see, the same thing I saw in my ex's eyes. Jealousy, possessiveness, and obsessiveness. I turned away from him. I closed my eyes to take a deep breath.

# Henson Dreamier

I opened my eyes past Hunter and saw Julius sitting in the car, just waiting. I sighed. Poor Julius.

"Telling you not to come over didn't stop you from driving thirty minutes over here." I raised my voice at him. "I said no because I wanted to spend time with Sasha before leaving for my weekend with you." I put my head down.

"What?" He moved closer to me. I couldn't allow him to touch me, or it would weaken me.

"Hunter, you're going to see me with a lot of men. I'm the owner of a company, and I meet a lot of different men. If I say that I'm with you, I'm with only you. You should believe me. You're not the only one that will find me attractive or want to fuck me." His eyebrow rose when I said that, but it was the truth. "I want this to work, but it won't if you think you're going to curse out every man you see me with." He smiled at the thought. "I'm serious, Hunter." He was quiet for a moment.

"Okay, Zollah, I apologize…" he said, easing his arms around me, "but I can't change overnight."

"I know but jealousy. It's something you don't have to be with me," I said, accepting his apology. I leaned in and kissed him. I wanted him to know that there was no other man but him. He pulled back the hug and stared at me. He walked back toward the door.

"Where are you going?" I asked.

"Back inside to apologize. I just needed to calm down. Plus, I haven't seen Damon in ages. I want to see if he's still Pretty Ricky." I tried so hard to hold in that laugh, but it came out. Hunter used to call Damon that. Pretty Ricky.

"Hunter," I called out his name.

"Zollah, I promise," he said, placing his hand over his heart.

"Okay." We entered the house, and Damon was sitting on the couch watching Sports Center. He got up from his seat when he heard the door open. Sasha was in the kitchen cleaning up.

"Hey, Darkness," Sasha said from the kitchen. Hunter's eyebrows rose in question.

"I'll tell you later," I said.

"If it's not Wealthy Kid Grayson," Damon said, and I laughed. They had made up names for each other that summer. As I thought about it now, they were always going back and forth.

"You still Pretty Ricky I see, but with a tan." Damon laughed, and they gave each other a handshake and a hug.

"What have you been up to these past ten years?" Hunter asked. They sat on the couch and talked. I watched them from the kitchen where Sasha and I cleaned the kitchen and drank wine.

"Damon is home for good… well, at least for a while," Sasha said.

"That's great news." I was excited even though I didn't sound like it. It would be great having him back home. I liked it when he was only a drive away. I looked over at Damon and Hunter laughing and talking about sports. I looked at Sasha, and my heart ached. I had all the people I loved in my life, and there were only two people missing. My sister and my brother.

"You still haven't heard or found anything about Brooke or Ryan?" I asked, finishing my glass of wine.

"No, which is very odd. It's like they fell off the earth after leaving Texas." Sasha had been looking for them since we moved back to California. There was no social media or no records of them. "Don't worry, Hope. I'll find them." She even sounded discouraged. Sasha could use that mind and those fingers and could find anything. Well, hack into anything, but I didn't want to use that word.

"I know you will, Sasha." I gave her a hug.

"Well, I have a long day ahead of me tomorrow. I'm going to bed," Damon said, placing his empty wine glass on the table. "Hunter, I'll see you later, and thank you again," Damon said. His eyes fell on me. When he headed upstairs, I wasn't surprised that he was sleeping here tonight. He had always been welcomed in my house, and it wasn't the first time we had slept under the same roof.

"I'm heading to bed also. You kids behave. Lock up when you're done," Sasha said, following Damon. Hunter was next to me with his arms around me.

"Thank God you'll be with me in New York this weekend," he said.

"Maybe," I said as he pulled back. He turned to head back into the living room, and I followed.

"Where is your phone?" He stopped, and I almost ran into him. He turned to me.

"In my purse." He lifted my face up with his finger so our eyes could meet.

"What have I told you about time and being punctual? Being noticeable of time, being observant. I guess you won't learn until you get punished," he said. My eyes lit up. I wanted to be punished. I reached my hands out to touch him. "Oh no, Baby Girl, your punishment isn't mind-blowing sex. Your punishment will be waiting for this good loving." He grabbed my hand in his, moving it toward his manhood. "I know you want this. Don't you?"

"Yes, I want it," I begged. His hand slipped inside the waist of my pants. He rubbed my wetness.

"Oh yes, you want it." I did. I was nice and wet, wanting him inside me. His hand rubbed slightly against my pebble. I came instantly. He pulled his hand from my pants and licked his finger. My God, he turned me on. He pushed me backwards until my back was up against the wall.

"You want it so bad. I can smell it on you. I want you to think about what you did. How I wanted to fuck you crazy in the middle of your living room." His body rubbed against mine. "How I was going to make you come until you needed a plumber for water damage." I came from just the thought of it. He kissed me, and I was going to attack him. He pulled back and stared into my eyes with a smirk.

"See you tomorrow, Mrs. Grayson," he said as he pulled away from me. It was like snatching a bandage off. He opened the front door and headed down the steps to his truck where Julius was still waiting. He got inside, and they drove off. The only thing I could do was smile at him. The man was driving me totally insane.

I checked all the doors and windows before I headed upstairs to my room. I lay in bed thinking how Hunter could just leave me like this. I was horny and frustrated. I was mad that Hunter reacted the way he did. I hated that Hunter had jealous ways. It reminded me of HIM, and I hated thinking about HIM.

Life with HIM was exciting at first. I was young, fun, energetic, fresh, talented, and pure, not something most fourteen-year-olds could say. I met HIM in a time of my life when I needed someone to take care of me. I didn't have anyone after my parents left. HE came along and swept me off my feet. He had loving, wonderful things to say to me. He was young, rich, and in charge, and I loved that about HIM. He wasn't my age. I was fourteen years old, and he was nineteen. He was the son of one of the most powerful men in Florida. I had traveled there one weekend with my modeling camp/agency. He said when he first saw me, I took his breath away. All he wanted to do was take care of me. Then he soon became obsessive of me. I didn't notice at first how Sasha, Sophia, and I booked so many gigs. It was because of HIM. He kept me working and making money. I loved HIM, but after we had sex for the first time, things changed. I wished I could have seen how controlling, possessive, and abusive he was before it was too late.

I saw the world with HIM. Even though most of it was a blur. The fancy jets, the huge hotel suites, and expensive parties I attended with HIM. HE took me to Las Vegas for my birthday. By that time, I was growing apart from HIM, but I would do anything to keep my friends working and bringing in money. I would do any and everything to keep HIM happy, my friends happy, and totally forgot about myself. There was a hot party on the strip of Las Vegas. By this time, I had stopped drinking for a while, and HE didn't like that. HE made me drink that night. I was stuck between a rock and a hard place. HE made me laugh, but HE made me cry more. Then I realized to deal with HIM, I had to be intoxicated or even high. I needed it to keep my sanity, I wanted things to go back to how they were when we first got together.

Sasha said one night that she didn't like the person I was becoming. Drinking and smoking every day just to get by.

# Henson Dreamier

She had no idea what I was protecting. She said that HE was using me, but I thought I was using HIM until Hunter came along. Then I would be out of there. Then she had told me that he was messing with other women. I just kept saying to her that HE wouldn't do that to me, but really, I didn't care. I knew better not to ask or to question HIM. HE told me to never question what HE did or who HE talked to. If I did, I would be punished for it. HE had built me up to never be jealous. I wanted out, but I knew I couldn't just leave. I had planned so many times to escape but never did until I just couldn't take it no more. If I didn't lose… the last person I lost was the last straw. Hunter was different; he would never put his hands on me. Well, not in a violent kind of way. He must be different, for my sanity, for my heart. My heart wouldn't allow me to fall for another one like HIM, but Hunter did scare me tonight. He must know that I wanted only him. He was all I ever wanted.

I was going over my past and present and how my past may conflict with my life. How my future with Hunter may be in jeopardy. I couldn't help but cry myself to sleep, thinking that I may lose Hunter. Thinking about what Dr. Stevens said about HIM finding me. I couldn't face him if he ever got his hands on me again. I didn't even want to know what He would do to me.

# BEST PLANE RIDE
# EVER

Hope, get up. You're going to be late for work, and you have a conference call at ten o'clock," Sasha said. God, was it morning already? I had my back toward the door. She came over and pulled the covers off me and sat on my bed. She looked over and saw dry tears on my face. "Did you cry yourself to sleep last night?" she asked. I pulled the covers over my face.

"No," I lied. She snatched the covers off me and the bed.

"What happened with Hunter?" she asked.

"Nothing, it's just... me. I was going down memory lane last night, that's all," I said, sitting up in bed.

127

"Hope, you have to stop doing that to yourself. I know you can never forget what happened to you and what you've been through. But I didn't get you out of there for you to not enjoy your life. Now, it isn't just me HE has to fight to get to you. It's me, Damon, and Hunter. I know that Hunter will never ever let you go again." She pulled me into a hug. "You're going to be okay. Now, go shower..." she said, wiping my face with her hand, "and get dressed. Are your bags packed?" she asked.

"No, he said that I didn't need to bring anything heavy. Anything I need will be available in New York." I got out of bed and brushed my hair back from my face as I walked to my bathroom.

"Lucky bitch," Sasha said.

"I heard that," I said as I closed the door. I didn't know how long I was in the shower, but when I got out, I felt like a brand-new person. I put on some black high-waist pants with a short-sleeve, white button-up shirt, some black peep-toe shoes, and a wide black belt. I brushed my hair into a ponytail. I grabbed my purse and headed for the kitchen. When I made it to the bottom of the steps, Damon was sitting at the breakfast bar eating.

"Good morning, Damon." I smiled, sitting next to him.

"Morning, Z," he said. Sasha placed a plate in front of me. Sasha was a best friend everyone in the world should have, and she was mine... and Damon's. We ate and talked about what the plans were for today. I told Damon about my business trip, and he told me about meeting his manager then going house hunting. That was music to my ears that he was staying, at least for a while. I finished my food, grabbed my things, and headed for the garage door.

"I'll see you guys when I return. Now behave yourselves until I get back."

It was 9:43 when I pulled up in front of EQ Skyscraper. Rodney was there waiting like always. I noticed that ever since he saw me with Hunter, he avoided eye contact. His conversations were short with me. Yes, no, maybe, okay. I wondered what the hell was going on with him, but I didn't have time to ask.

"Good morning, Rodney. How are you?"

"Great," he said.

"Is everything okay?" I asked.

"Yes," he said as he walked toward my truck. "Oh, Mr. Grayson said to park your car next to his for lock up, since you won't need it for a couple of days." That was the most he had said to me in days.

"Yes, thanks, Rodney. I appreciate it," I said as I turned and walked inside the building with a smile on my face. I pushed the button for the elevator, the doors opened, and I was on my way up. I stepped off the elevator, and Aimee wasn't at her desk. I headed back to my office, opened the door, and stopped in my tracks. My office was consumed with roses.

"What the hell?" I stepped inside, and Aimee and Melissa were there. "Who sent these?"

"Do you have to ask that question? This office has been bored but since Hunter, we have gotten so much excitement around here," Melissa said. How much did he spend on roses? I moved toward my desk and a fancy vase with roses and a note. I reached for the note, and my hand was smacked away.

"Don't have time for that right now. Your conference call starts in one minute." Melissa cleared my desk to make some room. She set out the necessary paperwork I needed for the call with Mr. Miles, Carmen's lawyer. We needed to discuss preparations for the photoshoot and the interviews. Mr. Miles had said that Carmen wanted her headliner Lirpa Summers to have her own interview.

We set the date for a month from now. I checked my calendar, and everything was good to go. Mr. Miles said that I would have the time of my life at the club. The photoshoot would be early Saturday morning, and the interviews would be on Sunday. The conference call lasted about an hour. After hanging up with Mr. Miles, I called upstairs to my manager and informed her of the arrangements. Abby Newman was a good colleague; she ran Javier magazine to a T.

The rest of my morning was just setting up follow-up meetings and sending emails. It was almost noon when I called it quits. I asked Aimee to send the remaining flowers downstairs to the lobby for anyone to take home. I kept the beautiful glass vase with the note.

"Is there anything else you'll need before my return?" I asked.

"No, we have the rest," Aimee said as they both left my office. I cleared my desk and turned off my computer. I almost forgot about the note on the vase. I pulled it off and smiled as I opened it.

*To Baby girl*

*Words cannot explain how sorry I am for the way I reacted last night. I will try my damn best to be on good behavior, I promise. I hope you enjoyed the roses. They smelled delightful, just like you. I can't wait to spend the weekend wooing you. See you soon.*

*Love H*

I couldn't wait to spend the weekend with him either, and I wondered about it as I grabbed my things. I locked my office door and headed to the elevator.

"See you girls on Monday," I said as the elevator doors opened, and I slid in. I pushed the button for the top floor. I'd never been on his floor, let alone inside his office. I had no idea who or how many people worked there. I felt nervous as the doors opened. When I stepped off the elevator to this huge lobby, there was a lot of space for clients in the reception area.

And just like his home, his furniture was coffee, cream, and white. It was very elegant with soft jazz music playing. The lobby had three flat screen TVs on the wall, one in each of the three corners. One TV had a diagram of some building being built. The second TV played Sports Center. Typical man. The third TV played the news. There were four cream-color couches. Four brown loveseats, and the rest were cream-color chairs. I walked straight ahead to the receptionist desk. She was a pretty blonde-haired girl with ocean-blue eyes and full lips. I had seen her come and go in this building but never knew she worked up here.

"Hello," I said to the girl, but she didn't look up from her computer. "Is Hunter Grayson available?" She finally looked up.

"Oh, I'm so sorry, Miss Hope. I wasn't paying attention," she said, fumbling with the stuff on her desk. She looked surprised.

"It's okay. Is Hunter busy? If so, I can wait," I said, pointing to a chair.

"Oh no, you can go in." She pointed to the right of her. "Down the hall, straight back. The last door straight ahead. You won't miss it."

"Thank you," I said as I followed her directions.

I passed a couple of people waiting and took the hall down. I noticed the paintings on the wall and smiled. They were beautiful, and they were also familiar. Hunter had

132

amazing taste. I stopped in front of one painting and noticed the signature. I smiled to myself. I reached the last door, and it read President Hunter J. Grayson. Just the name sent chills up my spine. I turned the knob, then pushed the door open, and all I saw was space. I was totally jealous. My eyes traveled in his office, looking for him. He wasn't alone. A lady sat in the chair in front of his desk, wearing a red business suit. They both turned to look at me.

"Oh, Hunter, I'm sorry. I didn't know you were in a meeting. I can come back," I said, closing the door.

"Don't be silly," he said, getting up from his seat. He came over to give me a hug and a kiss. He grabbed my hand in his and led me back over to his desk.

"Hope, this is Mandy. Mandy, this is Hope." We shook hands. I was taken aback by the name he chose to use to introduce me. He didn't use Zollah. I guess he noticed that I didn't go by Zollah here.

"Nice to meet you," I said.

"Likewise," she said, but I could tell she didn't mean it as she looked me up and down.

"Mandy oversees Best, Asher's part of the company. Asher is out of the country right now. She's taking over until he returns from the Dominican Republic," he said, never taking his eyes off me.

"Mr. Grayson, I have everything I need until you return. Email me if you need anything, and I'll see you on Monday." She smiled as she walked toward the door. Then she turned to me. "Nice to meet you again, Hope." I turned to Hunter and wrapped my arms around him.

"The Dominican Republic. Isn't that where you just came from?"

"Yes, I was there for two years."

"I heard it's lovely there," I said.

"It is. Would you like to go one day?"

"Sure, I'll go anywhere with you." I leaned to kiss him.

"So, are you ready to go?" he asked, pulling back the kiss.

"Yes." He let go of me and went over to his desk. He cleared some things off, then picked up his desk phone.

"Yes, Marcus, is she ready to go?" He paused for a response. "All right, be up in ten minutes," Hunter said before hanging up. "Let's go, Baby Girl," he said, holding his hand out for mine.

He locked up his things and shut down his system. Then he turned out all the lights. He pulled me toward the back of his massive office. I was sure in need of an upgrade. I thought we were going to head for the elevator, but he pulled me behind his desk toward an emergency exit.

# THE LOVE I CRAVE

"Where are we going?" I asked once we were in the white stairwell. The only thing that had color was the red fire extinguisher.

"You'll see." He smiled as we took the stairs two flights up. Was he leading me to the roof? When we got to the top and exited the door, I thought it was the exit to the roof. I was wrong. It was another floor. As we walked down the hall, I heard this noise. I had no idea where it came from. The floor had just one room, and it was filled with small TVs showing video recordings of the entire building; I assumed it was the security room. The noise got louder the closer we got to the end of the hall.

"What is that noise?" I asked, but he said nothing. He pushed open the emergency doors, and I saw where the noise was coming from—a black and grey helicopter with Grayson on the side of it. I had never flown in a helicopter before. I was kind of nervous.

"Mr. Grayson, everything is ready to go."

"Thanks, you have everything you'll need for takeoff?" Hunter asked.

"Yes, ready whenever you are, sir." He turned to look at me. "Miss Hope, it's a pleasure. I'm Marcus." He held out his hand as he introduced himself.

"Nice to meet you, Marcus." Hunter led me to the helicopter. Marcus got in front as I got in the back, and Hunter strapped me in with a smile on his face. "You're enjoying this way too much."

"I know. I got a little excited for a moment. I like the sight of you tied up."

"Why am I not surprised?" Hunter finished strapping me in and climbed in next to me. I could imagine what he was thinking.

He handed me some headphones to put on my ears to keep the loud noise to a minimum. As the helicopter took off, I was filled with excitement. I was nervous, but the LA sky was beautiful. Flying over the city this way was much better than a plane. We could see much more of the city. It only took us twenty minutes to make it to LAX. I'd never seen helicopters land at the airport before, but I guess everything was an exception for Hunter Grayson. We didn't land where all the other planes were. We landed in the back toward the grassy area. The helicopter wasn't even all the way on the ground when Hunter jumped out, holding my bags in his hand. He had done this hundreds of times, it seemed like.

He came over to unstrap me, as I pulled the headphones from my ears. He helped me out and walked hand in hand over the grassy area. There were only four private planes. The sign above read Best Airline, which I had heard before in passing. Hunter turned to me, and I smiled. I thought about his office and where he said Mandy handled the Best part of the company. One of the private planes had A.B. airline on it, and the other one had H.B. airline on it. That one further out had the steps down. There was another further back, but it looked like it was being worked on, as it was covered with some kind of tarp.

"Hunter, Best Airline," he responded to my silent question.

"You know we could have driven to the airport," I said.

"I know, but I couldn't show off my helicopter." I laughed. "Plus, my wife gets nothing but the best. Besides, we'd be still stuck in traffic," he said, and he was right about that. He held my hand as we took the steps up. Hunter ducked his head to get inside.

I was in awe. The plane was beautiful, and everything was white inside. The place was like heaven. I had flown in private jets before but nothing this high end. There were eight comfortable chairs and a TV with a small refrigerator in the corner. The plane had eight windows with little white curtains.

"This is nice," I said, turning around to see the place.

"Thanks, it was a gift from my best friend."

"Asher bought you a damn plane."

"Yes. He owns the airline, and I own a percentage of the company. He got me this when I left for Dominican Republic," he said. Wow, who gets a private plane as a gift? You get clothes, a watch, shoes, or maybe even a car, but not a plane. Marcus came through the door with another guy who went into the cockpit. Marcus informed us that we'd be taking off in five minutes. We sat in the seats next to each other, as we put on our seatbelts.

"You know you're doing a wonderful job wooing me," I said. He looked at me with that smirk, making me want to jump his bones. God, the man was sexy as hell. He reminded me of Lance Gross, but Hunter had more muscles, and his eyes were brighter.

"I know your panties are wet right now," he said, smiling. Dear God, those beautiful teeth.

"No," I lied.

"Zollah, I know when you're lying."

"How?" My eyes widened.

"That's my little secret."

"I don't like secrets," I said as he laughed. Five minutes passed, and we were speeding down the runway. I'd forgotten how fast these small planes were. My body was pressed hard against the seat. I exhaled once we were in the air. We rode in silence for a moment as we floated across the California sky.

Twenty minutes in the air, Marcus came over the speakers to tell us that we were free to take off our seatbelts and move around the cabin. Our flight would be five and a half hours. I quickly unfastened my seatbelt and grabbed my bag from under my seat. As I was about to get up, Hunter grabbed my arm.

"Where are you going?" he asked.

"To freshen up and change into something more comfortable," I said. He unsnapped his seatbelt in one motion.

"Let me show you the way," he said with that look, and I knew exactly what that meant. He moved in closer to me and kissed me. As soon as his lips touched mine, I knew I would give in. Then I thought about last night, and how he was here to torture me. I pulled away from him.

"No," I said, turning to walk away. "You're not getting any." He grabbed me by the arm and pulled me back to face him.

"I don't like being told no," he said, his hand sending chills from my arm down my stomach to my pants. God, I couldn't let him touch me there. If he did, it would be all over. His hand slithered inside the top of my pants, his gaze never leaving mine.

"No panties on, umm… nasty, nasty girl," he said, removing his hand from my pants. "You're making me hard."

"You're always hard, and I don't wear panties all the time," I said as I felt his hands grip my white shirt. Then once again, I was out of a good shirt. My buttons went flying across the cabin.

He leaned in and whispered in my ear, "You're always wet for me." I pushed him back enough to take off running to the bathroom. He was on my tail, but I was a step ahead of him as I closed the door in his face.

"Too slow," I said through the door.

"Zollah, open this door now."

"No. Remember what you did to me last night before you left."

"That's nothing compared to what I'm going to do to you if you don't open this door," he demanded.

"No, Hunter."

"No? Okay, I got you," he said as I heard his footsteps move away from the door.

I smiled as I turned around and noticed that I wasn't inside the bathroom. I was inside a bedroom. A bedroom inside a private plane. The bedroom had a full-size bed in it. I moved in closer to the bed and noticed another door inside the bedroom—the bathroom. There was another door inside the bathroom, and before I had time to react, I saw Hunter coming toward me with the biggest smile on his face. At that moment, I knew I fucked up. My eyes widened as I saw him enter the room. He had the belt from his pants in his hand with his pants around his knees.

"Too slow, huh?" he said as I tried to run. I tried to climb over the bed, but I was too slow. "Oh no, you don't," he said as he grabbed my leg, dragging me across the bed.

"I think you've waited long enough for your punishment," he said as he ripped every piece of clothing off me.

"No, not my pants." I drew the line at my high-waist pants, but of course, he didn't pay me any attention.

He climbed on top of me, holding my arms down. There was no point in fighting him. He was stronger than I. I looked above my head to see what he was doing with my arms—he was tying them to the bed. When I noticed that, my heart beat hysterically. I had to breathe in and out and tell myself that I wasn't with HIM. Then he slid down the bed and tied up my feet on either side of the bed. Not my feet too.

"So, baby girl, how would you like to be punished?" he asked. I was quiet for a moment, wondering if this was a trick question or not.

"I didn't know I could choose. What are the options?"

"Smart girl, but I can't say what the options are." He looked around as if he were looking for something.

"Hunter, I don't need to be punished. I'm a good girl," I said with a smile, playing into whatever, he had planned.

"I don't think so. I think you've been pretty naughty," he said. He got up from the bed and left the room. Hunter was gone for a minute. I tried to shake my arms free. Nothing there, so I tried the feet. Nothing. Hunter came back with some things inside a bowl and set them on the side of the bed. Then he went to lock both doors. I focused on what he brought. I saw strawberries, whipped cream, chocolate syrup, and ice cubes. What in the world was he going to do with those things?

"Umm, Hunter, what are you going to do to me?"

"Nothing really, just going to turn you into a human sundae," he said. He set everything around me. "I'm a little hungry, in the mood for some dessert."

My arms were tied together, and my legs was tied apart. He sat Indian style between my legs. I just stared at everything he was doing as my heart raced with anticipation. Not knowing what he was going to do freaked me out. He must have seen the anticipation in my eyes. He got up from the bed and pulled out a blindfold. Where the fuck did he find that?

"Nosy rosy," he said, tying the blindfold over my eyes. Once he was done, he trailed his finger down my neck past my breasts. He didn't stop until he got to my feet.

"You don't need to see what I'm going to do to you. The anticipation alone will kill you. Zollah, the more you fight, the harder it will be," he said.

"But I'm scared," I admitted. Not exactly scared of him or what he would do to me. I feared how he would make me feel. Scared of how my body would react to him. I couldn't see what he was doing, but I felt his lips on mine.

"You don't have to fear me. I'll never hurt you or let anyone hurt you. If it becomes too much for you, choose a safe word, and I will know when to stop," he said. I tried to think of a word that would suit us. So, I thought about where we first met.

"LABA," I said.

"LABA it is."

The room was in complete darkness and immediately, my other senses kicked in. I could smell his essence. I could hear his feet walking back to the end of the bed. Minutes passed when I felt something cold on my breasts. At first, I thought it was the ice cubes, but it didn't feel that cold. The cold never subsided as I felt something cold on my navel. Then I felt a cool feeling on my kitty, then something slipped inside.

"Oh." I moaned. Then I heard a squirting sound. Whatever it was, he sprayed it on my cave, my navel, then my breast. From the sound of it, it sounded like whipped cream. Then I felt what I thought was the chocolate syrup. He squirted it in the same place as the cream. Then for a moment, I heard and felt nothing. I imagined how I looked decorated in strawberries, cream, and syrup.

"Zollah, you look so delicious, I could just eat you alive, and that's what I plan to do." I felt his hands massaging my feet. Then my thighs, then my arms. I heard nothing for a moment, and the anticipation was killing me. I felt the end of the bed move, and I knew where he was. I felt one long lick on my kitty, and I came. "Yes, that's my girl."

How could one lick make me lose all control? Maybe it had something to do with the coldness of my insides. How could someone have so much power over me? That's what I feared. The effect he had on me. As he did what he said he would do, eat me alive, I remembered that I was on a plane, flying in the sky, toward the other side of town. He was eating the strawberries and licking the cream and syrup from my kitty, sending my eyes rolling to the back of my head. He was doing it so good. I tried to close my legs but realized I couldn't.

"Hunter, please," I begged.

He sucked on my pebble as his fingers worked my insides. My eyes continued to roll as I came for what seemed the hundredth time. Hunter had a magical tongue that loved doing magic tricks on my body. My mind felt light as a feather. My heart raced a hundred miles an hour. He sucked and licked me crazy as he took one finger out of my kitty and stuck one in my back door.

"Oh, fuck," I screamed and exploded. My head fell back on the bed, and I slipped into unconsciousness.

# NEW YORK CITY

I awoke to the sound of a slurping noise. I opened my eyes, and I didn't have on the blindfold. I looked down and saw Hunter licking the whipped cream off my stomach. I noticed the cold things on my nipples were strawberries.

"Finally awake," he said.

"What did you do to me?" I asked.

"Nothing. I just wanted to try something out and let me tell you. It went better than I expected. You will have to learn discipline." He laughed to himself as he continued to lick my body clean. My mind was still a little foggy from the explosion.

"How long was I out?"

"Ten minutes maybe," he answered.

"Ten minutes." That wasn't bad.

"That must have been a powerful orgasm." He laughed again to himself. I was happy he found this amusing. He had just finished eating the strawberries from my breasts and was now back at my kitty.

"Aren't you tired?"

"Never." He knew how to make a sister feel good, but I wished he would stop. I couldn't take another orgasm that knocked me out. He licked and sucked on my cave, sending waves of pleasure through me. Pains of pleasure shot through me with every lick.

"Please don't make me pass out again," I begged. I tried to fight, but I was still tied up. His tongue went from my pebble to my kitty repeatedly. "Shit," I moaned.

"The more you fight it, the worst it will be," he said. He was right. He finally crawled up my body. His eyes burned in mine, taking each breast in his mouth at a time. He slid right in me, nice and slow.

"Oh," I moaned, accepting him inside me as if I had a choice.

"Oh yes, you feel so good. Nice and juicy." He moved in and out of me. He felt so good in me, like he didn't belong anywhere else. I wrapped my legs around his waist locking him in.

"Zollah. Please never give my pussy away." I gasped. He begged as he moved in circles. I tried to stay here with him, but his words took me to the one person I hated to think about. Those were his words every time he was inside me. My mind almost left Hunter to go with HIM. but I reminded myself again that this was Hunter. His eyes kept me centered.

"I'll never. It's yours always." What I said must have turned him on because he picked up his pace.

"Yes, mine," he kept saying. He leaned back, and I felt his hands on my legs. He unfastened the straps on them. I didn't hesitate wrapping my legs around him. Then he leaned forward and untied my hands. Then he placed his hands under my ass and lifted me up. He went deep inside, and I screamed out.

I felt like a puppet, and Hunter was the puppeteer. He was controlling me, making me do whatever he wanted me to do. I wrapped my arms around him as I kissed him. I had to, to prevent from screaming out again. I knew Marcus and the co-pilot heard me screaming for my life. I was now free to take control of him. So, I unwrapped my legs and arms from around him. I pulled back the kiss. I pushed him back and flipped him over, so I was straddling him. He had no chance to react as I slid down on him. I rode him like a mechanical bull at a rodeo. I was out of control. I wanted to make him come as many times as he made me.

I had to take the control back. I kissed and licked his chest. Then I kissed him passionately on his soft lips. The taste of strawberries, whipped cream, syrup, and me. I pulled back enough to work just his head and slowly circled my kitty, sending his eyes rolling back in his head. I worked his head, then slid all the way down on him. He moaned out my name. I loved the way he said it. His moans sure sounded good to me. He sat with his chest against my breasts as he kissed me. We kissed as if it would be our last time. Our bodies were hot and sweaty.

"Baby girl, I fucking love you," he said; his eyes gazed into mine as we came together.

"I love you too," I muttered, as he emptied himself inside me. Our bodies went limp as he held me tight in his arms, and we both fell on the bed. I cradled up in his arms, and we just lay there in silence for a moment. We stared in each other's eyes, and I could tell he wanted to ask me something.

"What's on your mind?" I asked. He was quiet for a moment before he spoke.

"The guy you were with at the time you came to LABA," My body tensed up, and my breath caught in my throat. I couldn't go there, not now. His arms tightened around me. "How long were you with him?" Okay, this was an easy question, but it wasn't. I hated thinking about HIM.

"Nine years," I said, not looking at him. "Remember I met him when I was fourteen. Two years before I met you." I lifted my head back up to face him. "Until three years ago." I closed my eyes to get rid of the pain in my heart.

"He's the only other man you've been with?" he asked his hands rubbed up and down my arm. I shook my head. "What did he do to you?" he finally asked. I knew he had been wanting to ask that since he first saw me. His hands ran traces all over my back. Then I knew what he was referring to. I opened my eyes and saw the look on his face. It was filled with hatred.

"Some really bad things, and I can't talk about it, about what he did to me." A tear rolled down my face. He sat up and hugged me tight in his arms.

"It's okay," he said. Why was it so hard for me to talk about HIM? He had done a hell of a number on me. I was broken into thousands of pieces. Since meeting Hunter, it was like he was putting pieces back together. I closed my eyes for a moment, and I saw a little girl. She had big russet eyes that shined bright and long, thick, curly, brown hair like mine. I opened my eyes, seeing the same eyes staring at me. I didn't know how long I had my eyes closed, but I couldn't open them until the pain went away.

"Hey," he said.

"Hey."

"Are you hungry?"

"A little."

"Let's freshen up and get something to eat," he said, getting up from the bed, but I just laid there. "What?"

"I can't move my legs," I said as he came over and lifted me up from the bed and carried me into the bathroom.

I was quiet as a mouse and couldn't say a word. I just watched him wash me. He had so much love in his heart for me. His eyes met mine.

"Stay with me." I didn't know what made him say it, but he did, and it worked. My mind stayed here with him. Those words meant a lot to me. When he was done washing me up, he washed himself. He held my hand and led me back into the bedroom. He left the room for just a moment and he came back with a gift bag. "I got you something," he said, sitting next to me on the bed.

"You didn't have to."

"I know, but I wanted to." I watched him get dressed in some black sweats and a white t-shirt.

When he was done, I took my attention to my gift bag. I opened the bag and found fitted pink and grey sweats. He also bought pink leopard panties and bra. I slid them on, and they fit perfect. Then I put on the sweats, and they fit nice and tight. Then there was a white t-shirt with different color lettering on it. The shirt was cute because it read, 'I Kissed A Millionaire, and I Liked It.' Then he got me some pink, white, and grey Nikes. The exact same as his, just a different color. I put everything on and made my way back inside the cabin.

"I think I bought those pants a little too small. Your ass looks damn good in them."

# THE LOVE I CRAVE

"No, you bought these just right." I gave him a kiss. He had a bag full of my ripped clothes. What would he do with those? He set them aside as I took my seat. Hunter went to the small refrigerator and pulled out two ginger ales and two salads.

We sat and enjoyed our meal quietly for a while. I had no idea how long it was until we were due in New York, but then Marcus came over the intercom and said we had two hours left on our flight. After I finished eating, I laid my head on his shoulder and thought about how happy I felt. Hunter made me forget that my past would come back to haunt me. What would I have done to be with Hunter if I were still with HIM? There was no way possible I would've been able to leave HIM. Not over his dead body. Hunter worked on his laptop reading emails from Asher. He worked for a while before shutting down his laptop. He wrapped his arm around me and squeezed me tight.

I thought he was going to sleep when he asked, "How was your childhood?" he asked. My childhood was something I didn't mind talking about.

"My childhood was amazing. My mother was a nurse, and my father was a music teacher. We lived in a nice house on the beach in Sacramento, California. I had my own room, and everything in it was yellow. It was my favorite color at the time."

"What's your favorite color now?" I thought for a second.

"Black." I paused before continuing. "You know I'm the eldest child. My little sister Brooke and my little brother Ryan looked up to me. I was an honor roll student. I played the piano, and I danced and sang around the house." Looking back at that time of my life made me feel good. It was the time in my life when I was the happiest.

"My life changed the day my siblings and I rode to that foster home. I cried myself to sleep every night, thinking about my parents. I woke up every morning thinking it was just a nightmare, but I was living the nightmare. Foster care is where I met Sasha and Sophia, but you know that." I was quiet for a moment as I thought about that time. He knew this, we'd had this conversation before. It was long ago.

"Ms. Langley waited for my grandparents or an aunt or uncle to come for us. I told her that no one would come for us. My parents were all we had. After a couple of months, Ms. Langley enrolled us in school. My life was turning semi back to normal. Just when I thought things was getting better, that's when I took another shot to the chest." I paused for a moment, thinking about that time, holding back the tears. I was too emotional right now. "That day when that family came for Brooke and Ryan, I'd never seen them react the way they did. Ms. Langley had told them that they were going to leave with this nice family. They ran to me and held on tight. I didn't know what was going on. They kept saying, 'Don't take us away. Don't take us away.' I begged them to let me go too. But the family said that I was too old. They didn't want me." I felt Hunter hold on to me tight as he could.

# THE LOVE I CRAVE

"I begged and asked if I could keep in touch with them. I explained to the family that they were the only family I had left. If I couldn't go, at least I could talk to them on the phone and write. They agreed, and I did keep in touch for the first few years. After that, I never saw or heard from them again. That night they left, Sasha found me on the floor of my room crying. I stayed there for two days with no shower or anything to eat. After a few days, I was finally up and myself again."

"At lunch one day, Sophia and Sasha found a flyer for modeling camp. You needed to be fourteen years old with a 3.0 GPA to get accepted. I didn't want to do it, but I didn't want to be in foster care all my life. So, I did, and right after that, I met HIM, and my life changed forever." I put my head down.

"I'm sorry you had to go through so much at such a young age. Losing your parents then your siblings. Then Sophia." SHE, the one I would never talk about ever. "I wish I could have been there for you," he said, lifting my face up to his.

"It's okay. Hopefully, one day, I'll have your family in my life, then maybe I can finally remember what it feels like to have parents or even a family," I said as he kissed me passionately.

"Don't worry, my family will love you. Just as much as I do."

"I hope so." I kissed him back. I loved moments like this when I could lay in his arms and tell him things about me and not be judged or afraid. I could talk to him about anything except HIM.

"What about your grandparents?" he asked.

"Both of my grandparents disowned my parents when they got pregnant with me. They were from Vancouver, I do know that much. They gave my parents some money, and they took off to California. My father told me a little about them. Only that they own a chain of restaurants in Vancouver. I never knew about the money they left us. I thought they spent it all raising us, but apparently they didn't." I squeezed him tighter in my arms. "Thank you, for that." We just held each other in our arms. Apparently, my parents had left money for Brooke, Ryan and me. That was part of the money he gave me. We were quiet for a moment, until another question came.

"So, Sophia? I haven't seen her since New York. What happened to her?" he said, and I could feel my chest tighten. It was painful to think of her, but I could. I missed her so much. She was my best friend. The images of her beautiful face came to mind.

"She died."

"How?" he asked because he cared. He knew Sophia and knew she was my friend and that summer, she became his.

"Alcohol, sex, drugs, life." A tear rolled down, and Hunter took his thumb and wiped it away.

# THE LOVE I CRAVE

"All of that took her away from me, Hunter. It was her birthday; she died the morning of her birthday. We had a big party the night before. She died in her sleep. I guess that was a good thing, but I miss her so much. I lost so much in my life, which is why I keep a distance. I run, thinking I should leave first before they leave me. That's why I'm scared of you, Hunter. It's been five days, and I can't live another day without you. You've held a place in my heart since the first day we met. And you've held that place even after my heart has been played, cheated, abused, broken, and shattered. You're slowly putting the pieces back together." I gazed into his eyes. "Please don't stop healing me," I begged him.

"I'll never stop healing you, loving you, protecting you, or fucking the shit out of you," he added, and it made me laugh.

"Sounds like you're making a vow," I said.

"Call it what you want, but I'll never stop loving you. You never have to worry about anything again. Nothing and no one can keep you from me, never again."

"Stop licking your lips. It's making me weak in the knees." He licked his lips again, slowly this time.

"Naughty, naughty boy."

I climbed out of my seat and got down on my knees in front of him. I snapped his seatbelt off in one motion and pulled down his pants to his ankles. I slid his manhood between his boxers. He was nice and hard. I looked up at him as I slid my mouth over him. My mouth watered instantly. I wanted to let him know that he wasn't the only one good with his tongue. I licked my tongue around the tip of his head. Then Marcus came over the speakers to tell us to buckle our seatbelts; we'd be landing in twenty minutes.

"Okay, stop it and get in your seat. Put on your seatbelt," he ordered, but I didn't listen. I picked up the pace and added one hand to the motion. "Stop, Zollah," he yelled out, then moaned. I used my other hand to play with his two friends underneath his manhood. "Oh shit, stop."

"Not until you cum," I said between licks.

"Oh, you're going to get it," he said as the plane began to lose altitude.

"You first."

"Shit." He couldn't help himself but release himself inside my mouth. I didn't want to leave any evidence, so I swallowed all of him. Once I was done, I sat back down in my seat. I wiped my mouth with the back of my arm. Nothing like a nutritional shake. Hunter just stared at me after he fixed himself.

"You still don't listen," he said, putting on his seatbelt.

"I should tell you now that I'm not a good listener. On the other hand, you taste delightful. Sweet and salty." Not long after that, the plane landed at JFK. We grabbed our things and walked through the terminal. Terminal P was for private jets and planes only. We walked out hand in hand, smiling from ear to ear. There weren't that many people around, but they all were staring. He held onto me tighter as we exited the glass doors of the airport.

As we came out, there was a black Suburban parked in front with a tall, chocolate man standing next to it. I was checking out my surroundings when I noticed a girl. She was next to us in a heartbeat. She held a microphone in her hand. I gasped.

"Hunter Grayson," the girl yelled his name. "I'm Lisa from TMZ," she said as he turned toward her. He placed his arm around my waist, pulling me closer.

"Evening, Lisa," he said, looking directly into her eyes. Lisa's words got caught as she melted before him.

"He has that effect on me too, Lisa. Don't feel bad," I said as she snapped out of it. Hunter smiled.

"We haven't seen you in New York in a while. What brings you back home since you've returned from out of the country?" she asked. She knew a lot about him.

"Well, Lisa, I'm here for business." He turned to me. "And pleasure. I'm here to show my lovely lady a good time in the city that never sleeps," he said. He walked toward the truck, and Lisa followed.

"She must be a special lady," Lisa said.

"Yes, she's the love of my life, and you'll never see another on my arm," he said as we reached the truck. The driver opened the door for us.

"Well, where is one of the places you'll be taking her this weekend?" Lisa asked.

"Martin's tomorrow night," he said before closing the car door. We pulled out of the airport and headed over a bridge.

"That was exciting. Do you always have that effect on women?"

"Yes, but only one matters." I laid my head on his shoulder. We drove until we stopped in front of this building that looked like a hotel.

"Where are we?" I asked, looking out the window.

"At my penthouse, I own the building."

"Of course you do." The driver got out to open the door for us. Hunter placed me on the curb then went to speak to the driver, and then he was back in my arms.

"You have two places?"

"Yes, I'm from New York, but when I found you in California, I bought that beach house knowing that one day you wished to have one," he said, holding the lobby door open for me.

The lobby of his penthouse reminded me of a lobby to a hotel. Spacious and marvelous, it had a big chandelier on the ceiling. There was a couple of people sitting in the lobby just relaxing and talking.

"Hey, Mr. Grayson. Welcome back, may I take your things?" the guy behind the front desk asked.

"Thank you, Chris, but I have…" He looked at me. "Everything I'll need."

"Well, if you need anything, let me know. Oh, and your private elevator has finally been fixed."

"Great news, Chris." Hunter pulled me along to the back side of the lobby. We passed four elevators before we stopped at one that read PH.

He pushed the button for the elevator, and the doors opened instantly. We entered, and there were only three buttons. L for lobby, P for penthouse, and the red one for emergencies. Soft music played as he pushed the button P, and the doors closed. We couldn't keep our eyes off each other. He was my man, and I admired every inch of him. His lustful eyes. His soft, sweet lips. His long tongue, his strong hands. His broad shoulders. Damn, I was so turned on, and I licked my lips. That delicious chocolate bar between his legs. His abs of steel.

Ding! Damn, saved by the bell. We stepped out into the foyer. The foyer cream-colored walls were covered with beautiful, recognizable paintings. A huge fish tank and the table that had a vase with flowers on it covered the floorspace. We walked up to the door, and I noticed that the door didn't have a knob. Instead, there was a black, flat keypad. It was like an iPad attached to the wall. Hunter leaned in and pushed a few buttons before he turned to me and said, "Put your right hand up there please." He pointed to the box.

"For what?" I gave him a suspicious look.

"For the key to my place."

"I have to give you my fingerprints for a key to your place? No, thank you. You can keep your key. I don't want it," I said, folding my arms over my chest. He laughed at me, which I noticed he did a lot. Was I a comedian or something?

"I told you that you can trust me."

"Yeah, yeah, yeah." I was skeptical. I stood there looking at him, trying to figure out what to do. Fingerprints were a different story.

"Please, pretty, pretty please." He had made this sad face. Oh my God, he looked like a wounded puppy. I hoped he didn't make that face every time he didn't get his way. Let me say, he looked damn good.

"Okay, anything for you," I said, putting my right hand up to the box. It made a noise, then it said, 'Remove hand please.' I did what it said. The box made more noise before it said, 'Raise hand again.' I did, and after a few moments, the box said, 'Thank you, Zollah. Doors open.' The door popped open, letting us in.

# THE LOVE I CRAVE

"All the money in the world, and you couldn't get a lock with a key," I said as I entered his apartment.

"Only three people have keys. You, me, and my mother." He closed the door behind us. The air was on, and it smelled of strawberries and cream. The wall on the far side of the living room was all glass from floor to ceiling. I could look out to the whole city of Manhattan. Every piece of furnishing in here was black, but all the walls were white.

"This is a nice place you have here." I walked over to the windows that looked out to the city.

"Thanks, you're always welcome here." He came up behind me and kissed my neck. "What do you want to do now that the sun has gone down." I looked at my watch, and it was six o'clock.

"I don't know; this is your town. Take me somewhere. I want to dance and get something to eat. Then come back here and make love to you," I said.

"Sounds good to me, but I have to go inside my office to make a couple of calls. Make yourself at home. I had ordered you some things. You can find them through the second door on the left," he said as he disappeared into his office.

I smiled as I walked down the hall. There were pictures of his family on the wall. I passed a bathroom on my right. Then I passed a linen closet. I finally made it to the second door on the left. I felt like Carrie Bradshaw. There were clothes and shoes everywhere. He said he had ordered a few things. This was more than a few things. This was ridiculous. One half of the closet was my things, and the other half was his.

How much did he spend on clothes? I wanted to know but didn't want to ask. Then I thought about it. At the rate he was going with ripping clothes off me. I might need every piece of clothing. I slowly walked through the closet, touching everything. There was satin, cotton, denims, and silk. There were jeans, dresses, skirts, blouses, ballgowns, leggings, and tunics. From Versace, Vera Wang, Liz Claiborne, HLS, Marc Jacob, and anything else you could name. For a moment, I was happy spinning around in the closet. I always fell for men who spoiled me rotten, but also wanted so much control over me. What did that say about me? Was it because I lost my father at such a young age? I closed my eyes, knowing that Hunter was different. I felt some arms wrap around me.

"Jeans and pumps tonight," he whispered in my ear. "We're going to one of my favorite spots," he said. He kissed my neck and rubbed my breasts. One hand squeezed my nipple, and the other hand traveled down my pants.

"If you keep this up, we won't make it out to dinner," I said.

"Sorry. I can't help myself."

"You better at least until I have eaten." I pushed him off me. "I'm going to take a shower."

# THE LOVE I CRAVE

"Not before I give you your punishment for disobeying me on the plane," he said, holding up a bra and thong set.

"Oh, I love this punishment." I snatched them from him.

He grabbed me by the hand and led me to his bedroom which was freaking amazing. I didn't recognize the room at first, but once I looked around, it took me back ten years. In the middle of the room, there was a California king-size bed that I had to step down to get in. The drapes around the bed were black and sheer. He had paintings on the wall, and the mirrors on the ceiling caught her eye. How exotic was that. I gazed around and noticed he had no TV. He led me to his huge bathroom. The shower was separate from the jacuzzi tub. He slid the glass doors to the shower back, turned it on for me, and handed me a towel from the rack. When I started to undress myself, he smacked my hand out of the way.

"I'll do that for you," he said as I watched him slowly undress me, admiring every inch of my body as if he had never seen it before. "You're so beautiful and sexy," he said as his fingers traced the scars on my body. I didn't feel it because those spots were so numb. He leaned in and kissed one of them. "I'll shower after you. Women take the longest to get ready." I turned around to get in the shower as he smacked me on the ass.

"Hunter."

"I'm sorry; it asked for it," he said, leaving and closing the door behind him.

# BUY YOU 4 A NIGHT

I was ready to see Hunter's favorite place to hang out. I was in the living room waiting on Hunter who wasn't ready yet. And he said women took the longest to get ready. I decided to wear blue skintight jeans that look painted on. I wore a red corset that pushed my breasts up, making them look bigger than what they are. Then I put on a black, tight half blazer. With some red pumps. I selected a diamond necklace set with the earrings and bracelet to match.

I blew my hair out, leaving some out in the front as I put the rest in a ponytail. I was drinking a glass of wine when I heard the bedroom door open. I turned around to see Hunter walking in. He had on blue jeans with a black Polo button-up shirt with some black Polo casual shoes. He stopped when he hit the living room. His eyes widened, looking at me up and down.

# THE LOVE I CRAVE

"You look stunning," he said, laughing.

"What's so funny?"

"I think I bought the wrong size jeans. I mean they're really hugging you. I didn't think you would choose to wear the corset as a shirt."

"Is it a problem?"

"No, you're perfect." His eyes ate me up, and the way he looked at me made me weak in the knees. I finished my glass of wine and placed it in the sink. He grabbed my hand, and we made our way out of the apartment to the elevator.

"Do you have on the set I gave you?" I looked over at him. The look he gave told me that he had set me up, but it was just panties and a bra, right?

"Maybe I do, maybe I don't," I said, winking at him. He turned to face me as he pulled something from his pocket. It was small and black; it reminded me of a key fob.

"I can find out," he said, and something made me take a step back. He winked back at me as he pushed the button. All of a sudden, I felt a vibration on my clitoris and my nipples. I gasped, falling back against the wall of the elevator.

"What the hell?" His lips curled into a big smile. Then I realized he was too happy when he passed the set over to me earlier. Why hadn't I realized that it was a set up. He said punishment in the same sentence as he handed it to me. My knees buckled as it sped up.

"Hunter, please I'm going to come," I begged for him to stop. I bent over to try to stop myself from coming. He pushed the button, and the vibration stopped. My attention snapped his way.

"You have it on." He burst into laughter.

He put the remote back in his pocket, and I was speechless. I wanted to smack him across his gorgeous face. Now I knew why he said it was punishment. If I said anything or did anything that he didn't like, I would be punished for it. The doors opened, and I got myself together. Hunter grabbed my hand.

"Are you okay?"

"Now why would you do this to me?"

"I guess you'll be on good behavior tonight." I was mad that he found this amusing. We held hands as we stepped out of the elevator and through the lobby. The night New York breeze felt good, and the city was lit up. We hopped into the truck as we rode through the city. Even the air smelled different from California. In February in New York, it was cooler than home. It was freaking wintertime. Something I wasn't used to.

As we rode through the city, I thought about being on good behavior tonight, or the button would be pushed. I had to come up with a way to get him. Since Monday, he had done things to me that... I would never forget. The man had me open. We pulled up to this place called Dreams. It wasn't what I expected. From the outside, it looked like a simple brick building with windows and a simple sign, which was okay with me. Hunter opened the door, and he helped me out. The night was alive, and people were walking up and down the street. The men and women looked at Hunter as he wrapped his arm around me. Hunter led me to the door, and I stepped into a small area where they were checking IDs.

"Good evening, Mr. Grayson. Long time no see," the man checking IDs said.

"Good evening, Eddie. How are you?" Hunter asked.

"I'm doing great. What are you doing in town?" he asked.

"I'm here with my lady. She has a business meeting tomorrow," he said. Eddie didn't bother to check our IDs. He opened the second door for us, and we walked inside to the hostess stand.

"Your table is ready, Mr. Grayson." the girl behind the hostess stand said. She held a clipboard as she looked from him to me. I could tell she wanted to know who the hell I was. "Follow me." The inside wasn't what I expected either looking from the outside. She led us to a table on the far side, but we were stopped by a man.

"Hunter Grayson, long time no see," the short man said. He was wearing a blue suit with his loosely tied grey tie. He had to be in his thirties with dark eyes.

"Anthony Fisher, it has been a long time. How's the family?" Hunter asked, holding his hand for a handshake.

"Great, Melanie is doing lovely. We're expecting our fourth child. Other than that, life is good, and you?" he asked as he looked at me. The way he stared at me stirred me the wrong way. It made me uncomfortable, and Hunter felt it. He squeezed my hand in his as he moved me from one side to another to see if his eyes would follow, and they did.

"Well, you know, I'm still a workaholic." Hunter turned to me. "Hope, this is Anthony. Anthony, this is Hope." Again, he used the name I go by at work, not my real name.

"Nice to meet you," I lied. We shook hands. I didn't want to, but I didn't want to be rude. His hands were rough.

"It's a pleasure to meet you." He stared at me so long, it was uncomfortable.

"Enjoy your night." Hunter pulled me with him.

We made it to the table, and he pulled out the chair for me. The waitress didn't take long to come over and take our orders. I ordered a glass of wine and a glass of water, as Hunter ordered water and a glass of ginger ale. I didn't want to think about why Hunter didn't drink. I wanted to know who in the hell did it. Was it a jealous girl or a jealous boy? Who would do something like that? While we waited for our dinner, we listened to a lady play the piano, and it took me back to wonderful and dreadful times in my life. Playing the piano had always been a passion for me. My parents signed me up for lessons when I was five years old. I'd played ever since. It'd been years though since my fingers caressed the keys. I missed that as well.

"So, what is your meeting about tomorrow at Martin's?"

"I'm trying to get Martin's into Javier magazine," I said as he smiled at the name. "We have special features inside the magazine about nice, elegant, and fancy restaurants and jazz clubs, and the amazing stories behind them. Melvin suggested that I visit first before deciding to put Martin's in the magazine," I said, taking a sip of my wine.

"Martin's is a wonderful place. I'm sure you'll love it." He took a sip of his water. "If you land the job, will you have to return for the interview and the photoshoot?" he asked.

"Yes. Abby will be there, she's my manager. Lucy will do the interview, and Bobby will do the photoshoots. They both are great. I'll just be there to oversee everything, just to make sure everything goes the way I want it." I said happy to talk to him about my job.

"It sounds fun and interesting. So, how many celebrities have you interviewed?"

"Not many, only a handful of them. Right now, all I do is major businesses and a celebrity here and there. Landing one of the richest celebrities would be wonderful for Javier. We're doing great, but we could do better." We talked a little more before our food arrived. It wasn't bad at all. I ordered chicken, while Hunter ordered fish. The band was finished playing, and a DJ was now setting up. I had finished my food and wanted to freshen up.

"I'm going to the restroom. I'll be right back."

"Hurry back." He kissed me as I got up from my seat, and I followed the sign toward the restrooms. As I walked, all eyes were on me, even those eyes I met earlier. I wondered if Hunter noticed. Of course he did.

I entered the bathroom, and there were a few girls inside. They stopped talking once they saw me. I ignored them and went into the stall to use the bathroom. I heard the girls whispering. Well, they tried to whisper, or they wanted me to hear them.

"Hunter hasn't been here in years and when he comes back, he's with a girl."

"A girl with those scars. I wonder where he found her."

"Probably on somebody's pole." They laughed as they left the bathroom. Now I would have been wrong if I stepped out of the stall and karate chopped them in the throat. I never backed down from a fight, even when I knew I would lose. Things like that never bothered me, and I wouldn't let it start. I just laughed and finished up in the stall. I could have told them bitches that I owned my own company, and that he found me ten years ago, before I started dancing on a pole. I washed my hands and freshened up my lipstick before giving myself one last look in the mirror. I had my head down and wasn't paying attention to where I was going when I bumped into someone.

"Anthony, I'm sorry. I wasn't paying attention," I said.

"It's okay. I wasn't paying attention myself," he said as two other men joined him from the restroom. They all were staring at me. It made me wonder if I had something on my face. Even the other two men stared very uncomfortably.

"Hope, this is Roger." He pointed to the tall guy with the popping blue eyes. "And this is Bruce." He pointed to the other guy in the slacks and the dress shirt.

"Hello, it's a pleasure," I said but didn't shake their hands. I was getting ready to walk past when Anthony grabbed my arm. It wasn't rough, but his touch took me by surprise. I turned around to face him and looked at his hand on me.

"I apologize if I have given any offense. I was wondering how long you've known Hunter?" Anthony asked. *None of your fucking business*. But instead, I said.

"A long time," I said, being short. I wouldn't tell him anything about us. I didn't even know this man from Adam. I wouldn't have him all in our business. Not to mention he gave me the creeps, and I couldn't trust him. I looked at the other guys with him. They looked like creeps.

"I've never seen Mr. Millionaire with anyone, especially anyone as beautiful as you," Anthony said. From the tone of his voice, I could tell he was very jealous of Hunter, especially by the way he called him Mr. Millionaire.

"Sorry for the surprise."

I tried to walk away, but the two gentlemen blocked me. I knew if I didn't make it back to Hunter soon, he would come looking for me, and I didn't think that would be pretty. The bathroom was around the corner from the dining room area. So, he couldn't see the restroom from our table. I had been taking self-defense classes since I moved back, and I was hoping I wouldn't have to use it on any of it on them. It seemed like the right thing to take up after running from HIM.

"Well, I know you aren't Hunter's girlfriend; he never had one of those. So, what are you, a hooker from the escort service? I heard he likes those. What is he using you for?" he asked. I took a step back as my eyes widened, recalling what he just said.

"You have some nerve. Do I really look like a fucking hooker to you?" I moved closer because I was about to knee him in the nuts.

"Don't get offended. If you were a hooker, I would like to buy you for a night," he said. I lifted my hand to smack him across his face, but the vibration took over my body, and I gasped. The vibration went from low speed to high speed. I hunched over, trying to prevent myself from falling over.

# THE LOVE I CRAVE

"Shit," I said as Anthony bent over to help me up. "Don't you touch me with your hard ass hands. You asshole…" I was cut off by a familiar voice.

"Is there a problem here?" I heard Hunter say as the vibrations stopped.

It took me a moment to catch my breath and sit up straight. They all looked toward Hunter and backed up with scared looks on their faces. I turned to look at Hunter, and I saw a look on his face I'd never seen before. Now I could see why they looked scared. It made me wonder how long he was standing there. Did he hear everything Anthony said to me?

"No, there isn't any problem. I was just asking who she was." Anthony said, backing up some more.

"Were you? I think it is none of your business. I thought I heard you say something about me," Hunter said, moving closer to them. His face was red, and his eyes burned with fire. I pulled him back.

"They thought I was a hooker and wanted to buy me for a night," I said. I was mad at the way they were talking to me, but the look on Hunter's face scared me. I also wanted to know what Anthony meant by Hunter liking escorts. I wouldn't dear ask though.

"A hooker?" He raised his voice. "For real, Anthony? I don't think your wife would like the fact that you purchase hookers while she's at home, carrying your child. Is that what you do, keep her knocked up so she wouldn't come out? So, you can hoe your ass around. Anthony, I thought we've come too far for this. I should..." Hunter moved closer to Anthony. I just knew that Hunter was about to knock him on his ass. His hand was balled up into a fist. I pulled Hunter back; I didn't need Anthony to ruin our night.

"Hunter, don't worry about them. They're just three pig-headed men who get off on degrading women." I turned him to face me so I could look into his eyes. He looked at me as if he just realized I was there. I grabbed him by the hand. "Hunter," I called out his name. Nothing. "Stay with me." I used the exact words he used for me. Then I leaned in and kissed him. For a moment, there was nothing, then I felt him kiss me back. I knew this would bring Hunter back to me from whatever dark place he was.

"Come, let's go back to our table," I said as he wrapped his arm around my waist. He turned to those three idiots.

"And no, she isn't a hooker or a girlfriend. She's my wife, and if you're ever in the same place as her, I suggest you turn the other way. She won't be able to stop me from fucking you up the next time," Hunter said as we turned and walked away. When we got back to our table, the first thing I did was find my waitress and ordered a shot of Patron. I turned to look at Hunter to make sure he was okay, but of course he was staring at me.

"Are you okay? Did they touch you?" He was scared to ask.

# THE LOVE I CRAVE

"No, Hunter, I'm fine. I'm stronger than I used to be."

I could see behind his eyes that he was still upset. I kept thinking why Anthony would think I was a hooker. Did Hunter go out with hookers? This wasn't *Pretty Woman*. The waitress came back with my shot. I downed the shot, and Hunter stared at me drink.

"Let's dance."

"Not yet," I said.

"Why? When is a good time when you're drunk?" he asked. I gave him a look. I didn't want to be offended and say something to make us argue.

"No," I said defensively. My attention went back to the people on the dance floor. The word wasn't even all the way out when I knew I shouldn't have said no. Then I felt the vibrations. I jumped up from my seat. He grabbed my hand with a smile.

"Finish your wine," he said.

"But we're coming back," I said, and I saw his face.

"Never leave your drink unattended. Someone might…" He stopped and at that moment, I knew what he was about to say, and I understood why. So, I downed my glass of wine and set the glass back on the table. There was something serious behind him not drinking.

"If you're going to drink, Zollah, you have to be responsible about it." I didn't want to get into it, so I just said okay. He pulled me onto the dance floor. The DJ was playing the Cupid Shuffle. The moves were easy. Then he played the Wobble that made everyone get on the dance floor.

I enjoyed watching Hunter dance. He moved with so much grace and sex appeal, it turned me on. HIM never wanted to dance at all. I had to stop thinking about HIM. Ever since I had been back with Hunter, I couldn't seem to stop thinking of HIM. After we danced through a few more songs, we headed back to our table and grabbed our things.

"Don't forget the check," I said as he smiled at me as if I had said something funny.

"I don't get checks when I go out. They send it to my accountant, and she pays it," he said as we walked out of Dreams. The truck was there waiting for us as we hit the curb.

"What is the driver's name?" I asked.

"Adam," Hunter said as he realized he had never introduced us earlier. "He's my driver when I'm here in New York. So, you can imagine he gets a lot of days off, I pay him nicely."

"How often are you here?" I asked on our way back to his penthouse. Hunter was from here, so I could believe he came back often for business and to visit his family.

"Once or twice every three to six months. It's been a long time since I've been out of the country."

"Your family still live here, right?"

"Yes, my mother is a lawyer. My father has retired from the military. He owns a few properties here and in California."

"What about your brother and sister?"

"My sister Leena is a doctor. My brother Emanuel is a fashionable asshole. He owns a chain of boutiques and clothing stores all over the world." I laid my head down on his shoulder. "I bought my parents a house in California for when they come visit me.

"So, everyone in your family is making money," I said.

"Yes, but I'm the wealthiest one," he said as we walked through the doors of his building.

"Of course, you are."

"I invested a lot of my money growing up. My sister is the oldest and has been volunteering in a hospital since she was ten years old, I think. I was young when my parents got me a lot of stocks and bonds. I did a lot of things such as giving blood and sperm for money. I gave money for charities. I was worth hundreds of thousands of dollars by the time I was eighteen," he said. When he said donating sperm, it took me back to a time in my life that I never wanted to relive again. I remember him telling me this that summer at LABA.

"I knew I wanted to be successful as a child, but when I met you, I knew I needed to be successful because I wanted to take care of you in all ways possible. I was determined to find you, Zollah, and I wouldn't stop until I had you in my arms again," he said, holding me tight. I looked up in his eyes.

"And there's no place I'd rather be," I said.

# WHERE IS SHE?

My eyes opened slowly as the sunlight shine through the window. I tried to move and realized I was in a bear hug. I couldn't sit up, but I could turn around. Hunter looked so beautiful in his sleep. I knew why he was sleeping well. We made love last night. It was all hot and sweaty. It was powerful, sending us crashing. He made love to every part of me. My mind, body, and soul. It was ten o'clock, and I was starving from all that cardio last night. Hunter adjusted himself in his sleep, and I was finally able to squeeze from the bed. I used the restroom first, then I went into the kitchen. There was nothing to eat, so I called Chris. I ordered us breakfast and a few things to go inside the apartment to munch on while we were here.

While Hunter slept, I decided to pull out my laptop and do a little bit of work before Martin's tonight. I called Melissa and talked to her for a quick moment. She told me I had a few emails that I had to answer. She also told me that a lady had come into the office not too long after I had left yesterday. She had written five books and would like to talk to an agent about getting them published. Then she said that a man came in today looking for a job for the newsletter. She had sent me an email of his resume. Once I finished talking to her, I went through my emails. I answered and replied to some. Then I decided to call Sasha to check up on her.

"Hey, what are you doing?" I asked when Sasha answered the phone.

"Nothing. Just hacked into your company computer to see your schedule for the next week. So, you'll be on time. What's good with you?" she said. It was seven o'clock in the morning in California. Why in the hell was she up early on a Saturday? I had told her about everything from the plane ride to last night at Dreams, and how Anthony thought I was a hooker. She burst out laughing.

"I would have read him good. Hooker… What did Hunter say?" she asked.

"I have no idea what he would have done if I weren't there. I'd never seen him look so evil. He was going to kill that dude. I saw it in his eyes. He was trying to find a way to kill him without getting caught," I said.

"What is this asshole's last name?"

"Anthony Fisher. His wife's name is Melanie. They're on baby number four."

"Ummm," she said as we skipped the subject. I was done sending and responding to my emails.

"So maybe we should go to a doctor to see why you keep blacking out. I know it's been some years, but you seem like an amateur," she said.

"I wouldn't say blacked out. I'd say I had an orgasm that made me fall asleep on impact," I said, which she found funny. I was naked lying on Hunter's couch, waiting for Chris to deliver the food. Maybe I should put some clothes on.

"I don't care what you call it. I want one or some or whatever. And you were out for what, ten minutes? Bitch, that's a nap," she said as we both burst into laughter. "I'm so happy for you especially after what you've been through. Have fun now. I got to go. Damon is dragging me out jogging," she said.

"Jogging," I said, shocked Sasha hadn't worked out in a while. Then to think of it, me either.

"Yes, he hasn't been here forty-eight hours, and he has me working out. I need a new friend," she said.

"Okay, well, you two have fun. I'll call when I'm on my way home," I said as we hung up the phone.

I lay back on the couch and closed my eyes, waiting for Chris. I wanted to close my eyes for just a little while. I was still exhausted from last night. I felt myself drifting away into a deep sleep. Then I opened my eyes, and I wasn't in Hunter's living room. I blinked my eyes again, and nothing changed. I sat up and took a good look around. Noooo, I said to myself when I realized where I was.

I noticed I didn't sit up from a couch. I sat up from a bed. Then I turned to notice that I was wearing a night gown. I shot another look around the room and noticed I was in HIS bedroom at HIS family estate. The one HE and I shared together. The fireplace was burning, and the TV was on. I tried to figure out what night it was. I'd had plenty of nights alone. HE was out with God knew who doing God knew what.

I looked at myself in the mirror. I'd seen the scars that Hunter once asked about that I couldn't talk about. I had to be twenty-two and on the verge of killing myself to get rid of the pain in my heart. I gazed toward the TV again and noticed that Love and Basketball was on. Then it came to me what night it was, and I knew immediately I didn't want to be here. I couldn't relive that moment again. I tried to get up from the bed, and my whole body was sore. I was in so much pain physically and emotionally.

I heard the door open and slam shut. I jumped when I saw HIM come through the door. He was standing there looking at me like I disgusted him. I kept saying to myself that I didn't want to be here. It was like I was there watching myself go through it again. As I looked over at HIM, I wondered what I saw in him. He walked over to me like he wanted to hit me, which wasn't surprising. As the moments passed, I realized that tonight was the night I got fed up. I asked the first thing that came to mind.

"Where is she?" I yelled at HIM. I knew I had some drugs in my system, but my mind wasn't playing tricks on me. "Where is she?"

"Don't worry about it. She's in a better place," HE yelled back at me. HE and the doctors told me that she had passed but in my bones, I didn't believe it. I hit his chest repeatedly with my fist.

"Please, I'll be good. Please let me see her," I cried as I pushed HIM back.

"You lied to me. You tried to hide it. Thinking that I wouldn't find out, you sneaky bitch," he said, raising his hand, and smacked me across my face. I fell back on the bed.

"Please," I cried out. The smack didn't hurt as much as they used to. I think my body has gotten used to it. "Please let me see her. I'll do whatever you want," I cried and begged for him to get off me. He stood there undressing himself.

"So, you think you're going to leave me now. After what you've done to me. You can't leave me, and I will never let you go. No one is to have you. I will kill you and whoever is to think you belong to them. I can't live without you. If I can't have you, no one can," HE said as HE climbed on the bed with HIS naked body.

"Please let me see her. I won't leave you," I pleaded.

"You know what I want, MP. I want that sweet pussy," HE said to me, trying to lift my nightgown up.

"No, I'm bleeding. I can't," I cried, pleading with HIM. HE forced my legs apart. I screamed out, but HE put HIS hand over my mouth. My heart ached. How could he do this to me. HE took something away from me when he knew I'd suffered enough? Knowing I'd lost so much in my life. I knew HE couldn't possibly love me. No one had ever hurt me as much as HE had.

I loved HIM, and I didn't know why. HIS hands on me were forceful and aggressive. My body was numb from HIS touch. I wanted HIM off me, far away from me, but all I could do was think about her.

"Please let me go. Let me see her." My heart sank lower and lower in my stomach.

"Shut up, you ungrateful bitch. I gave you the world. You needed and wanted for nothing," HE said as HIS hand found its way across my face again.

HE ripped my nightgown, trying to lift it up. HE wanted to have better access to me. HE held my legs down with his. I felt HIS hands between my legs. I tried to close them, but I couldn't. HE was stronger than I. I was weak. I closed my eyes tight. I couldn't look at HIM anymore when HE was about to rape me. I couldn't fight him anymore. I had lost her, and I refused to lose anything else. All I wanted to do was die

# THE LOVE I CRAVE

If I did die, I could see my parents again. I wanted to see my mother. I wanted her to hold me and tell me that I deserved better than HIM. I wanted to see my father. I wanted him to hold me and tell me I was his little girl, and I deserved better. I knew dying was my only way out. My only way away from HIM. If I died, I'd never see HIM again. It'd been a day since HE had taken her away from me. And all HE could think about was sex. How could HE be so freaking selfish? I felt HIS hands on me again.

"No, please," I cried.

I felt HIS manhood between my legs. Just when I thought HE was going to put it in my kitty, HE slipped it in the back door. No oil, no creams, no ointment, no nothing. I felt my insides rip open as I screamed at the top of my lungs. I screamed for hours, and no one came to save me. I was crying so much, I was drowning in my own tears. All I kept asking was, "Where is she? I want to see her. Where is she?"

Then I felt myself being shaken uncontrollably, and my name being called. I wasn't sure if it was from the nightmare or what. I paid attention to the name. HIM never called me Zollah. HE stopped after we had sex the first time.

"Zollah, wake up," someone called out my name. I didn't recognize the voice. All I could do was scream.

"Please let me see her. Where is she? Please tell me," I begged for HIM to tell me. I knew she was real. HE couldn't take that away from me. Then I drifted back to someone shaking me and calling out my name.

"Baby girl, wake up." I knew that name. My eyes popped open, and I jumped back. I looked around to see that I was in Hunter's penthouse. Then I turned back to look at the man in front of me. It wasn't HIM; it was Hunter.

"I fell asleep. I'm sorry." Tears filled my eyes. I hadn't had a nightmare this severe in a while. Why now? I put my knees to my chest, holding them with my arms. I inhaled and exhaled repeatedly.

"Are you okay? You were scaring the shit out of me. You were screaming. 'Let me see her. Where is she. Let me see her. Where is she.' See who, who is she?" he asked, and I couldn't speak of it, not ever. Less than a handful of people knew who she was, and they never spoke of it again either. I couldn't tell him who she was not right now. I'd tried hard for the past four years not to think about it because it hurt so much. He saw it in my eyes that I couldn't talk about it.

He sat on the couch next to me. He pulled me into a hug and held me tight. I cried in his arms thinking of her. Was she real or was she just a fragment of my imagination? I knew she was real; I spent months with her. I knew she was real. Hunter's arms felt good around me. He was slowly easing my pain. I was slowly getting HIM and SHE out of my head. I held him tighter.

# THE LOVE I CRAVE

"Hunter, I'm still scared of HIM," I confessed. HE had so much of a hold on me, and it wasn't a good one. "I don't want to be afraid anymore," I said.

"Baby girl, you don't have to be afraid of HIM. I'm so sorry he hurt you and you had to go through that, but I won't let HIM hurt you ever again," he said, and he meant it. He kissed me on the forehead. He looked into my eyes, and he wanted to ask me a question, but the doorbell rang. He turned to face the door. His posture tensed. I felt as if he would go to the door thinking HE was there.

"I ordered breakfast for us, but I'm not hungry anymore," I admitted as I turned away from him.

"That was sweet of you. Let me get the door," he said, but I didn't let him go. I felt as if I did, I would never see him again. "It's okay I got you." He picked me up and carried me into the room. He placed me gently on the bed. "I'll be back," he said, staring me in my eyes. I nodded.

He left as I heard his footsteps walking back into the living room. I heard him talking to Chris, then I heard the door close. Moments later, he entered the room with a tray of food. He set it down on the dresser next to the bed. He climbed in next to me and pulled the covers over us. He wrapped his arms around me. All the hurt and pain seemed to go away for the moment.

"I just want to lie here all day in your arms until it's time for my dinner meeting." I laid my head on his chest.

"I can hold you forever, running my fingers through your hair. Rubbing my fingers up and down your arms and back." He paused for a moment then took a breath. "It kills me to see you crying. I hate it."

"One day, the crying will stop, and it will only be happy tears," I said, listening to his heart beating. We were quiet for a moment. I heard his stomach growling. I lifted my head to look at him. "Go ahead and eat your food before it gets cold."

"Not until I know you're okay," he said.

"Hunter, I'm fine." He gazed at me for a moment before he sat up and decided to eat. He grabbed the tray from the dresser. He peeled the plastic wrap from the plate with his omelet on it. The smell lit up the room. Watching him eat was a sight to see. By the time he finished eating, I was a little hungry. He peeled the plastic from another plate full of fruit. Cantaloupes, pineapples, blue berries, kiwi, oranges and my favorite, strawberries.

"Baby girl, you need to eat something. Let me feed you some fruit."

"All right." I sat up next to him as he fed me fruit. One bite of the fruit, and a burst of flavor hit my mouth. It was delicious and fresh. "That's fresh." I knew fresh fruit when I tasted it. We were quiet for a moment as we enjoyed each other. My eyes traveled around his room, and I noticed something he didn't have in here.

THE LOVE I CRAVE

"Do you have something against TVs in your bedrooms?" I asked.

"I want nothing to distract me in here," he said with a smile, and his eyes burned in mine. I swallowed the fruit. I knew exactly what he meant.

"Well, can we at least put one in my room in LA? I love lying in bed watching porn," I said, giving him a wink, and he began to choke.

"Porn, you're such a nasty girl. We can make our own videos," he said, placing the tray back on the dresser as he turned to face me.

He pulled the covers over us as we lay in the bed as I just stared at him. I noticed that his mind was traveling to another place and time. I wondered what he was thinking. Was it that he wanted to leave me because of my crazy past and my crazy nightmares? My mind was on the verge of going into a deep place when he called my name.

"Zollah." His voice was low and full of nerves.

"Yes," I answered. He was quiet for a second. I felt the question he was going to ask me. He was scared to. Not knowing what my answer or reaction might be.

"The—" He stopped. He lifted my face up to his so I could look into his eyes. "The scars are from HIM, right?" he asked. As soon as he said scars, I felt the stab in my heart. I couldn't look him in the eyes. I put my head down, but he lifted it back up.

"Don't worry about it," I said, putting my head down, and he pulled it back up again. "Don't worry about them." I was trying to control myself.

"Look at me and stop saying don't worry about it." He raised his voice at me. "Are those scars from HIM?" he asked again with bass in his voice. How could I look into his eyes and say yes?

"Yes, they are." He closed his eyes, then took a deep breath. His anger was building. He looked at me how he looked at Anthony last night. He tried to calm himself. He was highly pissed off.

"What did he do to you?" he asked, demanding an answer, but I couldn't give him one. If I told him, that meant reliving each scar. The scars were healed, but they still hurt.

"I can't talk about it, not right now," I pleaded. I took a deep breath, waiting for my heartbeat to slow down.

"All right." He was quiet, but I could tell a question still bugged his mind. "Did you run away from… HIM?" His hand stroked my hair from my face.

"Yes, I had to escape." His body tensed up from my response.

"I would have never found you if you would have never run away." He kissed my forehead. "How did you get out?"

# THE LOVE I CRAVE

There was only one word to answer that. It was plain and simple. "Sasha," I said. He held his breath for a moment. My hand laid on his chest.

"So, it's Sasha I owe everything to."

"You owe her the world." We just lay there with no more words.

Sooner or later, I would have to tell him everything. I silently cried myself to sleep thinking I would have to relive it. How would he react? All I wanted to do was enjoy the time I had with Hunter. Tomorrow wasn't guaranteed to anyone. These last six days had been amazing, and I wouldn't change that for anything. That's what I thought about before sleep found me.

"Rise and shine, sleepyhead." I opened my eyes and saw Hunter staring at me. He kissed me softly on the forehead. "You're even more beautiful when you wake up," he said as he played in my hair.

"You're so sweet, making me feel good with stinky breath."

"Well, I have a chocolate peppermint if you want to freshen your breath." He gave me a seductive look. I laughed at the chocolate peppermint.

"You're so nasty, but it sounds good to me," I said, climbing on top of him. I slid down his chest as I opened my mouth wide to please his manhood, licking the tip and using

191

my hand to massage him as I sucked. I worked him nice and slow.

"It didn't take you long to get to the cream feeling," he said when I was done.

# MARTIN'S

Hunter and I showered together with no frisky business. I followed Hunter from the bathroom to the closet. I couldn't keep my eyes off him. His chocolate skin still had water glistening down his back and arms. I wanted to be the white towel wrapped around his waist. He was finger-licking good and should be on the cover of a magazine. Something like GQ or Bachelor. Maybe Javier... a lightbulb went off. I was to discuss that on further notice.

"What's the dress code for Martin's?" I asked, finally taking my eyes off him. I looked over my choices.

"Classy and elegant. It's a very upscale place. You'll need a ballgown, and I'll need a tux. You could pick me out something if you want." He looked up at me.

"Really?" I had no idea why that excited me so much. I moved around the closet looking at everything twice.

There was so much to choose from. It took me about twenty minutes to find us something. I chose a beautiful red, long-sleeve gown. It was low cut and fit tight from the breast to the lower waist. Then it flowed the rest of the way. My dress was made by Emanuel G. I'd never heard of him before. Then I chose a black tux for Hunter with a white shirt and a red bowtie. I handed it to him as he left to get dressed. I went into the bathroom and blew my hair out straight. Then I flat ironed it out and curled it. Hunter had all the accessories here for me. I didn't have to worry about if they once belonged to another female. Everything had tags on them, and I hated to look at the prices.

Once I put on my dress, I chose what type of jewelry I would wear. It was from Winston Jewelry. Hunter never saw the dress I picked, and I couldn't wait for him to see it. I put my lipstick on, then applied some light makeup. I hadn't worn a lot of makeup in the last three years. HE made me wear too much makeup that I sometimes looked like a drag queen. As Sophia said, a clown. I also wore a lot when I tried to hide my black eyes. I felt so artificial with HIM. Like nothing about me was real. My personality, my clothes, my hair, my face, my nails, even my life seemed so fake.

I gave myself one last look in the mirror then I headed out of the room. When I entered the living room, Hunter wasn't there. I headed for the kitchen when I heard him speaking on the phone. He must be in his office. So, I crept down the hall. Luckily, he had carpet, so he didn't hear me coming. As I got closer, I heard him say, "No, it's a surprise." I heard him put the phone back on the receiver. I turned to enter his office. He was getting up from the chair behind a desk. When he looked up and saw me standing there, he stumbled. We both stared at each other as we admired one another. I had amazing taste. He looked like a shiny new penny. I walked in to get closer to him.

"I've never been rendered speechless before. You look breathtaking," he said, lifting his hand to touch me but quickly put them behind his back.

"What's wrong?" I asked.

"If I touch you, that beautiful gown will be torn to pieces. We wouldn't make it to Martin's on time." He kissed me with his hands behind his back. "Let's go, baby girl," he said as he pulled me by the hand. He had given me that name when we met at LABA years ago, and he still called me that.

When he closed the door to his place, I noticed the foyer had new roses and a new vase on the table. The vase was shaped like a person. I got closer for a better look at it. It was a… a glass naked lady, but it didn't look raunchy. It looked elegant with the white roses extending from it. Hunter pushed the button to retrieve the elevator. A couple of seconds later, the doors opened, and we stepped inside. I couldn't keep my eyes off him.

"Can I take a picture of you?" I asked to be polite. I never took pictures of HIM. We had taken many together when we first got together.

"Zollah, don't be ridiculous. Of course you can." He leaned up against the wall of the elevator and posed for the picture. Oh my God, it looked like the cover of GQ magazine. I looked at the picture and mumbled to myself, "Fine ass."

The elevator doors opened, and we stepped out and walked up the hall toward the lobby.

"Mr. Grayson, your ride is here," Chris said as he turned to face me. "Miss Hope, you look lovely."

"Thank you, Chris."

"Hey, Chris, can you take a picture of us?" Hunter took my phone and passed it to Chris over the desk.

"Of course, sir." Chris came from behind the desk and held up the phone. "Ready?"

Chris snapped a picture, then looked at it. "Lovely." He handed the phone to me. I turned to look at the picture. Chris got the full length of us with me on Hunter's left side.

"Let me see." Hunter leaned in to look at the picture. He smiled, then took the phone from me. He was pressing buttons, and I didn't know what he was doing.

# THE LOVE I CRAVE

"Chris, I just sent you the picture. I would like it blown up and hung up over the fireplace. Please and thank you," he said as he handed my phone back.

"Yes, sir. Immediately. Have a great night," Chris said. Hunter grabbed my hand as we exited the lobby. I was surprised to see a black limo out on the curb waiting for us.

"Hunter, you didn't have to get a limo," I said, but I was still thinking about the blown-up picture of us that would be hanging above the fireplace in the lobby of his building. Now I had to digest that we were taking a limo to Martin's.

"You look too beautiful to show up at Martin's in a truck," he said as the driver opened the door for us.

"Good evening, Mr. Grayson, Miss Hope."

"Good evening, Adam," I said as Hunter and I got inside the limo.

The limo was big and totally different from the last time I rode in one. The seats were black and red with a small flat-screen TV that had a movie playing. In the mini fridge, there was a bottle of Patron Silver waiting for me. Yes, a drink to get the party started. I moved to fix a glass when Hunter said, "Move. I got you." He opened the lid and inhaled the essence of the bottle. "Wow!" I laughed. He grabbed a glass and poured and sat next to me. He handed me the glass, and I took a quick sip. "You look like Cinderella going to the ball with her Prince Charming." He nibbled on my ear.

"Hunter, when are you going to tell me why you don't drink? Who did it?"

"When you tell me who SHE is or even who HIM is," he said.

"That's not fair." *That was totally fair.* "You not drinking couldn't be worse than my story of HIM or even SHE," I said.

"How would you know?"

"I don't know. I will if you tell me."

"Good try." He continued to nibble on my ear. I took that as we both weren't ready to talk about it yet.

"I want you to open up to me, and it's not about the drinking incident. I mean that was…" He was quiet for a moment. "It's about after. What became of me and the things I had done because of it. I've let go of most of my pain, but you're still holding on to yours. I want you to believe me when I say I'm not going anywhere. I'll take you anyway I can have you." He held up my hands in his. He moved in closer to me. "Just you. You can have no fingers." He kissed my fingers. "No arms." He kissed my arm. "No breasts." He leaned in and kissed the top of my breasts. "No legs. All I want is your heart and your soul," he said as I stared into his burning eyes.

"Don't make me cry," I said.

"Only happy tears with me," he said. I finished my glass.

"So, you own EQ Skyscraper, the building here. What else do you own?"

"More than you know," he said as we pulled up in front of Martin's. The outside was lit like a Christmas tree. It was huge on the outside, it reminded me of a place I had once been in Florida. There was a line of limos that trailed the front. They were all waiting for their time. The cameras flashed from every direction. The red carpet was laid out. It was live here in New York.

"Is it always like this at Martin's?" I asked, excited.

"Always. Thursdays thru Sundays are his busiest. It's one of the best places in town," he said as it was our turn on the red carpet. A guy with a red jacket that read Valet opened the door for us.

"Let me out first, so I can help you." I shook my head. Hunter got out, and I prepared myself to do the same. I got a glimpse of reporters, TMZ, paparazzi, and flashing cameras everywhere. This relationship was sure to go public, and I didn't think I was ready for it. I swallowed my nerves because I couldn't afford to freak out.

I accepted Hunter's hand and got out. The yelling women calling out 'Hunter Grayson. That's Hunter Grayson. Who's that? Who's he with?' I was on the curb when the cameras flashed. His arm found its way across my lower back. Hunter took about three steps when he stopped to pose for the camera. I stood up straight, my right arm against my hip with my right leg extended out in front of me, showing the slit of my gown. My modeling days came back to me as if they never left. Hunter pulled me along. We followed the line of people trying to get inside.

We moved swiftly on the red carpet. I saw Lisa standing there from TMZ. She smiled as she had her video recorder on us. I turned to her and smiled. We finally made it inside Martin's. The inside was like a golden palace. As soon as we came through the door, I saw an older guy standing there, greeting his guests. He immediately stopped talking when he saw us walking in.

"Well, if it isn't Hunter Grayson. How long has it been since I saw you?" the man asked.

"Too long, too long," Hunter said as they hugged each other.

The older guy pulled back and looked at me. "And my God, who is this angel that flew in with you?" I smiled at his compliment. He held his hand out for mine. I accepted it as he kissed it.

"Melvin, this is Zollah Hope. Zollah, this is Melvin, the owner of Martin's," Hunter introduced us. I had only spoken to Melvin over the phone. I didn't know this was him, but he sure looked like a man who owned the place. With his salt and pepper hair, Melvin was almost as tall as Hunter, and he wore an all-black tux.

"Miss Hope, I have a dinner meeting with you this evening. How lucky am I."

"Very, it's a pleasure to meet you," I said.

"Follow me inside." Melvin led the way. He turned to Hunter as we walked. "I'm so happy for you, son. I know she's special for you to have brought her here."

Hunter just didn't know of Melvin. He knew him on a personal level. I checked out his place while they talked. We walked further down the hall full of pictures of celebrities who must have been here before. Their autographs were on the pictures. When we stepped inside the ballroom, it was amazing. It was like a golden paradise. The tables were covered with gold tablecloths. Each table had a different centerpiece. Gold chandeliers hung elegantly from the ceiling.

I heard Melvin talking inside his earpiece. Someone must have said something to him. "Yes, in a minute, Karla. Wait until things calm down," he said as he brought his attention back to us.

"I have guest coming to join us," Hunter said. I turned to look at him.

"Guest?" He never said anything about a guest. I hoped it wasn't his parents. God, I wasn't ready to meet them just yet.

"I have a close friend of mine and his fiancée joining us. I haven't seen him since I left for the Dominican Republic. I wanted to check in on him before I head back to Cali."

"Who is he?"

"His name is Michael Long, and his fiancée's name is Phallon Mason. They live here, and I've known Michael for years."

"I can't wait to meet your friends."

Melvin led us next to the stage in a private booth. We were front and center but a little to the side. I checked the time, and it was 7:35. The place was crowded. Everyone was dressed to impress. Melvin spotted a waiter and called him over.

"How can I help, Mr. Melvin?" the waiter asked.

"Eric, how many tables do you have tonight?" Melvin asked.

"Not enough, sir." Eric looked about twenty-one or twenty-two years old.

Melvin smiled and said, "Good answer. Would you like to assist our table? We have two others joining."

"Sure, more tables mean more money for school," Eric said as he looked over at us and smiled and greeted us.

"What are you in school for?" I asked.

"Journalism," he said.

"A wonderful field. I own my own publishing company. When do you finish school?"

"Next year," Eric said.

"Great. Well, look me up when you finish school," I said.

"Cool, thank you," he said, pulling out his writing pad.

"You're not trying to steal one of my best employees, are you?" Melvin said.

"No, sir. I wouldn't do such a thing." I smiled, and so did Eric.

"So, what are we having tonight?" Eric asked just as I saw two people walking toward us. A tall gentleman and a woman wearing a pearl-pink gown. Her hair was in slight curls. Her eyes were all on her man, smiling at something he must have said.

"There they are." Melvin slid out of the booth and stood up from his seat. Hunter did the same.

"Hello, Michael." Melvin gave him a handshake and a hug. Then he turned to the beautiful woman in the pearl-pink gown. She wore long diamond earrings and a necklace to match. He reached out for her. "Phallon, it's a pleasure to see you again."

"How are you, Melvin?" Phallon asked.

"Baby girl." That took my eyes off Phallon and back on Hunter and Michael standing there. Michael wore an all-black tux. The two men standing next to each other looked so damn good. I shook my head and got out to give Michael a handshake. I would drool if I stared too long. "This is my friend Michael, and this is Phallon," Hunter introduced us.

"It's an absolute pleasure to meet you," Phallon said as she pulled me into a hug. I was taken by surprise that she would be so friendly. "I'm sorry, I just had to hug you." By the way she looked at me, I felt as if she had waited a while to see Hunter with someone. I wondered if she had heard about me.

"Let us sit so we can order," Melvin said as we all filled in. Phallon and I sat in the middle of the booths while our men sat next to us.

"I'll have a Jack and Coke," Melvin said as he turned to Michael.

"I'll have a double shot of Remy on the rocks, and Phallon will have some Volet."

"Zollah, what would you like to have?" Melvin asked.

"This is your place. I'm your guest; what do you suggest? This is still an interview. Give me your best champagne," I said.

"This is an interview?" Phallon asked.

"Yes, I want Martin's to be in next month's issue of Javier. So, if I began to ask you all questions, don't mind me. I'm here on business and pleasure," I said. Phallon smiled.

"All right, Eric, give the lady a glass of..." I cut him off.

"A bottle," I corrected him with a smile as Melvin turned to look at me and Hunter.

"Hey, my lady knows what she wants," Hunter said.

"I see. Miss Hope will have a bottle of our famous cherry bloom champagne, and Hunter will have a glass of ginger ale," Melvin told Eric.

"I see you haven't forgot," Hunter said.

"I can never forget a man who doesn't drink," Melvin said as I turned to look at Hunter. I wondered how long it had been since he had a drink.

"Me either." Michael laughed.

Eric left to get the drinks while we looked over the menus. Everything all sounded delicious. I looked over the wine options as well. I let everyone give their order before me to see what they liked. Michael ordered the steak with potatoes and asparagus. Phallon and Hunter ordered the salmon with rice and broccoli. I ordered the chicken breast stuffed with crab and shrimp. It came with potatoes, and I chose asparagus.

"I love Javier magazine. I mean I only just found out about it, but I read them online. When Michael told me, we were going to dinner with Hunter and his girlfriend. I wouldn't miss this for anything," Phallon said.

"I'm happy to meet some of Hunter's friends."

"You look beautiful in red. Just to think I was going to wear red, but Michael bought me this dress. How could I turn down something so stunning?"

"And you do look stunning in that dress. What color is that, pearl pink?" I asked.

"I don't know, but that's exactly what color they call it," Phallon said as we both laughed.

Eric had returned with our drinks. Hunter turned to the rest at the table. "Be back in a moment." He leaned in and kissed me on the cheek. He got up from the table before taking a sip from his ginger ale. I watched as he entered the door that read Employees Only. My attention went back to the bottle that Eric had opened for me. I couldn't wait to taste this cherry bloom champagne. Eric popped the cork and poured me half of a glass.

"Taste," Eric told me. He handed me the glass, and I took a sip. My eyes lit up. I placed the glass back down on the table. I looked between Eric and Melvin.

"That is the best champagne I've ever tasted, and I've had my fair share of champagne." It was like a burst of cherries exploded in my mouth. Eric smiled, filled my glass up, and placed the bottle back in the bucket of ice. He left us just as the band began to play on stage and the lights dimmed.

# THAT VOICE

Miss Hope, I want to ask you so much about you and Hunter, but I know you're here on business," Melvin said.

"Me too, but it's none of my business," Phallon said, taking a sip of her wine. I looked at all of them at the table. They all were filled with excitement and concern. It wasn't that they were being nosy; they all just cared about Hunter. I was curious as to why he didn't tell him about us.

"Well, what is it you would like to know?" I asked.

"Hunter once told me about a girl he fell in love with years ago. That she was the one he couldn't have, the one that got away. That one day he would find her and marry her. Is that you?" Michael asked as he took a sip from his glass.

"That sounds like it could be me." I smiled, taking a big sip from my glass.

"How long has it been?" Melvin asked.

"About ten years. Better late than never, right?" I said.

"I'm happy he found you. I've never saw a glow in him before. There was always this darkness surrounding him," Melvin said and paused for moment. "I don't know how much you know about him or his past, but he's a good man, and I want you to take care of him." Melvin took another sip. He grabbed my hand on the table and squeezed it a little. "He deserves it."

I could tell that Melvin had known Hunter for an awfully long time. He knew more than I knew, but I wouldn't dare ask him. I wanted to hear it from Hunter's mouth. I turned to see that Michael had the same agreement on his face.

"I love Hunter, and I want nothing but the best for him. We take care of each other. I've had a troubled past as well, and we'll get through this together," I said as I ran a nervous hand through my hair.

"Good. Now that that's over with, let's get to the real reason you're here, Miss Hope. What made you go into publishing?" he asked.

"Wow, that goes back to my modeling days when I used to rock the runway. I loved being on stage, but I loved the work behind the stage more. The modeling school I went to published a small newsletter. I used to travel the world and at the end, my best friends and I used to interview the models, producers, and the designers about the shows. Once we finished the interviews, we would edit the notes and send them over to the newsletter. The editor loved me and sooner than later, I was graduating from high school and attending college to follow my dreams. I attended a few colleges but finished at UCLA. Then I hit rock bottom and struggled for a while. Then one day, my knight in shining armor came and saved the day," I said as I finished my glass. The jazz band had finished playing, and now a lady was on stage reciting poetry. The poem was called "The Signs of Life."

"Living in that life and being in that career, I can see you having a rough life," Melvin said.

"Who hasn't?" Phallon said.

"You're right about that. I can see you being a model. Have you ever thought about being a writer? Your life seems so interesting," Melvin said.

"No, I don't have the time," I lied. I had the time but putting my life on paper for the world to see would make everything I'd been through real, and everyone would know.

"Always make time for the good things in life," Melvin said as I poured another glass. "Hope, you only get one chance in life to get it right. Make the best of it," and he was right. At that moment, I thought of my father and what he would think of me. Would he be proud of the woman I had become?

Melvin and I could have talked forever. He was funny and highly intelligent. He kept a smile on my face. Eric returned with another bottle of champagne since I had finished the first one. I gazed at my phone, and it was almost nine o'clock. Hunter had been gone for a while now. That must have been an important call he had to take. There was a lady on stage, different from the poet. This lady was singing and had a beautiful voice. Where the hell was Hunter? I hoped he returned before the food came. I turned to look at Michael and Phallon who were enjoying the singing.

"I guess it's time to tell you a little about myself and how this place came along," Melvin said as he sipped on his second Jack and Coke.

Melvin and his twin brother Martin grew up on the streets of New York. Their parents had divorced when they were ten years old. Martin had taken it harder than Melvin. He said Martin was the life of the party and loved to have fun. He was intelligent, energetic, but he was sneaky. Martin stayed in a lot of trouble once their father moved out. He spent most of his time in the streets, staying out late and hanging with a wrong group of boys. He stopped going with their father on the weekend. When he started doing drugs, Melvin saw a major change in him. He started with weed then by twenty, he was on the hard stuff. By twenty-five, Martin was strung out of his mind, selling his things for money just to buy more drugs. Melvin and Martin's parents loved jazz music; they grew up listening to all kinds of music, but jazz was their favorite. Martin always talked about owning his own jazz club. Martin also loved poetry and the blues.

Martin died at the age of thirty. I could relate so much to this story. I'd heard plenty of troubled stories in my life. For Melvin, what hurt the most was that he felt him die that night. He said he literally felt a sharp pain in his head like a bad migraine. Melvin and his mother bought a life insurance policy on Martin when he was twenty. Their mother paid for the funeral and gave the remaining money to Melvin. From that day, he worked on opening a jazz club in honor of his brother.

"Enjoy your food, and I'll go fetch Hunter," Melvin said as he finished his drink and slid out of the booth. I smiled as he excused himself from the table. He walked through the same door Hunter did almost an hour ago. The lights dimmed more, and there was a single spotlight on the stage where Melvin came out. Melvin stood on stage and grabbed a microphone. I looked around the room, and Phallon was smiling at me as if she was trying not to say something.

"Thank you so much, ladies and gentlemen for coming out tonight. How are you all doing?" he asked as everyone made noise and clapped their hands. "We have a special guest singing tonight. He hasn't sung here since he was about eighteen years old. He has one of the kindest voices I've heard in a long time. He is here dedicating a song to the love of his life. I'm happy to introduce him tonight. I'm so proud of the man he has become. It's a pleasure to have him back for the fifth time, I think. Please welcome Mr. Hunter Grayson," he said as the crowd clapped. My head snapped toward the stage.

"What the hell?" I said as I dropped my fork on my plate. Did he just say Hunter Grayson? My attention went to Phallon and Michael as they clapped with the rest of the crowd. I grabbed my glass and took a few sips. When my eyes met Hunter's, I got chills all over. He looked as if the stage was made for him.

"Hello, everyone. I'm happy to be back here. I was going to sing a song that I've been working on for a long time, but it isn't ready yet. So, I'm just going to sing a song that I love. So, I hope you like it," he said as music started playing.

I noticed the song immediately. How long had he planned for this? I thought performances were booked in advance. I guess not for Hunter Grayson. My heart raced. I got chills, and my stomach filled with butterflies when I heard the voice. Hunter's voice. He wasn't nervous at all. The last time I heard it is when we sang together that day in New York. Words couldn't express how I felt right now. I stared at the audience, and all the women were under his spell. That's what it felt like to hear him sing. Eric came over and poured another glass. Those few words of the song hypnotized me. Every word hit me. Hunter had a beautiful voice, and he almost sounded as good as the person who sang the song.

I felt his words travel through my body. I felt his hands on my skin. His lips on mine. I turned back to look at Hunter. I didn't even notice I was out of my seat, standing next to the stage. The song came to an end, and he hit that high note and the gates of heaven opened up. The crowd went wild. Hunter received a standing ovation.

"Encore, encore," the people screamed. He took a bow on the stage as he thanked everyone. I was in his arms the moment he stepped off the stage. He lifted me up and spun me around.

"I fucking love you," I said, landing a hell of a kiss on him. For a moment, it was just me and him. No one else in the world mattered for that moment. When I pulled back the kiss and opened my eyes, I saw flashes all around me.

"I love you more," he said as he took my hand.

"That was amazing. I haven't heard you sing in a long time. It was very refreshing and sentimental. You're full of surprises, Mr. Grayson." I wasn't hungry anymore for food. I was hungry for him. All I wanted to taste was him. I could put him on a plate and sop him up with a biscuit.

"Let's eat, say goodbye to them, and head home. I want to make love to you as many times as I can before the sun comes up," he said. He didn't have to tell me twice. We held hands as we made our way back to the table.

"Wow, Hunter, you have an amazing voice," Phallon said.

# THE LOVE I CRAVE

"I would trade a few things to have a voice like that. I would love to sing Phallon to sleep at night," Michael said. I smiled at the thought. Hunter could sing me to sleep any night.

Phallon and I talked while we finished our food. She told me she was an accountant. We exchanged numbers and said we would keep in touch. My eyes kept darting over to Hunter. I couldn't keep my eyes off him. Overall, I gave Martin's five stars. The food was good, and the champagne was delicious. I wondered if I could find that champagne in LA. Sasha and Damon would love it. Once we were done, Eric returned to the table to clean up. I knew that being with Hunter meant I didn't have to pay for dinner, but at least I could leave a tip. So, when Eric returned for the rest of the dishes, I gave him a handshake and thanked him for his service. I snuck him a couple hundred dollars in that handshake.

"Thank you so much, Miss Hope. I appreciate it, and I'll be looking you up next year," Eric said.

"I look forward to hearing from you. I know how it is working and putting yourself through school." It was nice to help someone out. We didn't have all this money for nothing.

"Were you being a naughty girl trying to steal Melvin's employee?" Hunter looked down at me as we left the dining room.

"Hunter, I wouldn't do anything like that," I said with the big smile on my face. Melvin stood in the lobby talking to a lady. He saw us and excused himself.

"So, Hope, did you have a wonderful time here at Martin's?" Melvin asked.

"Yes, I did. The food was excellent, and the champagne was outstanding. Where can I find that cherry bloom champagne back home? My best friends would love it," I said.

"That is my specialty champagne. It took me five years to create it. I'll see what I can do for you. I'll call you on Monday morning," he said.

"I'll be expecting your call, Mr. Melvin. Thank you for everything," I said as Hunter and I couldn't get out of there fast enough. Hunter and I said goodbye to Phallon and Michael as our limo was there waiting for us.

We made out in the back of the limo like it was prom night. Adam had to let us know when we arrived back to Hunter's place. When we got inside the elevator, I just stared at him holding his tux jacket over his shoulder. His tie was loose, and the two top buttons of his shirt were undone. I turned to get in front of him.

"I want you." I gripped his shirt with both hands hard and tight where the two buttons were undone. I yanked it open, and buttons flew all over the elevator. He had a shocked expression on his face.

# THE LOVE I CRAVE

"Look at you, baby girl," he said as our lips met. We kissed aggressively, wanting each other. Our hands were all over one another. The damn elevator took forever. Our bodies were pressed tight together, and I couldn't breathe. The doors opened, and we never took our bodies apart. Somehow, we made it out of the elevator, almost tripping over the table and the vase. Then my eyes widened at the vase. I couldn't break such a beautiful piece. We finally made it to the door. His back was against the door, and I put my right hand up against the keypad.

"Door unlock," the keypad said. Oh God, I was happy that I didn't have to stop kissing him to find a key. That would have killed me. The door popped open, and we fell inside to the floor, laughing. Hunter kicked the door shut with his foot. Then he turned over so he could get to his feet.

"Come on, let's go to bed so I can get you out of this dress." He picked me up and carried me to the bedroom, never braking eye contact. I'd never looked at a man the way I looked at Hunter. Something surrounded him that made my eyes twinkle with desire and admiration. Once we entered the bedroom, he threw me down on the bed. I giggled like a little child as he came over and tickled me. It had been awhile since someone had done that to me. I laughed hysterically.

"Someone's still ticklish."

"Stop," I said, laughing. He stopped after a few seconds. He went over to the nightstand and pulled out a remote. He pushed the button and turned on some music. Silk came through the speakers. I could swear I heard it playing all over the entire place. He stood at the hood of the bed, undressing himself as I watched.

"Come here," he said, looking amazingly sexy with his manhood at attention. I got up from the bed and walked over to him. He slowly walked around me, admiring all of me. I felt his hands on my back. I heard the zipper of my dress being released. The zipper stopped right above my ass. He peeled it off me like a banana peel. Thank God he didn't rip it.

Hunter took off each piece of jewelry. He leaned into me, pushing me back onto the bed. Obviously, he wanted me to leave my shoes on. His lips met mine, and his sweet tongue devoured me. His lips traveled my body from head to toe, making me squirm underneath his touch. His hands were big, long, and strong. When they touched me, they were soft and sensual. We made love all night long. He had me screaming his name until the fat lady sang. We passed out a little after three in the morning. By that time, I swear the neighbors knew his name. We slept like babies in each other's arms. I had an amazing weekend in New York City, and I would be back sooner than later. New York would eventually be a second home to me as well. I closed my eyes a happy camper. This was the life I had been craving.

# MOMMA MIA

My head was ringing. I couldn't have drunk that much last night. I turned in the bed when the ringing stopped. It wasn't long before the ringing started again. I crept my eyes open and knew it wasn't my head ringing. It was a cell phone on the bedside table. The ringing stopped, and I relaxed. Not even a minute later, the ringing started again. I turned around to see Hunter's eyes wide open, lying next to me as if he didn't hear the phone ringing.

"Are you watching me sleep?" I asked.

"Yes, I am, and it's a beautiful sight."

"They say people who watch people sleep are crazy."

"I can agree because I'm crazy about you," he said, and I tried not to smile but failed.

"Are you going to answer that?"

"No, it's been ringing all morning."

"It could be important," I said.

"I doubt it. My brother, my sister, my father, then my mother. They probably heard I was in town." I looked at him as if he were crazy.

"You didn't tell your family you were coming home. How rude," I said. I couldn't go home and not see my family. Maybe I felt that way because I didn't have a family. No mother, no father, no sister or brother. I wish I could rush home to see them.

"If I did, then we wouldn't have had enough time alone, and I know meeting my family is too soon for you. My family is a little aggressive," he said. Well, I guess the apple sure didn't fall far from the tree.

"Aggressive is the new in." I smiled as I pulled the covers back and climbed on top of him. "I feel special that you wanted me all to yourself." I leaned in and kissed him. I turned and noticed the time. It was going on one o'clock in the afternoon.

"How long were you watching me sleep?" I asked.

"Not long, about an hour."

# THE LOVE I CRAVE

"You really are crazy?" I said as I slid down on him. I greeted my morning breakfast sausage. My chocolate peppermint, he called it. CP was at attention, waiting for me to come and swoop him up.

"I love wake and bake," he said as I took him in my mouth. My lips, mouth, and tongue made love to his manhood. "Damn, baby girl," he moaned. I took my tongue and played with his tip. Then I slid my mouth down on him again. I repeated that process until he lost control, and I swallowed all of him.

I knew he'd be hungry when he got up, and I wanted to feed my man. I headed down the hall toward the kitchen. I had asked Chris for a few things yesterday when I had ordered breakfast. He brought some ground turkey, spinach, and peppers. I looked in the cabinets and found some lasagna noodles and some tomato sauce. Then I found all types of cheese in the refrigerator. So, from what I had, I decided to make some lasagna rolls. I had made them years ago in college.

I found three pots. One I used to boil the noodles. I used the other two for the spinach and the ground turkey. In about a half hour, it was finished. I also threw some garlic bread in the oven and chilled some wine on ice. I must have my wine.

I looked at the time, and it was going on three o'clock in the evening. I couldn't believe Hunter was still asleep. I decided to freshen up for dinner and then decided to wake Hunter. As I was heading out of the kitchen, I heard the door say, 'Door unlock.' My entire body shut down. My feet were like boulders on the floor. My mind caught a blank spot. Then I remembered Hunter saying that only I and his mother had keys. So, I knew it was his mother. I slowly turned around when I heard the door close. The clinking of heels sounded, and there she was. Hunter's mother was beautiful. She was tall, dark, slim with a long, flowing, teal dress on. Her hair was short cut like Toni Braxton. Her eyes connected with mine. We both stood there with shock on our faces. When I pictured meeting his mom for the first time, this wasn't how I imagined it. I was naked with nothing but Hunter's t-shirt on. And I was standing in front of her with bed hair.

"Mrs. Grayson," I timidly said, trying to cover myself up. "I apologize for my appearance. We weren't expecting you. At least I wasn't. I should go and put some clothes on," I said as we both just looked at each other. She stared at me as if she were staring at a ghost. Could she see right through me? She came closer inside the living room and set her purse down on the couch. She looked around the kitchen.

"So, it's true. Now I see why my son has been ducking my calls," she said, standing there as if she wanted to tell me off.

"I'm sorry. What is true?" I asked.

"That my son had travelled home and didn't think to call his mother. And for you to be here in this place I know you're not just any girl, and he hasn't involved me with that little detail either." I didn't know what she wanted me to say to that.

"I guess he thought I wasn't ready for such an introduction." I smiled. "Things are moving quite fast with us, but he did it for me. Don't be mad with him." Mrs. Grayson said nothing as she looked around his house. I guess she was looking for a sign that I lived here.

"What is that smell?" she asked.

"I made Hunter dinner before we leave for California—" She had cut me off.

"You cook?" she asked, surprised. She moved closer.

"Yes, dinner is ready if you would like to stay. I will wake your son." I was going to kill her son. If he would have just answered the phone, I could have avoided this awkward first impression. I took a couple of steps backward toward the hall. It was polite to ask her to stay, right? I was new at impressing the in-laws. HIS father always traveled, and his mother was never around. Her mind checked out a long time ago. I had become HIS mother.

"That will be great, Zollah. I'll make the table." I turned back and gave her a caring smile, then continued down the hall. Then I stopped when I realized she called me by my name. I turned back to face her in shock.

"You know who I am?" I asked.

"When you date someone as wealthy and important as my son, your life is front page news. Everyone would know your name," she said. For a moment, I wondered what that meant. How did she find out? Then I thought about all the cameras and people inside and outside of Martin's last night. My heart sank.

"Thank you." I had no idea why I said it.

"No, Zollah, thank you," I heard her say as I continued down the hall. Why would she thank me? I chose something from the closet to slip on. When I entered the room, he was still asleep, so I decided to take a quick shower before waking him up. I tossed the clothes on the end of the bed. Once I was done, I put on a comfortable dress with some cute sandals. I sat on the bed, leaned in, and kissed Hunter on the lips.

"Ummm," he said, smiling. "You sucked and rode me to sleep, Mrs. Grayson. You get big brownie points for that." He turned to face me in the bed. His hands found their way around my waist.

"I have a bone to pick with you, Mr. Grayson."

"I got a bone for you." He tried to pull me on the bed.

"Oh no, you don't. We have company."

"What?"

"Come, dinner is ready."

# THE LOVE I CRAVE

"Dinner is right here," he said, pulling me on top of him. I couldn't have sex with him with his mother in the next room.

"Your mother is in the kitchen setting the table for dinner," I said as I pulled away from him.

"Is she really?" He stopped and sat up from the bed, then he looked sad. "So, this means I won't be getting any of your dinner. I'll have to wait."

"Yes, your mother is waiting. Get dressed." I got up off the bed. It took him no time to wash his face and brush his teeth and toss on some clothes. I sucked back all my nerves as he held me, and we walked out.

We walked into the kitchen, and his mother was putting the final touches on the table. She had taken out the fine china from the china cabinet. She lit candles around the table. When she turned to see us standing there, Hunter placed his arm around my waist.

"Hunter, son," she said, walking toward us. She held her arms out for him.

"Mother, what a surprise," he said, pulling her into a hug.

"Is it really a surprise? You left me no choice when you wouldn't return my calls." She pulled back and turned to look at me. "Now I know why. I had to see for myself."

"Had to see what?" I asked as we moved toward the beautifully set table. She went inside her purse and pulled out a paper.

"This." She placed a newspaper in my hand. I opened the newspaper, and my stomach hit the floor. My knees almost followed. There we were on the front cover of the Style and Entertainment section, sharing a passionate kiss. There was another one of us as we stepped out of the limo. Hunter was over my shoulder, looking at my reaction to the newspaper with a smile, and I wanted to scream.

"I can't believe it." Well, yes, I could. Dr. Stevens wasn't the only one who had told me this relationship would go public. I couldn't show how scared I was right now. I would keep my composure. I knew messing with Hunter would get out there, but front page? I was about to open it up to the page to see what they said about me, but his mother took the paper from me. Was it something she didn't want me to see?

"Enough of that, let's eat. I want to try whatever it is that smells so divine," she said, putting the paper on the breakfast bar. We all sat at the table and said grace. We all passed around the casserole dish, putting a roll or two on our plates.

"This smells good," Hunter said as he inhaled the aroma. "What is it?"

"Lasagna rolls. I learned how to make it in college," I said.

Things were quiet for a moment while we ate. I was totally losing my mind at this table, but I wouldn't let them see it. I was sure Sasha was reading the paper by now and freaking out for me. Sasha read different papers from Florida,

Washington D.C., Atlanta, and New York City. I had no idea what state of mind HE was in, and I knew that sooner or later, He would have a way of finding me, and this just gave Him a clue.

HE had some family here in New York, but they were distant and probably wouldn't call him to let him know I was here. HE had burned a lot of bridges over the years. HE may or may not be on his way here. It had been three years and the words he said to me kept repeating in my head.

'I will never let you go. If I can't have you, no one can. I will kill anyone who has been with you or thinks you belong to them.' If anything ever happened to Hunter because of me, I would die. My thoughts were brought to a halt when Mrs. Grayson said something.

"This lasagna is really good. I've never had rolls before, and I've had my fair share of pasta," she said.

"Wow! Thank you," I said. That was a good thing coming from her. I hoped that made up for finding me naked in her son's kitchen.

"She's right, baby girl. You did an amazing job," he said, devouring the food as if he hadn't eaten in days. Mrs. Grayson saw the way he looked at me and decided to break the contact.

"So, Zollah, what a unique name you have," she said.

# Henson Dreamier

"Thank you. My mother named me after her best friend she left behind in Vancouver," I said. I had asked my mom once about my name, and that was the story she told me.

"What do you do? Where do you work? I would have looked it up myself, but I rushed over here so fast after my husband had gotten the paper. My son wouldn't answer the phone," she said. Now I knew where Hunter got his tendency to invade on people's privacy from. She smiled at her honesty.

"I own a publishing company in LA." I poured myself another glass of wine. His mother held up her glass, telling me she wanted a refill as well. "Hope's Publishing Company. I also have a magazine called Javier and a newsletter called LA News," I said, sipping my wine.

"Wonderful! You have a career and not just a job," she said, sipping her wine. "How long have you two known each other?" she asked, looking me straight in the eyes. I turned to look at Hunter, and all he was concerned about was his food.

"It's a long story, but we met ten years ago at summer camp."

"LABA?" she said. The shock and concern on her face told me she knew something or was concerned about something. She stopped chewing her food. She looked at her son. There was something there in that look, but I had no idea what.

# THE LOVE I CRAVE

"We fell in love all those years ago and promised each other after we had lived life, we would find each other. Your son has helped me in more ways than possible. And I will always be grateful to him for that. And you can be sure I never gave a rat's ass about his money, not ever," I said as Hunter finally looked up at me. It was the gospel truth; I knew what having money was like, and I knew what not having a pot to piss in or a window to throw it out of was like too. I took another bite of my food. Mrs. Grayson gazed into her son's eyes, and it was like they were communicating without talking. It was weird. She finally turned back to me.

"That sounds romantic." She was quiet for a moment, then she said. "I guess I would have never known if the two of you didn't show up on the cover of NY daily entertainment page." She sipped her wine. "Oh, and you two will be on the cover of Loyal next month."

"What?" I said, trying hard not to choke on the food I had in my mouth. I knew that being with Hunter would be a spotlight on our relationship, but not so soon. My palms were sweating, and my throat tightened as if HIS hands was around my neck, choking the life out of me. I had to breathe.

"Yes, my son is an extremely high commodity. Every man wants to be him, and every woman wants to be with him." She stared at me while I soaked that in.

"Mother," Hunter said, finally coming up for some air.

"I know being with you won't be easy, and neither will being with me. We both are still learning each other, but I can tell you, Mrs. Grayson, I'm not going anywhere." I stared at her to let that soak in. She finally smiled at me.

"I see. I'm happy that Hunter has found someone he can bring home. I've never met a girlfriend ever. I thought for years that something was wrong with him. That he was afraid of commitment, or he just enjoyed the company of the same sex." I couldn't help the wine that came out of my mouth. I grabbed my napkin to wipe my face.

"Mother," he said. I burst out with laughter. Hunter turned to look at me as if I weren't supposed to be laughing, but I found that to be hilarious.

"Hey, I'm being honest," she said, taking a sip, then turned to look at me.

"I want you to be ready for this life. This won't be an easy relationship. If you two love one another like you say you do, then be ready for the crazy, jealous-ass women. Now that they know he's not available, they're going to come after him even harder. You know women want what we can't have," she said as she answered the question I was about to ask. "So be ready to cut a bitch. I'm just saying." We all burst out into laughter. I had no idea his mother had such a potty mouth on her. "Don't be surprised, Zollah, by the way I speak. I do nothing but speak truth."

"I'm happy, and I will do the same as well, Mrs. Grayson," I said.

"Please call me Carrie."

"All right, Carrie," Hunter said.

"Oh no, it's Mother to you, smartass."

"Okay, Mrs. Carrie," I said.

"A girl who can cook, own her own business, and has manners. What is the downside to you?" she asked. Now what was I supposed to say about me that would be truth?

"The downside to me is that I have no parents. They died when I was twelve years old. I may have some daddy issues. My sister and my brother were taken from me in foster care. I lived a... rough life, one that I had to run from." I saw Hunter staring at me. He wanted to know how much I would go into my past.

"Anyway, I joined a modeling school and became a model and travel the world. Then I met someone who turned my life upside down." I put my head down. "I went to college and graduated. A few years after, I started my business, and now here I am," I said, taking big sips of my wine. I didn't want to lie to her. I saw her get up from her seat.

"Oh, poor child." She came over and hugged me. Shock covered me like a blanket. I gasped from the feeling that took over me. It was a tight, motherly hug, one I hadn't received in a long time. It felt good, and it told me everything would be okay.

"It's okay, Mrs. Carrie. I'm stronger than I look," I said.

"I know, honey. You have to be to have been through so much. You have to be strong to deal with my obsessive, possessive, demanding, and controlling son," she said.

"I'm still here, you know, Mother," he said.

"Why are you, son? You've finished your dinner. Are you waiting for dessert?" she asked.

"Actually, I am, but I can't get any until you leave," he said, getting up from the table. He dumped his plate in the sink.

"Hunter," I said.

"What?" He turned to me. His mother was standing with her mouth wide open.

"I think you've had enough dessert, don't you think?" I said as I met him at the kitchen sink.

"Never," he said, lifting me up and spinning me around.

"Hunter, put me down." I tried to yell at him, but I was giggling. He gave me a sad look before putting me down.

"I want you so bad, Mrs. Grayson," he whispered in my ear. I melted all over as he stuck his tongue in my ear.

# THE LOVE I CRAVE

"I'll leave my two out of three favorite ladies alone. I'll be in my office, arranging our flight back home." I turned back to Mrs. Carrie.

"I apologize," I was saying when she cut me off.

"Don't be. I've never seen him so happy before. He has always been so private and shy about things." She shook her head. "Ever since that summer at LABA, he returned home a changed person, and it wasn't a good change. He's the baby of the family. So, I'm a little overprotective." Her eyes locked with mine. "What happened that summer?"

"Nothing that I know of. We spent every day with each other until I left. If anything happened, it happened after I left. I left a couple of days early. I don't think us having to leave each other was what was wrong with him," I said.

"Oh, hmm." Her mind wandered. That made me think of what may have happened after I left, if he had been drugged the night I left. Hunter and I had drinks the whole summer. There was a party the night I left. "What had happened between then and now?" I asked her.

"Have you ever seen Hunter have a drink? Alcoholic one?" I asked to get an idea of how long it had been.

"Never," Mrs. Carrie said as she cleared the table. My mind raced of what he had said to me. He had done things as a result of what happened to him. Did it have anything to do with the escort service Anthony mentioned?

"You don't have to do that."

"It's okay. I'm not that bougie that I cannot help with cleaning my son's place. Don't let the expensive clothes and jewelry fool you, Zollah. I'm from D.C.," she said. I smiled. I had gone to college and met a group of girls from D.C. They were cool, but they didn't take anything from anybody.

We both cleaned the table and the kitchen. We sat together and talked and drank glasses of wine. We talked about my company and Sasha, who I wanted her to meet. I told her how I was here on a business trip. We finally cut things short, and she gave me her number and told me to keep in touch. She went inside Hunter's office and said goodbye.

I wasn't all the way in his office when he was up and out of his seat. His arms were around me, and I put my arms around his neck. He lifted me up, and I wrapped my legs around his waist. He carried me, using one hand to knock the things off his desk. He slowly laid me down on the desk.

"Finally, knowing you were naked all this time under that dress has been driving me insane," he said, pulling my dress from my shoulders. He kept going until my dress was on the floor. He stripped his pants off and pulled his shirt over his head.

"Does your dick ever go down?" I asked.

"Not since we've been back together. You have that effect on me," he said, spreading my legs apart.

# THE LOVE I CRAVE

He didn't hesitate to dive headfirst in me. Damn, this man, he was gifted in all kinds of ways. I turned my head to the right and noticed that his floor-to-ceiling windows were bare. I was sure everyone with a place this high up could see us. Just the thought of him devouring me with his mouth while someone watched turned me on. When he finished with his tongue action, he didn't hesitate to slide right into home base.

"Shit," I screamed out.

He circled his hips inside me, making my eyes roll in the back of my head. His mouth found my breast. My nipples hardened under him.

He pulled me down to the edge of the desk, so my ass hung over. Oh my, he felt so damn good. He had a wonderful pace as he pulled in and out of me. Once he was done with that position, he quickly turned me around so he could enter me from behind. He lifted my right leg and placed it on the desk as he took me from behind. His hand slid in front of us and found what he was looking for. He rubbed my pebble until I was screaming his name. His other hand wrapped my hair around his hand. I exploded.

"Yes, baby girl," he whispered in my ear as he joined me as heaven opened its gates. When we were done, he turned me around so our lips could meet. "Let us go shower before our flight home."

"But you wore me out. I'm tired," I whined.

"You can sleep on the plane."

"I think I'm scared of that bed now," I said with a smile.

"Don't be. You two will be seeing more of each other," he said with a smile. We showered, and I grabbed a few things from my closet to take back home. Hunter had pulled a Louis Vuitton luggage set and gave me one to put the extra clothes in. When we left, I took one last look at the place.

"Don't worry. You'll be back," he said, closing the door behind us.

"I know," I said as we passed the vase. It was still here.

"Hey, I need this vase. Can I take it with me?" I asked. I wanted that vase because it was one I had never seen before. I didn't have a special place for it yet, but I knew I would.

"You can have anything you want. I'll have Chris ship it to Cali," he said, pushing the button to the elevator. The doors opened, and we were on our way.

The flight back home was long and tiring. I slept most of the time while Hunter worked on his laptop. I thought I worked too much, but I guess I didn't. I was happy though that he was working because that meant he paid me no mind. My kitty needed a couple of days of relaxation. Julius was at the airport waiting for us when we arrived. It was four in the morning, and I knew Julius wanted to be home in his bed.

Once home, I unlocked the door, and the alarm went off. I put the code to cut it off. Julius had just driven off, and I closed the door behind me and locked it. I put the alarm back on. I pulled my suitcase over to the steps. I wanted to stop in the kitchen for something to drink. I fixed a glass of orange juice and when I closed the refrigerator door, my heart jumped out of my chest.

"Sasha, you scared the shit out of me. I thought you were asleep," I said, holding on to my chest.

"How can I sleep when my best friend who has been doing God knows what all weekend, creeps in the house at four in the morning," she said, pouring her a glass of orange juice.

"Sorry, our plane just landed, and Hunter dropped me off," I said, sitting at the breakfast bar. She stood on the other side, facing me.

"So, the cover of New York Daily, huh?" Sasha smiled, but I saw that she was nervous as well. I didn't want to think about it. I knew in my bones HE was sitting somewhere, staring at the front page.

"Sasha, I'm scared, and I don't want to be," I admitted. "I love Hunter so much that it scares the shit out of me. I feel like that sixteen-year-old again." I felt my eyes tearing up. "Our relationship has gone public, and HE will find me." I couldn't say the rest. Just the thought of HIM finding me and taking me away from Hunter left me speechless. Sasha came around to my side of the breakfast bar.

"No, Hope, don't go there. You're the happiest I've seen you in a very long time. Hunter wouldn't let anything happen to you. It's about time you realize that you're not that same girl anymore. You have grown and changed in the last few years. You have to tell Hunter, you must," she was saying when I cut her off.

"Sasha, I don't know. If HE comes back, you know the effect HE has on me. One look in his eyes, and I will be under his control again." I told myself not to freak out.

"Hope, you have to be strong. You're not going through this alone. When it all comes down to it, you'll fight. You'll fight for your love and life with Hunter." Sasha hugged me tight in her arms. We sat quiet for a moment, drinking our juice.

# SOPHIA PATRILLI

What's wrong?" I asked. Sasha was quiet for a moment before she spoke.

"This upcoming weekend is Damon's premiere party."

"I didn't forget," I said. I didn't forget and didn't realize how fast two weeks went by. I could tell there was more she wanted to say. "What is it, Sasha?" I asked. I thought about what this month was and what today was.

"Well, this weekend is also Sophia's birthday and your charity event." She put her head down. I set my glass down on the table. I didn't forget about the premiere, but the charity event slipped my mind. It was the first time it was being held in Florida, and I told myself I was going. Florida was a place I never thought I would ever go again, but the state had a high rate of children who needed help. I wouldn't let my fear of HIM get in the way of business.

"Sophia would have been twenty-seven years old," I said as it hit hard. I didn't forget her; it just hurt to think of her. How could I forget her birthday? I'd been so wrapped up with landing these clients and getting laid by Hunter, it just slipped my mind. Where did my priorities lie?

We had planned for a whole year for Sophia's birthday party. We had worked nonstop for it. We had planned everything to a T. We were young and ready to take on the world but weren't ready for the consequences. We had white tents, and a DJ. We had the pool open and the hot tub. We had ice figures and balloons and flowers everywhere. She had a three-tier cake. Her party was alive, and everyone and their momma were there. People we knew or didn't know were there; even Damon was there. So many people, so many drinks, so much drugs. The drugs were good that night. We were having the time of our lives. No one cared about what tomorrow brought. I was so wrapped up in my own shit, I didn't recognize anyone else's. I was about to turn twenty-two and had made a huge decision in my life. A decision that should have gotten me killed. We all went to sleep about four in the morning. Sophia and Treyvon went upstairs to the room they shared. That was where I found her. I closed my eyes as the image appeared in my head. I had never felt death before until I walked into that room. I cried and screamed loud, louder than the times when I was being beaten and raped by HIM.

# THE LOVE I CRAVE

"Hope," Sasha called out, bringing me back from that night.

"Sorry, I was just thinking about that day. It seems like yesterday. Anyway, what do you and Damon have in mind?"

"Well, Damon suggested that we visit her grave with some flowers and candy. You have your charity banquet that Friday afternoon in Florida at the Chariot Hotel. Then we can visit her grave Saturday morning before our flight back for the premiere Saturday night," Sasha said.

"You sure we'll be back in time for the premiere?" She shook her head. "Okay, I can do it," I said, trying to convince myself. "Thanks for being such a wonderful friend. I couldn't ask for a better one," I said as we finished up in the kitchen and walked down the hall to my room. It was now going on six o'clock in the morning. There was no point for me to go to sleep when I had to be to work in a couple of hours.

I ended up falling asleep anyway after calling Melissa and telling her that I wasn't coming in today. I couldn't make it out of bed; I was exhausted. Sasha left about nine thirty this morning. I guess Damon was gone too. I was dead to the world, in a comatose-like sleep. Eventually, I heard my phone ringing nonstop, and I heard some banging on the door while the doorbell rang. What the hell was going on? I didn't bother to look at my phone. I wanted to know who was banging on my damn door. I finally made it downstairs.

"Who is it?" I turned to look at the clock on the wall by the front door. It was almost noon.

I didn't even look out the peephole when I heard, "Who the hell do you think it is?" It was Hunter's sounding pissed off. I unlocked the door and opened it as Hunter burst through.

"Hunter Grayson, what are you doing here?"

"I can ask you the same thing," he said, looking through the house as if he was looking for something. I wiped my eyes to get a good look at him.

"What?" I closed the door behind him.

"You're supposed to be at work. When I came downstairs to your office, Melissa said you weren't there. I've been calling all morning. I was so worried and scared. Why didn't you call me?" he said. Hunter looked like he had gotten plenty of sleep, while I looked like a zombie.

"Hunter, I'm tired. Plus, my truck isn't here. It's at the building. I thought you would have figured that out, but you're so filled with... I don't what you're filled with right now," I said, walking away from him. I wasn't trying to explain to this crazed man. He grabbed my arm and turned me to face him.

"Well, I was worried sick thinking something had happened." He paused as he looked in my eyes.

"Thinking what?"

"Thinking that you left, or that HIM or SHE came here." He stopped to breathe. He pulled me closer. "I was worried, damn it." His arms found their way around me.

"Why would you think that?" I asked.

"Because you ran from him, and I'm sure he'll come for you. Don't ever have me worry about you again. Do you know I would tear the whole state of California to pieces if anything ever happened to you? Do you?" he yelled.

"I'm sorry." I was sorry, but Hunter overreacted when it came to me. Maybe it wasn't overreacting because I would feel the same way if I couldn't get in contact with him.

Hunter let out a grunt of frustration. He picked me up in his arms, threw me over his shoulder, and carried me upstairs. He took his time going up the steps. He paused at the top of the stairs, waiting for directions to my room. This would be his first time in my room. He walked further down the hall. The door to my room was already open as he walked in. Anytime he carried me over his shoulder, I knew I was in for some sexual torture.

"I was going to punish you, but I'm just happy that you're okay," he said as he looked around my room.

"I think you should punish me. How would I ever learn if I'm not disciplined," I said. His attention came back to me with a smirk.

243

"Baby girl wants to be a naughty girl. I love it," he said, throwing me down on the bed.

I had nothing on but a t-shirt, but as soon as his hands touched me, the shirt was off. My breasts were exposed as they hardened from his touch. He removed his suit jacket, and the rest disappeared just as fast. He stood before me naked, looking delicious. His manhood stood at attention. I sat up from the bed while that one eye snake gave me a wink. Even though I was tired as hell, and I said my kitty needed rest, I wanted to be punished more than I was tired. He pushed me back on the bed, pulling my legs until my ass hung off the bed. He dove in headfirst before slithering inside me.

"Never have me worry about you again," he said as his pace picked up.

"Hunter," I begged.

"Promise me." What did he want me to promise him again? All I cared about was the orgasm that wanted to rip through me.

"Please," I begged as he pleased me with long and slow strokes. I was on the edge of exploding, and then he stopped again. I died inside. How could he deny me of my orgasm? It just wasn't fair, and it was straight up torture.

"Promise that you'll never have me worry about you again," he said as he dove in deeper. I screamed out. My eyes rolled back in my head. I should be cross-eyed by now.

# THE LOVE I CRAVE

"I promise, Hunter, I promise. I will never have you worry ever," I begged as he finally allowed me to come. I screamed as his hands found the roundness of my ass and lifted me up from the bed with my legs on his shoulders. He turned around with my back up against the wall. He looked into my eyes as he let me have it.

"Do you know how much I love you, Zollah? Do you?" he asked with one hand slightly around my neck. He was deep inside me, and I tried not to go back to the time in my life where this felt so familiar. I moaned yes.

"I don't think you do. I'll give up everything I have for you. All I ever wanted was you." He leaned in and kissed me as he fucked me hard and good. I was going through convulsions as he hit every spot I had inside me. He carried me back over to the bed as he made great love to me. He told me how much he loved me. How much life wouldn't mean anything to him without me to share it with. I felt the same way about him. Nothing else mattered but him. We both had waited a long time for this moment. When I woke up, I felt eyes watching me. I saw the worry all over his face, which made me worry. I hated to see him without a smile on his face. I sat my head up and placed my chin on his chest.

"Hey," I said.

"Hey," he said back.

"Are you okay?" I asked. He said nothing as he just looked off in space.

"I'm just thinking," he said, stroking my hair from my face.

"About what?" He finally met my gaze.

"The night we stayed together. The next morning, you took off. I just remember seeing you in a car riding away, and I never saw or heard from you again, until that day in New York," he said. I remembered that day I left as if it were yesterday.

"I had to go. I couldn't stay. I wanted to but couldn't."

"I thought that we were going to have one more night together."

"Me too, but now we have forever," I said. Things were quiet for a moment.

"So, HIM and SHE must have hurt you so much to the point where you can't even mention their names." he asked, and he was catching on. He wasn't stupid.

"Yes." We said nothing else as the room got quiet again. It was hard for us to have conversations about our pasts. Maybe harder for me than him. Our conversations about the past never lasted long. I must stop telling myself I couldn't and open up to him. I guess it wouldn't hurt anyone.

"I met HIM the summer of 1999. I had just turned fourteen. I was in Florida for a runway shoot. HE was like a breath of fresh air when I saw HIM. HE came backstage to meet me. HE said I was the moon and stars in his darkness, and that made me smile. HE knew all the right things to say to me at that time. HIS father was the owner of the modeling camp I attended." I was going to try not to give no names. I didn't want Hunter looking them up. If Hunter thought harder about that summer, he would know the name he sought.

"HE told me that HE wanted to protect me and show me a life a girl like me deserves. I believed everything HE said to me. He did show me a life, but it wasn't one I deserved to see." I had his full attention; his eyes never left mine. I knew if he was going to be with me, he deserved to know something.

"Our first couple of years together were great, but that summer I met you, something changed in me. When I went back home with HIM, I wasn't the same. HE was absolutely infatuated with me. I felt as if I were a piece of property to HIM. When I turned eighteen, I thought how I would leave HIM. I thought Harvard was my way out, but I was wrong. I knew it would be impossible. HE threatened me if I were to leave HIM. He threatened my life, my model career as well as Sasha and Sophia." I paused for a moment just thinking about that time.

"So, I continued to make HIM as happy as possible, while I was miserable. I've done a lot of things in my life that I regret, but it has made me who I am." I looked deep into his eyes, letting Hunter know I meant every word. "I've drank until I couldn't drink anymore. I've done drugs some, I was forced to do, some I just wanted to do to numb the pain I felt.

All those years I'd felt as something was missing from my life, and it was you. I wanted to feel whole again." He stopped me with a passionate kiss.

"I haven't mentioned HIS name since the day I left, and SHE was just she. She didn't have a name. Well, she did, but she didn't. I could never talk about her," I said as I laid my head back on his chest.

"So, SHE isn't Sophia?" he asked.

"No."

We were quiet just lying in my bed. It felt good to open up, but I felt myself going into a dark place. I had to tell him something. Maybe that would allow him to open up more to me. I wanted to know what made him make a huge decision of a vasectomy. Who the hell drugged him? I felt like a little bit of weight had been lifted. Hunter was quiet, and I didn't know if it were a good thing or bad. Hunter hated HIM just as much as I did, and I dreaded the day they both met. We dosed off for about an hour when he got up and said he had work to do. He asked me to go with him, but I knew if I did, there wouldn't be any work getting done. So, I decided to stay. Plus, I had some work to do myself. I walked Hunter to his car.

"Really? You had Julius waiting for you all this time?" I said, wanting to apologize to Julius. "Can you even drive?"

"I can, but what's the fun in that?" he said, kissing me before hopping in his car and leaving. I went back to my room and started on some work. I was sitting on the couch when the door opened, and Damon and Sasha walked in. I finally came up for air. It was almost six o'clock.

"Oh my goodness, I forgot to make dinner. I'm so sorry. I had some work to catch up on," I said.

"Well, I guess it'll be a carryout night then," Sasha said, entering the kitchen and pulling the menu from the refrigerator.

"I'm sorry," I said again.

"It's okay. It's the carryout; it'll be ready in fifteen minutes," Sasha said.

"Everything is ready in fifteen minutes," Damon said, laughing. I went back to work while I waited for dinner. As I finished my email for my charity banquet this weekend, it occurred to me that I had totally forgotten to tell Hunter about my trip to Florida. I'd have to tell him by Friday, or maybe tomorrow. Once I was done with my work, I showered, ate dinner, then headed to bed.

# I FORBID IT

It was Tuesday morning, and I was up feeling good. Today was a good day. As I lay in bed last night, I kept thinking that Hunter and I must find better ways to fight and communicate. Sex was always the answer to our problems. I knew sex couldn't fix anything. I also thought it could be from our past. What Anthony said about the escort services still lingered in my mind. Did he get girls from that kind of service? Hunter did say something about what had become of him after what happened to him. Maybe I should ask. What if he was some real live maintenance man? I smiled at the thought.

I also thought about how I would tell Hunter that I was going to Florida. After what I saw yesterday, I knew he would flip out or demand he come with me, which would be fine with me. I didn't mind his company, and I would feel safer with him. I was nervous about it, and he would make me even more nervous. I shook all of that from my head. I said goodbye to Sasha and Damon sitting at the island. I opened the door to find Hunter walking up to my door. He called me last night to inform me that he would be at my house to pick me up. He was dressed in a grey and black pinstripe suit.

"Mr. Grayson."

"Great morning, Mrs. Grayson," he said as I closed the door behind me. He met me with a quick kiss. "Are you ready for work?"

"Yes, I am. Today is a good day."

"Your chariot awaits," Hunter said, pointing his hands toward Julius. Poor Julius. I accepted his hand, and he led the way. I got in first, and Hunter followed. I sat quiet in the backseat as Hunter stared at me like a piece of meat. I had to distract myself and him because I didn't want Julius to witness a fuck session in the backseat.

"I'm sorry, Julius, that you have to witness Hunter's crazy behavior," I said, looking at him in the rearview mirror. A smile came across his face.

"Actually, I find it quite amusing."

"Of course you do, but having you up at four in the morning, then have you wait while he..." I paused for a moment, thinking about what I was about to say. I had to change it. "While he went all Hulk on my door." I turned to

Hunter, and he was still looking at me as if he heard nothing we said.

"I had never seen him act like this before. Just when I was beginning to think he was a hard-cold bastard, he's actually a love-crazed teddy bear," Julius said. I turned to Hunter, then back to Julius, and I laughed. Love-crazed teddy bear was almost a perfect fit.

"So, are you two going to sit here and talk about me as if I'm not even here?" Hunter said.

"Sure are. I don't know what has gotten into you," Julius said.

"I know what has gotten into me," Hunter said as he turned to face me, his hand raising up to touch the side of my face.

"Hunter Grayson, stop that." I smacked his other hand away that tried to slide under my shirt.

We pulled up to EQ Skyscraper five minutes before nine. Wow, this was what it felt like to be on time. Julius turned back to say goodbye and gave me a polite smile. Hunter held out his hand for mine and helped me out onto the curb. No one rode the elevator with us anymore. When they saw us, they would wait for the next one, which was fine with me. I could make it to my floor faster without stopping on each floor. I had a feeling that just popped up in my mind. I needed to ask him this as soon as the elevator door closed behind us. I turned to face him.

THE LOVE I CRAVE

"Did you say something to Rodney? He doesn't even look at me anymore. He doesn't say things to me anymore. He doesn't smile that flirty smile at me anymore," I said as I saw his facial expression change. He didn't say anything to me, which confirmed that he did say something.

"Hunter, why would you do that?"

"I don't care for the way he looks at you. I could just imagine what he was thinking in his head about you." I cut him off.

"Do you want to know what I'm thinking in my head about you right now? That you're crazy and have lost your mind. You cannot go around threatening my friends or people that smile or flirt with me," I said, folding my arms over my chest. He moved toward me, and I backed up.

"You're really mad. You like him flirting with you?"

"No. I just hate to have someone scared to talk to me because the big bad wolf blew their house down."

"Talk to you. All he has to do is say hello, good morning, or see you later. He shouldn't say more than that." Was he fucking serious?

"Why shouldn't he? Rodney's a nice guy. We're friends."

"A nice guy. So, what exactly are you saying?" He didn't understand what I was trying to tell him. I saw him move away from me.

"All I'm saying is I have friends of the opposite sex, and you cannot control that. I told you this from the beginning."

"Control." He laughed. "You want to see control at its finest?" He dug his hand in his pocket.

"If I wanted to fuck Rodney, I could have done it already." In the moment it escaped my lips, I knew it was a mistake.

He pulled that key out so fast and stopped the elevator. Damn it, I was almost there. We were stopped on the twenty-seventh floor. I saw his facial expression turn to pissed off. I saw his eyes burning through mine. He came toward me until my back was up against the wall of the elevator.

"Say it again," he said in a stern voice. "Say it again," he said again, but I didn't want to. Not that I thought that he would smack me. "What did you say? If you wanted to fuck him, you could have done it already," He was up on me. I could feel his breath on my neck. He lifted my right leg up. I heard the zipper to his slacks.

"Hunter, no," I said, trying to put my leg down.

"You want to fuck Rodney, right? Well, I'm going to show you that no one can fuck you like I can," he said as he slid inside me.

"Shit," I moaned out. He lifted my left leg, wrapping them around him. He held my arms above my head. He gazed deep into my eyes and fucked me hard and rough. And when

I was about to explode, he stopped and slipped out of me. I nearly died. My legs hit the floor and gave out from under me as I fell to the elevator floor. He deprived me of an orgasm, one that I was looking forward to. Hunter fixed himself up and moved back over in the elevator. He pulled the key out and sent the elevator up.

"Don't ever say anything like that to me again."

I slowly got myself together and got to my feet. I snatched up my purse and bag. I stared at him, wanting to smack him across his face. I was about to say something when the doors opened to my floor. I was speechless as I walked out. Why did he always punish me with sex? I turned to look at Hunter. He had the biggest smile on his face.

"Have a great day, Mrs. Grayson," he said as the elevator doors were closing. I gave him the finger. I heard him burst into laughter behind the closed doors. I just stood there.

"Hope, are you okay?" Aimee asked.

"Yes, I'm great," I said, turning on my heels. I passed Aimee's desk and took the hall to my office.

"You had a delivery this morning," Aimee yelled out to me. I passed my door and stopped at Melissa's office. Melissa was at her desk waiting for me. She held my plans for the day, and I took them to my office. I opened my office door and saw two boxes next to my desk.

"What is this?" I yelled loud enough for Melissa to hear me. This must be the delivery I had this morning.

"A gift from Melvin. He sent you this note accepting your business agreement," Melissa said. That was great news. Now I would have to start on a contract immediately. I walked over to one of the cases. I had a feeling what was inside. It was the cherry bloom champagne. Melissa was there with the box cutter, and she sliced it open. My eyes lit up at the bottles lined up inside. I opened the mini china cabinet I had with glasses and took out three.

"Are you drinking during work hours?" Melissa asked with surprise.

"If you knew what I just went through, you wouldn't mind me having this." I never really drank while at work, but right now I needed it.

"What the hell happened?" Melissa asked.

"All I can say is Mr. Grayson has gotten under my skin," I said as I poured Melissa and me a glass. I took a sip, then another one, and I felt better.

"What did he do to you on that elevator?" Melissa asked, and I just smiled.

"All I can say is that I love that man. Wait... how did you know?"

"Aimee yelled back that the elevator was stuck on the twenty-seventh floor."

# THE LOVE I CRAVE

"Hmmm."

After we had a few glasses, I sent one out to Aimee for her to taste. Then I had to go to work. The first thing I did was call Melvin and thank him for the opportunity and for the champagne. I flipped through my calendar to see what date was good for the both of us. We set the date for the second week of March. So, I had two weeks to get everything together. After talking to Melvin, I called upstairs to my magazine to inform them of the upcoming events. My manager Abby would choose a group for New York. The day went by fast because I had so much work to do. By the time I got home, I was exhausted.

Damon was still living with us and was home when I got there, so he had prepared dinner. Spaghetti was the only thing he knew all of us would like. He also made good salads. I made sure I called Hunter to check in before going to sleep. I didn't need him banging on my front door. We both talked about how our day was at work. I told him about Melvin agreeing on the contract. We talked for about two hours before I begged him to let me sleep. He did, and I dosed off at eleven. I slept all night without a single nightmare. I woke up refreshed and ready for work.

Wednesday was busy as well. I had two meetings that morning. I'd been making it a habit of making it to work before nine. When I entered my office, I had flowers and candy waiting for me. Hunter had left a note saying how much he missed me, and how his bed had been so lonely without me in it. So, I decided to have lunch with him upstairs in his office. It was noon when I traveled up. He had the table set up with candles and flowers. He looked so damn fine in his burgundy suit. He had soft music playing in the background. He had a table in there full of food. Hunter pulled out my seat for me.

"You have a lot of my favorites here," I said, looking over the table.

"I have a wonderful best friend. She has all the good information. Her name is Sasha," he said as my eyes lit up. He sat across from me. I knew Sasha would tell him anything, but I knew the one thing she or Damon would never talk about, and that was HIM and HER.

"Hunter, we could have ordered takeout. I'm not that hard to please,"

"I know. That's what makes me love you even more," he said as he dug in.

"How's work going?" I asked.

"Good so far. I'm waiting on my inspector to call me back about the new hotel. I want to be sure it's okay to proceed. He had run into a little snag. He's due to return my call in an hour. Then if he says it's a go, I'll have to be prepared for an important trip to the Dominican Republic to meet up with Asher." When he said that, I looked up from my plate.

"Dominican."

"Yes," he said.

"When is this trip?" I asked. I hoped it wasn't a trip that would have him gone too long away from me.

"Probably sometime in April. March is a busy month for me."

"Oh," I said. He must have felt that I was disappointed.

"What's wrong?"

"That's so far away. Would you have to stay as long as you did?" I asked.

"Hey, don't worry. I'm taking you with me this time," he said. My eyes lit up.

"You are? I'm the luckiest girl in the world." I knew I looked too excited right about now. So, I had to calm myself.

"You said you wanted to go, so I'm taking you with me," he said, taking a bite of his bake chicken wings, then he scooped up some rice with his fork.

"I don't want to be in the way of you handling business."

"You won't be in the way." He got up from his side of the table and moved to my side,

bringing his plate with him. "You seem so far away." He paused, then asked me about work.

I told him about my day and my trip to Vegas coming up, then about my set date to return to New York. I was hesitant to tell him about Florida. I knew how he would react. I would start off with my charity banquet before I told him where it was. Maybe knowing it was for charity, he wouldn't be so clouded. So, I told him about the charity event and about Sophia's birthday and going to visit her burial site. He stopped eating. I was close to him, so I could feel him tense up next to me. He placed his fork down and asked me where Sophia was buried. I placed my fork down on my plate. I looked him deep in his eyes and said Florida. His eyes widened, and his eyes burned. His voice was so loud, I knew the whole damn building heard him.

"Like hell you are. You aren't going anywhere near HIM or Florida. Fuck Florida," he yelled. I leaned back in my seat to stare at him. He was furious, and I could see it in his eyes.

"I'm not going there to see HIM. I'm going to speak at my charity event, then I'm going to the gravesite."

"But it's still in the same state as HIM, and I forbid it," he said, and I picked up my fork. He continued to eat his food as if the topic were finished.

"Forbid it. Hunter, I'm a grown woman. I was telling you and not asking you. You can't—" I didn't finish because he cut me off. I wasn't trying to argue with him.

"Damn it, Zollah." He slammed his hand on the table, and I jumped. "You're not going. *I.forbid.it,*" he yelled.

"I'm going." I put my foot down.

"No, you're not." He got up from his seat.

"Hunter, I have a charity event I have to attend. You know how that is. I'm quite sure you have charities." He was quiet for a moment. He turned back to look at me.

"Zollah…" He paused as his body shuddered. He was scared, and I wasn't sure if it was because of what may happen to me or what he may do or become if he lost me.

"I'm going whether you like it or not." I calmed my voice. I got up from my seat and walked over to him. I stood in front of him. "Just tell me how you want me to do this, and I'll obey. I'll do whatever to make you feel comfortable with me going." I reached out for him. I didn't want to argue with him, but I knew I had to compromise with something to make him be okay with the idea of going back to Florida. Hunter was quiet for a moment. He thought hard about what to say. I grabbed one of his hands in mine, and I touched his face with the other.

"My rules, my plane, my hotel, my car, and my security," he said so firmly, and I wasn't going to disagree with what he wanted. I was still going, and that was all that mattered to me. I pulled him into an embrace.

"Thank you. Why don't you come with me?"

"If I could, I would, but I have some important meetings this weekend," he said. I pulled him back over to the table so we could finish our lunch. "I'll arrange everything. Just let me know when you want to leave and which one of my hotels you want to stay in. I'll email a list of them."

"How many are there?" I asked, picking up a piece of pineapple to pop into my mouth. There was nothing like fresh fruit. Then I grabbed a fried wing and dumped a little hot sauce on it.

"I have twenty-six hotels," he said with a smile. That was a lot of hotels.

"Twenty-six," I said surprised. That was a lot for someone who was still in his twenties. "How old were you when you built your first one?"

"Eighteen. It was a birthday present for myself," he said, and I thought there was nothing in this world I could get a man who had everything. He bought himself a hotel for his eighteenth birthday, and his best friend bought him a private jet. "Eighteen. At that age, people are going off to college or finishing high school, and I was out here opening up hotels. I had my mind on a plan and the promises I made to a certain girl." I didn't say anything, just smiled.

"What else do you own?"

"I own a few gyms all over California and New York. I have a few restaurants, a couple of nightclubs, a golf course, a few apartment buildings, a few office buildings, a couple of studios, a few other things. Oh, and I'm opening up my first resort with Asher," he said.

"You're a busy man and must have thousands of people working for you. How do you oversee so much?"

"I have a wonderful team working for me." Wow, I knew he owned a couple of things, but damn. How did he even have the time to live? Well, I was sure he had done more living than I had. I had existed for so long I didn't know how to live. That was something I had to learn how to do when, for the past three years, I had been looking over my shoulder, never driving home the same way just in case someone was following me. I could say I had slacked up a little in the past few months, and now that I'd be all over papers and magazines, I needed to be more careful. I looked up to see Hunter staring at me. He whispered in my ear, "I want you."

"You're such a horny devil," I said, leaning in to kiss him. He was quick as his hands found the roundness of my ass, and I slid out of my seat and straddled him in his.

"I knew you wanted it." He smiled. I shut him up with another kiss. I had my arms around his neck as his hands massaged my breast. I felt his manhood harden underneath me, and I ground on him when a voice came over the intercom in his office.

"Sorry to interrupt, Mr. Grayson, but the inspector is on line two," his receptionist said.

"Thank you, Stephanie. Give me two minutes," he responded. Saved by the bell. Then he turned to me. "You're so lucky; you were about to get it." I climbed off his lap to fix my clothes. "Since I won't see you this weekend, you'll be spending the next couple of days with me." I was fine with that.

"I have to go anyway. I have another meeting. Thank you for lunch; it was great," I said. I was about to leave when I noticed how much food was left. So, I decided to fix Aimee and Melissa a plate.

"I'm going to take this with me," I said, carrying two plates out the door with me.

"Greedy," he said.

"Well, if I'm going to spend the next two days with you, I'm going to need my strength. See you later."

Once I was back downstairs, I handed Aimee her plate, then I gave Melissa hers.

My meeting didn't last long, and my day was almost over. I had a few emails to send, along with some thank you notes. It was past five o'clock, and Melissa and Aimee had gone home. This was the first time in a long time that I'd been alone in my office. After finishing my emails, I shut everything down, cut off my lights, and closed my office door. I walked down the hallway and pushed the button to the elevator. When the doors opened, a man stepped out wearing a black hoodie and some dark jeans. I wasn't sure if he had the right place. He pulled the hood from his head, and I stopped in my tracks. My heart sank to my stomach. My purse and phone slipped from my hands onto the floor.

# THE LOVE I CRAVE

"You thought you could hide from me forever, did you? I told you I would find you wherever you were," HE said, walking closer to me. I backed away from him. "I'm going to kill you, but not before you watch me kill him first. You love him, do you?" HE said as I kept backing up down the hall. I ran to my office, but he grabbed me by my hair. "You gave another man what's mine," he said as he grabbed me between my legs. I fell to my knees as he dragged me along the floor.

"Please don't hurt him. I'll do whatever you want," I screamed, trying to get out of the hold he had on me.

"You're begging me not to kill him. You should be worried about yourself." He stopped dragging me across the floor. He bent down to his knees and inhaled my scent. I felt his nose rub against the scar on my neck. My stomach tightened, and vomit formed in my throat. He smelled my hair where it was wrapped around his hand. I was on the floor fighting for my life.

"MP, I missed you more than life itself." HE used the fingers from HIS free hand to run along the top of my blouse. Those gray and brown eyes stared down at me as if he saw nothing but nightmares. HE moved so fast and before I knew it, HIS hands were around my neck. It was tight, but HE had choked me tighter to the point where HE smacked the shit out of me before I dared slip away. HE smelled me again, from my neck and further down to my breasts, then my center. The man was absolutely demented. HIS eyes snapped to mine.

"You have definitely been giving my pussy away, MP, and now you must be punished." HIS hands tightened around my neck. I was trying to fight him off, but I couldn't move. HE was too strong. My eyes widened when I felt my life slowly slipping away, and the only thing I could think about was Hunter and how I couldn't say goodbye to him. How I would never see him again. What would he do?

"Zollah, wake up." My head popped up from my desk. I looked around frantically and noticed I was still in my office. Then I saw Hunter and fell back into my chair. I looked around the office again, catching my breath. I must had fallen asleep typing emails. "Are you okay?" Hunter leaned over me. His hands reached out to me, but they never made contact.

"HIM, he was here waiting for me by the elevator. He was about to…" I paused, taking a moment before continuing with something else. "He said he was going to kill you." I shook my head. That was all I could say before my body went cold, and the numbness took over, and I was shielded with darkness. I couldn't move my body; I couldn't move anything. I'd had nightmares before, but this one seemed so real. I knew from that nightmare, HE knew where I was, and HE was coming for me.

"No one else is here. It's just me and you, baby girl." He knelt in front of me, pushing my chair away from my desk. "I'm taking you home," he said. I had no words. I just shook my head. He looked me in the eyes. "Stay with me."

# THE LOVE I CRAVE

Hunter shut everything down and took out his phone to call Julius. He told him to meet us in the garage and not the front. He turned to me, his eyes filled with much concern, and I didn't even have the voice to tell him I was okay. I would be just lying anyway. He grabbed all my things from my desk, put them in my purse, and wrapped it around me. I tried to get up to move some part of my body, but I couldn't. I was cold and numb. Hunter picked me up in his arms and cradled me like a baby. It had been a long time since I felt this way, and I tried to shake it off. I laid my head on his chest and closed my eyes. I felt the elevator stop, then moving, then a door closing, and then moving again.

"We're home." I finally opened my eyes to Hunter's voice. "You can go on ahead home for the night, Julius."

"Are you sure she'll be okay?" Julius asked. Hunter paused before getting out of the truck. He stared at Julius with a clueless face.

"No, Julius. I don't know. I don't know shit." He turned back to look at me, and I had no words. All I could do was reach out to him. I touched his face with my hand and smiled. "She'll be fine." Hunter grabbed me and carried me to the door. Julius had the front door open. Hunter took me straight upstairs to his room. He laid me down on the bed as he went to the bathroom. I was here physically, emotionally, but mentally, I was gone. Well, part of me was gone. Sasha said it was hard at times, bringing me back to reality after having a nightmare or when the darkness took over. Julius stood in the doorway staring at me. Hunter came out of the bathroom. "You can lock up for me and head home," he said to Julius.

"Are you sure she doesn't need to go to a hospital or something? She looks sick." Julius asked.

"Thanks, but I can take it from here. Oh, and I need to have a meeting with you in the morning," Hunter said. I heard Julius leave and put the alarm on. Hunter came over to the bed to undress me. I just lay there looking at him, waiting for the darkness to fade. I could reach to touch his face in the car, maybe I could sit up. "Zollah," he called out, moving my hair from my face. "Do you know where you are?" he asked. I looked around the room to the bed to the man before me. I opened my mouth to speak, and sound finally came.

"I'm home."

"Yes, you are." He smiled, but then it quickly faded.

"Though I'm not sure if we're about to take a bath or have sex." I looked at him undress me. A laugh escaped his lips.

"All right then, you're coming back to me."

Hunter went back inside the bathroom, and I heard the water shut off. He came back out naked as well. He lifted me from the bed and carried me to the bathroom. He slowly put one foot in at a time. He sat, and the water was warm. We sat in the tub with his back up against the jacuzzi tub and my back up against his chest. I laid my head back on him. We were quiet for a moment, and I wondered what was going on

# THE LOVE I CRAVE

in Hunter's head. I didn't know where to even start to talk to him. *What can you say after something like that?*

# MEMORY LANE

**H**unter and I laid back in the tub. He used his hand to trickle water over my arms. I had finally calmed down from that terrible dream. I didn't want to think how it would be if HE found me and if it would happen like that or worse. I was speechless for a while and couldn't come up with anything to say to him but that I was sorry. I closed my eyes and took a moment to focus on my breathing and to clear my head. I didn't know how long we sat quiet. When he finally spoke, his voice was sad and scared, and he tried to hide it.

"Zollah, are you sure you want to go to Florida this weekend?"

I opened my eyes. To be honest, I wasn't sure if I should go, but I must. My professionalism was on the line, and I couldn't back out now. "Yes, I must go." I should have expected for him to ask.

"Please talk to me about HIM. It's killing me inside to see you like this," he begged. I felt his worry for me. This was a first to have a man feel the pain I felt.

"I'm sorry, Hunter, but I can't." I turned just so our eyes could meet. "To tell you what he did to me means I have to relive it, and I can't do that, not right now. When I think of HIM and the things he had done to me, I go into this cold, dark place of numbness. I want to kill myself. I want him to kill me, so I can be free and no longer hurt. You see the scars." His eyes landed on the scar that came from the side of my face down my neck. His hand ran down it. I could feel the tears forming in my eyes. I wanted him to let it go and let us get past this. "They've healed, but there are hundreds more scars that you cannot see." He placed his hand on my heart. I closed my eyes to take him in.

"Damn it, Zollah. I want to kill him," he yelled. Then the tears fell. I knew he wanted to kill him, and I knew he would if he was given the chance. I never mentioned who I was with but once that summer, and it never came up again. If Hunter really thought back to that time, he would know exactly who he was. I hoped he never remembered.

"Hunter, don't be mad. I—"

"How can you say that? HE has made your life a living hell, and I can't..." He paused. Oh no, was he going to say

271

that he couldn't accept me with all of my baggage? This was what I wanted to prevent. Hunter leaving me because of my past.

"Please don't say that you can't be with me."

"That's not what I was going to say. I will never leave you. I just can't take you being so afraid of HIM," he said as I put my head down. "Zollah, you have to be comfortable talking to me about your past. If you can't do that, what do we have besides successful jobs and amazing sex? No, please stop crying. You know I can't stand that." His thump wiped the tears from my face before pulling me closer. I turned to face him with my legs wrapped around him. I sucked up my tears because I knew it was time to put on my big girl panties. I laid my head on his chest and listened to his heartbeat. The fast-thumping sound was like music to my ears.

"When I was a little girl…" I finally said after I didn't know how long. "I never knew where I would be in my life as an adult. My parents sheltered me a lot growing up and kept me busy. They took us everywhere. We used to have so much fun, and all the places we went, there was always music. I never saw how cruel the world was or how cruel people could be, not until I entered foster care." His arms tightened around me.

"My mother and my father were the only children, that I know of. They were disowned by their parents, my grandparents. They were young; my mother was sixteen, and my father was seventeen when they traveled from Vancouver to California. They started a wonderful life here; it wasn't easy, of course, with them being so young and alone. They never talked about the bad stuff, mostly the good parts of their lives. I was four years old when my mother had Brooke, and Ryan came two years after that. I was an honor roll student, and I rarely got in trouble." I paused, thinking what to say next. I wanted to make a long story short. I wanted him to know what I'd been through before HE came into my life.

"I was home helping my sister and brother with their homework. It was after six o'clock, and my parents were late getting home. So, I fed the kids, gave them a bath, then sent them off to bed at eight. I was twelve years old. Brooke was eight, and Ryan was six. There was an earthquake that day. My parents were in a car accent on the freeway. They died on the spot. I was worried when they never came home. I was scared because the kids were scared after the earthquake." I paused again, thinking about that time. I had taken care of my siblings always. The fact that I couldn't and hadn't in years was the worse feeling.

"There was a knock on the door about ten o'clock that night. I wasn't going to answer it, but I had a feeling I needed to. There were two police officers and a lady from social services. They came in and asked me where my parents were. I told them that they never came home. They asked for a picture of them, and I showed them. That's when they told me that my parents had passed away earlier that day. I'd never experienced a broken heart before, until that day. My heart shattered into a million pieces." I had to get myself together and not burst into tears. Going back to that day wasn't as hard as it used to be, but that shit still hurt like a bitch.

"They kept asking us if we had any family we could contact. I kept telling them that we had no one, that my parents were all we had. The lady from social services asked me to pack a bag of clothes; she had a place for us to go. The worst part for me was telling Brooke and Ryan that Mommy and Daddy were dead. Mrs. Langley, she was the mother of the foster house, she thought that someone would come for us. By September, no one came, so she had to enroll us in school. I hated foster care but if I had never gone, I would have never met Sasha and Sophia." That was the only good thing that came out of that place. The place was old and always cold. In winter, Brooke and Ryan would sleep with me so we could use each other's body heat to stay warm.

"We were there for two years when some couple came and decided to be foster parents to my sister and brother. I was reading a book while Sasha and Sophia went hunting for something at the mall. I heard them screaming, saying, 'No, you can't take us.' I asked Mrs. Langley what was going on, and she explained everything to me. I cursed and fussed, telling her that she was a total bitch for taking them away from me. I asked the couple if they could take me too. They said that I was too old." I burst out laughing, just thinking that a fourteen-year-old was considered too old.

"I felt like my heart was shot out of my chest again. When they left, Mrs. Langley couldn't control me. I went into my room and destroyed everything. I smashed the TV. I took all the sheets off the bed. I broke the lamps. I kicked holes in the wall. I screamed and cried. I fell to the floor and balled up into the fetal position. I cried until I felt numb. I cried until I passed out, and I prayed for death. I had no idea how long I was on the floor. Sasha and Sophia had finally gotten the nerve to come in my room. They found me lying there. They tried and tried to get me up off the floor, but I wouldn't move. I didn't want to move. They said I was there for three days. They brought me food, but I didn't eat. They hugged me tight and told me that everything would be okay.

"They finally got me up off the floor. They bathed me and clothed me; they even washed my hair. They did my hair and my nails. I wasn't there anymore. I was dead inside. They took me downstairs and got me something to eat because I hadn't eaten in days. They were talking across the table while I ate. Sasha pulled out this flyer to this summer camp for modeling. You had to be fourteen to eighteen years old. You had to have a 3.0 GPA, which was good because I was on the honor roll. Once the camp was over, they would choose twenty-five models to travel the world. Sophia said that it was my ticket out of foster care. I didn't want to go; all I wanted to do was find my sister and brother. Then Sophia asked if I wanted to be here until we were eighteen, just to be thrown out on the street without a pot to piss in. I thought about it. What did I have to lose when I'd already lost everything." The dumbest shit I could ever think of. I did lose everything but not my life, which I had to worry about the moment I let HIM into my life.

"So, I agreed to go, and I made the best and worst decision of my life. I met HIM that summer. By the end of the summer, I was HIS girlfriend and happy as ever. We would travel from Friday through Sunday for modeling, and I would spend my time with HIM. Just in a little time, I fell in love with HIM. Maybe it was the things he did for me. All of it went away when I met you two years later. That's when I finally recognized what love really was." I stopped. I lifted my head and looked into his eyes.

"You're a strong woman, Zollah. Some women don't make it out of situations like this. I'm happy I have you. I hate that you've suffered so much loss." He leaned in and gave me a passionate kiss, one that told me he would be there for me no matter what. That he would do anything and everything to have me and keep me safe.

"I love you, Hunter, and I have to take the life with HIM one day at a time. I will tell you, I will," I promised. Now it felt good to say but to think about that place HE and I stayed...

"I love you more. Now let's wash up and head to bed." There was nothing sexual about Hunter washing me up; it was all about taking care of me and being there when I needed him the most.

# THE LOVE I CRAVE

"I think I can walk on my own now," I said as he reached out and pulled me into his arms.

"Don't worry about it. I'll carry you through hell and back if I have to."

"You say the sweetest things."

"I mean everything I say to you, and I will never lie to you or hurt you."

"I know."

We got in bed facing each other, and he wrapped his arms and legs around me. I smiled because I couldn't move a muscle. We were quiet for a while, just listening to each other's heartbeat. There was no place I would rather be but in the arms I'd craved for so long. I closed my eyes and wanted to drift off to sleep. I prayed that no nightmare came to haunt me. Hunter was the one who broke the silence this time.

"After spending the night with you that summer at LABA, when you just picked up and left the next day, I was so mad and upset. I had this feeling that I would never see you again," he said, stroking his hand through my hair. "That night, Asher and I went to a party a girl had in her room." When he paused, I was scared that he would tell me that he slept with another girl that night. That should be the least of my worries. I left and had sex with someone else. It wasn't my intentions, but I did have a boyfriend, but we never had sex. So, of course HIM would choose that night to take my virginity.

277

## Henson Dreamier

"Asher and I were drinking at the party. Everyone was. The girl who had the party was fixing my drinks. She did so well, you could barely taste any liquor. As the night went on, she sat next to me and kept talking about you," he said, and I was surprised. I had no idea who the hell he was talking about.

"Me?"

"Yeah. As I look back on it now, she said she had been trying to get my attention all summer, but I paid her no mind. She must have seen us together every day after that first party. She asked me who you were and if you were my girlfriend. She made up lies about you. I knew they were lies, but I had no idea she would stoop so far." I wanted to ask what lies did that bitch try to conjure up about me, but I let him talk. "As the night went on and people left, she started to come on to me. I kept telling her that I didn't want to go there with her, but I guess she couldn't or wouldn't take no for an answer. Asher had left with some girl to do you know what. I started to fill dizzy." I looked up at him. He wasn't looking at me; he just stared into space.

"The next thing I knew, I was passed out and didn't remember a thing. I woke up the next day with my head ringing and my clothes messed up. I couldn't remember anything, not until I made it to my room. Asher had been looking for me all morning. I had told him what happened, and he made me something his mother used to get him to make her the mornings she woke up hungover. It was a concoction so she could remember what happened the next

278

day. The drink was nasty as hell, but it brought back everything from the night before." He paused for a moment before he continued.

"What she did to me that night changed me forever. I wasn't the same after that. That incident triggered other things that one day, I would want to talk about, but not yet. I'm quite sure my mother asked you about it." He looked at me, and I looked away.

"Yes, she did. She's just worried about you," I said as our eyes connected again.

"Of course she is."

"Who was she?" I asked because I was going to kick that bitch's ass. I was going to go kung fu panda on her.

"It's not a big deal, Zollah. It was years ago." Easy for him to say.

"She drugged you, Hunter. It's... something no one should have to experience." I knew exactly how that felt. I knew what being taken advantage of felt like. It was something you couldn't control because you were so numb and drunk that you couldn't even move even if your life depended on it.

"So is abuse," he said.

"Hunter," I said, not knowing how tormented he had to have been after experiencing something like that.

"Zollah, I wanted to open up to you and tell you things in my past that have affected me. Just like you, we have to take one day at a time," he said. But I tried to think about what girl in her right mind would do something like that.

"And I appreciate it. Thank you." I kissed him. Tonight was the first night we spent together that didn't end with hot, mind-blowing sex. We just held each other and slowly drifted off to sleep.

I was the last one to get up the next morning. I woke up to the smell of breakfast in the air. When I opened my eyes, Hunter was standing in front of the full-length mirror fixing his tie. He was dressed in his grey suit that made his eyes scream at me. I lay back to just watch the view. Hunter was one tree I loved to climb. I thought about last night and how we were able to open up to each other. It was a good thing, right? I knew this wouldn't be easy, and he was right. We must have something more than successful careers and powerful sex.

"Good morning, baby girl. Time for work," he said, walking over to me. I didn't even notice he was done with his tie and had walked over to me. He kissed me on the forehead. I pulled the covers from me and climbed out of bed. I pulled him into a hug.

"Hunter, I just want to say that I'm happy. Happier than I've ever been in a long time, and I wouldn't change anything we have and will share together. I understand that we both have stuff that we've been through. I want to be there for you always. You've shown me how much you love me, and I want to show you," I said as my eyes never left his.

"The night you came home with me and agreed to be with me showed me how much you still loved me. I love you so much it hurts at times. All I want is for us to be honest with each other," he said.

"I'll always be as honest as possible with you," I said as we shared a kiss. After that, I went to my room to pick me out something to wear. I chose me a pair of beige slacks with a black collar shirt and black pumps. I headed downstairs for breakfast. When I entered the kitchen, Hunter was already eating.

"Good morning, Zollah," Mrs. Phoebe greeted me as I entered the kitchen. She had on her white apron and a smile on her face. She was such a sweet old lady, but I would never call her old to her face.

"Good morning, Mrs. Phoebe." I sat next to Hunter at the island. She set my plate in front of me, and I ate my eggs and bacon. I didn't say much; I just watched Mrs. Phoebe go around the kitchen, putting the clean dishes away from the dishwasher and putting the dirty ones in. Hunter was done with his food, and he just stared at me as if he were still hungry.

"Finish up. Julius should be here any minute," Mrs. Phoebe said, refilling my glass of orange juice. I stopped eating the moment I thought about Julius seeing me that way last night.

"Julius is heading straight to the office this morning for a meeting. I'm driving," Hunter said, and Mrs. Phoebe dropped a dish in the sink. She turned around to look at him so quick, I was sure she had whiplash.

"What did you say?" she asked again to make sure she heard correctly.

"MT, what's wrong with you? I can still drive, you know."

"Nothing. I'm sure you can." She turned to stare at me like I had an answer to what she was looking for. I sat back and wondered what the big deal was. To think about it, I'd never seen him drive before. I wasn't sure if he had a license. "I mean you haven't driven since you came home from college or was it the Reserves? It just took me by surprise, that's all." Reserves, I thought. Did he join the Army Reserves? And what did MT mean?

"I know." He smiled to himself. "Today, I feel like driving." He turned to look at me and kissed me on the forehead. "Baby girl, you have ten minutes." Hunter left me, and he headed into his office. I turned to Mrs. Phoebe.

"MT?"

"Oh, he has been calling me that since forever. It stands for mom number two. He has known me for a long time since he was a little, snotty-nose boy."

"Are you okay?" I asked because she was staring off into space, and I was sure I could see her eyes watering up.

"Never felt better, darling," she said as Hunter came out of his office.

"Ready?" I shook my head and got up from my seat. I had finished off the last bit of my orange juice. I picked up my purse from the couch. Hunter had my hand, pulling me toward the garage door.

"Hunter, you're not driving that toy of a car, are you?" she asked just as he opened the door.

"It's a luxury car," he said.

"It's a piece of metal, and you drive carefully with that girl in the car," she yelled from the kitchen.

"Yes, ma'am," he said as the garage door closed behind us. When I entered the garage, there were two cars. One was a black, four-door Mercedes with red interior and rims. It was shiny as if it had just been washed this morning. Then there was another car that had a cover over it.

"Can you still drive?" I asked, skeptical.

"I can drive as good as I can fuck," he said, and I rolled my eyes at him. He turned and smiled, pulling the cover off the car and revealing a black car that was sure a piece of metal. My eyes popped out when I saw that car. Mrs. Phoebe was right. At first, I thought it was a batmobile, and he was Batman, and I was Batgirl, and we were about to go all vigilante in Los Angeles. Nope, it was an all-black Lamborghini. My mouth hit the floor because I had never seen one with my own eyes.

"Mrs. Grayson," he said as he slid the door up, waiting to help me inside. A Lamborghini with the butterfly doors. Just like the Mercedes, the interior was all red. Red was sure to be the man's favorite color.

"This is a sexy car. What's her name?" People always seemed to name their cars females. I named my car Silvia because she was a silver beauty, and she floated like a spaceship.

"Piper," he said, and a chill went up my spine. I looked up at him as he held the door up for me.

"You named your car after me?"

"You named your magazine after me."

"Touché," I said as he helped me inside. He slid the doors down with a thump. I watched him walk around to the driver's side to get in. The inside of the car was spectacular. The dashboard was laid out with all sorts of screens and new technology. The red seats were leather, and it smelled brand new.

# THE LOVE I CRAVE

"Seatbelt, baby girl." I was so busy admiring the car, I didn't bother to put it on.

Hunter pushed a button to start her up. The car roared to life, sounding like a werewolf in the night howling at the moon. He hit the gas, and it pushed forward fast. The car floated as if it were an airplane in the air on autopilot. We stopped at a light, and we were in the middle lane. Hunter reached out for my hand, and I accepted it. I looked to my right, and the guy in his car next to us stared at the car, drooling over it. I turned to my left, and there was a car with a female who was also drooling, but I wasn't sure if she was drooling over the car or my man. Hunter smiled at her and gave her a nod, and the light turned green. He hit the gas, and the car rushed forward, leaving the two cars in the dust. Such a show off.

We pulled up to the building, and the look on Rodney's face was priceless. Not just his face but everyone standing in the front of the building. It was like we were at a car show. Everyone tried to look inside to see who it was. I turned to look at Hunter, and he was smiling from ear to ear. There was nothing like seeing a smile on the man you loved. Hunter pushed a button for the doors to lift. I thought that was so cool, and so did everyone else who had crowded around. He told me to stay, and he would help me out. It wasn't the fact that I was low to the ground; I could still let myself out, but he wanted to be of assistance, and I was going to let him.

"Mr. Grayson, holy shit, this is a nice ride." Rodney came off the curb to get a better look. Could a man have an orgasm from just looking at a car?

"Thanks, Rodney." He passed Rodney in front of the car. Hunter gave him the keys but told him he didn't need it to drive; the key just had to be near the car. Rodney looked at the keys like he couldn't believe he was about to get behind the wheel of such a car. Hunter walked around the car and held out his hand for mine.

"Should I even drive this? I'm scared," Rodney said. Hunter helped me to the curb and put his arm around me. I looked around as people gawked over the car.

"Go ahead, but a scratch on her means a scratch on you." Hunter smiled. I didn't even bother to speak to Rodney. Never come between a man and his car. Hunter held me close as we entered the building through the glass doors. We caught the elevator by ourselves, holding each other until the doors opened to my floor. I would get used to riding the elevator alone with no stops.

"Have a good day." Hunter gave me a quick kiss as the doors opened to my floor.

"You too, Mr. Grayson." The doors closed.

"Early again. Wow," Aimee said as she handed me sticky notes full of messages. I left her and headed back toward my office. It was Wednesday, and I needed to call Sasha on our plans for Florida. I had to tell her the arrangement Hunter and

# THE LOVE I CRAVE

I agreed to. He was very overprotective, and I could see why. HE was very overprotective with me too, but I knew in my heart things would be different with Hunter. For me to go to Florida, I had to do what Hunter said, and I was sure Sasha didn't mind saving some money on the flight and the hotel. I stepped into my office, and Melissa already had my plans for the day on my desk. I turned on my computer, pulled my chair back from my desk, and sat. I placed my purse on my desk and scanned through the messages as I called Sasha.

After our conversation, she didn't care about the security that would be following us. She was the best friend ever. We chose to stay at Grayson's Palace which was thirty minutes from the gravesite and twenty minutes from the charity banquet. After talking with Sasha, I went straight to work. I had a lot of work to do if I planned on missing a half day of work on Thursday. I wanted to call Hunter to let him know of the arrangements, but I knew he was in a meeting. So, I went over my calendar again. I had two weeks left before my Vegas trip. I wondered if Hunter had a hotel there. I was sure he did. He'd be a fool if he didn't.

After a few conference calls, I had to finish working on my speech for the charity function. I didn't understand why it was taking me this long. I'd always known what to say. Maybe my mind was clouded right now. I'd been trying to keep myself busy and not think of HIM, but it was hard getting so close to going back. My day went by fast and before I knew it, it was five o'clock, and I was ready to head home. My office phone rang, and it was Hunter telling me he was on his way down. I finished up my last-minute emails and shut everything down. I headed out, shutting my office door behind me. I walked out to my reception area and found Aimee and Melissa chatting.

"What are you two still doing here?" I asked. They had been adamant about getting out of here at five on the nose, and here it was almost five-thirty.

"We were waiting on you," Aimee said, looking from Melissa to me.

"You don't have to wait on me. I'm done now. You all can go," I said as they stared at me as if I were speaking another language. "Are you two okay?" I asked just as the elevator doors opened, and Hunter stepped out. When I saw him and the way he smiled when he saw them waiting, I had an idea of what was going on.

"Good evening, Mr. Grayson." Aimee said.

"Evening, ladies," he said as he held the elevator doors for us to get in. I looked around at the awkwardness in the elevator, but it could just be me. Hunter was beside me on one side of the elevator, and Melissa and Aimee were on the other side. I broke the silence.

"Did he tell you to not leave me alone and to wait for me?" I asked them, and they didn't say anything, but the look on their faces told me all. I didn't go any further. I just smiled and squeezed Hunter's hand. I couldn't blame him; he was a protector at heart. We all headed down to the lobby and out the door. Rodney was there waiting with Hunter's car.

"Who in the hell is driving that special-edition Lamborghini?" Melissa asked. I didn't hear what she said. It was Lamborghini than a bunch of letters and numbers. I focused on the crowd around the piece of metal.

"That would be me." Hunter said as Rodney handed him the keys. The doors to the car were already up on both sides, so everyone got a good look at the interior.

"Of course, why would I ask? Shit, I want to be like you when I grow up," Melissa said as she walked over to the car, squeezing her way through the audience.

"You know your cars I see," Hunter asked.

"Since I could talk. My father owned a dealership and a mechanic shop. He used to take me to work with him. He taught me everything about a car. I was the son he never had." She smiled. I saw Rodney and Aimee talking over on the side.

"I'll have to test drive this one day," she said giggling.

"Over my dead body," Hunter said, and Melissa shook her head as she named things that were inside the car.

Hunter walked me over to the passenger side, and I climbed in. He came around and got in the driver's seat. The audience backed up as the doors went down on both sides.

On the way home, we talked about work and the trip. After that, I could tell he was quiet because he was worried about me.

"Hunter, I'm going to be okay," I said.

"You fucking better be okay. Plus, I'm sending Julius with you. He'll protect you," he said.

"But who will drive you?"

"As you can see, I can drive myself. Plus, it's only for a couple of days."

"We have to be back for Damon's premiere. Sasha and I are going as his dates," I said.

"And what lovely dates he will have." He lifted my hand up to kiss it. "When we get home, I'll call Marcus with the arrangements," he said.

"Sasha picked Grayson's Palace."

"She has amazing taste." I loved when he smiled. I just stared at him with his pearly white teeth.

"What?"

"I want to suck you off while you're driving," I said as he turned to me with shocked eyes.

"Nasty girl," he said. Well, that wasn't a no. I reached over and unbuckled his seatbelt and his pants before his manhood burst through his boxers, almost taking my eye out in the process. He rolled the windows up as my mouth wrapped around him. My mouth watered instantly around him. He was a chocolate peppermint. He had slowed down once we reached the highway. I went to work on him in his car. I felt frisky and couldn't wait to get home to have a piece of him.

"Shit." His moaning made me get more into it. I tried to make him come before we got home. I felt like I was on a race against the clock. I won, and I was just wiping him from my mouth as he pulled into the garage. Mrs. Phoebe's car was still here, and I wondered if something had happened. We took a moment to get ourselves together before going inside. Mrs. Phoebe had the house smelling good.

"Food's in the oven, kids. Good night." We smiled as she headed out. She was gone before I could even open my mouth to say anything. Well, I was glad I didn't have a chance to say anything. I didn't want to be talking with dick on my breath.

We washed our hands and sat to have dinner together. When we were done, I cleaned the kitchen so Mrs. Phoebe wouldn't come here in the morning to a dirty kitchen. Hunter went into his office and called Marcus about the travel arrangements. He was still in the office when I headed upstairs. He came in just in time to catch me undressing. He came through the door as his clothes were falling off him. It was like he snapped his fingers, and his clothes disappeared. I laughed as he tripped over his slacks at his ankles. I found that to be the funniest thing as he crawled over to me, pulling me down with him. Let's just say sex and carpets didn't mix.

# ZOLLAH BEST

I handled everything I needed to before two o'clock. It was Thursday, and I had to do the final arrangement for the team trip to Vegas. I wanted to make sure I got everything out of the way. I was done by three o'clock, then I headed home. I had to pack for the trip. Hunter requested to have clothes shipped, but I told him that was unnecessary. He said he'd be over later to check in on us. Damon was home when I got there. He was in the kitchen, drinking wine and making a big bowl of salad with all the fixings.

"What's up, Damon," I said as I came through the door.

"Hey, Z. You ready for Florida?" he said, looking up for a moment before he was back to tossing the salad with the wooden spoon.

"I can't wait to visit Sophia." I tossed my purse on the couch and made my way to the kitchen. "I miss her."

"Me too." Damon stopped to pour me a glass of wine. I sat and thought about Sophia for a moment. I pictured her beautiful skin and her big smile. I never thought Sophia would be the one we'd say goodbye to. I just knew it would be me. Funny how things could transpire.

"You think we could hit the strip when we get there. I know it isn't safe to be hanging out, especially with you know who roaming around."

"Well, I have you to protect me, and Hunter is sending Julius as security."

"I know; he told me." I looked up at him, wondering when they had time to talk. "He's scared."

"I know he's scared that something will happen to me."

"No," Damon said as he took a sip then placed the glass down on the island. "He's scared of what he might do if something happened to you. Two different things." I sat back with my glass in my hand. I'd seen Hunter angry before, just once that summer. I never thought about what Hunter would do if he found HIM or if HE came for me. Hunter would try to protect me. I swallowed the thought of something happening to him.

"I think it should be okay. As long as we're back before your premiere," I said.

# THE LOVE I CRAVE

"I'm the life of the party," he said.

"You are until I walk through the door," I said, sipping my wine. I had always been the life of the party, Sophia and I. Sasha was more reserved and would get crazy if she had tequila. I used to love it when she got wild.

"How was work?" he asked.

"Busy, but hey, it's work." I watched Damon, and he was feeling good. He was smiling and had the music on low in the background. Hmm, maybe it was the premiere, or did he get laid? This was his first big premiere back home.

"And how are things with you and Wealthy Kid Grayson.?" he asked like the big brother he was.

"Don't call him that."

"Why not? That's what he is, and he seems to have no problem with me calling him that."

"Exactly how often do the two of you talk?" I asked. He said nothing; he just sipped his wine then changed the subject.

"Sasha should be home. Then we can eat, get drunk, and pack." His words weren't all the way out when Sasha came through the door. I turned toward the door.

Sasha came in looking like a sun shining day in a yellow halter dress and some white Jimmy Choos. She set her things next to mine on the couch and came over to the kitchen. Sasha looked hot, and I wasn't the only one staring.

Henson Dreamier

"Trick, you look cute. Who are you looking hot for?" I asked as we gave a quick hug as if we hadn't seen each other in weeks.

"Florida and my damn self. It's been a long time," Sasha said, sitting next to me. Damon passed her a glass of wine. Every time I looked up at Sasha, I saw the light that surrounded her. She had been my savior. I kept all the abuse and drugs a secret for as long as I could, but Sophia and Sasha didn't know how bad it was and how deep I was in until it was too late.

"Since I'm saving money on my flight and hotel, I decided to do a little shopping." She took a sip from her glass. "So we got security coming with us this time," she said as I rolled my eyes.

I wouldn't put it past if Hunter had called her and gave her an earful of how important security was. Just as I was about to say something, a song came on the sound system. I looked around to see where it was coming from. The same song played the first night Hunter and I met at the club. I walked over to the couch, and the sound came from my purse. I pulled out my phone and answered it.

"You're sneaky. When did you have time to make yourself a ringtone?" I asked.

"Each time I fuck you into a coma." The sound of his seductive voice gave me chills. I rolled my eyes because that wasn't a lie, and I wasn't sure if it was a good thing or a bad thing.

"What do you want, Mr. Grayson?" I said playfully.

"I was calling to tell you I'm running late. I'll have to meet you at the airport. There's a storm passing over Texas into Louisiana, so you'll have to board early. Are you packed?" he asked.

"Yes," I lied. I had taken something out, but I put them in my carry-on.

"Good. Julius will be there at six thirty for pick up. No later," he said.

"Okay. I'll be ready."

I hung up and turned to Damon and Sasha. I wanted to get back to what I was saying before my phone rang, but I didn't have time for that. I told them Julius was on his way, and we all separated to rush and pack. We didn't have time to eat our salads. So, we drank all the wine.

Julius knocked on the door at 6:29. I could see Hunter must have had that talk with Julius about being punctual. When I opened the door, I didn't even recognize Julius. Usually, he was dressed in a black suit. Now, he stood before me in black Polo jeans and a white Polo shirt. He had a fresh haircut and was groomed nicely.

"Mrs. Grayson," he said as I let him in.

"Julius, you can call me Hope or Zollah; either one is good," I said. Damon came downstairs with his and Sasha carry-ons. Julius walked over and helped him.

"I got it. You can grab Z's next to the door," Damon said as they carried the luggage to the car.

Sasha went through the house, unplugging things. Julius was the first one back inside.

"Anything else, Hope?" Julius asked.

"Nope, that's it." I smiled. "You chose to call me Hope," I said.

"Well, I realize that everyone calls you Hope, and Hunter is the only one who calls you Zollah. So, I didn't want to call you what he calls you. Just out of respect," he said.

"It's cool," I said as Sasha walked over. "Julius, this is Sasha my best friend, and that's Damon out there. He's my other best friend." His eyes lifted to look at Sasha. He stared at her for a moment; he sure liked what he saw.

We didn't have time to eat, so we packed up the salads in four containers. Julius left as Sasha and I locked up. She waited for me as I turned and noticed what she was looking at.

"Look at this here," Sasha said.

"I told him not to do this," I said. There was a limo waiting for us.

"Hey." I felt Sasha's arms around me. "Stop thinking so much. It's just a limo. Luckily, he didn't send the helicopter," she said.

"Oh God, no," I said.

"He wants to spoil you. Let him." She grabbed my hand and led us to the limo. Julius stood at the door waiting for us to get in, then he was the last to get inside. I noticed he was a little more at ease. He was still in protective mode. I could see two guns under his jacket, one on each side. The limo pulled out, and we were on our way to the airport. Ten minutes into the ride, Julius opened the small refrigerator and pulled out a bottle of my favorite champagne.

"Yes. Thank you, Julius. I totally forgot," I said as he opened the bottle, and I grabbed three glasses.

"Remember I told you about the cherry bloom champagne. This is it," I said to Sasha. "It's so delicious."

"I'll be the judge of that," Damon said as Julius poured our glasses.

"None for you?" I asked Julius.

"No, I'm on duty. Maybe I'll have one on the plane," he said with a smile as I saw him eyeing Sasha.

"Let us make a toast," Sasha said.

"Here's to the coolest Spanish fly we've ever met in our life. She kept it real and told you nothing but the truth. To a girl who looked so mean but deep down, she was funny, smart, and had the most beautiful blue eyes. She wasn't just our best friend, she was our sister. She was your ride or die bitch. To Sophia Patrilli," Sasha said as we toasted. We all sipped from our glasses.

"Wow, Z, this is good," Damon said.

"Good? This is marvelous," Sasha said, handing Julius her glass. "Can I have another please and fill it up to the rim this time? Thank you." She smiled at him.

"No problem. I'll pour all your troubles." He poured her another glass. He couldn't keep his eyes off her.

By the time we got to the airport, we had finished the whole bottle of cherry bloom. We were laughing and giggling when the door opened, and the driver let us out. I felt nice and ready to party. But no, I was about to fly across to the other side of the country. There were four bottles left, so I told everyone to grab one. The driver opened the truck to the limo and grabbed our luggage, and Julius helped him. They took the luggage on board. I didn't even bother to look up. I figured Hunter was letting us use his plane. Something had told me to look up. I noticed the plane was a little different. Asher's plane read Asher's Best. Hunter's read Hunter's Best with the logo of Grayson Industries.

This one was different. The colors and the lettering were different. Under the windows read Zollah's Best. On the lower part of the front where the pilot sat, it read Hope's

Publishing. I immediately stopped in my tracks. I was taken aback. I saw Hunter stick his head out of the plane.

"You like it, Mrs. Grayson?"

"Hunter, what have you been up to?" I said, putting my head down. I saw Sasha looking at me. She told me again not to go there. "Yes, Hunter, I love it," I said as I made my way up the steps of the plane. To my plane. How many women could say their man bought them a plane?

"Come, we have a schedule to keep." I wanted to admire my plane, and I was nervous. I lowered my head to go inside my plane, and it was lovely. Everything inside was yellow and white.

I had ten comfortable chairs with small TVs on the back of the chairs. On the right side, I had a table that we could sit and do work. Hunter gave us the tour. I had a bedroom like his did, and when I saw it, a chill came over me. Hunter sensed it and smiled. I had a nice-size bathroom.

Marcus came over the intercom to say that we had ten minutes before takeoff. We all took our seats, Sasha and I in the front, Damon and Julius behind us. Hunter stood in front of us and told us the plans.

"You should arrive in Fort Lauderdale about one a.m., two at the latest. That's still early enough for you to hit the strip if you want. The hotel has all your arrangements ready. Just give them your name. You'll be staying in the presidential suite. It has three bedrooms. I guess Sasha and

Zollah will share a room and let the men have their own." He gave a little smirk.

"The charity function is tomorrow at two p.m. You'll have enough time to go to the gravesite. The premiere starts at nine p.m. on Saturday, so you have to be in this plane no later than one thirty p.m. Did you all bring clothes for the premiere?" he asked.

"No, we plan on going shopping there," I said.

"Cool, so the limo will be here when you get back to take you to the premiere," he said.

"Thank you, Hunter," Damon said, holding his hand out for a handshake.

"No problem." He shook his hand. He turned his attention back to me. He went into his pocket and pulled out something. He handed me a black American Express card.

"Hunter, I'm okay," I said.

"Take the card," he demanded.

"No, I don't need it," I said. He gave me a stern look. I gave him one back.

"Thank you, I'll take it," Sasha said as she took the card and put it in my purse.

"Thank you, Sasha," he said as he gave me one last look before he walked away to the door.

# THE LOVE I CRAVE

"I'm about to leave you guys. I put extra bottles of champagne in the fridge, along with something stronger," he said. I got up from my seat and followed him out. He turned to me and stared me in my eyes.

"You be careful, Zollah, please." He moved in closer to me. I could feel his breath on my neck. "If you're not on this plane by one thirty Saturday, I'll be on my way to Florida on the first thing smoking to raise hell in Florida if anything happened to you. Do you understand me?"

"Yes, sir. I have Julius here to protect me." I smiled, letting him know that he didn't have to worry. I leaned in and kissed him. His lips were soft and sweet, making me miss him already.

"I love you," I said when he pulled back the kiss.

"I love you more," he said as he walked slowly down the stairs. Once he was off, I pushed the button for the stairs to come up. Marcus came over the intercom, telling us it was time for takeoff.

I sat in my seat and buckled my seatbelt. The plane backed out of the terminal, and just like that, it took off down the runway. The speed got my anxiety going every time. My heart sank in my chest but loved the thrill. I couldn't wait to land in Florida. Even though I hate what happened to me there, it was my home for years. I wanted to hit the Miami strip. It had been way to long. A half hour into our flight,

Marcus came over the intercom to tell us it was good to move around the cabin.

I got up from my seat, turned, and noticed that Julius had gotten up as well. He asked me if I needed help with anything. I shook my head no, and he sat back down. I pulled out the salads and passed them around. Sasha grabbed two bottles from the fridge and four glasses.

"I'll have that glass now," Julius said as Sasha handed him a glass. He took a sip of the cherry bloom. "Wow, Hope, that's amazing. No one will tell if I have more than one," he asked. We smiled.

"No," we all said at the same time. We all sat and had our salad and glasses of champagne. After we finished eating, I realized that I had to look up some emails. I looked around and noticed I left my laptop.

"Shit, I left my laptop," I said.

"Don't worry about that. Hunter installed three laptops inside." Julius came over to my seat. His hand went toward a hidden compartment on the side. He pulled out a laptop.

"How thoughtful of him," I said as Julius still knelt on my side.

"That he is." He looked up at me. "He's a good man and has been a wonderful friend. I've never experienced or seen love like you two have before, and I want it." He stopped for a moment. "Sorry if I'm talking or saying too much, but I like you for him. I can tell that you love him the same as he loves you," he said as he broke eye contact. He turned and saw Sasha listening to our conversation.

"Thank you," I said.

"Anytime. Now I'm off the clock until we land. Do y'all want to watch a movie? Hunter loaded I think every movie that has ever came out on this thing," he said as he went over to the wall next to the cockpit.

"What y'all want to watch?" I asked.

"Something funny," Damon said.

"The new Will Ferrell movie I heard is funny," Julius said.

"Anything he does is funny," Sasha said. Julius put on the movie, and we turned off our overhead lighting. I sat alone while I did some work and watched the movie. Julius sat next to Sasha, and Damon sat on the other row of seats.

We got our laugh on. That Will Ferrell was a trip. We had three hours left and of course, Sasha wanted to spice it up with some Truth or Dare. I hadn't played that in years. Now I didn't care about spilling my shit, but Julius was here. I knew there would be no questions about HIM, but Julius had no idea. Maybe Hunter told him about it, or maybe not.

"Sounds like fun," Julius said.

"Okay," I said as we refilled our glasses.

"I'm going first, and I want to ask Julius."

"Okay," I said as if I were going to have a problem with that. This game was going to get interesting.

"Truth or dare," she asked Julius.

"Truth," he said. She made a face as if she were disappointed. Did she want him to pick dare?

"Okay, is it true that when you were younger, you had an affair with a married woman?" she asked him, and I gasped. Why in the hell would she ask him that? I had to realize she was the queen of gossip. The look on his face was priceless. Damon and I looked at him.

"Where do you find your information?" he asked.

"I do my homework and to think, it only took me five minutes," she said.

He was quiet for a second then said, "Yes, it's true." I was shocked. "I was young and dumb, and I didn't know she was married until I had already fallen for her. I've learned from my mistakes," he said, smiling.

"So, are…" Sasha was cut off by Julius.

"Only one question. It's my turn. My question is for you. Truth or dare?" he asked.

"You're single and ready to mingle. Is it true that the last relationship you were in was over a year ago." he asked. The look on her face was priceless. It was quite funny.

"I see I'm not the only one who has been doing his homework," she said as she looked at me. What the hell did she want me to say?

"Yes, it's true," she said as their eyes connected for a moment.

"So, you..." Julius was saying when Sasha cut him off.

"Only one question," she said as they both smiled. For a moment, I felt they needed to be left alone. That Damon and I should leave the room.

"I want to ask Damon. Truth or dare?" I asked him. Of course, he picked truth. "Is it true that you slept with Tracy Duncan, one of your clients?" I said. This was something I'd been wanting to know for a long time. Well, I knew I just wanted him to say it.

"You're a painter?" Julius asked.

"Yes," Damon said as he looked at me.

"I would love to see some of your work," Julius said.

"You have. Hunter has them all over his office, his house, and his apartment in New York, and he doesn't even know." I laughed.

"He doesn't?" Damon asked, surprised.

"Yes, but that's not the question," I said.

"How did you know that?" he asked.

"Remember we were supposed to meet up at Louie's that night? You were running late and so was I. I stopped by to see if you had left already. I saw your car and used my key to enter. You'd finished her painting. I guess she was paying you off," I said as we laughed.

"OMG, juicy stuff," Sasha said, sipping her champagne.

"So, I just left and went to Louie's."

"You didn't say anything when I got there," Damon said.

"I figured you didn't want us to know. So, I didn't say anything," I said. We all were quiet for a moment.

"Well, I slept with Tracy. One of the best experiences in my life," Damon admitted.

"Was she?" I asked.

"Yes, she was older and had a lot of experience," Damon said.

We played a few more rounds of Truth or Dare. It just turned out to be a questionnaire between Julius and Sasha. So, Damon and I just quit. Then we decided to play I've Never. Julius didn't know how to play, so we taught him.

"You have to say something about yourself. We have to decide if it's a lie or not. Like I'll say I've never been to a therapist before, and if you say it's true, then you would have to take a shot because its false. If you had said false, then I would've taken the shot. We usually do it with tequila, but champagne will do," I said.

"Hunter said he put two bottles of the strong stuff," Sasha said. She raided the cabinet. Sasha pulled out a bottle of Patron. Julius sat next to Sasha with the biggest smile on his face. He was really feeling her.

"This sounds very interesting," Julius said as he pulled out four shot glasses.

"I'm going first." This was hard. They knew everything about me. What could I make up that was believable?

"I've never had sex in a car before," I said. Everyone was quiet at first. Their eyes went from left to right, looking at each other, trying to figure it out.

"False," Damon yelled out. I was shocked. I thought after all these years he would know. Sasha thought long and hard. Sasha and Julius agreed with Damon.

"Nope, I never did," I said.

"What?" Damon asked, shocked. "You never?" He looked at me sideways as if I were telling a lie.

"Take your shot first," Sasha said. "It's the rule." He grabbed his shot and down it quick.

"Well, I thought you would have been experienced something as minor as having sex in a car," Damon said.

"Well, I'm quite sure Hunter will help you with that. The way y'all been going at it like two horny teenagers who just can't help themselves," Julius said. I couldn't do anything but smile because it was the truth. I was just surprised at Julius saying more than three sentences.

"Okay, who's going next?" Sasha asked.

We played that game for the next hour before the plane shook. We must have hit turbulence over New Orleans or something. Marcus came over the speakers to tell us to put on our seatbelts. We were running into a storm. We suffered through another thirty minutes of turbulence before we could unbuckle our seatbelts. I was exhausted, so I took a nap, especially if we were going to hit the strip in Florida. Julius put on another movie. Twenty minutes into it, I was asleep.

I woke up to the sound of Marcus over the intercom, telling us that we were about to land. I woke up nice and refreshed. I was ready to go on the streets of Miami. Once we stepped foot off the plane, Julius was back in protection mode.

"All right, I'm back on the clock," he said with a smile. I'd seen another side of Julius. It was nice. He was a nice guy.

# FLORIDA

W e made a pit stop to the restrooms to freshen up. I fixed my makeup and my clothes. I had on blue high-waisted jeans and a white blouse with blue leopard-print Jimmy Choo shoes. I let my hair down from my ponytail. It was dark, but I still put my Marc Jacob sunshades on. Yes, I wore my sunglasses at night.

When we stepped foot out of the airport, there was a black Excursion waiting for us. Just like Hunter Grayson to go big. Julius and Damon put our bags in the trunk. Julius hopped in the front seat behind the wheel, and we all hopped in the back. We headed straight over the bridge toward the strip. The Miami strip was lit up. The first place we went to was Fat Tuesday's. Julius drove around for ten minutes looking for a parking spot. We pulled into a spot just as someone pulled out and we walked two blocks.

"Slushies." Sasha smiled. The strip was lit, and everyone was out as if it were midday. People were everywhere dressed in mini dresses. Oh, how I missed this place. We passed fancy cars having a show across the street. Julius walked next to me, looking all around. He was on duty.

"How are you doing, sexy?" a guy said as we walked by to get inside. I smiled and kept it moving. Julius gave him a look, and the guy walked as if his ass was on fire. I slowed down so I could be next to Julius.

"I hope you don't have the same effect on women. If you do, we have a problem. How can I ever find you a lady if that's your M.O.?"

"Are you looking for someone for me? If you are, my biological clock is ticking." He smiled as we both smiled at one another. "What about your girl Sasha? She seems like my type." He turned to look at his environment as we walked into the club. He checked out everyone's faces as Sasha went to find us a table.

"And what type is that?" I asked him to bring his attention back to me.

"Someone beautiful and successful but mysterious. That's Sasha."

"Is it really? Well, I don't think you're ready for her," I said.

# THE LOVE I CRAVE

"I don't think Miss Sasha is ready for me, and I'm not just talking sexually," he said. We walked toward the back of the club to our favorite spot where we used to sit. I looked around at the place to find nothing had changed. I checked behind the bar and saw the same bartender.

"Okay, ladies, what poison are we choosing to indulge?" Damon asked.

"You don't remember?" Sasha asked.

"Oh, I remember. I just thought we were having something different. Strawberry melon for you." He pointed to Sasha. "Call a Cab for you." Damon headed over to the bar.

Kim, the bartender, didn't notice him at first. When she did, her eyes lit up. She used to have a thing for Damon. I took my eyes away from them and focused on the scenery. It wasn't as crowded as I remembered it being. People sat around drinking and laughing. We enjoyed each other until we were walking sideways.

After leaving Fat Tuesday's, we walked to the hotel. The Grayson's Palace sign was lit up. As I checked us in, the bellhop grabbed our bags from the trunk. The lobby was filled with black-leather furniture with huge TVs on the wall. The place screamed elegance. It had Hunter written all over it. I walked up to the counter.

"Hello, I'm here to check in," I said to the older lady behind the desk. The lady looked up at me.

"Yes, how can I help you?" She gave me a look as if I didn't belong. I was on the verge of saying something, but Sasha cut in.

"Yes, Zollah Hope," she said. The lady's facial expression changed. She looked between the both of us, not knowing which one of us was Zollah. Her eyes locked on mine; I must have had the look on my face.

"Mrs. Grayson, I'm so sorry." She stared at me for a moment, taking me in. I guess she had waited all night to see how I looked. I was quite sure I didn't look like they imagined. Who was the scarred beauty on the arm of Hunter Grayson? Gina shook her head clear and apologized again. She typed in a few things on the computer before heading toward the back wall to retrieve a key from a lockbox.

"You're going to take the last elevator down the hall. That will take you straight to the penthouse suite," she said to us, pointing down the hall.

"Thank you, Gina," I said.

"You're welcome. It's a pleasure to meet you, Mrs. Grayson," Gina said. The name Mrs. Grayson was one I could sure get used to.

"You can call me Hope," I told her before heading toward the elevator.

I was quiet on the way up. A lot was crossing my mind right now, like how much my life had and would change forever. My life was moving fast, and it wasn't long ago I was dancing with Hunter on the dance floor. Now I practically lived with him. He had bought me my own private plane. I didn't know what to do, but just take one thing at a time. The doors opened to the elevator, right into Hunter's private suite.

"My goodness. This place is amazing," Sasha said.

"Better than anything I've ever stayed at in my entire life," Damon said, looking around at the place. It was spacious with huge, white-leather furniture. The dining room had a huge table where we would have breakfast. The living room fireplace was lit with a fifty-inch television above it.

"There's three bedrooms, two on this side of the room, and one on the other side. That one…" Julius pointed to the single room, "has the king-size bed with a bathroom in it.

"Sasha and I will take the big room. You and Damon can have your own rooms. I'm tired, so I'll see you all in a few hours," I said as I headed straight for the room. After I grabbed my luggage, I headed to the room, took out my pajamas, then hopped in the shower. Once I was done, Sasha got in. I lay down in the bed and pulled out my phone. It was almost four in the morning here, so it's almost one back home in California. I wasn't sure if he was asleep or not, but I had to call.

"Shouldn't you be asleep, baby girl?" Hunter's voice came through the line. It made me feel so good.

"I should, but I couldn't go to sleep before hearing your voice."

"You miss me. I miss you."

"I miss you so much, Mr. Grayson."

"I'm happy to know you're okay. You need to get some rest before your charity event. I have some work I have to finish before I hit the sheets," he said.

"Hmm, hit the sheets. That sounds good."

"Oh no, you don't. Don't get me all horny with you a thousand miles away," he said.

"Sorry, I can't help it."

"Good night, baby girl. I'll see you on Saturday night."

"Good night," I said before hanging up. I was asleep before Sasha got out of the shower.

I woke up to my alarm going off. I turned to get my phone. The time said 11:32am. Oh my God, I was tired. I hit the snooze button, meaning in five minutes, it would go off again. I closed my eyes and tried to go back to sleep when I heard laughter. I opened my eyes and turned around. I saw Sasha smiling.

"What's so funny?" I asked.

"You're still the same. Hitting the snooze button three times, then turning it off. When you could just set it for the exact time," she said.

"I'm happy I amuse you." I smiled then inhaled. My eyes widened to the smell of hot cakes and maple syrup. "You smell that?"

"No," she said, sitting up on the bed, sniffing the air.

"I smell breakfast and coffee." I got out of bed and went to the bathroom to brush my teeth and wash my face. When I opened the door, the smell hit me. My stomach growled. Who the hell was cooking breakfast? I knew it wasn't Damon. I thought for a quick moment that it was Julius until I saw a tall, white man with a chef uniform on. I stood still and leaned to my side as Sasha came up beside me.

"There's a fine man in the kitchen cooking breakfast."

"I can see that." Sasha smiled as she walked past the living room into the kitchen. "Good morning." She sat herself down at the island. "It smells wonderful in here."

"Good morning, ladies," he said as he finished whipping up something in a bowl. He set the bowl down and fixed us two glasses of orange juice. "Mimosas." He handed us two glasses.

"Thank you. I would say no but what the hell," I said.

"I'll have one as well," Damon said as he walked in wearing his pajamas. We all grabbed our glasses and had a seat on the couch while we waited for the food to be ready.

"What time is your charity banquet?" Damon asked.

"At two," I said.

"And from there we're going to the cemetery?" Damon asked.

"Yes." We sat talking when the other door opened, and Julius came out. Oh my, he was looking fine in a wife beater and sweatpants. I wasn't the only one who was looking. Sasha melted in her seat.

"Good morning, everyone." Julius turned to the chef. "Morning, Colie," he said.

"Good morning, JuJu. I didn't know you were here," he said as he finished fixing breakfast. Sasha and I looked at each other.

"JuJu," we said.

"Hey, don't call me that." Julius looked at us.

"Sorry, but that's what I heard," Sasha said.

"And he's the only one who can call me that. He's been doing it since he could talk," Julius said. When he said that, it made me think how old Julius really was.

"Colie, that's your name?" I asked.

# THE LOVE I CRAVE

"Yes, I'm sorry. My name is Colie Smith, and I'm the head chef here at Grayson's Palace," he said. Damon went over and held a conversation with Colie while Sasha questioned Julius.

"Looks like you've been up for a while?" Sasha asked Julius.

"I have been. I hit the gym this morning," he answered.

"After going to bed at four. You have good stability," I said.

"You work out even when you don't have to," Sasha said as she admired his body.

"Well, I have to let out some stress," he said. She was about to say something when Colie said that breakfast was ready. We all sat at the table as Colie laid it out buffet style.

"So, JuJu, how have you been?" Colie asked.

"I've been good, no complaints," Julius answered.

"That's good. Are you still looking for Mrs. Right?' he asked. Julius' eyes went to Sasha.

"Yes, I am, but I'm taking it one day at a time," he said as we said grace.

We ate, and it was delicious. I had a little bit of everything. I was stuffed but had to put my game face on. I was happy I was only making an appearance. I didn't have to stay for the banquet. I was going to show my face, make a speech, and then we were out. I wanted to get to the cemetery at a reasonable time. I was dressed and ready to go. Of course, Julius was waiting for Sasha and me.

It didn't take us long to get to the banquet hall at the Hillson Hotel. It was a little after one p.m. when we arrived. My charity name was Sophia's Angels Foundation. It was for young children who were being abused or molested by their parents or parents' friends and had nowhere to go. The organization helped any child in any kind of situation. We went right on in and headed straight to the table they had for me and my guest. Opening ceremony started with new clients who gave donations to the charity. The CEO of the charity handed everything over to me. After everything I had been through, I never finished the speech.

I placed the paper down on the podium and looked out at the crowd. I was nervous at first until I looked over at Sasha and Damon, who had been with me through it all. I just started with what I knew, and that's what I did.

"Thank you all for coming today. My name is Zollah Hope, and I'm the founder of Sophia's Angels Foundation. I started this charity three years ago. I grew up here in California. My parents were disowned by my grandparents, and they ran away from Vancouver to California. My parents were very young when they had me, but they loved me unconditionally.

"I started the Sophia's Angels Foundation for abused and abandoned children because I was once a child in foster care.

# THE LOVE I CRAVE

I met two of my best friends there who inspired me to start this. We have been through a lot together. Growing up for us was different, but we've all been through similar things.

"The Spanish fly Sophia. That's what we called her. Sophia A. Patrilli had a lovely family until her mother died of cancer. Her mother had been hiding it for years. Sophia's father took it hard when his wife died. He drank himself into oblivion every day. He didn't recognize his friends and co-workers creeping upstairs to molest and rape his daughter. Sophia loved her father, but she loved herself even more. So, she decided to leave home. She lived on the street for a while before she ended up in foster care."

"Then there's me. My parents died in a bad car accident when I was twelve years old. My sister, brother, and I entered foster care, and we were later separated. Not only did I lose my parents, I lost my sister and brother too. I was lost, but I had Sasha, Sophia, and Damon in my life." I stopped to think back to those times.

"This charity, this organization is for all the children out here. You can overcome any struggle you have in life. Never let this world we live in eat you up and spit you out. Be strong and go after what you believe in. Today is Sophia's birthday so I'll be leaving here and going to visit her. She would've been twenty-seven today." I smiled at everyone out there. My life had evolved into something amazing.

"I want to thank each one of you for coming today. In the past three years, we have helped save thousands of children, and it's all thanks to you all. I want to let you know that I will be opening another location in Detroit, Michigan. There are a lot of children there who need help. I want to thank you all again for coming out." Everyone stood to give a standing ovation. It took about twenty minutes to make my rounds to the very important people. Then I was out in the truck, on my way to the cemetery.

We stopped by the candy store and got her favorite candy—Skittles and Jolly Ranchers. At the cemetery, we found her in no time. She was laid to rest next to a woman named Nancy Buttercup. I would never forget that name. Her tombstone read, An Angel Gone Too Soon. Sophia Angel Patrilli born March 2nd, 1984. Home March 2nd, 2007. Julius stood over to the side while Damon laid out a little blanket. We three sat and popped open the candy. We went straight into good times with Sophia.

We had a ball going down memory lane. Damon was there a lot with us. Wherever we went, he seemed to follow. Even when we moved to Florida, Damon got accepted to a school there. We talked about her for a couple of hours. When a man walked up, my heart skipped a beat for a second. I couldn't recognize the man. Julius stepped in front of him before he got too close.

"Excuse me, sir, this is a private party."

"I've seen him somewhere before," Sasha said as she leaned into me. Damon stood up to help Julius as if he would need it. The man's eyes were full of tears.

# THE LOVE I CRAVE

"I'm sorry to disturb you, but my name is Monroe Patrilli. I'm Sophia's father." My eyes widened at the man standing before me. "I've been coming here every year on her birthday since I found out. Sorry we haven't met sooner." He paused for a second as he gazed around at us. "I can come back later if you like."

"Julius, it's okay. Let him pass. Mr. Patrilli?" I said, getting up from the blanket.

"I didn't know she had such amazing friends. I mean I knew she had someone who loved her. To give her this amazing barrel and tombstone. Thank you," he said.

"You're welcome." I moved in closer. "My name is Zollah, but everyone calls me Hope. This is Sasha, and this is Damon. We were her best friends. Sasha and I met Sophia in foster care in California," I said.

"Then y'all moved to Florida?" he asked because he had no idea what his daughter's life consisted of once she left home.

"Yes. We all did. How did you find her?" I asked.

"Well, after I sobered up, I realized she had run away. I lost her twice, the day she ran and the day she died. About five years ago, I hired a private investigator to find her. It took him a month after she had died. I was devastated," he said, and we all were quiet for a while. "I've been coming to see her ever since," he said.

We made space for him on the blanket as we told him stories about Sophia. We had lightened up his day. He said he had learned so much about his own daughter. When it was time for us to leave, Mr. Patrilli looked like he wanted to say something more before he left.

"I was wondering…" He looked at all of us. "Never mind," he said.

"What is it?" I asked as he looked at all of us there, but his eyes were focused on me.

"I wanted to know if it was possible to get her moved to California. I was looking into it myself, but it's a lot of money. I can pay almost half, but I can't…" I cut him off.

"Don't worry, Mr. Patrilli. I'll pay for everything. I'll call you with further information. Leave your number with Julius," I said. This was something I had been thinking about off and on for a while.

"It's a wonderful decision. I should have thought of it first. I'll pay for it," Sasha said.

Damon added that he would help also. Mr. Monroe had given his number to Julius, and we hopped back into the truck, headed back to the hotel. We had stayed up kind of late. It wasn't that late, but I was tired as hell. When we got back to the room, I climbed in bed and went straight to sleep. I woke up to something falling on the floor. I jumped up and out of bed. Sasha was right behind me.

324

"What the hell was that?" she asked. I quickly looked at the clock, and it was ten o'clock in the morning.

"I don't know," I answered as we opened the bedroom door. We slowly walked up the hallway. I could hear noise coming from the living room. A lady was talking to someone. Sasha and I stepped out into the living room, and the whole place was turned into a damn clothing store.

"What the hell?" I said as I saw Julius come from behind the rack of clothes.

"Don't freak out," he said. I must have had it written all over my face.

"Hunter figured you wouldn't make it out for shopping. So, he had a designer send over some clothes to the hotel. The stylist is here to help. He said pick something and make your way to the damn airport." Julius tried to say it how Hunter would, and I laughed.

There were designer dresses hanging everywhere. There was a small section of tuxes. But every kind of ballgown was in the living room.

"My name is Phynix, and I'm the designer Mr. Grayson sent over." Before we got started, Julius came back over with a message that our flight at one thirty was pushed back to four. He said something about the weather. "We have two hours to pick out something. So, let's get started," she said, and Sasha and I went on the hunt like Red October. We had one side while the men took up the other. Of course, they didn't need as much space as we did.

I looked on every rack and the first thing I saw was this white dress. It took my breath away. It was the perfect dress, but it wasn't for right now. I eventually found a black spaghetti-strap dress. It clung to every curve I owned. It was the one. I pulled that from the rack and tried it on. It was perfect. Hunter knew my size. Sasha found a navy-blue strapless dress that fit her just right.

As Phynix waited for Sasha and me to dress, I couldn't seem to keep my eyes off that one-strap white dress. It was calling for me. It flowed to the ground. It was a beachfront dress, and I loved it. I walked back over to it. I touched it and admired it. When I saw that dress, I thought of my day. The dress I would wear on a beach, confessing how much I loved the man in my life.

"You love that dress, don't you?" Sasha came up behind me and asked. I smiled because I did love it, and I wanted it.

"It's beautiful," I said as I looked at the price tag; it made my mouth dry.

"Why don't you get it?" she asked.

"It's a little past my price range. I don't have that type of money to just buy a twenty-thousand-dollar dress," I said. I felt guilty for even loving it the way I did. I never wanted a piece of fabric as much in my life.

# THE LOVE I CRAVE

"First of all, you need to start treating yourself and stop cheating yourself. Besides, Hunter will be paying for it," she said, waving his card in front of my face.

"I don't want him to think I'm just using him." I snatched the card from her. How did she even get it out of my purse?

"He would never think that. He knows you're not that girl. It's your size by the way, you should get it," Sasha said, pulling it from the rack. I wanted to try it on.

"I can't. Let's go. We have a plane to catch," I said as I grabbed all my things for us to leave. We needed to get back in time for Damon's premiere. It was four o'clock when we boarded. I was heading back to California where my heart was. As soon as I sat, my phone rang. I smiled and knew it was Hunter.

"Hello, Mr. Grayson," I answered with a smile.

"Hmm, you knew better not to miss this flight. You saved the people of Florida the wrath of Javier," he said.

"He sounds dangerous. Would I ever meet him?" I asked.

"I hope you never get the chance. I missed you so much. Have a nice flight, and I'll be at the airport waiting for you, baby girl," he said, skipping the subject.

"Hunter."

"Zollah," he said my name without saying anything.

"Hunter, tell me who Javier is. I want to know."

327

"No."

"This is my plane, right? It moves when I say it moves," I said.

He gave me a sarcastic laugh before saying, "Stop playing, girl." He was quiet for a moment. I tried to figure out what he was thinking. I knew he was finding a way to punish me.

"Zollah Piper Hope Grayson, do not play with me. If that plane is not in the air in five minutes, you don't want to know what I'm going to do to you. You haven't seen anything yet. I'll tie you up and eat you alive. Make you squirt until you can't no more. Make you suffer and wait for that electric orgasm you'll be screaming for. Have you screaming LABA all night long because you wouldn't be able to handle it. Now you have three minutes to get that plane in the air. Or I'll be there in three hours, and you don't want that." He hung up the phone on me, and I sat there flabbergasted.

"Are you okay?" Sasha asked as she stood in front of me while I sat. I looked up at her, and she sat next to me.

"It's nothing," I said. She turned to me, taking a moment before she said anything.

"They're two different people, Zollah. We all have an alter ego in us." I didn't think HE had an alter ego. Twenty-four hours a day, he was crazy. Well, he did have his moments when he was the sweetest guy. The things Hunter said to me were the same things that HE would say to me with maybe a little more bitches in it.

"How did you know I was thinking that?" I asked.

"I know you, and I heard the conversation. Hope, he's not HIM, not by a long shot. Hunter really means well. He wants to keep you safe. There's no harm in blaming that," she said, and I understood that part. I wanted to. "You're scared, and you have the right to be, but what you need to know is Hunter and HIM are two different people with many similarities." I looked up at her and smiled.

"Now, bitch, get this plane in the air before you get in trouble. Unless you're trying to get in trouble on purpose. Nasty girl."

"No, I wouldn't do no such thing." I got up and pushed the button for the stairs to go up. We all cuddled up in our seats. Julius had put a movie on before sitting. Halfway through the movie, I looked around, and I was the only one still awake. So, I closed my eyes and drifted on a memory. I woke to a ringing phone that I heard Damon answer. His voice sounded still asleep.

"Hello." I couldn't hear the other end, but whoever it was, he was surprised to hear from them. Damon was instantly alert. "Okay, sure, thank you," he said and hung up the phone.

"Who was that?" I asked.

"It's about time we get ready. We'll be landing shortly. I'll go first," Damon said as he grabbed his things and walked toward the bathroom.

Twenty minutes later, Damon came out as Julius went in. Damon wore a black tuxedo. He looked sexy in his cufflinks. Another twenty minutes later, Julius came out with a navy-blue suit. It almost matched Sasha's dress. I saw the way Sasha looked at Julius as we passed. She had wet herself.

"I saw that," I said as I got undressed in the bedroom.

"You didn't see anything, missy." Sasha talked about the color of his suit and how she thought he had done it on purpose. She admitted to how she found him attractive. She thought about pursuing whatever may come of it. Even if it was just great sex.

"I think you should go out with him. From what I can see of him, he seems like a cool guy," I said.

"I'm thinking about it."

Sasha entered the shower first. We were dressed and putting our makeup on when Marcus came over the speaker to say that we were about to land. I was excited to be able to support Damon in something so important to him. This was my first premiere, and I wanted Hunter to see me in this dress. Julius was all drooling from the mouth when I came out of the bathroom.

# THE LOVE I CRAVE

We sat and put our seatbelts on. It took us twenty-five minutes to land. The doors weren't opening fast enough for me, after pulling into the terminal at LAX. The stairs slid out, and I saw Hunter standing there. Julius, Damon, and Sasha went down first, then me. I saw Hunter standing next to that Lamborghini with the butterfly doors. The door to the driver's side was up. Hunter must have enjoyed driving himself around since Julius had been gone. He looked fine and sexy as hell in his wine-color tuxedo and bow tie. Then the door to the other side of the Lambo went up, and I saw a beautiful lady get out of the car. I stepped down the stairs and walked over to the Lambo.

"Zollah."

"Mrs. Carrie, it's a pleasure to see you again." I gave his mother a hug. I couldn't keep my eyes off Hunter. Wine was another color that looked good on him.

"You look beautiful," I said to Mrs. Carrie.

"So, do you. I like that dress," she said.

"Thank you. Let me introduce you. This is Sasha Jordan and Damon Solomon. They're my best friends."

"Mr. Damon Solomon, the man of the hour," Mrs. Carrie said. I noticed that Hunter hadn't touched me yet. Was he trying to punish me? They took the conversation over to the limo that was waiting for us. Hunter and I stood alone.

"So where are you going looking all sexy?" I asked.

"I'm going with my mother to an event tonight."

"A very formal event I see." Hunter kept his hands in his pockets. I moved in closer to him. I watched him tighten up.

"So, you're not happy to see me, Mr. Grayson?" My pointy finger ran up and down his chest. He looked down at me and smiled.

"I'm ecstatic to see you, Mrs. Grayson. I'm just thinking of your punishment. Today is the last night you sleep away from me." His eyes burned fire, and it turned me on. That made me want him even more. I grabbed for his manhood, but he was quick and blocked me.

"You have a hard head, Zollah," he said.

"Well, I'm trying to give you a hard head." He burst out laughing. I didn't think I was being funny. I tried to give him the sad puppy look, but it didn't work.

"You should go before you're late. Come on, Mother," he said loud enough for her to hear. I gave her another hug before Hunter helped her inside the car. I walked over to the limo.

"That car is so sexy," Damon said.

"Yeah, he is." I gave one last look back at Hunter as he drove off. We got inside the limo and headed to the premiere, which was held at the Ford Center. The whole ride there, I kept thinking about what Hunter would do to me.

# THE LOVE I CRAVE

It was nine thirty when we pulled up at the Ford Center. There was small line of limos, so it took us no time to get to the front. Cameras flashed here and there. I took a deep breath as the driver helped me out. I stood next to Damon on his right side, while Sasha stood on his left. We stood there for about a minute while the cameras flashed. There were reporters out with the paparazzi. Once we were done, we moved further down on the red carpet. Damon trailed off a little for a short interview. It felt amazing to be here to support my best friend. Now I was spotted by Entertainment TV.

I did a small interview. They asked me questions about my company. I turned my head toward the front, and I could have broken my neck when I saw that Lamborghini pull up. What the hell was he doing here? Everyone went crazy when Hunter got out and helped his mom from the car. My tongue was stuck in my throat. I turned back to the interview, but I couldn't focus.

"I'm sorry. What did you ask me?"

"About your magazine. I was saying how we love the black history tribute you did in February issue of Javier." An easy question. I didn't know what to do if they asked about Hunter.

"Thank you. It was something I've wanted to do for a couple of months. Happy to dedicate this issue to black history month," I said.

"Well, we loved it." I turned my head and noticed Hunter getting closer. Sasha came up behind me and rescued me from making a fool of myself. I was getting flushed just looking at Hunter.

"Do you see what I see?" she asked.

"Yes, I do. He thinks he's slick." I turned back to look for Damon, who was looking at us. He must have been telling them who he brought with him. I saw Sasha spin around me and move out the way. I felt someone creep up behind me.

"You look divine in that dress," Hunter said as I felt his sweet breath hit the back of my neck. I melted, standing right there. I hated that he had that effect on me. I was about to say something when a guy came up on us.

"Mr. Grayson, a picture please," the guy asked.

"Sure," he said, and in one motion, his hand was on mine, pulling me up on him. We both turned toward the cameraman. He took a few pictures as others crowded around. Hunter standing so close to me was doing something to me. I cut the pictures short and left him standing right there. Damon was done as we made our way inside.

# LAS VEGAS

Saturday was a hell of a night. Damon did a wonderful job at the premiere. He shined like a star. I couldn't focus half the night with Hunter stalking me. His eyes harassed me the whole night. He kept sneaking up on me and saying lustful things. He tortured me the whole time. Then he had the nerve to say he'd see me Monday after work. He said he had something for me. I knew what he had, and I wanted it. At least I thought I did.

Hunter had used his mother as an excuse to leave early. We had gotten home about three in the morning. So on Sunday, I tried not to think of Hunter. I cleaned my room and the house from top to bottom. Sasha said I was a mad woman. I sat on the couch, eating the dinner that Sasha had cooked. She was in the kitchen on the phone and her laptop. She had been on those things all damn day. She was surely up to something. Damon was gone doing God knows what. Everyone had something to do, but me. It was getting late, so I said my goodbyes and was asleep by nine.

My alarm went off at eight thirty a.m. Monday morning. I got up without hitting the snooze button. No Sasha waking me up. I wanted to get to work and get my day started and over with. I got out of the shower and knew what I wanted to wear, a black trench coat dress with my red bottoms. I only wore this dress once before. I flat ironed my hair and threw on some makeup, then my accessories, before putting on my Marc Jacobs.

"Good morning, everyone," I said with a smile on my face.

"Wow, don't you look hot," Sasha said.

"Thank you." I poured a glass of orange juice and grabbed my keys from the side table.

"I know you two are up to something. I don't know what it is, but I don't like surprises."

"Yes, you do," Damon said.

"I know I do, but..." I didn't finish before leaving.

I pulled up to the building at nine thirty as always. Rodney climbed in once I climbed out. I saw a little girl about thirteen years old walking with her mother. I smiled at her as I caught her eye. She stopped in her tracks. She whispered something in her mother's ear. I was about to open the door to the building when the little girl came up behind me. I turned around and she was holding a magazine.

"Are you Zollah Hope?" she asked.

"Yes, I am. Who's asking?" I asked as I let go of the door, and it closed. I turned to face the little girl.

"My name is Angelica, and I saw you on Entertainment TV Saturday night. I was watching it with my mom, and now you're on this cover of Loyal magazine." I looked at her as if she were speaking another language. I took the magazine from her to look at it.

"Well, I'll be damned," I said. There we were on the cover. Hunter and I at Martin's that night. To be honest and not biased, it was a great picture of us. I stared the cover in awe.

"Can you sign my copy please?" she asked.

"Of course," I said, shocked. I wasn't sure what was going on here. I was signing an autograph. "Would you like a picture as well?" I asked, not knowing why, but the little girl looked ecstatic.

"That would be great, if it's okay with you," she said, pulling out her phone.

"I'll take that for you, princess." I heard that familiar voice. I didn't need to look up to know who it was.

"OMG, you looked mighty sharp on the cover, Mr. Grayson." Angelica came in for the picture. He smiled.

"What a beautiful picture, princess," he said. I smiled as he took the picture. The little girl and her mom went on her way as Hunter opened the door for me. I stepped inside and didn't stop until I reached the elevator and pushed the button. The doors opened, and I stepped inside first, then Hunter followed. I was quiet as a mouse, but I felt his eyes burning a hole up my dress.

"So, you decided to go back to your modeling days with that little ensemble," he said.

"I must look like I just walked off the runway. You like?"

"Yes, I do. You look sexy, beautiful, and exotic." I moved in closer to him. He found himself trapped in the corner.

"Stop the elevator, I want to taste you," I begged, and he gave me a seductive smile.

"I have a meeting at ten a.m. I need to be focused."

"Hunter, stop playing with me. I suffered enough. Don't you think?" I asked.

"No, Zollah, I can't. I will tell you why later," he said as I put on a sad, puppy dog face.

"Looking at you in that dress is making me feel like I chose the wrong time to do what I did." He paused for a moment as he gazed at me. "Come here, baby girl?" he said with his arms out.

"Are you sure everything is okay?"

"I've never been better. I promise," he said as the doors opened for my floor.

"I love you."

"I love you more," he said. I got off the elevator and watched the doors close with him behind them.

My workday consisted of last-minute business for the Las Vegas trip. By noon, I had everything ready to go for Friday. Then I pulled my schedule for the next few weeks. This weekend was Vegas, and next week was back to New York. Then in two weeks, the Dominican Republic. I called Melissa in to tell her of the plans for this weekend.

"Now find me a copy of this Loyal magazine please." Melissa smiled then pulled out a copy from behind her back.

"I knew you had a copy," I said.

"I'm surprised Sasha hasn't called you yet," Melissa said.

"She's probably still reading right now," I said as I went through the pictures. There was a picture of Hunter and me in New York and a few from the premiere on Saturday. I was scared to hear what they had to say about Hunter and me. There were pictures of us kissing at Martin's and the Ford Center. I closed the book.

"What did it say?" I asked her because I knew she had already read it.

"It said that Hunter Grayson has never been out with a woman. They said he's had a few eye candies, but nothing this serious. They say only his mother and sister have been seen with him at important functions. They wanted to know what the relationship is between the two of you. Of course, they spoke about how rich he is. That you have been with him every time he's seen now. That he never smiled until now. Are you with him because of his money? They wonder where he found you. They had spoken about your career and your charities. They wondered where you came from. That's about it," she said. We conversed for a while. When she was about to leave, she asked me if it was okay if she rode on the private plane to New York. I didn't have a problem with that.

For the rest of the day, I tried not to think of Hunter, but he was infecting me. At five, Melissa and Aimee headed out. I called upstairs to his office. He wasn't there. His receptionist Stephanie answered the phone. She said that he had already left the building. He had left a message telling me to come straight home. Who was he to tell me what to do? When I got downstairs, Julius was waiting for me.

"I did drive my own car," I said.

"Hey, I just take orders. I don't give them. Now get in the car. I got you some cherry bloom in there.

"Yeah," I said as he held the door open for me to get in. I poured a glass and enjoyed the ride. It seemed like it was taking forever to get home. I felt as if I was going in slow motion.

"Hope, you stopped traffic today in that dress," Julius said.

"Thank you."

"So, what's up with your friend Sasha? I want her," he said. I figured that out already.

"Then why don't you ask her out? I'm sure she'll say yes."

"I sure will," he said as we pulled up to the house. Julius helped me out of the truck. "See you in the morning."

"Later, Julius." I used my key to open the door, which was already unlocked.

I walked in and placed my things down on the couch. The house smelled like a gourmet restaurant. Soft music played in the background. I walked into the kitchen, and Hunter was over the stove.

"You cook now?" I said.

"I can do whatever you want. I'm like Tony Toni Tone. Whatever you want, girl," he said, singing to me. Standing next to him, Hunter turned around with some sauce on a wooden spoon. He lifted it up to my mouth. The flavor exploded on my tongue.

"That tastes amazing," I said as he made our plates, and we sat.

He wore some grey sweatpants and a tank top. God, he looked good. We had a nice dinner with lovely conversation. After dinner, he cleaned the kitchen. He turned off everything, and we went upstairs. I entered his room, saw his bed, and immediately wanted him on it. I smiled just thinking of the times we had on that bed.

"Come with me," he whispered to me.

"Where are we going?"

"It's a surprise."

"All right," I said as he covered my eyes with the blindfold. He grabbed my hand and led me out of the room. We traveled down the hall and stopped. I heard keys jiggling and a door open. The room was a little warmer than the other rooms. He pulled me next to the bed, lifted me up, and laid me on my back. He opened my straps and buttons, and my dress fell to the sides.

"No bra or panties. Hmmm, you're always ready for me." I could feel his hands travel over my stomach and breasts. He massaged my body from head to toe. Damn, he made me feel good. Every touch, I melted.

# THE LOVE I CRAVE

"Open your mouth," he said, and I did. "Wider," he demanded. I felt him put something in my mouth. I concluded that it was a ball gag. My mind wanted to drift away to a place that wasn't good to me, but I stayed focused on the moment at hand.

He set me up and removed the dress, then laid me back down. He removed himself from the bed. I heard a drawer open then closed. I felt him climb on the bed, and his hands rubbed against my thighs. He forced my thighs apart. His hand rubbed my clit. I felt his tongue on my cave, and my entire body tingled. I moaned to myself as he massaged my insides with his finger. I backed all the way up on the bed with nowhere to go.

"Where are you going?" he asked, pulling me by the legs back to him. "Don't move again, or I will tie you up." He went back to work on my cave.

I couldn't take it and moved all the way up the bed again. In vampire speed, my legs and arms were tied up. I wanted to call out to him. Let him know how good he made me feel. Just when I was about to explode, he stopped. I heard this buzzing noise like a vibrator. I felt the vibration on my cave. I tried to move instantly. He removed the ball gag from my mouth, and I screamed out. Every time I was about to explode, he would stop. I wanted to cry and beg for forgiveness for whatever it was I did.

"Hunter, please," I begged.

"Oh, now it's please," he said as he put his finger back in me, and the vibrator worked my clit. I squirted everywhere.

"You can squirt all night, but you better not come until I want you to." I looked at him as if that were the stupidest thing I had heard. Weren't they one and the same? He bent over and popped one of my nipples in his mouth. Time passed, and I didn't know what time it was. I was tormented for what seemed like days. It took almost until morning when I came. Then I passed out.

For the next couple of days, the same thing happened to me. On Thursday, I was so exhausted. After falling asleep at work on important phone calls, I convinced Hunter to let me stay at my house to spend some time with Sasha and Damon. After seven o'clock, I was no good to them.

On Friday evening, I was on Hunter's private plane, flying to Las Vegas. There were no freaky things going on. It was a short forty-five-minute ride. Paparazzi waited at the airport when we left the terminal. Cameras flashed until we were safe inside our truck. We rode to one of Hunter's grand hotels here, Ceaser's of Grayson.

The inside was marvelous but not better than the one in Florida. This one had the Vegas atmosphere. We caught the elevator up to one of the two penthouse suites. I was still a little tired, so Hunter ran me a bath and ordered room service. Then he walked me across this penthouse but still no lovemaking. I hadn't felt him inside me all week. I was on the verge of losing my mind even though he still pleasured me.

# THE LOVE I CRAVE

He made love to my body without even having sex. We made out like two teenagers who had skipped school. I woke up after noon and was refreshed. I opened my eyes to find myself lying on the couch next to him. He was doing some work on his laptop.

"How did I get in here?" I asked.

"I didn't want you looking for me when you woke up. So, I brought you in here with me." He smiled.

"That's sweet. I guess I should do some work too." I pulled out my laptop and sat next to him. I checked my emails to see if there were any changes. Then I checked my schedule for the interviews and the photoshoot. The interviews were scheduled for Sunday, and the photoshoot for tomorrow. If things went well, I could finish both in one day and be home on Sunday. I received an email from Mrs. Carrie telling me I looked amazing Saturday. I sent a thank you and finished my work.

"Are you hungry?" he asked. The only thing I was hungry for was him, and I couldn't seem to have any.

"No, not really," I said. We both went back to work. All I could think about was the last week and how I'd been tormented. I had been eaten alive. I'd been deprived an orgasm for hours. I'd squirted so much, I soaked the bed. I was officially addicted to him. To this man who had done all kinds of things to me.

I thought about that room he took me in, and I'd never seen the inside of it, which was probably full of freaky shit. I'd used a vibrator on myself plenty of times, and it had never felt the way he did it. I wondered how the room looked inside.

"Hunter," I called out.

"Yes, baby girl," he said, never taking his eyes from the laptop.

"What is that room at your house? The one I never saw inside?" I asked.

"You mean our house," he said.

"Okay, our house."

"And that room is none of your business," he said as he went back to work. I wanted to say more to get him to tell me, but he was a hard nut to crack. I didn't want to provoke him. My thoughts were interrupted by his cell phone ringing.

"Do you want me to get it?" I asked as he jumped as if his ass were on fire.

"No, I got it." He went over to the kitchen counter and grabbed his phone. He looked at the number, smiled, then answered it. Who was on the other line that had him smiling like that?

"Hello." He was quiet for a moment before continuing, "Okay, you have everything you need. Email me the arrangements," he said before hanging up the phone. I wanted to ask who it was, but I felt a slap across my face. I blinked my eyes to determine if it really happened. He sat back down next to me, and it felt like something fishy was going on. Sasha and Damon had been acting weird.

What had he done for us not to be having sex? I had too much on my mind right now to figure this shit out. I worked for a couple more hours. Hunter ordered room service while I lay back down. Working had tired me out, but I thought it was because of the lack of sleep I'd been getting.

I woke up from my nap and noticed I wasn't in the same room. Why did Hunter keep moving me like a piece of furniture that he didn't know where to put? I looked around the room, and Hunter was nowhere to be found. I noticed old eighties furniture and at that moment, I knew where I was. I was in Vegas, but it was years ago. I panicked because I didn't want to be here. I was at HIS father's hotel.

I turned toward the door when I heard it open. There HE entered with a girl. A girl I'd seen before, and she was surely drunk. They looked more comfortable than they should. HE had been gone all evening, and HE returned drunk and high off God knew what. HE told me that I wasn't allowed to stay out late. I could see now that he wanted to go out and do HIM. When HE saw me, it was like HE had forgotten I existed. The girl saw me standing there.

"Who the hell is she?" the girl asked.

"Oh, that's my wife," HE said with that smile on his face. The one I fell in love with, and now I couldn't stand that damn smile. I felt when HE said that, but that wasn't the worst HE'd said to me.

"The question is who the hell are you?" I yelled. I was getting fed up with HIM. I regretted it as soon as it left my lips.

"She is a good friend of mine," HE said.

"Why is she here?" I asked.

"She's here to make me feel good since you haven't in a while," he said, and the girl burst into laughter. We had been together for years now, and I was miserable as hell. I wanted to leave HIM, but I was afraid to. He turned to her.

"Excuse me for a moment. Make yourself at home," he said as he grabbed me hard by the arm. HE pulled me into my bedroom which wasn't the master suite. I knew what was coming once we entered that room. HE threw me down on the bed. I backed up to the headboard.

"Please, I'm sorry," I begged.

"No, you're not. I told you about questioning me," HE said, unbuckling his belt. My heart raced. I felt myself about to cry from what I knew would happened.

"Get your ass over here," HE said, but I didn't move. "Get your ass over here now before I throw your ass out the fucking window," HE yelled, and I obeyed.

# THE LOVE I CRAVE

"Now you want to cry. Those tears mean nothing to me," HE said as he yanked my shorts down to my ankles. His manhood popped free of his boxers. He looked at me and saw that I was still crying, and HE smacked me across my face. The tears came down even more, but I made no sound.

"Turn around so I won't see you crying." I did as I was told. HE took me from behind, making me tighten up. "Loosen that ass up and let me in some more," HE said. Tears constantly fell from my face, but I made no sound. I was used to that. HE took me in my vagina and ass. HE didn't stop until one of them was bleeding. HE wrapped his hands around my neck, choking me.

"I fucking love you. I love you so much. You're mine and don't you ever forget it. Do you understand that I love you and if I can't have you, then you won't live to love another?" I was losing consciousness. I didn't know what hurt the most, my ass, my throat, or my heart. I was going under when I heard my name being called.

"Zollah, Zollah, wake up!" My eyes popped open, and I saw Hunter standing there looking at me. I jumped back on the couch.

"It's okay; it's just me," he said, reaching out for me.

"No, don't," I said. I had no idea what I would do if he touched me right now. I saw pain in his eyes. He was hurting because I was hurting. I was stuck in the corner of the couch with my knees up to my chest. Hunter slowly sat on the couch, staring at me.

"What did you see?" I asked.

"You were coughing as if you were choking. You were crying in your sleep." When he said that, I began to cry.

"I'm sorry."

"Oh no, baby girl, don't be sorry. It's not your fault. I'm scared for you," he said, wiping the tears from my eyes.

"I haven't had a nightmare in a long time. They just became frequent once I started seeing you," I admitted. "Maybe it's because I'm happy now. I guess." I thought about what I said and wondered if it made sense.

"We should go and see Dr. Stevens," he said, and I was flabbergasted. I didn't remember telling him I was seeing a therapist, but nothing was a secret with Hunter. "I want to go with you. If it's okay?" he asked. It was a good way to be slick. To ease his way into one of my sessions so he could finally find out.

"That would be okay," I said as I felt the pain and heartache release me. I dropped my legs and unfolded my arms.

"Thank you," he said.

"No, thank you," I said, opening my arms to accept a hug from him. He leaned in and gave me a long, tight hug. He felt so good in my arms.

"Hunter, can I ask you something?" I said as he pulled back.

"Sure," he said, turning off his laptop so I could have his undivided attention.

"What was this place before you bought it?"

"It was some old eighties hotel. I bought it from an older man. The owner Bishop Troy, something Troy," he said. My heart sank in my stomach. I remembered HIM telling me that some rich asshole was trying to buy his father's hotel. Who knew that rich asshole was Hunter? It was truly a small world out here, and things were closing in on me.

"Why you ask?" he asked me as I looked into his eyes. I couldn't say why I asked. If I did, then I'd have to talk about HIM. Then he would know exactly who had scared me.

"No reason. I just don't remember seeing this place when I came here some years ago," I said.

"This was my twenty-first birthday present to myself," he said. *Who gives hotels for their birthday?*

I wondered if HIM had found out about Hunter and me. I didn't know what I would do if HE found me. If HE did something to Hunter. I couldn't live without Hunter. I felt my breathing pick up. I was on the verge of losing my mind. I needed to calm myself down. *Okay, Zollah, get yourself together. It's time to be strong.*

# CLUB CANDY

I'd forgotten how much I loved Las Vegas. The streets were lit up, and every place was alive. They lied when they named New York the city that never sleeps. In Vegas, no one went to bed. They were up all night gambling their life earnings away. People were out walking the streets. Vegas was in fact Sin City.

I stared out the window as we rode past all those amazing places. We slowed down in front of this huge brick building. The two-level building stood alone on the strip with a wall of windows. A huge sign read Club Candy.

On the outside walls, huge picture frames hung with pictures of girls. They must be the girls who worked here. One frame was bigger than the others. Lirpa Summers was their headliner and my God, she was beautiful.

"Name please?" a man asked as we entered the club. He must have been the bouncer.

"Zollah Hope and Hunter Grayson." I turned to look at Hunter.

"Yes, Miss Hope and Mr. Grayson. Right this way." He led us inside the double glass doors.

When we stepped through them, the lights were dim. We had to walk down a flight of stairs to get to the main floor. When we got to the bottom, we were escorted to our table. The walls were cream with different color light fixtures on them. We stopped at some doors, and I turned to look at myself in the mirror that was on the wall.

Damn, I looked good in this purple and black striped dress. The front was low cut, showing off just enough cleavage. I wore a big black belt that went with my black Jessica Simpson stilettos. I left my hair down because Hunter loved it that way.

"You look sexy." I snapped out of my own moment and turned to Hunter.

"Thank you, I try." I smiled as the security guard stopped, and a lady escorted us the rest of the way to our table. The place was nothing how I imagined it would be. It was better. We came in on the top level, and I could look up at the amazing glass ceiling. That had to be a thick piece of glass or hard rain or an earthquake would shatter it. Hunter's eyes followed mine.

# THE LOVE I CRAVE

"A glass ceiling... hmmm. Never thought of it." He squeezed my hand and smiled. The look on his face told me he was thinking something naughty, and it included glass ceilings. The hostess led us to a table in the front row, right in front of the stage.

"Ms. Hope and Mr. Grayson. You're Carmen's guest for the evening. You're seated in VIP section 1," the girl said. "Thank you for choosing Club Candy. My name is Nina, and I will assist you tonight." She couldn't keep her eyes off Hunter. She was hypnotized by him. I just smiled because I knew my man looked finger-licking good. Then she finally turned to me.

"Can I start you with something to drink?"

"Yes, I will take a ginger ale and a glass of water. My lady will take whatever your specialty is," Hunter said, knowing that I wanted to taste their specialty drinks because I was here for business.

"We have three special drinks to offer. We have Club Cash, which is good. Ecstasy is okay if you like coconut, and Ryder, is a one hitter quitter," she said, waiting for an answer. I was about to say what I wanted, but Hunter answered for me.

"She'll have all three but save the hitter quitter for last." My eyes shot to him. I couldn't believe it.

"You know me well." I smiled as Nina excused herself. I looked around at the place again. The stage was the biggest

I'd seen so far. It took up most of the floor. There was a section for the band that was now playing some soft music as people came in. The bar along the long wall by the stairs.

The next floor up had two sections. One section had tables, but the other side had none. I could tell that room was standing room only, which that space was probably cheaper. Nina came back with two glasses and a bottle of champagne.

"Carmen sent this over," she said as she opened it and poured me a glass after Hunter told her that he didn't drink. Why did everyone make a face when they found out he didn't drink?

"Thank you," I said as I sipped my drink.

"Would you like to order something to eat?" she asked, and Hunter looked over the menu.

"Fish or chicken?" he asked.

"I'll have chicken," I replied.

"I'll have the rotisserie chicken breast dinner and the lemon salmon dinner," he ordered and passed her the menus. As Hunter ordered the food, I noticed that every time we ate out, he ordered fish. *Does he not trust chicken outside of his house?*

"Enjoy the show. Thank God it's Friday." She smiled before leaving us. Another server brought us our drinks. The lights dimmed, meaning the show was about to start.

# THE LOVE I CRAVE

Once the show started, the place was alive. The show started with a song. Carmen was on stage singing and dancing with the other ladies, who I might add looked good. I wondered if she had it in their contract for them to work out. A question I may add to the list. There were about twelve girls at the most. After the opening act, a few different girls performed.

Our food arrived, and it was delicious. I loved the sautéed asparagus. Hunter said he enjoyed the salmon. Lirpa Summers was the last to perform. She sang a powerful love song first, and it almost brought tears to my eyes. She had an amazing voice. I wish I sang like that. I was told I had an amazing voice. HE said that my voice was one of a kind. Then for her second song, she did a classical and modern number. It was beautiful.

Her third number was sexy. She chose a guy to perform with. He looked to be a mix with black and Latino. He was fine. She placed him in a chair that sat in the middle of the stage. Her song of choice was intoxicating. The way she danced for him. It was powerful. She flipped on him. She crawled all over him. The way she moved made me want to hit the gym. She had all kinds of moves. I turned to look at Hunter, and he was so into the show. He was turned on, and so was I. After that performance, there was a fifteen-minute break.

# Henson Dreamier

The last number was amazing; it got everyone dancing in their seats as all the girls came out for a dance. They received a standing ovation.

"Did you enjoy the show?" I asked Hunter.

"Very much so," he said as he kissed me on my lips. I moved closer. I wanted to eat him up. We kissed and didn't notice someone walking up.

"Ms. Hope." I turned my head from kissing Hunter.

"Lirpa," I said, standing up. "I enjoyed your show. You're an amazing dancer and singer." She shook my hand.

"Thank you," Lirpa said.

"Umm, this is Hunter Grayson," I introduced them. Hunter stood up to shake her hand.

"Hello, Mr. Grayson," she said, smiling. He had that effect on everyone with a vagina.

"Hello," Hunter said.

"I just stopped by to say hi, and that I'll be ready for my interview. This is the first time I'll be in a magazine. I mean I've been in the newspaper, but Javier is amazing." I turned to look at Hunter. He smiled, knowing my magazine was named after him.

"Don't worry, you're in good hands," I said as a guy walked up. I didn't notice him at first until he was next to Lirpa.

# THE LOVE I CRAVE

"Yes, she is." The guy smiled at her, and I got it now. They were together.

"Everyone, this is my boyfriend Tyler. Tyler, this is Ms. Hope and Mr. Grayson." We all said hello.

"Well, I will see you fine people tomorrow." She grabbed Tyler's hand, and they walked over to the bar.

Carmen came over to say hello before we left. She apologized for taking so long. I told her that it was okay; I knew she had a place to run. She said that she'd be ready in the morning. She asked what time I wanted to start. I said the earlier the better.

After speaking to Carmen, we left and headed back to the hotel. I felt nice from those three drinks I had. That Ryder was the best one, but Ecstasy was very fruity and tasted good. Hunter tormented me again tonight. It wasn't very long because he knew I had a long day tomorrow.

It was seven in the morning when I woke up. Hunter was still sleep, so I started to do some work. I had some emails to answer and phone calls I needed to make. I called my photographer to let him know what time to be at the club. I called Bianca to let her know the plans. It was almost nine when I hopped in the shower. Hunter joined me, but there was no freaky shit, which was good. I needed to be focused and not drained.

"I'm going to come watch you work," he said.

"You don't have to. I'm going to feel bad for not paying you any attention," I said as I got dressed.

"It's going to be like I'm not even there. I have my own work to do. I won't bother you," he said as he put on his shoes.

"You never saw me at work. I can be very bossy," I said.

"Not bossy. But the boss, and it looks good on you," he said. I smiled as we walked out the door. I got to Club Candy at eleven in the morning. Bobby was there setting up for the photoshoot. Carmen set me up at a table for me to work. Lirpa set up a spot for Hunter to squeeze into.

Bobby started taking pictures of the place. Once that was finished, we had the photoshoot for the girls. They had changed their clothes a hundred times, it seemed like. Carmen dressed in a breathtaking all-black gown. She looked amazing. Once everything was done, we had time to add in the interviews, so my staff could head home early if they wanted. Before the interviews started, I had time to check in on Hunter.

"Are you okay? Do you need anything?" I asked.

"No, baby girl. I'm good. Go back to work," he said as he kissed me on the cheek. I smiled, then headed over to Bianca who was doing the interview. I sat in just in case there was any more questions I wanted to ask. Bobby had packed up his things, and he asked me if it was okay if he could go and enjoy Vegas. I said of course; his job here was done.

# THE LOVE I CRAVE

Lirpa had lived an interesting life, and I enjoyed her story very much. I asked her if she wanted to write a book. I would be honored to publish it. Carmen's story was amazing too. She had been through hell and back. They both had suffered loss.

The club opened at seven, and we were done at five o'clock. That meant my job was done tonight. I thought that maybe Hunter and I could fly home tonight. I wanted to sleep in our bed. By the time we got back to the hotel, I was exhausted. We showered and lay in bed. Hunter wrapped his soft arms around me.

"You looked sexy at work today," he said.

"Did I now?"

"Yes, I was hard the entire time."

"You're always hard," I said as he smiled, and we both went to sleep.

I woke up Sunday morning still feeling tired. Hunter had ordered us breakfast before heading to the airport. All my staff had gone out on the town last night. I told them that my plane would be leaving at two the next day. Hunter and I were on his plane by noon. It was three o'clock when we finally made it home. We lay in bed for the rest of the day. It was amazing.

Monday morning, Julius dropped me off at my house to pick up my truck. I made it to work on time. Melissa handed me my file, and I went straight to work. My team upstairs had already emailed me the pictures and the recordings of the interviews. It took all day for me to choose what I wanted for the magazine. It was four o'clock when I came up for air because Hunter called me.

He told me he had a last-minute business trip that came up. That he'd be leaving tomorrow and would return on Friday. Then I had to remind him of my business trip coming up this weekend. I had to return to New York. Martin's would be my next project. He told me to go ahead without him, and that he'd see me Sunday. I asked him where he was going, and he said to New Orleans. There was a problem with the construction for his new hotel. I felt as if he was up to something. Not like he was cheating, but something. I didn't ask; I was too scared.

Once I was done, I sent my revised email back upstairs. I closed up and headed home. Sasha was the first one home, so she made dinner. Hunter surprised me with a visit. We all sat and enjoyed dinner. Hunter stared at me the entire time. He kept telling me how much he was going to miss me. He laid kisses all over my face.

"You two make me sick," Sasha said, smiling.

"This love right here comes once in a lifetime," he said, kissing me again. Never taking his eyes off me.

"I hear that," Damon said as he sipped his wine.

After dinner, Hunter and I headed to my room so he could have dessert. He ate my kitty until I couldn't take it anymore.

# THE LOVE I CRAVE

I wanted him inside me. I went to grab at his manhood, but he slapped my hand away.

"Not today." He pleased me until I went to sleep. I woke up the next morning, and Hunter was gone. There was just a note he had left on my pillow. I smiled and read it.

"You're so beautiful when you're asleep. Like Sleeping Beauty but way hotter. I love you. See you on Sunday. Julius is at your beck and call. Use him please."

"H."

By Wednesday, I finished editing and sent it back to Abby. By the end of the day, I had the finals done. When I got home, Sasha was running around like a chicken with her head cut off. She was in her room packing up a suitcase.

"Where are you going?" I asked.

"I have to go out of town on some business," she said. I looked at her if she were joking. Sasha rarely traveled for work.

"So, you and Hunter are going to be out of town."

"Yeah, I'm thinking about hiring some new people. I'll be back on Friday," she said.

"Well, I'm leaving on Friday. So that means I won't see you until sometime next week. I'm leaving for New York."

"Okay," she said, and I could tell she was hiding something. I'd known her too long. "I made fish. Let's eat and try this new wine I bought," she said as she walked out of the room. I stood there for a moment thinking.

"No, they wouldn't do that." My mind almost took me to a place it shouldn't be. Sasha or Hunter wouldn't do that to me, would they? *No, I'm overthinking this.*

# HUNTER'S FAMILY

E verything was ready for sendoff on Thursday. I had sent the story over to the printing company. I had one meeting and four conference calls. After that, I headed home. I felt lonely. Luckily, Damon was here to keep me company. I missed Hunter like crazy. I got off early so Damon and I could go house hunting. He had looked at plenty of places in Beverly Hills and Los Angeles. He said he didn't want to move too far away from Sasha and me. He had found a couple of houses he liked, but no final decision yet. Of course, he was welcome to stay with us as long as he wanted.

When we got home after dinner, I asked him if he wanted to fly to New York with me on Friday. He was down, so I called Melissa to tell her to meet at my house so she could leave her car in the garage. Julius was due to pick us up for the airport at noon. Damon and I went to sleep until a little after ten o'clock. I usually didn't sleep this late with Sasha around.

Melissa had woken us up. She was ready to go. She hadn't been outside of California so she was excited. Not long after she showed up, Julius came with the truck. We got to the airport five minutes before noon.

"Hope, you have your own private plane. How come I'm just finding out you're keeping secrets?" Melissa asked.

"No." I smiled. "I just forgot to mention it."

"Ready when you are, Hope," Marcus said, greeting us inside.

"Ten minutes, Marcus, and we'll be ready," I said as we took our seats. I put on my seatbelt. Ten minutes, we were in the air on our way to New York.

We arrived in NY about six p.m. We settled in at the hotel. Melissa and I shared a room, while Damon and Julius occupied the other two rooms. I called Mrs. Carrie once I got settled. I told her that I was in town, and she sounded excited but a little funny as well. She wanted to meet for breakfast in the morning. I informed her that I had to work tomorrow at Martin's. She offered to pay for dinner later that evening.

After I showered, I was ready to go out, and I was starving. So, I asked Julius to take us to Dreams, the place Hunter used to go to all the time. He knew exactly what I was talking about. Everyone got dressed to go out. When we arrived, we ordered dinner and shots of tequila. After eating, we partied the night away. We left just as they were closing. We got back to the hotel around four in the morning, and I went out like a light. I woke up to my phone ringing. I didn't want to get up to answer it, but I knew who it was.

"Hello," I answered.

"Rise and shine beautiful." That voice woke me immediately.

"Hey," I said, turning to see the time. "How is your business trip going?" I asked as I sat up in the bed. It was almost nine o'clock.

"It's going. These assholes are trying to get more money out of me. Don't worry, I can handle that."

"What happened?"

"They're saying what I ordered cost more than what I paid. So, they want me to pay the difference, but I won't," he said.

"Oh well, it's not your fault. That's their problem."

"I got us on this end. You have a long day ahead of you. You need to get up and get ready. I scheduled us an appointment with Dr. Stevens before we leave for the Dominican Republic," he said, taking me aback. Why was it important we go before the DR?

"All right. Sounds good," I said.

"I have to go. Love you."

"I love you more," I said as we hung up.

I got up, took a shower, and dressed. I called my team to wake them and let them know that we were heading to Martin's about eleven. I hung up from them and called Melvin, who said he was already at Martin's, and he was ready whenever I was. I told him that Melissa was coming with me. He said his nephew Conner was coming in later to help around the club.

Julius was ready to take us to the club. By the time I got there, Keith was setting up, and Lucy was getting the questions together for the interview. Melvin brought in some pictures of Martin, his brother, so we could use them in the magazine. The place was still as amazing as the last time I saw it. Everything didn't take long to finish, and we were done by four.

Melvin invited us for dinner later. I wanted to decline because I had nothing to wear. Then I thought that I could stop by Hunter's penthouse to pick up a gown for Melissa and me. I knew I had one she could wear. Julius pulled up in front of Hunter's place. Melissa and I got out and went inside. As soon as I walked in, I saw our picture over the fireplace.

"Wow, Hope, you two look amazing," Melissa said as I walked up to the desk.

"Good afternoon, Mrs. Grayson. Mr. Grayson didn't tell me you were coming to stay," he said.

# THE LOVE I CRAVE

"Chris, I'm just stopping by to pick up some things. Is it okay if I go up, or do you need to call Mr. Grayson?" I asked.

"Oh no, he would have my head if I called him for something like that. Head on up," he said.

Melissa and I made our way up the elevator. Once inside, I called Mrs. Carrie to let her know that I and some friends were having dinner at Martin's tonight. She was delighted and said add her and two others to the reservations. The doors to the elevator opened. Just looking at the foyer made me shiver. The way he had me in here gave me flames. I put my hand up to the pad.

"Hello, Zollah. Door open."

"That's nice. I might have to invest in one of those," Melissa said as she looked around. "So, this is how a multi-million-mogul lives." I led the way toward my closet which had its own room. I pushed the doors open, and Melissa stopped in her tracks.

"Living life like it's golden. Are all these clothes yours?" she asked as we stepped into the closet.

"Yes, he kind of went overboard ordering clothes for me. Pick anything you want. Unless I like it, then you have to choose something else," I said, smiling. Melissa was like a child on Christmas morning.

"We're about the same size, right?" I asked.

"Yes, I'm just a little taller," she said.

369

# Henson Dreamier

I chose a beautiful, one-shoulder, champagne-color gown with black Jessica S. pumps and a black handbag. Melissa chose a black strapless gown with red pumps and a red handbag. Her dress had a little train attached.

"You can keep the dress, but those I need back," I said, pointing to my red pumps. We headed downstairs to the truck. Damon and Julius were waiting patiently. We went straight back to the hotel to get ready for tonight.

I called Melvin to tell him to set us a table for nine. He said that Mrs. Grayson had already called and requested her favorite table. He would be expecting us around nine. I lay down for a while, but I was scared to go to sleep, thinking I might drift off to another time in my life. I missed Hunter so much, I didn't want to have any more nightmares.

Then I thought about the time I visited Vegas with HIM. How could I have put myself through that much heartache? Then I kept thinking that I needed to stay with HIM to make more money rather than working at some restaurant. If I would have left HIM, HE would have killed me. Now looking back at it, I was dying slowly each time I decided to stay. HE had already killed me on the inside.

I remembered meeting HIS mother maybe ten or eleven times. The first time I saw her, she was quiet and timid. I saw her off and on living at the Troy Estate. A year passed, and I saw her again. She knew who I was, but she didn't. She almost looked like a zombie. She aged five years and lost some weight. She was on drugs, the good prescription kind.

# THE LOVE I CRAVE

They had millions on top of millions, so I know she had the good shit.

A few times after that, I figured out what was going on. Mrs. Troy lived in the same estate. Mr. Troy treated his wife like shit. He had his mistress living there too. The mother wasn't in her right state of mind to say something. She kept locked away. How creepy was that, living in the house with your wife and your mistress? HE was just like his father, and I realized I was becoming HIS mother. I lost myself in HIM. I was alive when HE was gone. When HE stepped in the room, HE took all my life away.

Sophia had the good blood of the family. She had Treyvon HIS cousin. He was cute and had personality. He treated Sophia so good. HE would say don't worry about my bitch. Worry about yours. How I wished HE would have treated me the same way. Treyvon tried to say something to HIM about it, but there was nothing anyone could do. Treyvon had respect for women; I guess it skipped a couple of bloodlines. Treyvon and Sophia loved each other so much. They were made for each other. I guess HIM seeing HIS father beat HIS mother made HIM think it was okay.

\*\*\*

# Henson Dreamier

We stopped in front of Martin's at nine. It was alive just as it was the last time I was here. The cameras were flashing as we got out.

"Was it like this last time you came?" Melissa asked.

"Yes," I said as we posed for the camera. Damon was in the middle, Melissa on his left, and I was on his right. Then we took the long red carpet up to the front. Melvin had our table ready for us. We weren't there long when Mrs. Carrie walked in with her guests.

"Hello," I greeted her with a hug.

"Hello, darling." She pulled back the hug and just stared at me. I strangely stared back.

"Oh, I'm sorry. This right here is my husband Dustin, and this here is my son Emmanuel," she introduced us.

"Nice to finally meet you both," I said, shaking their hands. Mr. Grayson looked young and dapper. "This is my best friend Damon, and this is my assistant Melissa."

"And I'm Melvin, the owner of this place. This right here is my nephew Conner." We all sat at a long booth up against the wall. Before sitting, I walked up on Julius.

"Are you going to sit with us? No standing tonight. I got a seat for you."

"I'm good, Hope," he said.

"Julius, every time I see you, you're working. Sit and have a couple of drinks and relax," I said.

"I can't drink and drive," he said.

"Okay, how about you get twisted tonight, and I'll drive." I grabbed his arm and led the way to the table.

I sat between Mrs. Carrie and Emmanuel. Melissa and Conner sat next to each other. Damon and Melvin sat next to each other. Mr. Grayson sat on the other side of his wife with Julius next to him. I saw Eric walk past, and I waved him down.

"Mrs. Grayson, I see you brought back company with you," he said as I smiled at him calling me Mrs. Grayson, but they all looked at me as if he was mistaken.

"Yes," I introduced him to everyone. "Do you mind?" he cut me off.

"Of course, I will take care of you. I'll be right back," he said as he walked away. Once Eric returned, he took our drink and food orders. I had to have my cherry bloom champagne.

"So, you're the one who stole my son's heart. Had him waiting on you. What was it, a thousand years?" Mr. Grayson joked.

"Yeah, I thought he was a cupcake, but it seems like my little brother knows how to pick them," Emmanuel said, taking a sip from his cognac. Emmanuel favored Hunter just a little. His eyes were darker, and his skin was lighter. I smiled and wanted to say something, but I ignored him.

"We both were waiting on each other," I said.

"So, you were here on business?" Mr. Grayson asked.

"Yes, but business is over, and now it's time to party," I said, holding up my glass.

"Party girl, so how does my brother feel about you drinking when he doesn't?" Emmanuel asked.

"Hunter is fine. He knows what I enjoy. It's not like I'm a lush," I said as I finished my champagne and poured another glass.

"A career woman, party girl, and funny. I like," Mr. Grayson said.

"I told you you'd love her," Mrs. Grayson said as they shared a kiss.

"So, Emmanuel, what it is you do? I know you don't get paid for good conversation," I asked as I looked around the table. Melissa and Conner were deep in conversation. Damon and Melvin were still talking.

"I own car dealerships. A few hair salons and boutiques. A few studios. For your information," he said, smiling.

"Hmmm." I sipped from my glass, turning my head back to the talented people performing tonight.

# THE LOVE I CRAVE

"A lot of talent here tonight. I'm sure you can get one of them in that studio of yours," I said. We all gathered our things to head out. It was going on two in the morning.

"Is this how it feels to have an annoying little sister you can't get rid of," Emmanuel said.

"Does that mean you approve of me dating your brother," I said as he turned to look at me, like I didn't know what he was doing. We made it to the curb, waiting for our cars to pull up.

"It was nice meeting you, Zollah. I'm sure you'll make a wonderful addition to the family. Leena can finally have the sister she always wanted." He gave me a hug before he hopped inside his silver BMW sports coupe.

"Take care, everyone," Mrs. Grayson said as she and her husband got inside their 1975 Jaguar. It was beautiful and classic.

"Okay, peoples, let's mound up," I said as I got behind the wheel of the truck. I drove straight to the hotel and passed out as soon as my head hit the pillow.

We made it to the airport at ten. I tried to sleep on the plane, but I was anxious. So, I just pulled out my laptop and did some work. When we arrived at LAX and the doors opened to the plane and I saw Hunter standing outside, my knees buckled. I couldn't believe my eyes. Hunter wore sweatpants and a t-shirt, with some Jordan's and a North Face jacket. What the hell. He looked so damn good. I'd never seen

375

him dress like this outside the house. I ran down the steps and into his arms. And my God, did they feel good. The way he looked at me was like he missed me too. He squeezed me tight.

"I missed you," he whispered in my ear.

"I missed you more," I said. We held the hug for a moment before pulling away. He smelled good. I wanted him, and I wanted him now. It had been two weeks since he'd been inside me. Oh my, how I missed it.

"Let's go home," I said, and the smile on his face was priceless.

"Yeah, baby girl, let's go home." He turned to Julius. "Take them home."

"My car is parked at your house," Melissa said as she gave me a hug.

"I'll see you in the morning. Bright and early." She smiled as she walked away.

"I'll see you tomorrow, Damon," I said.

Hunter and I hopped in the Lambo and headed home. It was a nice evening out. I wanted to stay outside and enjoy the weather, but all I wanted to do was be in his arms. I hoped and prayed I didn't have any nightmares. I laid my head back and stared out the window.

# THE LOVE I CRAVE

"It's a nice day out tonight,"

"It is now since you're home," he said.

When we got home, dinner was ready, and it smelled delicious. He had some wine on ice. He knew I liked my wine cold.

"Wow, Hunter!"

"You deserve a nice meal and a glass of wine. You worked hard this weekend. You completed a job and scored big," he said, taking my suitcase and putting it in the closet.

"Scored big?"

"Yes, with my father and brother," he said.

"I see someone called you."

"As soon as Emmanuel got inside his car last night, he called me. He told me to marry you like yesterday," he said, wrapping his arms around me.

"You should listen to your brother," I said as I kissed him "Did you cook?"

"No."

"Doesn't matter." I smiled.

We sat and enjoyed dinner. I had three glasses of wine. It was one I hadn't tasted before. It was quite lovely. I washed the dishes while Hunter dried them. He wanted to put them in the dishwasher. I told him I liked to wash my dishes myself.

"Do you want to sit outside and enjoy the evening breeze?" he asked.

"That would be nice. I want to change." I ran upstairs, did a quick wash up, and put on a summer dress. I was back downstairs in ten minutes. Hunter opened the patio door. I stepped out first, and I could never get used to stepping out of my backyard and hearing the beach brush against the sand. The stars were shining bright. The moon was a crescent. Hunter closed the door and led me to the swinging bench. He sat first, and I lay with my head on his lap. He put a little blanket over me. I could get used to this every night.

"It's so beautiful out here," I said.

"Yes, it is," he said as he ran his hands through my hair. I felt like a baby getting rocked to sleep.

# DR. STEVENS

It was Monday morning, the twenty-sixth of March, and I was the first to wake up. I lay there for a moment, staring at Hunter snore like a bear. This was the first time I had heard him snore. He must be exhausted. I crept out of bed, hoping I didn't wake him. I couldn't deal with his horny ass this morning. I needed to get to work at nine. I had a lot of work to do. I had an appointment with Dr. Stevens one day this week. So, I wanted to get as much work done as possible.

I left the room and went inside mine to shower and dress. After showering, I wrapped the towel around me and went inside my closet to find something to wear. I wanted something different. So, I chose a pair of Versace light-blue, skintight jeans. A white button-up shirt with a blue suede blazer with shoes to match. I put my hair in a ponytail with some bangs. I looked in the mirror, and I still had my baby face. I applied my makeup and my earrings, and I was done. I opened the door to my bathroom, and Hunter was standing there. I jumped back.

"Boy, you scared me," I said as I held my chest.

"You scared me when I woke up and you weren't there," he said as I walked past him. He stopped me inside the closet. He turned me around to face him, as he wrapped his arms around my waist. He leaned in and kissed me.

"I apologize. I wanted to shower and get ready for work. You looked so peaceful, I didn't want to wake you," I said.

"I didn't get the chance to have my breakfast before breakfast," he said.

"What's before breakfast?" I asked, and I knew I shouldn't have. This man seemed to have a one-track mind when I was around.

He closed the closet door behind us and pushed me further in. Okay, I knew this was going to happen as soon as he found me missing. The man was a horny little devil.

"Pull your pants down," he demanded.

"Hell no. I want to be at work at nine," I said, backing away from him. I tried to move past him and head for the door, but he caught me. I guess I wasn't fast enough.

"So, you're going to deny me when I haven't tasted you in a week. Are you serious?" he asked. I got out from his embrace. He was coming toward me as I backed up. I came up short when there was nowhere else to go. My back was up against the shelves.

"Nowhere else to go, baby girl," he said with a smirk.

I felt his body against mine, and heat inflamed me. This was a problem; every time he touched me, I wanted him, and I got all moist. All I wanted to do was shower, eat breakfast, and go to work.

"Please, Hunter, I don't want to black out, pass out, or even faint," I begged him. He burst into laughter. I felt his hands on me. They easily slipped under my shirt and squeezed my breast. Each pinch at my nipples made my knees weak.

He began to unbuckle my pants and just like that, they were down to my ankles. He did all that without breaking eye contact. He leaned in with a smile, saying that he was about to get lucky. He kissed me as his hand massaged my cave. Why, why, why did he make me feel this way? His thumb rubbed against my pebble, while his finger entered me.

"Always wet and ready," he said as he kissed me again. He lowered the kisses to my neck, then my breasts. "Oh God, I'm going to explode." His lips were so damn soft. He lowered himself down some more until his lips were faced with mine. He lifted me up as he ducked his head between my legs. I wrapped them around his neck.

# Henson Dreamier

He dove in like he had entered a pie eating contest. This man had a magic tongue to go along with his magic stick. I moaned uncontrollably. I was on the verge of losing it. It had been a week since he tasted me, but it had been weeks since I felt him inside me. My eyes rolled back in my head. I had no idea what he was doing to me. The feeling was unbearable. This man never got tired. The energizer bunny had nothing on him.

"Oh, shit. Fuck!" I screamed out. My body went limp from that explosion, and that didn't stop him. He sucked on my pebble, and his tongue worked my cave.

"Hunter, please stop," I begged, and he didn't obey. My head slammed against the shelves, and clothes fell as I tried to hold on for dear life. He didn't stop until another tornado ripped through me. I knew the whole neighborhood heard me screaming. Let alone, I knew Mrs. Phoebe heard me.

After we were done, I did a quick wash between my legs, and Hunter got in the shower. I went downstairs to see what Mrs. Phoebe was cooking in the kitchen. As soon as I hit the bottom step, I could smell the food in the air.

"Good morning, Mrs. Phoebe," I said as I sat at the breakfast bar.

"Morning, honey. You look nice. I don't think I've ever seen you in jeans before," she said.

"I haven't really worn jeans since I started my business. I just felt like jeans today," I said. My kitty rubbed up against my jeans. I felt like I wanted to come on myself. Maybe today wasn't the day to wear jeans.

"I know you're hungry," she said, smiling. My eyes widened. I knew what she was smiling at, and I felt embarrassed.

"I'm sorry that you had to hear that," I said. I felt like I had said this too many times before.

"Don't be. It's about time I hear some noise around here. For years, it's been a ghost town," she said, placing my plate in front of me. French toast with butter and strawberries and scrambled eggs with cheese and sausages. I dug in.

"So, how's work going?" she asked, making Hunter's omelet.

"It's going wonderful. I actually have a ton of work to do, and Hunter has made me late."

"Well, all you have to do is tell him no," she said, and I almost choked on my orange juice. Was she kidding? She had to be telling a joke.

"Oh." I wiped my mouth. "I'm sorry. I didn't know that's all I had to say. I'll remember that the next time."

"Are you okay? Do you need me to perform CPR? I heard you choking," Hunter said as he came from out of nowhere.

"No, I'm fine," I said as Hunter sat next to me.

"What happened?" he asked.

"Nothing, honey. Eat your omelet." Mrs. Phoebe placed his plate in front of him. She looked at me and smiled.

"Is that how it's going to be? Keeping secrets," he said.

"Oh, and you're not keeping anything from me?" I asked, looking at him. He stared back at me. He had a certain look on his face as if I caught him.

"No," he said with a smile. I knew he was lying.

"Eat up. Julius will be here soon," she said as I handed her my plate. Hunter was almost done with his food when I noticed what he had on. He had on blue jeans with some Nike boots. A black button-up shirt. I had to think about what day it was.

"Why aren't you dressed for work?" I asked. He turned to look at me.

"Because I'm off today. I have a few things I need to handle before I leave for DR." I gave him a look.

"You're up to something, Mr. Grayson. You better be lucky I love surprises."

"I know you do." I grabbed my purse from the couch. The front door opened, and Julius walked in with a smile on his face.

"Good morning, everyone." He came in and walked behind the island. He leaned in and kissed Mrs. Phoebe. "Good morning, Mother," he said.

"Good morning, son. Did you call your father? He said he left a message for you last night?" she asked.

"No, I plan on doing that once I drop Hunter and Hope off," Julius said. I was still trying to comprehend what was going on. Did Julius just say mother?

"Mrs. Phoebe is your mother?" I asked with a shock look on my face.

"Yes, she is," he said, drinking the glass of orange juice his mother gave him. "She's the reason I look so good."

"I can see the resemblance now since I'm paying attention." I glanced between both of them.

"Well, Mrs. Phoebe, you raised a wonderful son," I said. She gazed over her son, knowing she did do well.

She leaned into me and said, "All he needs now is a wife and some babies." We laughed.

"Ready to go?" Hunter said. I turned to give Mrs. Phoebe a hug before following behind Hunter to catch up. He waited for me at the door, and we walked to the truck together.

When I finally made it to work, I got straight to business. I had a lot of editing to do. The story would be released in next month's issue of Javier. Melissa kept up with the surveys of the magazine. She said people were asking for a beauty and hunk of the week. I didn't want to go there. To do that, I had to get back into the modeling industry, and I wasn't sure if I wanted that. I'd run that decision through my head for the past year.

I was done with the editing by one o'clock and sent the edits downstairs. Once I was done with that, I decided to check my schedule for the next two weeks. When I pulled it up, I didn't even recognize it. As of Wednesday, I was off for the next three weeks. I knew damn well this was wrong. I had no meetings, no trips, and no conference calls. I had a lot of work laid out for me for the next few days. Fifteen conference calls. Seven today and eight tomorrow. Six meetings for today and tomorrow. What the hell was going on?

"Melissa," I yelled her name. She took her precious time coming in. When she did, she was pushing a food cart like in the hospital. The food cart had a plate of fruit, a garden salad that looked delicious, crackers with cheese, and an energy drink.

"What the hell is going on with my schedule? It has me off for three weeks. I'm not taking off three weeks. Why am I working like a slave for the next few days?" I asked. Melissa just stood there, fighting the truth.

"I don't know, Hope. I just do what I'm told. I didn't change your schedule," she said, walking toward the door. "You have your first conference call in ten minutes. So enjoy your food." She smiled as she left. I smiled back as I pulled the cart closer to my seat.

# THE LOVE I CRAVE

I ate a couple of bites of fruit before I began my salad, with my schedule going through my head. I swallowed my food and picked up my phone. I had to get Mr. Grayson on the line. He answered on the first ring.

"Yes," he answered.

"What are you doing?" I asked.

"Minding my business. I thought you had some work to do and would be too busy to call me and be nosy," he said.

"Nosy," I repeated. "Did you have my schedule changed?"

"No."

"You lie."

"Never," he said.

"Then who changed it?" As soon as the words left my mouth, I knew who did it. The same person who had hacked into my work schedule if I could remember. It all made since now. Hunter had everyone under his wing right now.

"Hunter Javier Grayson, are you being sneaky?" I asked, finishing up my salad. Okay, I was calling everyone out. Sasha was the only one I knew who hacked into my shit. She couldn't change my schedule without Melissa's help. I took another look at my schedule and noticed what this Saturday was. I'd been so busy, I didn't even know that my birthday was Saturday.

"Y'all planning a birthday party for me?"

"Bye, Zollah," he said as he hung up on me. I couldn't believe he did that. I smiled and finished up my food. That man made me crazy but in a good way. Melissa came in like clockwork in ten minutes with the file. I downed my energy drink and was ready for these crazy few days.

It was seven o'clock, and I was finally done with my day. Melissa stayed to help me do some work. Hunter must have told them to never leave me alone again after the last incident. When I walked through my front door, I was beat. Sasha and Damon stood in the kitchen in a weird position. They were trying to hide something from me.

"I'm too tired to even ask. I'm going to bed," I said as I walked past them and went to my room. I knew they was planning something for my birthday. I stripped off my clothes and climbed in bed. I turned on the TV and watched fifteen minutes of RuPaul's Drag Race before I passed out.

I woke up to my alarm going off. When I went downstairs, no one was there. I just smiled and poured a glass of orange juice. I grabbed a yogurt and a banana and was out the door.

I made it to work at nine. I got straight into it. I was refreshed and ready. I had a meeting at nine thirty, one at eleven, and one at two. After that, I took a few conference calls. At lunch, Hunter had it brought to me again today. My manager sent the final printing of Club Candy. I checked and sent it back. Then she sent me the finish of Martin's piece. I made a few more corrections, then sent it back.

I had fifteen minutes to myself between my busy ass day. I called Hunter to see what he was up to. He hadn't called me at all today. Aimee said she saw him earlier, and he wasn't dressed for work. I called, and Stephanie said that he was in a meeting that just popped up. I invited Melissa in and asked her about Conner. I'd been so busy, I didn't have a chance to ask. She said that they hit it off. They had been talking every day, and he would visit soon. He was twenty-six years old and had a five-year-old daughter. After we talked, I thought it would be a good time to be nosy.

"Are they planning a birthday party for me?" I asked. She was quiet as a mouse. "Tell me, or I'll kick you out," I threatened her. I wasn't serious, but I wanted to know something.

"Hey, that's not fair. I'm sworn to secrecy. I would die if I gave it up," she said. Those were the words of Hunter Grayson.

"So, you'd rather be fired by me, then die by Hunter?" I asked.

"Yes, I love my life," she said. "Besides, Hunter will give me a job upstairs if you fire me." She smiled and left my office as I went back to work. When I was finally done with work, and I remembered that we had a session with Dr. Stevens.

Stephanie, Hunter's receptionist, called me back, telling me that Hunter was finally out of his meeting. I finished everything and closed up. I looked over my office. It was the last time I would see it for three weeks. I took the elevator upstairs. Stephanie said I could go straight back. When I opened the door, Hunter came out of the bathroom, fixing his clothes.

"What the fuck are you doing?" I cut myself off mid-sentence. I couldn't believe what I just said. I saw the look on his face. "I'm sorry. I didn't mean it," I said, backing away from him. I just knew a slap was coming, but nothing happened.

"It's okay." He moved closer to me. I moved back further and had my head down. He slowly moved in front of me and lifted my head with his finger. "I was just cleaning up for our visit with Dr. Stevens." I felt like an idiot. I felt tears form in my eyes. I wasn't with HIM anymore.

"No, you're not going to cry," he said. I couldn't believe I reacted that way. Maybe I needed a vacation and a visit to Dr. Stevens. How could Hunter deal with me going through all these emotions?

"I'm sorry," I said as he hugged me. "It's just that we haven't spent a lot of time together. I haven't had sex in weeks. To be honest, you're driving me insane but in a good way." He smiled at me and kissed me.

"We have to go, but if everything goes right, you'll finally get what you want. This dick." I smiled as he led us out.

We arrived at Dr. Stevens at 6:20. Ten minutes early. She was ready for us to come in. I entered, said hello, and went straight to my relaxing couch right next to the bookcase. Hunter stared at me.

"She always sits there. She talks more when she does," Dr. Stevens said as she pulled out her notepad. We all got relaxed before we began. I wouldn't be doing much talking today with Hunter here.

"So, I believe we're here because you two want to be together even with all of her baggage," she said.

"Well, Dr. Stevens, I'm here to understand why she can't tell me who HIM is or even who SHE is. She's strong and an amazing woman. But she's weak when it comes to HIM," he said. *Damn, he doesn't hesitate, does he?* We hadn't been here three minutes. I was quiet for a moment as they both stared at me.

"I want you to know how dangerous it is to know about HIM. I don't want anything to happen to you. It will kill me."

"I'm in more danger not knowing who he is, Zollah I have a lot of businesses out here, and he could work for one, and I wouldn't know. I'm in more danger that way," he said. He was right, but HIM wouldn't work for anyone but himself.

He lived off his family fortune. He was a spoiled brat. I hadn't even thought of that before. Hunter could have run into HIM already. He owned hotels all over, and HE could have stayed at any one of them. Now I was afraid. All this attention I was getting from the media. HE was sure to find me. If Hunter used his brain the way I knew he could, he would have already figured out who he was.

"You're right."

"I've told Zollah that to let you in, she has to forgive HIM for what he has done. That's the only way for you two to move on. That goes for the both of you," she said.

"I want her to be able to sleep without being awakened by nightmares. She wakes up afraid of me touching her because she's thinking of HIM," he said as I saw Dr. Stevens writing something down on her note pad.

"Zollah, how frequent are your nightmares?" she asked.

"I've had six or eight since we've been together." Two or three was more than enough.

"Now, Hunter, how many nightmares have you had since getting together?" she asked as my head turned to look at him. I had never known for him to have nightmares.

"I haven't had a nightmare since being with her." He sounded upset and sad. I took my eyes off him and looked at Dr. Stevens.

# THE LOVE I CRAVE

"So, since the two of you have been together, Hope, your nightmares have started, and Hunter, your nightmares stopped?" she asked, writing it down. Hunter and I looked at each other. What could Hunter be having nightmares about? Well, he was drugged and raped at seventeen years old. I was sure that would leave a mark on him.

"I can see myself opening up to Hunter. I already told him about when my parents died, and when Brooke and Ryan were taken from me and were adopted. I stopped the story at the part where I met HIM." I put my head down, playing with my fingers.

Things went quiet for a moment. I watched Hunter as he watched me. We went on about each other for a while. Dr. Stevens asked us numerous questions. I felt as if we were taking a compatibility test.

"Now I'm going to speak hypothetically. If you two were to get married, do you think the love you have for each other will outlast the earthquake your past will have on both of you? Are you two ready for that?" she asked. Marriage. If I had the privilege to marry Hunter, I wouldn't let anything come between us. "Because just when you're the happiest, that's when the shit hits the fan."

How could things get any worse than what they were? If HE came back for me, I wouldn't know what to do. That would be the worst thing that could ever happen to me.

"I'm willing to walk through fire with and for her. To walk to hell and back for her. Is she willing to do the same for me once our past comes out?" he asked the question to Dr. Stevens but looked directly at me.

"I love you, Hunter, forever. I'm not with you because of the sexcoaster we have. A lifetime is all I ever wanted with you and if walking through fire will get us through the past, then that's what I will do," I said. He came over and sat next to me.

"Forever is all I ever wanted," he said, holding out his pinky finger. Did he really want to pinky swear? I stared into those eyes. He was head over heels in love with me, and I saw it. I felt it. He wanted to protect me from the world and everything in it. I put up my pinky finger and wrapped it around his.

"Forever is all I'm asking," I said as he smiled at me, and I smiled back. He leaned in and kissed me, and I wrapped my arms around his neck.

"Now I want the two of you to think about what we discussed. You have to be open and honest with one another. If your love is as strong as you two say, it will last forever, and no one will be able to come between that." Dr. Stevens wrote down a few things. "Come see me after your little vacation," she said.

"Yes, ma'am." Hunter and I left.

# THE LOVE I CRAVE

"Go on home, and I'll see you in the morning," Hunter said as he and Julius pulled out of the lot. I was about to start my car up when I thought about what Hunter said. It was sticking to me like glue. He was right. I was putting him in more danger by not telling him. HE could be happy out there. HE could have found someone else and be married with children. Maybe in the next week, I could grow some balls and tell him everything. Hunter sent me a text.

"I love you, and I want you to believe that I will and can make you happy. Can you believe that?" I sent a text back, saying just two words. "I believe."

I was about to call Sasha when I felt someone watching me. I looked up and saw a lady in a car across the street from me. She had tears in her eyes as she stared at me. I felt sorry for her. I had no idea why she was crying, but I wanted to console her. As I stared at her, I noticed her features. She kind of looked like me but a little lighter in skin. Something told me to get out of my car and go over there.

I cut the engine and began to walk across the street. She was shocked that I was coming toward her. She wiped her tears and pulled off. When she did that, I felt a knot form in my stomach. Something weird was going on. What did that mean? Who was that girl? I hopped back in my car. Something in me wanted to follow her, but I chose otherwise.

# DOMINICAN REPUBLIC

I pulled up to my house and eased my way into the garage. I cut the engine off, grabbed my things, and got out. I could hear music blasting as I came through the door. Sasha was in the kitchen cleaning up. I could smell food in the air. It was nice to come home to a clean house and dinner.

"Hey, how was your visit with Dr. Stevens?" Sasha asked. I put my things down on the couch and headed to the breakfast bar when I noticed my luggage next to the chair.

"It was good. We talked with one another about what we needed to do to have a successful relationship." I walked into the kitchen.

"Why is my luggage packed already?" I asked.

"Because you have a trip tomorrow, and you haven't packed anything," she said as I sat at the breakfast bar. She poured me a glass of wine.

"I could've packed my own clothes."

"You could have, but you've been too busy the last couple of days. So as your best friend, I did it for you," she said as she placed a plate in front of me.

"Of course, like you changed my work schedule. Had me working like a chicken with her head cut off, leaving me too busy to pay attention to what's going on around here," I said as I sipped my wine.

"Hey, I was just taking orders," she said.

"I bet Melissa said the same thing." I scooped up a forkful of food, chewed it, and then asked, "Where's Damon?"

"He's out handling some business for his movie," she lied. I could tell because she could never look me in the eye when she lied. I skipped the subject.

"So, what did you pack for me?" I asked.

"Everything you'll need for your vacation," she said. I was finishing up my food when the door opened, and Damon came in with some bags.

"Ladies, I want some," he said, dropping the bags on the couch.

"Some of what? Food and wine? I'll get it," I said as I was about to get up.

"No, I'll get it. Just relax and enjoy your wine," she said.

It was cool to sit down and relax with my two best friends. We listened to some oldie but goodies. It was a little after one in the morning when I crawled into bed. I was tired as hell. It felt like I had just dosed off when I felt a kiss on my cheek. For a moment, I thought I was dreaming. I ignored it until I felt another one. I opened my eyes and found a man lying next to me.

"Hello, baby girl," Hunter said.

"What are you doing here? What time is it?" I asked, lifting my head up from the bed.

"It's time to go. Are you ready?"

"No, I haven't showered or brushed my teeth yet," I said, wanting to close my eyes again.

"You can brush your teeth but no shower. You have time to freshen up." I wiped my eyes and got up from the bed. I turned to look at the time; it was five o'clock in the morning.

Shit, I had just crawled into bed. Why were we leaving so damn early? I got up and brushed my teeth and did a quick wash up. Yup, I took a hooker bath. When I came out of the bathroom, Hunter was waiting patiently. He had set out an outfit for me. Pink leggings, a white flare tunic, and some all-white Converse. I looked up at him.

# THE LOVE I CRAVE

"That's cute," I said as I put on what he had picked out.

"I know what I like to see you in." He smiled. Oh my, how a smile could melt my insides. I brushed my hair and applied some gloss, and we headed downstairs. Damon and Sasha were at the door. I hugged them goodbye.

"Have fun," Sasha said. She looked teary eyed. What really was going on here? She acted like I wasn't coming back.

"Are you okay? I'm coming back, you know," I said.

"I know. I'm just happy for you," she said.

"See you later, Z," Damon said.

Hunter and I got inside his truck, and Julius dropped us off at the airport. We went through the private security and boarded his plane. My heart raced for some reason. Hunter handed our luggage over to Marcus who carried them aboard. We settled in as Marcus came over the intercom. Ten minutes later, we were in the air.

"How long is the flight?" I asked Hunter.

"Nine and a half hours," he said.

"Nine hours. That's a long time to be floating in the air," I said.

"It won't seem that long once you've slept. I can put you to bed." He gave me a wink and a seductive smirk.

"I'm sure you can," I said.

After two hours in the air, we decided to get some work done and pulled out our laptops. I emailed Melissa and Abby to see what was going on at the office. They gave me the rundown of the day. I told them that I'd be working for the next two hours.

"Shit!" I heard Hunter shout out next to me. From the look on his face, he was upset about something.

"What?" I asked, looking at his screen.

"This is some bullshit." I'd never heard him sound so frustrated before. "Someone bid higher than me on this studio."

"So bid higher."

"I want to, but the place isn't worth the money," he said, typing an email.

"Well, then let it go," I said, and he looked up at me. I could tell he really wanted it. I took in his expression and realized what was going on.

"You don't like losing."

"I see you're learning."

"Why not find another location for whatever it is you want to put there. If you don't want to lose it, well, I hope whatever it is you're putting will make a lot of money."

# THE LOVE I CRAVE

He moved in closer to me. He brushed my hair from my face. His eyes glowed, and I knew what that meant. I still had thirty minutes of work left. I was too tired to do whatever he was thinking.

"Have you ever thought about starting another business? If so, what would it be?" he asked. I was taken aback because I had been thinking about my dream since I was a child.

"I have actually, but…" I blushed. "No, never mind."

"I want to know," he said, squeezing my hand.

"I want to open a music school where kids can learn to play any instrument they want." I put my head down. "I used to love to play the piano. I used to take music lessons at school., but when HIM heard me play and sing, HE said that I was to only play for HIM. If I didn't, he'd break my fingers." I smiled at the same time as my eyes teared up.

"Don't cry," he said, wiping the one tear.

"They're happy tears. I swear they are," I said. Hunter leaned in and kissed me on my lips. That sent chills all over my body. He kissed me again with a little aggression.

"Can we have sex now?" I quickly got over being too tired. He withdrew the kiss. I wanted him, and I wanted him now. He burst out laughing.

"Not yet," he said as I made a sad face, hoping he'd give in.

"Don't do that. It's already hard for me to tell you no. Saturday, I promise. Now stop pouting and kiss me." I kissed him for about five minutes. "You want me to eat that kitty. You know I love doing that."

"I waited this long; three more days shouldn't hurt. It'll hurt, but it won't kill me," I said. We were quiet for a moment. "I also want to open a shelter for street kids. Kids who have run away from home or foster care. I know how hard it is; living on the streets is dangerous," I said.

"And you can have both."

"I shall one day." I went back to school where I used to play everything on the piano. I was five when I started playing. My father said that I was becoming a wonderful player. "Do you still play the guitar?" I asked.

"When I get a chance."

"We should play together again one day."

"I'll do anything for you if you haven't noticed by now. We'll play for each other again, and I promise you'll still have your fingers when we're finished." He smiled, being funny.

"That sounds like a wonderful idea. I need to get me a piano. I have one I've been looking at, but I've been too cheap to buy it. Maybe I would now," I said.

"Don't worry about that. Just make sure you're ready when you get it," he said.

"I will be." When I first played for HIM, that was the last time I played for anyone but HIM. I hadn't played the piano since I left his ass. I'd been taking my time on getting one. I put up my laptop and was getting ready to lie down. Hunter went back to work. He was a working maniac.

"I've never seen someone work as hard as you."

"I have to so we can live comfortably. Plus, I love making money."

"I own my own business too, and I don't make that much or work as hard. Hmm, maybe I'm not working hard enough," I said.

"You don't ever have to work as hard anymore," he said. I smiled, and he closed his laptop and followed me to the bedroom. We lay in bed and just took a nap.

I opened my eyes when Marcus came over the intercom, telling us that we had a half hour before landing. That was enough time for me to take a shower. So, I did and put on the same outfit as before. We pulled up to the terminal and walked out. A tall girl with cinnamon skin and curly brown hair stood by.

"Hello, Mr. Grayson. Welcome back to the Dominican Republic. Passports please." When she asked for our passports, I didn't even think about getting one. I knew Hunter was smart, and he had that covered. He pulled out two passports, had them stamped, and the girl handed them back. He grabbed me by the hand.

"Enjoy your visit," she said as he pulled me forward.

"You're a slick man, Mr. Grayson. How did you even get all the information you needed for my passport?"

"I have a best friend who knows everything." He winked at me. "You will always be taken care of." We hopped into a van with our luggage and drove twenty minutes before pulling up to this amazing resort. We got out just as a tall, brown-skinned guy walked up.

"It's about time you got here," he said as they shook hands and hugged.

"Hey, you can't fight air traffic," Hunter said. The guy looked familiar. I'd seen him before.

"Zollah, this is Asher Ross, my best friend and my business partner. Do you remember him?" Hunter said.

"Hello, Asher." I shook his hand. "We hung out all summer; how could I forget?"

"Zollah, it's a pleasure to see you again," Asher said.

"Call me Hope."

"Hope, it is." Asher led us inside the beautiful resort. Everything was nicely picked out, and the tropical colors fitted the place. The lobby was half inside and half outside. The sitting area had different-colored couches and chairs. He walked us through the lobby and out the other side that led toward the rooms.

# THE LOVE I CRAVE

A bellhop followed us with our luggage. Asher gave me the tour because Hunter had been here before. We walked along the path past the pool and a tennis court. Then we kept walking until we passed an entertainment lodge where shows took place every night. It was a nice evening out tonight.

The trees blew softly, and the stars shined bright. This resort was elegant. We walked back and took the elevator to the next floor up. Room number 520. When I walked in, I couldn't believe my eyes. This room was outstanding. The balcony looked out to the resort. All I could hear was the sound of the ocean. How could I go back to LA after experiencing a place like this?

"The night is still young. Would you like to get something to eat and drink?" Asher asked.

"Food sounds good," I said, closing the balcony door.

"Would you like to change for dinner?" Hunter asked.

"No, I'm fine. Should I?"

"No, you're perfect," he said as we left the room. We walked back toward the lobby, passing another pool and a few bars. We entered a restaurant call Dominican Grill and stopped at the hostess stand.

"Good evening, Mr. Ross, Mr. Grayson. Your usual table?" the hostess asked.

"Yes, ma'am," Asher said. The lady led us to a table as I noticed the restaurant was buffet style. As soon as we sat, the waitress came over to introduce herself. Her name was Heather.

"What would you all like to drink?" she asked.

"I'll have a rum on the rocks. More rum than rocks."

"I'll take a ginger ale." They all looked at me.

"A frozen peach margarita please."

"Would you like an extra shot with that?" she asked.

"Why not. I'm not driving anywhere," I said as I stood from my seat. They stood too. Such gentlemen.

I walked around, examining what I wanted to eat. I was starving. I grabbed two plates and filled them up with different things. I hadn't eaten all day, so I knew Hunter was hungry. As I walked along, I saw Hunter and Asher talking about something. I really wanted to know what was going on. I walked back over to the table and sat. They got quiet. I just smiled at them.

"I brought a variety of things for us to try," I said as I tried some of the Caribbean chicken. Hunter grabbed a fork and helped himself. Our drinks arrived at the table, and my margarita was delicious.

"Hope, we have a lot of activities here for you to do. We have horseback riding, jet skis, snorkeling, volleyball, glass-bottom boat, four wheeling." There was so much to do. I knew I wanted to go horseback riding.

"Jet skis sound good. I always stayed away from water. But now, since I can swim. I'll try," I said. I went back to eating and let me tell you, it was good.

"So, how is the business going over here?" Hunter asked Asher.

"Great. I thought it would be difficult, but it's good," Asher said.

"What about the vendors? The entertainment and performers?" Hunter asked.

"We have interviewed over two hundred people. We're narrowing it down to the seventy-five best."

"What about…" He was about to say something when Asher cut him off.

"Hunter, everything is good. Stop worrying yourself. You're here to get—" He stopped, then continued, "You're here to enjoy your new life with this beautiful lady here. How is Grayson and Ross going in LA?" Asher said.

"I'm getting outbid for that space." He gave him a knowing look.

"How?" Asher asked.

"I don't know; I thought no one wanted it. It's weird that someone is interested in it now."

"Have you looked into who's trying to buy it yet?"

"I have Jason on it." After that, there was no more conversation about business. Hunter asked about his family and how they were doing.

Asher said that his parents were getting a divorce after twenty-five years. He said it hurt at first, but his little sister took it harder. Ashley was devastated because she had just gotten married here on this beach. My face lit up.

"Here on the beach?" I asked.

"Yeah. I set everything up for her. I damn near planned it. She had other places she could have chosen: Bahamas, Aruba, here, or Jamaica," Asher said. I just fell in love with the idea of a beach wedding. I'd pictured my wedding a million times, and it never was on a beach.

"That sounds beautiful." I blushed at the idea.

"Is that something you would like one day? For us to get married on a beach?" Hunter asked.

"Why not. You know I love the beach," I said as he leaned in and kissed me.

"Okay, I will see you guys tomorrow." Asher got up and left the restaurant. We finished our food and went back to our room. We lay in each other's arms.

"I love you, Zollah,"

"I love you more, Hunter,"

# THE LOVE I CRAVE

I woke up to a craving feeling down in my kitty. I opened my eyes, and Hunter was having his morning meal before breakfast.

"Umm…" I moan.

"Good morning, baby girl," he said between licks. I spread my legs wider to give him more access.

"Good girl." He pleased me until he got tired, which was surprising. He seemed to never get tired. The man was a machine that took no charge.

I showered, and I opened my suitcase to see what Sasha had packed. There were things I'd never seen before. Most of the things had tags on them: bathing suits, summer dresses, shirts, skirts, and shorts. She packed flip flops, sandals, and high heels. I chose a yellow polka dot bikini with a yellow summer dress and some white sandals.

"You look like a sun shining day," Hunter said. "I'm just so used to you dressed for work."

"Well, you haven't seen anything yet," I said. Hunter put on his swim trunks, a white tank top, and a gray shirt. He had on some blue and gray Nikes. He looked different outside his work clothes.

There were only two places serving breakfast this morning, so we chose the buffet of course. After eating, we walked the beach hand in hand. We got on the conversation about our parents. He told me that he grew up in a house with a strict mother. He said that she wasn't accepting anything less than straight As.

I told him how my father was the strict one, and he accepted nothing but the best from us. My mother used to play music while she cooked and cleaned. We used to sing and dance around the house. I told him how my father gave us one day out of school. That day, he spent with Brooke, Ryan, and me. He would take us anywhere and everywhere we wanted. It was a secret, and I never told my mother.

I told him how my father put me in music school. He said that I had to learn to play an instrument. I was an honor student as well. I told them how I overheard my mother and father talking about how their parents disowned them. How they left Vancouver and never went back. I told him I never met my grandparents before. That I probably saw them and never knew it was them.

When we finished walking the beach, we went to the pool and did some swimming and cuddling and kissing. After that, we headed toward our room where we passed a rum tasting. I looked at Hunter, and he smiled, knowing I wanted to stop. They had six different rums that I tasted. Some were nasty, and some were good. The one that was specially made from the Dominican had a bitter after taste but was drinkable with a lot of ice and cranberry juice. By the end of that, I was tipsy. Hunter held my hand while we walked back, but I grabbed some jerk chicken from the grill stand first. The night was still early, and I was ready for whatever.

# THE LOVE I CRAVE

"Let's shower and get dressed for the night. I have something I want to show you," he said.

Okay, this was it. No, it wasn't my birthday yet. I was kind of freaking out. I wanted to know what he was up to. Hunter hopped in the shower first, then I jumped in. When I got out, Hunter had my clothes picked out again for me on the bed. Hunter already had on a white linen short-sleeve shirt and pants with some Timberland dress shoes, but they looked like tennis shoes. He put out a pink strapless summer dress. It was long and flowing. I smiled and put the clothes on.

"I think I still remember how to dress myself," I said as I brushed my hair.

"You feel like you're losing control of yourself. That you're not in control anymore." He smiled.

"Hmm." When I came out of the bathroom, I saw him stuffing things into his pockets.

"You ready?" he asked.

"More than I'll ever be," I said.

We left and headed toward the beach. I just loved this place. It was amazing here. The stars shone bright. The air was fresh. I watched Hunter's face the whole way there. He was happy about something. When we got to the beach, he helped me out of my white stilettos. He held my hand with one hand and my shoes with the other. We walked the beach and stopped when I saw three horses waiting. A white one, a brown one, and a black one. I chose to ride the black one of course; it looked so exotic for some reason.

Hunter and the guy helped me on the horse. Hunter got on behind me. Oh my God, I was getting wet just by him sitting behind me on a damn horse. I got it bad, let me tell you. We rode up and down the beach.

"Are you enjoying yourself?" he asked.

"I'm having the time of my life," I said.

"I'm happy you are," he said as we stopped at this yacht. He helped me off the horse. The yacht was white, black, and gold. It was amazing. A lady stepped off the yacht to introduce herself.

"Good evening, Mr. Grayson. My name is Tabitha. I will be assisting you tonight," she said.

"Hello, Tabitha," I said as Hunter hopped on board, then helped me back into my shoes.

Tabitha gave me a glass of champagne. The sun was going down, and the night was young. We ate dinner as the yacht left shore. We talked about college and what we wanted out of life, where we saw our businesses in the next ten years. After eating, we sat on the front of the boat. We were in the middle of the ocean. I sipped my champagne and enjoyed this wonderful night.

I could do this every day of my life. There was something about the beach I loved. My father used to take us all the time.

# THE LOVE I CRAVE

My sister and brother and I made sandcastles. Those days were amazing. I missed my parents like crazy, but I knew they were watching over me. I didn't think that at first, when I was with HIM. I thought that there was no God because he wouldn't put such a man on this earth. Or he wouldn't let me go through this.

The yacht stopped, and we just sat here. Tabitha took my glass from me. Hunter stood me up on my feet.

"Zollah, I want to tell you something," he said as he took my hand in his. He looked a little nervous, but he kept smiling. "I know you've heard me say this repeatedly. My life took a turn ten years ago at LABA for the good and the bad. I knew from the moment I saw you that I wanted you. I wanted to protect you from the world and the people in it. I knew you were the one for me. I never lied when I said that I would find you. It took me some time, but I was determined. Now that I have you, I will never let you go. I will love you through all your flaws. You made me want to be a better person." As he talked, he brought tears to my eyes.

He was speaking from the heart. I knew how he felt. I felt the same way. I heard the nerves in his voice. I saw him grab something out of his pocket. He lowered himself down on one knee. This couldn't be happening right now. Was this too early for us? But this was what I waited for.

"Zollah Piper Hope, will you please do the honor of being my wife and making me the happiest man alive?" he asked, and for a moment, I thought that this was a dream. This was something I waited so long for, and now it was here. I was speechless. My mouth was dry, and my heart was racing. I looked down at Hunter on his knee. The tears rolled down my face.

"Yes, Hunter, I will marry you," I said as he stood up on his feet.

"Thank God," he said as he took the ring out. I didn't even pay attention to the ring until he put that bad boy on my finger. I couldn't believe my eyes. It wasn't a regular-size ring or shape. This was the biggest ring I'd ever laid eyes on. It was a heart-shaped diamond.

"Oh my, Hunter," I said as I looked at the ring on my finger. I couldn't walk around with this bad boy on my finger.

"It's beautiful, just like you."

"Yes, it is." It glowed in the midnight hour.

I glazed in his eyes and laid one hell of a kiss on him. I loved him. I was in love with him. I wanted only him. I knew it had only been a few weeks since we'd been together. We'd been together for years in our heads. I had to come to realize that I didn't have to run anymore. If HIM was to find me, so what. What could he do to me that he hadn't physically, emotionally, and mentally already done to me?

I wanted forever with Hunter and if life blessed us with years together, I would be grateful. His eyes shined bright as they talked to me. We made out like two teenagers on the yacht as we turned around to head back to the resort.

# SURPRISE

Oh my, I was an engaged woman now. I couldn't believe it. All I could do was just stare at the rock on my finger. There was no way I could wear this sucker out in public. I would get busted upside my head; the ring was heavy as hell.

"I've never seen a ring more beautiful before," I said. I could be biased because it was mine.

"And you never will see another one like this exact one. It means that you wear my heart around your finger. I designed it and teamed up with Winston. The heart-shape diamond is called Zollah. When each heart shape is sold, you will receive a check. But that exact ring is only made for you," he said. I didn't have any words for that but thank you.

# THE LOVE I CRAVE

When we pulled back into shore, I saw a couple who appeared to have gotten married. They were taking pictures on the beach. They looked so happy as people stared as they walked by. Hunter took my hand, and we walked back to our room.

"I want a beach destination wedding in Jamaica. I hear it's lovely there,"

"Would you like to do that Saturday?" he asked.

"Do what?"

"Get married," he blurted out.

"What? No," I said as I stopped in my tracks. "I have nothing to wear. I have no family or any friends here. You have none of your family here," I said.

"Yes or no?" he asked. I took a moment to think about it. I wanted a wedding filled with people we love.

I said nothing as he opened the door for me. I was literally speechless and didn't know what to say. We lay down in bed. Hunter lay on his back with one arm behind his head. The other arm slid down his chest, and he grabbed his manhood under the covers. That beautiful thing was standing at attention. My eyes widened when I saw it. My mouth watered instantly. I wanted him, and I wanted him now.

"You're a freak." I smiled as I tried ignoring the way he made me feel.

"Yes," I said as I climbed on top of him. "Let's do it." He quickly flipped me over. So, he was on top of me. I guess this meant I wasn't getting any.

"Let me show you how grateful I am," he said as he spread my legs apart. He dove in headfirst. Oh my God, this man had me open like a 7-11. I passed out after the fifth time I came.

I woke up, and Hunter was on his laptop. I wondered what he was doing. If he was telling someone that we now were engaged. As he typed away, I thought that maybe it would be best to get married away from the United States. There would be less stress, no TMZ, no paparazzi. Our wedding would be broadcast all over the internet and the newspaper. We couldn't get married without telling our family. I would have to tell Sasha, or she'd kill me. I watched him work until I fell back to sleep. I felt arms around me as I woke up. We made out all morning until right before breakfast was almost over. We finally showered and headed to breakfast.

"Good morning," Asher said as he came up behind us. "I guess by that fat ass rock on your finger, congratulations are in order?"

"Yes, sir," Hunter said as Asher lifted my hand to look at the ring.

"Damn, blind me, why don't you." The lady next to him choked on her orange juice. I didn't even see her at first.

# THE LOVE I CRAVE

"It's beautiful, Hope. My name is Tange, Mr. Ross and Mr. Grayson's supervising manager here," she introduced herself.

"Thank you." I blushed. Asher and Tange went straight to the table while Hunter and I fixed our plates. He went to the omelet station which didn't surprise me.

As I walked back to the table, I saw Tange smiling at Asher. We sat, and I dug in, eating my bacon, eggs, and French toast.

"Asher, is Carrie ready to go?" Hunter asked, which drew my attention because of the name.

"It's ready when you are. I'll meet you there. I'll take the plane there and return here in Carrie," Asher said. I wanted to ask questions, but I was hungry and didn't want to be nosy. I couldn't help it.

"Where are we going now?" I asked.

"Jamaica," Hunter said.

"We're going there by boat?"

"Yes, is there a problem?"

"No, just being nosy. I'm down for whatever."

"I know you are." He smiled as we finished our food and walked toward the beach. I saw a bellhop with our luggage.

"We're not coming back?" I asked.

419

"No, maybe another time," he said as we walked up to this big yacht. It was black and white with the word Carrie on it. He named a boat after his mom. Hunter helped me up on Carrie. A man handed him some paperwork, which Hunter filled it out and handed it back.

"Come." He grabbed my hand.

He led the way to the bottom of the yacht. We entered a bedroom. I went in and sat on the bed. My mind raced with thoughts. I thought of what Dr. Stevens had said the last time I saw her. I replayed it in my mind. I thought about how many people would be upset that they weren't here to share this moment with us. Maybe we could have a small ceremony when we got back home. Then I thought about HIM and the things he had told me over the years.

"No one else wants you the way I do. No one else can have you. If you ever leave me, I'll kill you. If you ever give my pussy away, I'll kill you and them. If I can't have you, no one can." That was what I heard for nine years of my life. That played repeatedly in my mind as I watched Hunter put everything away. Then he pulled out his laptop. I couldn't wait to be his wife. I could finally have him inside me soon.

What had Hunter done to himself so he wouldn't be able to have sex for weeks? He did something while I was in Florida. I took off my shoes and got comfortable on the bed.

# THE LOVE I CRAVE

Hunter relaxed with his laptop on his lap. I just asked a question out of nowhere.

"Are we saying our own vows or reciting the original?" I asked.

"Whatever you want to do," he said, never looking up from his laptop. I closed my eyes to think about what I wanted. It wasn't long before I went to sleep.

I opened my eyes when I no longer heard the typing sound. I looked around, and I wasn't on the yacht. I was in Florida, and I was with HIM. It was one of his partners' rentals. This was right before I left for LABA. He had the house decorated with candles and roses everywhere. He had a chef fix his favorite dish. After we ate, we went into the living room. There was a piano there. I had never played for anyone before except my parents, Sasha, Damon, and Sophia. I played the piano and sang a song to HIM, and the boy lost his mind.

He told me that my voice was a gift from God, and that it would make a blind man see. My voice was only for his ears and his ears only. He said that he would wait to have sex with me until I was ready, but the way I sang that song to HIM, he had to have me. We didn't have sex, but we kissed and toyed with each other's body.

Then the scene changed, and we were at the estate having a party. I remembered that night as well. That was the first time I saw HIM flirting with someone in front of me. I got jealous and tried the same thing.

"What the fuck are you doing?" HE said as HE came over to me. I was surprised HE noticed because HE had left the room.

"Having a conversation. What the fuck are you doing?" I asked, drunk.

"Let me talk to you." HE grabbed me by the arm and led me upstairs. Something in me didn't want to go, but one half of me wanted to talk because I loved HIM.

"Do you have a fucking problem?" HE asked.

"Yes. Who is she?" I asked.

"You're questioning me now?"

"Who is she?" I asked again. I felt like there was something between them, when I saw them together. "Did you fuck her?"

"Don't ask me questions you don't want the answer to." To me, that meant yes. HE was avoiding the question.

"Great, now I can go out and fuck somebody else." At that moment, I knew those words were the wrong ones to say. HIS head snapped my way. HIS hand came up so fast, I didn't see it until it came across my face. I fell on the bed, crying. "I'm sorry." HE turned me to face him. I screamed at him before I attacked. HE smacked me again. I smacked him back.

# THE LOVE I CRAVE

The look on HIS face was utter shock. This time, HE used all HIS might to smack me again. HE threw me down on the bed, holding my arms above my head. "Let me go," I cried out.

"I'll never let you go. You belong to me," HE said, holding me down. I tried to escape the grip HE had on me. It was like something in HIM snapped out of HIS crazy trance. HE let me go.

"I'm sorry, MP."

"How could you hit me? I can't stay here," I asked, still crying. HIS facial expression changed.

"And where the fuck would you go? You have nothing. You are nothing without me. If you leave, you and your best friend's modeling career is over. You want to leave me for someone else. You want to give my pussy away."

"If I knew where he was, I wouldn't be here with you." I was upset. I wanted to hurt HIM just as bad as HE hurt me. He ran over to me.

"Who the fuck is he?" HE slapped me again. HE pulled his belt off with one hand as HIS other held me down.

"Please, no," I begged as HE tied my hands to the headboard.

HE pulled out his manhood. I yanked and yanked the belt, trying to get myself free. HE pulled my shorts off, spread my legs apart, and entered me. I screamed out at HIM. Sex between us in the beginning was slow and sensual. Now HE was being aggressive and abusive. He moved at a fast pace in and out of me.

"Please just let me leave," I begged.

"No, I'll never. You want to be with this boy. He'll never have you because I'll kill you first," HE said as HE smacked me across my face again.

When HE was done, HE stood over me. I cried, hoping it would get rid of the pain. HE paced back and forth, mumbling something to himself. HE came over to untie my arms. I wrapped my arms around myself. When HE came up and wrapped his arms around me, that made me cry more. I didn't want HIM to touch me.

"I'm sorry, MP. I just panicked. I never wanted to hurt you. I love you more than life itself. I'll never hurt you again." A piece of my soul left me that night, along with some of my sanity. "Do you still love me, MP. Will you forgive me?" HE turned me around to face HIM. HE leaned in and laid a hell of a kiss on me. Another reason I fell in love—HE was a great kisser.

"Yes, I do forgive you. Yes, I still love you," I said, and I knew I'd never forget. That night, I cried myself to sleep.

I started to believe after a while that I was doing something wrong. That I deserved what he was doing to me. I never questioned HIM again. I slept in the next day. Sasha and Sophia checked on me, but I didn't answer. I didn't tell them about that night, but they sure learned about nights after that.

"Zollah, wake up." I heard my name, and my eyes popped open. Hunter was leaning over me. I jumped up in his arms and squeezed him tight. He pulled back the hug. "HIM?" he asked. I shook my head yes. His facial expression tightened. He was mad; I saw it in his eyes. I got up and paced.

"I'm sorry."

"Why do you keep apologizing? He's the one I'm going to fucking kill," he said. I stopped pacing.

"No, you can't talk like that. If you do, then I'll lose you, and I couldn't bear that." I moved in front of him. "HE can't hurt me anymore, least not physically. You won't let HIM hurt me, and I won't either. Not anymore. I can protect myself. When I left, I joined a gym. I took self-defense classes, and I took lessons at the gun range," I said. Hunter made a face.

"The thought of you handling a gun turns me on," he said.

"Everything turns you on," I said as he pulled me into a hug.

I could see Hunter killing HIM and getting away with it. That's how much money and power he had. That wouldn't make my nightmares go away. That wouldn't make the pain go away. HE had done enough to me that I wouldn't let it draw a wedge between Hunter and me.

Dr. Stevens said that I had to forgive HIM to move on. How could you forgive someone who had done the things he had done to me? He made me do things you thought didn't exist. It was easier said than done. I thought about Sasha and how she was dragged around a drug whore house and passed around to drug dealers. I asked her how she moved on. She said she forgave her mother. Was that how you moved on? Sophia had forgiven her father after his friends had molested her. She moved on. They both ran away and ended up at the foster house where I ended up because my parents had died. I am going to be strong about this. I didn't escape a death sentence with HIM to be dragged back willingly. I had to fight.

# JAMAICAN ME CRAZY

It was Friday when I opened my eyes. I felt like a whole new woman as I stretched. I eased out of bed and made a mimosa. I slipped on my red robe and slippers and grabbed my shades as I left the bottom of the boat and came up the yacht. The sky was one of the perfect ones I had seen. I walked slowly to the edge of the boat and watched as we headed to shore. The water I could tell had changed to a crystal blue. I slipped on my shades, leaned on the rail, and watched the morning sky and the breeze through my loose hair.

I enjoyed all the refreshing me time I had, just enjoying the view. I smiled to myself, thinking about what it took to get to this moment and would I do it again. Would I go through life-threatening hell just for this moment in my life?

I wanted to cry happy tears. I had no idea how much time had passed before Hunter came out.

"Good morning, love of my life." I turned to see a glow radiating from him. I guess it was a good morning for the both of us. I smiled just like a schoolgirl as he kissed me on the cheek.

"It's a beautiful morning, isn't it?" I said, looking out as the shore drew closer.

"Yes, it is," he said, staring at me. Hunter and I watched as the shore came in better view, and I could hear music coming from somewhere. "We should get ready." He led me back down and twenty minutes later, we were stepping off Carrie. A lady and a gentleman were waiting for us.

"Good afternoon, Mr. Grayson. We have everything waiting for you." She turned toward me. "Mrs. Grayson." She smiled, and I said hello. I could get used to being called Mrs. Grayson. As of tomorrow, I would be.

Three other men stepped onto the boat to grab our luggage. The gentleman whose name tag read Thomas led us off the beach and toward a pool. There was a sign that read Welcome to Sandals. This place was more elegant than the other one. Everything about this place screamed Hunter. I wouldn't be surprised if he owned this place. He got behind the wheel of what looked like a golf cart. He drove us to our personal little cottage.

# THE LOVE I CRAVE

He opened the room and let me tell you, DR had nothing on this place. The cottage was huge. It reminded me of a little house. We walked into the living room. There was black antique furniture with a flat-screen TV and a gold and black coffee table. The kitchen was decorated with Jamaican colors. I went to look in the bedroom, the bed was in the middle of the room. We had to walk down steps to get to the bed. The bathroom had a huge glass shower with a bench in it. Then it had a Jacuzzi tub that sat outside and inside. I walked out back, and we had our own pool. The room was magnificent. I was all smiles, just like Hunter was yesterday. I checked the mini fridge, and they had all kinds of beer inside, but I wasn't a beer drinker. I was in dying need of a drink.

"You like the place?" he asked.

"Like it, Hunter? I love this place. I may never want to leave."

It was early morning, and Hunter and I had time to rest up before our dinner at four. Hunter pulled out our suitcases and unpacked our things. We had eaten something small to have in our stomachs. I took a nap and woke up with just enough time to do some work. I checked my emails to see what was going on. There wasn't much for me to respond to, so I showered and got ready for dinner.

"I have a surprise for you," he said when I got out of the shower.

"Another one? I don't think my heart can take any more," I said as he laughed. I walked further into the room and noticed he had already set out clothes for me. It was a turquoise-blue spaghetti-strap dress. It was low cut with a heart-shape neckline. It was fitted up the top and down to my lower waist, it flared out. I slipped on some cute sparkly rhinestone sandals. They went well with the dress.

"So, you own this resort?"

"Yes. I lived here for a while, getting it built. This is my personal cottage. I had it built like where we stayed when we were at LABA. This was my first resort; Dominican is my second," he said.

"You moved back from DR the day I saw you on the elevator?"

"Yes," he said. I was quiet for a moment.

"Where are we going?" I said as we passed another restaurant.

"To have dinner. I rented out a private hall for us," he said as he pulled out his phone. He punched in a few buttons as we walked up to this door that read, 'Bob Marley's Guitar Room'

"Open the door." He looked at me. From where I was standing, it looked like all the lights were out, and no one was home. I put my hand on the knob and slowly opened it. I felt the wall for the light switch but couldn't find it. The light clicked on, and my eyes widened with shock.

"Surprise!" The sound of loud voices erupted in my ear. I backed up.

My heart leapt from my chest. I couldn't believe my eyes. The room was filled with everyone that meant something to me. How could everyone fly here just in time for my wedding? I wasn't complaining. It made sense to me now. This was why everyone was acting strange. I was literally shocked. I knew Hunter was up to something. I saw Sasha, Damon, Melissa, Aimee, Jessie, and Dr. Stevens. Just when I thought I wouldn't share this moment with my friends. My dreams were coming true.

Mr. and Mrs. Grayson were here. So was Emmanuel and the girl from the pictures had to be his sister Leena. The guy next to her was her husband, I guessed.

"What are you two doing here?" I said as I hugged Sasha and Damon.

"We wouldn't miss your big day for anything," Damon said.

"Hell no, we wouldn't," Sasha said. I was in tears. I was thinking about my family. My mother and father. Brooke and Ryan. I missed them so much.

"Hope, that ring is blindingly big," Sasha said with a smile. "What is that, a three karat?"

# Henson Dreamier

"Hell no, that's a boulder. Can you even hold your hand up?" Damon said.

"That's a beautiful ring but so big. Why did he have to get a five carat?" Mrs. Carrie said, examining it. "The poor girl won't be able to go out in public with that thing."

I went around hugging everyone, including my friend Jessie who had been like a father to me. I met Leena and Hunter's grandparents. It was Mrs. Carrie's parents. Mr. Grayson's parents died a couple of years ago.

Asher was also there with Tange. I also met Bradley, Leena's husband. We mingled for a while, just talking and having a cocktail. I was in dying need of a drink and when I tasted it, it was gone just like that. I peeked over to see Hunter standing and talking to his brother. He looked over at me as if he felt me staring. He moved his lips, forming the words, I love you. I smiled and made my way around before dinner was served.

We all sat. Hunter was on my right with his family, and Sasha sat on my left next to Julius and the rest of my family. Before I had a chance to chow down, Hunter stood up with a glass of ginger ale. Everyone else's glass was filled with champagne.

"I want to thank everyone for coming all the way to Jamaica for this lovely occasion. All of you know how long I searched for this beautiful lady right here. I always wanted to make her my wife. Ten years since the first day I met her.

# THE LOVE I CRAVE

Eight years since I last saw her, but who's counting. There was a time when I almost had given up. As you all know, giving up isn't in my blood." He looked at his father. "Someone told me that if it was meant to be, it will be." He looked at his mother. "On that day when Jason had called me and told me he had found her, it was like a weight had lifted from my heart. Words can never express how I feel about her. So, thank you all again for coming. Now God is great, God is good, and I thank him for this food. Amen." He sat back down in his seat.

There was a complete moment of silence, all we heard were our forks and knives hitting the plates. I stopped the server and asked for a Bob Marley drink. It was a slushy one with three different Jamaican colors. It was delicious.

I leaned toward Sasha and said, "I have nothing to wear tomorrow."

"You have nothing to worry about. I got you like I always do," she said.

"I know this is last minute, but will you be my maid of honor?"

"Of course," she said with a smirk.

"Then we have to find you a dress," I said.

"Hope, don't worry. All you have to do is show up and say I do," Sasha said, and I smiled. How did I deserve such a great friend?

"How did you know I'd say yes?"

"You've loved him for too long. He makes you happy, and you make him happy. So, I knew you'd say yes. You would have been a fool to say no. I told Hunter that you'd say yes," she said.

"Do you think I'm a fool for marrying a man after being with him for what, two months?" I knew eight weeks wasn't enough time. All I knew was I didn't want to be with anyone else ever. I couldn't live without him.

"Yes, I do, but it's you and Hunter. You two have history, without having history." She burst out laughing at her own words. "If that makes any sense." I had no idea what she was talking about, but I understood where she was trying to go with that. We hugged tight.

"There's a club here on the resort," Melissa said. She sat next to Julius. "We can turn this party into a bachelorette party. Just us ladies."

"That should be fun," I said.

"Let us turn up tonight," Aimee said.

"Don't get too drunk and leave me at the altar," Hunter said, butting into our conversation. I turned to him. His eyes glowed, telling me he wanted me. If marrying him was a mistake, then it was the best mistake I'd ever make.

# THE LOVE I CRAVE

I smiled and said, "Never." I kissed him. Oh, how I loved the way my body melted when any part of him touched me. I closed my eyes, pulled back the kiss, and turned back to Sasha.

"I almost forgot," she said as she pulled out a bag from under the table. She pulled out a sparkled tiara with a bride on it. She placed it on my head, sticking me with a few bobby pins.

"Now you're ready to go. It goes good with your dress."

We left the Bob Marley Room and headed to the club. Just us ladies. The men headed to a show at the theater. The lights were low, with flashing lights of different colors. We found a table by a little stage.

"Hello," a guy said. "My name is Joseph." He looked up at the tiara. "Congratulations."

"Thank you."

I saw the bartender come over with two bottles of champagne and a special brewed rum. He lined up shot glasses, along with nine champagne glasses.

"If you need anything, let me or Nathan know," Joseph said. "Nathan is the bartender." He smiled and said hello.

There were a few people sitting around. People were also coming in and finding a place at the bar and the tables. Reggae music played from the DJ booth. It wasn't the kind of reggae I listened to at home. It was the hardcore, come fuck me music. I loved it. We all sipped from the champagne. Mrs. Fields and Mrs. Phoebe only had wine. Mrs. Carrie only took one shot and left the rest to the young girls. A half hour and three shots later, we were on the dance floor. We partied to some of our favorite music. I was having so much fun, enjoying everyone's company. It was a little after two when we left.

Mrs. Carrie told me that I was to sleep with Sasha tonight; I couldn't see Hunter until the wedding. It was fine with me. I didn't mind, but Hunter might be disappointed. She said she'd take care of her son. I wished I could be a fly on the wall for that conversation.

I was sleeping when I heard my name called. I thought I was going crazy. Sasha stayed on the ground floor. So, someone could've been calling me. I slowly peeked my eyes open. I saw a shadow by the patio door. I heard my name again. I got up and walked over to the door. I pulled the curtain back. I saw Hunter standing out there with a single white rose in his hand. I unlocked the door and let myself out.

"What are you doing here, Mr. Grayson? It's bad luck to see me before the wedding." Hunter held his hand out for mine.

"I had to make sure you didn't have cold feet," he said as we walked over toward a bench. It was so beautiful here. I felt like a princess. One with a dark past.

"I don't, do you?" I asked.

"No, but I had to make sure you didn't run for the hills," he said. I noticed he was leading us over to the pool.

"I'm not going nowhere." I blushed.

"I had to see you one last time before you become Mrs. Grayson. Officially." He smiled.

"Damn, and I thought you were coming for a booty call," I joked. He laughed.

"You're funny, baby girl. I'm not making love to you no more until you're my wife," he said.

"Well, I'm glad that's in like less than seven hours." He smiled but ignored what I said.

"That's one reason I held out on sex." His face turned serious. "The first reason." He paused for a moment, just enough for him to take his shoes off. I looked down at my feet and noticed that I had no shoes on. We sat at the pool and put our feet in the water. We turned to face each other. He gazed into my eyes.

"The first reason is because I had my vasectomy reversed. The weekend you went to Florida. I know you want to have children one day, so I did it." I looked at him as if he were speaking Chinese. He got what reversed. My brain was moving in slow motion, replaying what I thought he said.

"What?"

"I had to wait three weeks before I could be inside you again." He smiled. "You want little crumb snatchers one day, don't you?"

"One day? How about now day," I said as I charged at his lips. Oh my goodness, I wanted him. Everything in me tingled for some type of affection or touch from him. I pulled back the kiss.

"Hunter Grayson, I wanted nothing all my life but to be your wife and bear your children." I paused for a second. "You promised." I charged at him again with a kiss. I wanted him so bad. I kissed him with everything in me. My heart and my soul. I didn't break the kiss when I straddled him. His hands gripped my nightgown tight. I knew he wanted to rip it off, but he couldn't.

"I want you," I begged in his ear. I kissed and licked his ear and his neck. I bit his ear and his neck. He pulled me back. It was like ripping a bandage off. It hurt.

"Stop before I have to fuck you here in this pool," he said, looking at me. I saw it in his eyes. He was on the verge of cracking. He wanted it.

"Yes, fuck me in the pool," I said, getting excited.

"No…" He laughed. "Not until you're my wife." He stood up from the pool, his manhood standing at attention.

"See, even Javier wants some," I said, looking at his manhood with my mouth getting watery.

"Is that what you want to call him?" He helped me up from the pool.

"Yes, Javier is sexy. It can be an animal because you're one in the bedroom." I went to grab him down there. He caught my hand.

"Look at what you do to me," he said.

"I didn't do that. You did that to yourself when you told me we can have kids now," I said. He smiled and tapped my leg for me to get up. We walked back to Sasha's room.

"Where are you going, girl?" He followed me.

"Bye."

"You going to leave me out here?" he said.

"Yes. Do you want me to get your mother and tell her you're out here harassing me?" I said, standing at the door of the patio.

"Oh, you're playing dirty. Get my mother involved."

"Goodbye, Hunter," I said.

"Hold up. Take your rose." He handed me the white rose.

"Now get out of here. I need as much sleep as I can get."

"See you at the altar." He walked back down the grass passageway. I remembered that boy at LABA. He had the same walk. I would never forget it. I closed the door and locked it and climbed back in bed. I was so happy, a tear rolled down my face. I would finally have the family I wanted. I thought of that until I drifted off to sleep.

I woke up and stretched my hand out for Sasha, but the bed was empty. I turned over to check the time. It was still a little early. I didn't know what time I was getting married. I got up from the bed and walked over to the bathroom. I saw a note on the dresser. It was Sasha's handwriting. The note read.

"Don't leave the room and order room service. Be back soon." I threw the note back on the dresser and went back over to the bed to order room service.

My food didn't take long to get here. I also ordered a couple of mimosas. I was getting a little nervous. After I ate, I ran a bath to relax. I breathed in and out. My mind flooded with thoughts. What dress I was wearing. Where the location would be. I kept telling myself that I would tell Hunter everything. I was scared because once I did, I didn't think I could stop him if he went after HIM. What I had to say wasn't anything nice. Well, twenty percent of it has good parts in it.

I looked at my hands to see if they were wrinkled. My momma told me you weren't clean until you were wrinkled. I let out a sigh, thinking about my parents, wondering if they were proud of me or cursing me out, telling me I was crazy. I wanted to see my father smile and be in my mother's arms. I missed them so much, but I knew they were watching over me. I heard the front door open and voices getting closer.

"Okay, lady, it's time to get this show on the road," I heard Aimee say.

"Where is she?" Melissa asked.

"I'm in here," I yelled out from the bathroom. The door swung open, and Mrs. Carrie, Leena, Melissa, Aimee, and Sasha stood in the doorway.

"There you are." Mrs. Carrie came over and let the water out of the tub. Sasha grabbed a towel from the rack. I climbed out. They led me into the living room and sat me down in a chair. Sasha blew out my hair for me like she always did since we were younger.

"How do you want your hair?" Sasha asked.

"Curled and pinned to one side with that rose." I pointed to the rose on the nightstand. Mrs. Carrie grabbed the rose from the room. She looked at it.

"I guess my son paid you a visit last night," she said, turning the rose in her hands. I smiled and blushed. I couldn't help it; I had no idea why I was laughing.

"Yes, but I sent him away." I did after I tried to rape him by the pool.

"Umm hmm." She handed it to Sasha who pinned it in my hair. Leena told me to close my eyes while she applied my makeup. When I opened my eyes, I looked amazing. She didn't use a lot of makeup, just enough to enhance my beauty.

# Henson Dreamier

I sat there and looked at myself in the mirror. Leena went over to grab a dress from the bed. So did Melissa and Aimee. Sasha handed me a mimosa for my nerves before heading into the bathroom with the rest of the girls. I paced the floor, waiting to see them. I heard the bathroom door open. They all came out in red Chevon dresses. Sasha was the only one in a different type of dress.

"You ladies look lovely," I said, examining the dresses. "Who picked out the dresses?"

"Hunter picked out the color, but I picked the dresses and emailed the picture to see if they all agreed," Sasha said.

"Everyone looks nice, but what about me?" I said in a sarcastic way.

"Sorry," they all said. Sasha went over to the bed and pointed to the only dress left. "This one is for you." I went over and unzipped it. When I pulled the dress out, it was again another surprise.

"You sneaky bitch." I couldn't believe my eyes. I took it out of the dress bag.

"Oh, darling, that's a beautiful dress," Mrs. Carrie said.

I was holding the white dress that I loved in Florida. The one I wanted so bad but didn't get. I didn't want to pay that much for a dress even though I had the money. I couldn't wait to put it on. When I first saw the dress, I knew it was made for me. They helped me get dressed, and they picked out jewelry for me to wear. When they were done, I looked in the mirror, and I looked breathtaking. The one-sleeve white dress fit me perfect.

"Let's get this show on the road," I said.

We headed toward the beach. I felt like I was on the runway, modeling for wedding gowns. This dress was made for a beach wedding. Sasha had gotten me some white sandals that had silver rhinestones on them. We made it to the beach. We all climbed in a cart, and a girl drove us down the beach. I saw a few people a few feet away. The cart stopped before we reached the blocked area.

"Is someone walking me down or am I walking down by myself?" I asked.

"Whatever you want?" they asked. I thought for a moment.

"Damon," I said.

"Well, Damon, Julius, and Emmanuel can't because they're in the wedding party," Aimee said. Just as she said it, a light bulb lit up. I totally forgot. Someone who I looked up to. Someone who had been like a father to me.

"Jessie should do it. Do you think he'll mind?" I asked. I saw Tange come over and handed us bouquets.

"He'll be honored, I'm sure," Sasha said.

"I'll go get him, then we can get started," Mrs. Carrie said. I saw her walk down to the group. She said something to Jesse, and he looked my way. I tried to look for Hunter, but I couldn't see him. Jessie walked my way. He finally made it and stopped in front of me.

"You look magnificent," he said as he hugged me.

"Thank you, Jesse, so much for doing this for me. It means a lot to me," I said.

"Please, Hope, it's a pleasure. I told you that you were the daughter I never had." He held out his arm for me to take.

As I grabbed his arm, music came on, playing one of the songs I'd loved since it came out years ago. We walked and as we got closer, all I wanted to see was Hunter. To see if he was real. Leena walked down the aisle first. Then Melissa and Aimee. Then Sasha. I was beginning to lose my breath. I had my head down as I walked, listening to the song.

When I looked up, I saw Hunter standing there with an all-white suit. There was nothing sexier than a chocolate man in all white. He looked like a Greek god. Our eyes met, and I could tell his heart skipped a beat. It was written all over his face. My eyes watered because I could see Hunter getting emotional. I got to the beginning of the short walkway, and everyone stood. I couldn't believe I was getting married.

I finally made it to Hunter. I wanted to let go of Jesse and run into his arms. Have him take us somewhere where we could never be disturbed. I was fighting my emotions; I didn't want to cry and mess up my makeup. He was fighting his emotions too. The music stopped, and everyone sat. I saw Damon behind Emmanuel. He looked nice in his tan linen outfit. Everything was perfect right now. The weather wasn't so hot today. The pastor was tall with light-brown skin. He looked at Jessie.

"Do you give this woman to this man?" he asked. Jessie looked at me and smiled. He turned back to the pastor.

"I do," Jessie said as he handed me over to Hunter. When my hand touched his, I felt sparks inside me. After five mimosas, I felt wonderful. I wasn't nervous anymore. All I wanted in life right now was him.

# THE VOWS

I stood next to Hunter. His eyes were glowing. He smiled, and I knew that I made him happy. He made me happy, and I was in love with everything about him.

"You look..." He paused for a moment. He eyed me up and down. "You literally took my breath away." We turned to face each other.

"Thank you. You don't look so bad yourself. Sexy, handsome and..." I leaned in and whispered, "fuckable." He smiled. Lucky for me, we weren't inside a church. I'd be going to hell. Once we were quiet, Hunter and I just stared at one another. Eyes locked in the moment.

"Dearly beloved, we are gathered here today to spread the love that Hunter and Zollah share. We are here to bring this man and this woman together as one. Hunter met Zollah years ago where one day made them realize that what they felt for one another would last forever. Now, here we are. Here to share their special day." The pastor turned to me.

"Zollah, do you love this man?" he asked. I squeezed his hand in mine.

"With everything," I said. He turned to Hunter.

"Hunter, do you love this woman?" he asked him.

"More than everything."

"Now, would you to like to say your vows to each other?" he asked, and immediately I knew I wanted to go first.

"Oh, Mr. Grayson, I felt empty for so many years without you. One day at a time, I'm feeling whole again. You have been there for me in ways I could have never imagined. I knew that one day I would be standing here vowing my love to you. Telling you how much I loved you. How much I will be here to support you at whatever you want to do. I will work hard on our love as best I can, no matter what. Through the good times. The rough times. The tough times. I vow to love, honor, respect, and cherish you until my heart beats no more." I was teary eyed, hoping my makeup wouldn't run. The pastor turned to Hunter.

"Zollah Piper Hope." He smiled to himself. "When we first met, you were so caught up on my good looks. You tripped and fell on your face. I knew I had to save you. When I held you in my arms for the first time, and our eyes

447

connected, I knew… I knew you would be my wife. A spark was ignited when I spent that summer with you. I love you more than anything. You have made me the happiest man alive. I vow for the rest of my life to honor, respect, cherish, and make you a happy woman. I'm going to love you every day until forever." A single tear rolled down my cheek. Hunter lifted his hand and wiped it with his thumb. Things were quiet for a moment.

"After those words, there is nothing left for me to say. I now pronounce you Mr. and Mrs. Grayson. You may now kiss the bride." Hunter didn't wait for the pastor to finish. He kissed me hard. I wrapped my arms around his neck. I could kiss him all day without stopping. Hunter was the one who pulled back. We turned to face our guests.

"Mr. and Mrs. Hunter Grayson," the pastor said.

Music came on as we walked back down the aisle. I noticed a photographer taking pictures. The pastor led us over to a table where we signed our marriage certificate. The guests headed to the other side of the beach where we would be having dinner. The bridal party, Hunter, and I took pictures along the beach. Then they left for dinner while Hunter and I took more pictures. After like the hundredth picture, I was in dire need of a drink, and I was tired of smiling for pictures. So, we made our way to the reception.

At the table before eating, everyone said something special to Hunter and me. I felt so emotional, but I felt relieved. We ate dinner, and I had some champagne and a few shots of tequila. We danced the evening away. It was still early when Hunter turned to me and said he was ready to go back to the room. We said our goodbyes and headed back. We planned to get together tomorrow for dinner.

We stopped in front of our door. Pulling out the key, Hunter turned to me and smiled. He lifted me up in his arms and carried me over the threshold. He didn't put me down until we were in the bedroom. He put me on my feet in front of him. His hands ran up and down my arms. His head leaned into mine.

"You look beautiful in this dress," he said, his eyes glowing.

"You're not ripping this dress, or your ass is mine," I said.

"I won't," he said with a sexy grin on his face. "Stay right there," he ordered as he went to turn on some music. He came back over to me.

"Let me help you out of that dress." He touched my face with his hand.

I could feel the heat from his hand radiate from him to me. His hand slid down my cheek, then he caressed my neck and shoulders. Oh, I felt like I'd smoked a drug that didn't exist. He walked around me, and his hand touched my back and kissed the back of my neck. I gasped. He licked my back as he unzipped my dress and peeled the dress off me as his hands traveled over my body. My dress fell to my ankles, and he told me to step out of it. He came around and faced me again, admiring my body.

He moved his hands to unbutton his shirt. I moved them and told him to let me do that. I slowly undressed him, taking off his shirt first. Then I lifted his tank top over his head. My eyes gazed at his chest as his muscles rippled. I ran my finger from his cheek to his neck. Then I ran circles around his nipples with my finger then trailed down his stomach. I licked him just to see if he really tasted like chocolate. He sighed. I took my hands to unbuckle his belt. His pants fell down to his ankles, and he stepped out of them. My eyes met his, and I leaned in and kissed him.

"You have the softest lips I've ever kissed." He moaned from the kiss.

He picked me up and placed me slowly on the bed. I watched as he climbed on the bed. He sat on his knees at my feet. He took one foot in his hand and lifted it up. He opened his mouth and sucked on each one of my toes. He massaged my kitty and thighs. I loved the way his lips made me feel, like I was the only one in the world who existed to him. The effect he had on me should be illegal. Each kiss sent a tingle through my body, erecting my nipples. He made his way back down and stopped at my cave. One lick, and I came.

"Yes, baby girl. I love the effect I have on you," he said.

His lips made love to my body. I closed my eyes, and he took me to a place I'd never been before. Something was happening to me. I had no idea what was going on. I opened my eyes, and I saw us floating in the sky at night. While the stars shone bright, it felt as if all my emotions and senses took over my body. I could feel him touch me before he even touched me. I felt like a puppet, and Hunter controlled the strings, making me do whatever he wanted me to do. We lay on a cloud in the sky.

Things moved in slow motion. My body ached for a release. I flipped him over to return the same pleasure he gave me. I kissed him all over his body, from his neck to his manhood. I kissed it like it was mine, and I didn't want to let it go. I sucked his head, then took him all in my mouth. It seemed like forever since I had him inside me. I could tell he was about to explode. He stopped me and flipped me back over. So, he was on top. He sucked my nipples.

"Make love to me Hunter. I ache for you," I begged as he wasted no time entering me. He wasn't all the way in when I came.

"Oh my," he moaned as I opened my legs to accept more of him. I moved my hips with his. He moved slow in and out of me. He worked every inch of my insides. I closed my legs around him, securing him inside me. I wrapped my arms around his neck. I grabbed his ass to push him in more. His pace picked up, moving fast in and out of me, building up my orgasm.

I turned him over so I could be on top. I wanted to ride him until he let all of his seed inside me. I leaned back on him. He pinched and squeezed my nipples. My hips ran circles on the tip of his dick, then I slammed down to the base of him, accepting all of him. I did that repeatedly. I saw his eyes rolling in the back of his head.

"Damn girl, you're going to make me come," he moaned. I stopped and leaned forward, gazing into his eyes.

"Come inside me," I moaned in his ear. He sat up with his elbows.

"Are you sure you want this so soon?" he asked.

"I've never wanted anything more than being your wife and having your…" I paused to think about what he called them earlier. "crumb snatchers. I want a family. We're five years late," I said.

"Whatever you want, I want." I kissed him as I moved my hips, massaging his manhood with my cave. Our tongues fought with each other, and our bodies melted together.

"Shit!" Hunter said as he pulled me off him. He turned me around on my stomach. He slapped his manhood on my ass. It was firm and hard. He entered me from behind. We made love all night. Each time he came in me, he made sure one of those nuts would make a little Hunter or Zollah. There was so much sucking, licking, fucking, moaning, and screaming, I knew the neighbors knew our names.

We didn't go to sleep until the sun came up. This was the second time we made love until the rooster hollered. I was dead to the world when I woke. I turned left and right and no Hunter. Something told me to look down, and there Hunter was, with his head in my lap. Who fell asleep like this? He was sleep as I tried to move from under him, but one movement had him licking me again. I couldn't take no more of him. My kitty was sore, and my clit was swollen.

"Oh God," I moaned. Hunter was up now that I made a move. Everything on my body was sensitive.

"Hunter?" He said nothing to me. He just ate his omelet which was me. He got me all nice and wet before entering me.

"Shit," I moaned as he held my arms down on the bed. I tried to push myself away from him.

He made me feel too good. The more I moaned, the more he fucked me senseless. He used his finger to rub my clit, sending me squirting all over his hands. My eyes rolled in the back of my head as I screamed. I went out again.

We slept and had sex the entire day. I needed to come up for some air. It was seven o'clock when we left for dinner. I could barely walk. Everyone was already seated when we arrived. They were all smiles as we sat. Sasha and Julius sat next to each other. Damon was talking to Aimee. Everyone from the wedding was here.

"Glad that you two decided to come up for some air," Emmanuel said as he sipped from his glass. Conversation traveled the table, but all I could think about was my husband.

Hunter had his arm on the back of my chair. I laid my head on his shoulder. Dinner was buffet style, and I couldn't get the strength to get up. I looked up, and Sasha had brought me a plate and set it in front of me.

"Thank you," I said. I was starving; the only thing I'd had to eat was dick. That wasn't enough protein to keep me from passing out. Sasha probably knew what I had been through. I tore that food up, cleaning the plate like my father made me do.

"So, are you going to move in with him at the beach house?" Sasha asked.

"What?" I said.

"You're married now. You can't live in two different places. Plus, Hunter won't allow that," she said, and she was right. But I wouldn't want to live apart from him. I hadn't even thought of that. I was going to have to move out of my house.

"I guess I do. I married now," I said, sounding like Celie from *The Color Purple*. I couldn't believe I was married. I turned to look at Hunter who was staring at me. He kissed my forehead, my cheek, my lips, and my neck. My kitty was moist instantly.

"Not at the table," Mrs. Carrie said. I looked up and saw everyone smiling at us.

"Let's go back to the room." Hunter said, whining.

"But you haven't eaten anything, and we have guests at the table," I said, but to be honest, I was no good to any of them.

"All I want to eat is you." He kissed my lips, and heat took over my body.

"Nothing until you eat first." He looked at me for a brief second.

"Okay," he said, getting up from the table to fix him a plate.

"Don't come back to LA with something you didn't leave with," Sasha said.

"What?"

"The rate you two are going, you'll be pregnant in no time," she said. I looked at her. I didn't say anything. I didn't say that since we said I do. That's what we had been trying to do.

"No way." I smiled. Hunter returned with his food. He ate so fast I was surprised he didn't choke.

"I'm finished now. Can we go?" I stared at him in shock. He sounded like a whining child who needed to get his way.

"You're too excited to get back to the room," I said. I turned to Sasha who was talking to Julius.

"Okay, everyone." I stood. "We're about to go."

"Okay, you two." His mother gave us an eye. "We leave in the morning." She stood up from her seat and gave me a hug. It hit me that I had no idea how long they were staying. "Call me when you decide to come up for some air." I hugged Dustin, Emmanuel, and Leena.

"Yeah, we leave in the morning as well," Damon said, referencing to him and Sasha, Julius, Melissa, and Aimee. "I'm happy for you, Z. I truly am."

"Thank you, Damon." Then I hugged Sasha who didn't want to let me go. She held me like a proud mother who had raised her child and was now moving on.

"I love you, Zollah. He will take care of you. I know it," she said.

"I know." We would take care of each other.

Hunter and I walked back to our villa. He was on me before the door closed. We couldn't keep our hands off each other. We made love our entire stay. The remaining days consisted of us talking, swimming, horseback riding, relaxing by the beach and of course, I had all the beverages Jamaica had to offer. Sex on the beach was something I was looking forward to trying again in the future. We were there for almost two weeks. So, when I got my period, we decided it was time to go home.

When I walked through the doors of the beach house, I felt as if I was home. I had a boost of energy that came out of nowhere. I put my things down and flopped down on the couch. I saw Hunter looking at me.

"Come here," I said. He dropped his things and lay down with me.

"Welcome home, Mrs. Grayson," he whispered in my ear.

"I kind of missed this place," I said.

"That makes me feel good," he said. I was quiet for a moment.

"Hunter, can I tell you something?" I asked.

"Of course." He sat up a little. He lay on his side. He put his arm around the back of my neck. I lay on my back, looking up at him. I took a deep breath. Right now, I felt like talking about HIM. Well, not exactly about HIM. Just my time with HIM.

"You remember when we were in Vegas…" I paused as I watched him shake his head. "and I had that nightmare. It was about the hotel that used to be there. The one you tore down. I stayed there with HIM before."

"When?" he asked, his eyes wide open. I didn't know how he would take this. I didn't want him going off in a rampage.

"I think I was about seventeen or eighteen. I've blocked a lot out of my mind because they're too drastic to think

457

about. But things have changed, and things are coming back. It's like getting hit by lightning, and you suddenly remember things. I've never had anyone care for me as Sophia had and Sasha is now. I owe her everything. After I had our..." I cut myself off. I wasn't ready to discuss that with Hunter. Not yet.

"After Sophia died, there wasn't any need for us to stay. Sasha helped me run. She got me away from HIM. She planned everything. She had all our information transferred. She closed her bank account and opened a new one. She gave up everything to leave town with me. We couldn't fly out of Florida because HE would have that tracked. So one night, HE left and told me HE had a surprise for me, something I had been waiting for. HE said HE noticed that I looked empty inside, and that I was missing a part of me. I didn't care what HE had for me. I didn't stay to find out.

"When I left that estate, I had nothing but a bag and ten thousand dollars that Sasha had taken of my money. I snuck out through the emergency tunnels that weren't finished yet. So, it didn't have any cameras. It led to a road a couple of miles behind the estate. Sasha was there waiting for me. She had stolen a car. We couldn't take one of ours as they would be tracked. We dumped our cell phones. Sasha brought untraceable ones.

"We drove until the next night, going in the opposite direction. Then we ditched it at a shopping center. We needed another vehicle, so I stole one while Sasha was inside the grocery store. We made it to Georgia, then found some tractor truck drivers. We rode as far as they were going. We did that until we made it back to California. When I landed in California, I felt good for a change. But I had to keep looking over my shoulder. I knew that one day, he would come and when he did, it wouldn't be pretty," I waited to hear what he had to say. He was quiet, then he laughed.

"Zollah, you stole a car?" Out of everything I said, he focused on that.

"Yeah, I was young, and I would have done anything to get away from HIM," I said.

"You stole a car. That's so hot." I laughed as he leaned in and kissed me.

# SO YOU THOUGHT

It had been a whole month since I became Mrs. Grayson and let me tell you, it had been a little crazy. Somehow, it got out to the press that Hunter Grayson and Zollah Hope had eloped. Now, all the tabloids were having a good time with that. Some said that I was pregnant, and his parents made us get married, being that he came from a strong background and was worth millions of dollars. Some say he ran and married me because his parents didn't agree. People offered to pay me millions of dollars for our wedding pictures. What the hell was wrong with these people? There were so many things being said about Hunter and me. I would let nothing break my happiness.

Hunter brought home every pregnancy test there was. All of them had been saying the same thing. Not pregnant. Now this was freaking him out. Me, I was cool, calm, and collective. I told him it would happen when God said we were ready. He was convinced his vasectomy reversal didn't work.

The sales of my magazine had increased in the last thirty days. The last and latest additions to the magazine had put me in the top ten best magazines. That was music to my ears. Hunter just got back from a business trip to Arizona. I had no idea what kind of business was in the desert. We were looking for a property to buy, so I could start my music school. I'd always loved playing the piano. So, this was a project close to the heart, along with my children's shelter.

It was almost lunch time, and I was trying not to think about what people were saying about us. I had a couple of visits to see Dr. Stevens. I had one yesterday, and I was telling her about the tabloids. I told her I was taking baby steps on telling Hunter about my life with HIM.

Sasha and Julius had gotten close. Five weeks, Sasha kept saying. They had been a couple for five weeks now. She said she wasn't looking for a boyfriend. She had too much to worry about. She said that Julius was very funny and such a gentleman. She said she hadn't given up the booty yet. She was scared to have sex with him. Sasha didn't go farther into telling me why.

It has been a long time since escaping HIM. I was in a better place, in a different space in my heart. My mind was another thing. Sasha had reminded me of the journal I had written on that long journey back to California. The one where I talked about everything HE done to me. I exhaled at

461

the relief that I didn't have to talk about it, all Hunter had to do was read it. It is a dark, sad and explicit story. I was scared because it talked about who SHE is, and he was going to finally know the truth. The truth about what I done because I was selfish and craved for him. What would Hunter do? What would he say? I was picking up the journal when I got off work today.

"I'll be right back. I'm going to get something to eat. Do y'all want something?" I asked. Melissa and Aimee said no.

I left the building and headed to the crosswalk. I was craving for a cheesesteak. I could taste it on my lips. There were a lot of people walking the street on this nice day. In California, we had nice days every day. As I stood at the corner, waiting for the walking sign, something told me to look to my right. I looked over everyone until my eyes focused on a guy standing by the souvenir shop. He had on a black sweatshirt with the hood pulled over his head. He was turned sideways, so I couldn't see his face, but I saw his complexion. He was light skinned and short.

My heart raced. My eyes seemed to only focus on him. I wanted to see his face. I wanted him to turn and look at me. Just when he was about to turn my way, a girl came up to him. She held something in her hand that she had bought from the souvenir shop. He turned my way, but her head blocked his face. The way the girl smiled at him, I could tell she was in love with him. She leaned in and kissed him. A little breeze came along and blew the girl's hair from her cheek. I saw a birthmark on the side of her face, and my heart stopped. It couldn't be.

"Brooke," I yelled the name. I had no idea if it was her. She turned her head to see who was yelling. Our eyes met for a quick moment. *Oh my God, it is her*.

I moved through the crowd to see if I could get closer. I called out her name. I finally made it to the shop, and she was gone. Just like that. I looked around to see if I could find her, but she was gone. Who was that guy to her? Maybe I was seeing things. I ran across the street and grabbed my cheesesteak. I ran back upstairs to my office. I picked up the phone and called Sasha.

"I think I saw Brooke at the souvenir shop by my office." That was what I started with. No hello, no nothing.

"What?" she asked.

"Sasha, snap out of it. I think I just saw my sister here in California. What is she doing here?" There was a pause before she said something.

"Maybe she's here to find you. Or here on business or vacation. Did you say something to her?"

"I called out her name, but she was with this guy. Then when he saw me calling her name, he got her out of there. She disappeared just like that. Oh my goodness, I'm freaking out," I said.

"Okay, calm down. Let me hack into the security cameras at the shop and see what I can find. I'll call you back." She hung up. My mind was racing. *Where is Ryan? He can't be far.*

I was totally freaking out. I couldn't eat. I couldn't go back to work. I was about to call Hunter when Melissa came through the door.

"Here, Hope. I forgot to give you this earlier before you left for lunch. Some guy dropped this off." She handed me a white envelope. I smiled and thought about what my husband had in store. I sat back in my chair and opened it.

When I read it, I wasn't sure if I comprehended what I read. So, I read it again with my heart pounding in my chest.

*"So, you thought you could hide from me. I've waited for the day I would find you. I've let you have your fun, but daddy's home now. I can't believe you let someone else inside my sanctuary, inside my pussy. Do you know how that makes me feel? How it pisses me off. Then you go on and marry that mother fucker. I forgive you and want you to come home. If not, I'll kill him and still bring you home where you belong. I miss my sanctuary. Have you been looking for your sister, she is quiet lovely.*

*I love you MP.*

*Sebastian. "*

# THE LOVE I CRAVE

I shot up from my seat and grabbed my purse. I knew this day was coming. I was terrified, but not as terrified as I thought I would be. If I left town, he would follow me and leave Hunter out of this. I didn't want to see him hurt because of me. I ran out of my office to confront Melissa about the letter.

"Hope, what's wrong with you?" Aimee asked.

"Who dropped off this note?" I yelled. They both looked at me with concern.

"Some guy."

"What did he look like?" I asked, but I knew.

"Light skin. Short, wavy hair and grayish-brown eyes. He wore a black sweater with a hood. He said he was a friend from a long time ago." I gasped, my breath catching in my throat. The guy in front of the souvenir shop. It was HIM; it was Sebastian.

"Sebastian," I started choking. I felt like I was drowning. My knees buckled. Why was Brooke with him? I had to save my sister. I pushed the button for the elevator. Thank God, I didn't have to wait long. The doors to the elevator opened, and I stepped inside.

"Hope, where are you going?" Melissa asked.

"I have to find my sister."

"Your sister?" Aimee said.

"Something isn't right. It wasn't supposed to happen like this. I have to find Brooke and save her." I gave them one last look.

"Call Hunter now." I heard Melissa say to Aimee before the doors closed. I hoped I made it out of the building before he shut it down. I texted Rodney to bring my truck around and when the door opened, I ran out to find Rodney waiting for me.

"Hope, are you okay?" he asked as I closed the door. I turned to the building and saw Julius running out. I put Silvia in drive and took off for the highway. I was determined to lead HIM away from Hunter and find out what the fuck Brooke was doing with Sebastian. My heart sank at the thought of what he could be doing to her.

My stomach cramped as I thought of never seeing Hunter again. I dodged in and out of traffic. These people were in my way. I needed to find my sister and get her as far away from Sebastian. Where I was headed, I had no idea. As I sped down the street, I saw a white Benz following me. I wasn't sure, so I turned off. And so did they. I kept going, then made a left, and so did they. The white car had tinted windows, so I couldn't see inside. I wanted to cry, but that time was over. No more tears. Sebastian had my sister, and I would do anything to prevent Brooke from suffering as I did.

I was thinking of just pulling over and giving myself to HIM. This had to be Sebastian in this car. What in God's green earth was Brooke doing with him? She couldn't be with him. Then I thought about the way she looked at him outside the souvenir shop. She got it bad for him. Like I used to. I sighed.

My stomach tightened in a knot. My palms sweat upon the steering wheel. My stomach hurt so bad, and I began to feel nauseous. I hoped Sebastian wasn't doing the things to Brooke that he did to me. That would break my heart. Then I thought that if my sister were in love with him, how would she react to him being in love with me? Did he want to be like his father, with his wife and his mistress staying in the same house? I wanted to throw up. I felt sick.

I looked out of the rearview mirror. I didn't see the car anymore. I looked out the driver side window, and the car was there. I heard a horn beep and for a moment, I lost my train of thought. The car slammed into me, sending me flying off the road. I tried to take control of the wheel. I took my foot off the gas and turned my wheel to the left. That got me back on the road. Before I even got comfortable, the car hit me again. I sped up and changed lanes, and they followed me.

My phone rang, and I knew who it was. He was calling to tell me to come back and not to run away. The car came up and ran in the back of me, sending another car to slam into me. The truck kept going and hit a tree. And I knew I was gone. I heard my name being called. I tried to open my eyes, but that made my head ache.

"Zollah." I heard my name called again. I could recognize that voice from anywhere.

"Zollah, no." I felt like I entered a battle against Spartacus and got my ass whipped. I felt like I'd been cut. Death by a thousand cuts. Sliced and diced everywhere. I saw a flashing light, and someone lifted my eyelid to check.

"Please tell me she'll be okay." I heard Hunter ask.

"Sir, I'm going to need for you to step back."

"That's my wife," Hunter yelled. I pulled everything in me to speak. I needed to talk to him. I didn't want to leave this world without telling him. He had a right to know.

"Hunter!" I called out. My throat burned. A warm, metallic taste entered my mouth. *Blood.*

"Zollah, baby girl, I'm right here. We're going to get you out," he said. I was weak. I was losing consciousness, and it wasn't in a good way. I tried to keep my eyes focused on Hunter. He was my focal point but looking at his pain, I closed my eyes for a second. I didn't know how much time had passed before I was able to say something, anything.

"Hunter, I'm sorry." I felt numb all over, I couldn't move a muscle. I felt myself going under. Drifting to a place that would soon be my resting place. I had to tell him. I felt my heartbeat slowing down. "We had a…a baby…"

Stay tuned for

**THE LOVE I FEAR.**

Coming Soon

Find out if Hunter and Zollah can overcome what has been thrown their way. You will see the life Zollah had with Sebastian.

I want to thank everyone who has had a hand in this process. The Love I Crave was a story that came to me after reading books by E.L James. This book was one of the first stories I written all the way through to the very last book. I hope you enjoyed Zollah and are thirsting for more. Thank you for all the love and support.

www.ingramcontent.com/pod-product-compliance
Lightning Source LLC
Chambersburg PA
CBHW021118260626
47169CB00005B/1339